DEEP SPACE ACCOUNTANT

Mjke Wood ACRA

To Sarah

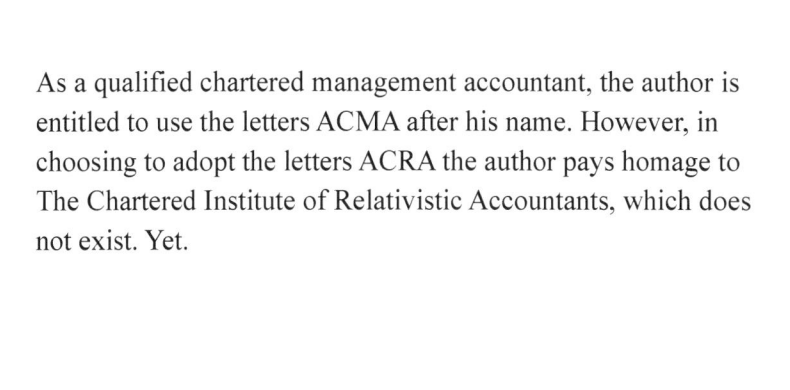

As a qualified chartered management accountant, the author is entitled to use the letters ACMA after his name. However, in choosing to adopt the letters ACRA the author pays homage to The Chartered Institute of Relativistic Accountants, which does not exist. Yet.

ONE

Elton found himself unmarked and floating through wide open space. The defence was split. Eight seconds remained on the clock, and it all came down to this:

Goal. Trajectory. Pig.

Hangball! It's all about belief.

He picked out Walther, moving along the meridian, in possession. They made eye contact.

Game on.

Walther rotated, arms windmilling, and released the pig with perfect timing. The pig rifled along an imaginary line intersecting Elton's own vector line.

Elton licked his lips. He rubbed his hands together. This was what it was all about. Glory. Triumph. How many years had they waited?

Goal. Trajectory. Pig.

And – at last – belief that was tangible.

He closed in on the hurtling pig; two hundred pounds of pink, low-friction, tactile-plastic-encased ballast. In the FHA rule book they called it a ball, but it wasn't round and it didn't bounce. Everyone else named it for what it most resembled: a pig – even though nobody knew what a pig was – something to do with Old Earth and sausages. Something from once-upon-a-time, something alive and not very nice.

Where the vector lines intersected, pig and player would meet and cross the goal line together. Three points. An outcome as inevitable as the movement of the planets in their orbits. An outcome driven by immutable laws.

Five seconds.

Elton's team trailed five points to six, but there were three points if you carried the pig over the line.

Victory was possible. No, victory was *assured*.

Unless Elton dropped it.

Because, as the pig drew nearer, Elton felt his body begin to twist.

"Use your legs!" Jim's voice, in his ear – Jim, his loyal and ever-present imentor.

"Shut it, Jim, I'm concentrating."

"You're losing it, Elton. You have axial rotation. *You have to use your legs!*"

Elton kicked and blustered and squirmed. His movement demonstrated all the qualities of a lifelong sports loser.

The gap narrowed.

No cheers. Few sounds, just the occasional squeak of Nikes off the Octahedron walls. Elton's team, Third Floor Finance, coming from behind. The KP Audit Atoms, on the verge of losing a hard-fought lead. Each could only watch the drama unfold, and pray.

Goal. Trajectory. Pig.

Elton.

Pig.

Impact!

Elton twisted, arms flailing in a desperate search for a catch. The pig smacked him in the face – a meaty, sweaty, prize-fighter kind of wallop – and ricocheted harmlessly away to one side of the goal. Elton bounced off to the other side.

Game over.

The hangchamber lights dimmed, leaving just the red safety lamps.

Silence from both teams. Then the KP Audit Atoms exploded into whoops and jeers of delight.

Elton's teammates gaped. KP were only in this league to make the other teams look good. They were ecstatic. The final game of the season and now KP Audit were only the *second* worst team in the Kenilworth Transit Hangball League.

The background whine of the ZG generators dropped in pitch. The sense of up and down emerged, and the players sank to what was now the floor. They left the hangchamber; KP leaping and high-fiving; TFF trudging, heads down.

Elton walked out last. Alone.

In the changing rooms, the smell of old trainers and sweat.

"Don't give up the day job," someone muttered.

"Why?" said another. "He's a crap accountant, too."

Walther came over to Elton and put an arm around his friend's shoulder.

"We'll get them next time, compagno. At least they didn't thrash us. We gave them a game tonight."

Elton pulled his shirt over his head and threw it onto the bench. It slithered down between the grey plastic slats into a netherworld of finger-burning steam pipes, darkness and dust bunnies. He dropped onto the bench and held his head in his hands, sprouts of glistening black hair sticking out through his fingers. His pale, wiry frame, all angular lines and jutting bones, gave him the appearance of a sad bundle of sticks.

"Why do we bother? Why do *I* bother? Who am I trying to kid, Walther? I can't play hangball. Never could. I'm quitting the team. The guys are right. I *am* an accountant." He said the last part in a loud voice aimed at his teammates. Then, in a quieter voice, "I do numbers. Finance. I should be more… serious."

"You can't quit, Elton. We're the guys; me and you, the Strike Force. We lost because the others didn't understand our tactics. One day the premiership scouts will spot us and our bean-counting days will be over."

It was a frequent line of make-believe.

Walther clapped him on the shoulder. "Let's shower and go up to the bar. Your shout. You owe us tonight, compagno."

A hangchamber is a truncated octahedron. An Archimedean solid consisting of eight hexagons and six squares. The Kenilworth Leisure Dome boasted four hangchambers, positioned around the lounge bar. The lounge's location at the hub created a fussy, hexagonal room with complex angled geometry for walls. Picture windows looked out into each hangchamber.

Elton hesitated at the door.

A mocking cheer went up from a large group clustered around a table near to the Chamber Four window. They'd seen Elton.

"Ignore them," said Walther. "Or then again we could go over there and fight them."

"Oh, perfect. You want to round off the day by getting our asses kicked?"

Walther shrugged and headed for a table at the opposite end of the room. Tonight they'd be drinking alone; their teammates had left by the back door. Elton weaved through the tables to reach the bar in the centre of the room. It was hexagonal, as were the tables and chairs, the mirrors and light fittings; even the drinks glasses.

"I hate it here," said Elton, after setting two drinks on the low table, taking a sip and dribbling beer down his shirt. "I hate these glasses. Whose stupid idea was it to do six-sided glasses? How are you meant to drink from this?"

"Well, I like to go for one of the angles. Then I just pour it down."

"I hate this room. It's all angles... and glass, and hexagonal floating lights. Everything's hangball. I hate hangball," said Elton.

"You don't."

"I do."

"Not very happy tonight, are we, compagno?"

"He's not very happy any night." The second voice came from Elton's beer-stained shirt. It was Jim, his imentor.

"You're meant to be supportive, Jim. And you're not meant to butt into conversations."

He turned back to Walther. "Does yours do that? Does your Jim keep sticking his oar in when you're trying to talk?"

"Yeah, all the time," said Walther. "I buy cheap clothes from the bodged AIs down the market, though. Most of their stuff's dumb, so you get to take a break from your Jim now and again."

"Is he with you now?"

"Yeah. Smart pants," said Walther, patting his trouser leg. "The shirt's dumb, though, so my Jim'll have to shout if he wants to contribute to our conversation. It's a cool shirt, don't you think?"

Walther pulled the shirt to stretch the wrinkles out so that Elton could read the writing across the chest.

Abel Bartholomew Smith: Shrinking the Sphere.

"Who's Abel Bartholomew Smith?"

"Protest singer. He's doing a gig in town in a couple of months, at The Revolution. You want to go?"

"It's not country, is it?" Elton asked.

"No. It's not country. Why do you have to put that tone on when you say 'country', like it's contagious? You have a real downer on good music, don't you?"

"I don't have a problem with good music, Walther. I just have a problem with your weird, Earthy cowboy music, that's all. I mean, the music's bad enough, but all that dressing up, the boots and the funny hats. It's… I don't know, it's kind of deviant if you ask me."

"Well I'm not asking you, and you don't have to worry. ABS is nothing like that. But he's good. Kind of profound. Songs with a message, yeah?"

Elton shrugged. "Okay, why not. It isn't as if we have much else to do. Life's kind of predictable these days: sleep, work, hangball, beer…"

Elton took a sip of his drink and pulled a face.

"Beer's terrible here, too. What are we doing, Walther? What happened?"

Walther shrugged.

"I'm thirty years old," said Elton.

"I know. Bummer."

"You are too, Walther. Well, almost."

"I have no problem with thirty."

"Really? Hand on heart? So come on, thirty years; what have we done? What have we seen? How many worlds are in the Sphere?"

Walther ignored him.

"I'm serious. How many worlds are there, in the Human Sphere of Influence?"

"Well, hey, number boy, I should think you'd have a better idea than me. Fifteen thousand? Sixteen?"

"I'm not talking about the whole bag of gravel; moons, planetissimals, asteroids – though you're well shy of the number: it was 27,018 as of last Thursday's *Data and Statistics Digest*."

Walther gave a wry smile and a hand gesture that said; there you go, see?

"Come on, Walther, how many *inhabited* worlds; proper

colony worlds?"

"Including the Ring?"

"If you like."

"Twenty-seven."

"Twenty-eight, actually, but the number's not important, not for what I'm saying, which is this: How many have *we* seen, you and me?"

"I can manage that one, compagno."

"Yeah, well even *you* can count to two, Walther. Do you remember the dreams we shared back on Erymanthus? Let's get off this dung ball? See the Sphere? Build a career?"

"We've *got* careers."

"We've got jobs," said Elton. "Not careers. I'm supposed to be gaining post qual. experience. I've been a passed finalist for *three years*, and I'm no nearer to CIRA membership than I was when I started. I'm supposed to *do* stuff. Finance. Post Qualification Experience."

"At least you *passed* your finals," said Walther.

"You could pass. You could bluff it if you turned up for the exams once in a while. But then why bother? You, Walther, are just like me. If you scraped through your finals you'd just be stuck in zero-experience, passed-finalist limbo for all eternity. Qualified but not qualified. We don't *do* anything, Walther. We count beans. When do we ever use the good stuff, like relativistic depreciation techniques, or WACC, or DCF?"

"What's WACC?"

"Weighted Average Cost of Capital, in… *you know what WACC is. You passed paper fifteen in your technicals before I did.*"

Walther pointed to his ear and twirled his finger. "In and out," he said. "Long gone. You're different to me, Elton. You *know* this stuff."

"I know the theory – *knew* the theory. I've never *used* any of it, and for me too it'll be gone soon. Poof." Elton waved his hand in the air with an effeminate flourish to indicate the nebulous quality of all accountancy knowledge.

"I want the letters, Walther."

"They're no big deal."

"To me they are. ACRA. I want my junk mail addressed to Elton D Philpotts ACRA. Associate Member of the Chartered Institute of Relativistic Accountants. I want to make my dad proud. I've done the work. I've passed the exams. But I have to demonstrate post-qualification competence before they'll make me a full member."

"Can't you just join one of the *ordinary* institutes?" said Walther.

"You know it doesn't work that way, and no. Boring. I'm relativistic qualified. I know the difference between the time value of an asset in local space, and that of an asset pegging along at near light speed. I can *calculate* it."

"Can you?"

"Okay, no. But isn't that the point? If I had the chance to apply some theory now and again. If I could put a real starship on an asset register, capitalise it, and see what happens when it zips off into the cosmos and its relative life dilates with time. Isn't that how we learn?"

"It's how we learn that it's time to get out more."

"I need to do this, Walther. I want the reward. I *need* that post qual. record of experience."

Walther set his glass down on the rickety hexagonal table. He gave Elton a look that suggested he was about to become serious. He pushed the beer glasses to one side, reached into his pocket, and took out his paper. He unfolded it on the table, smoothing out the creases. If it had been real paper it would have soaked up the spilt beer. Instead the beer stuck it down onto the surface by capillary action. The lettering flickered as the power cells reacted to all the surplus alcohol.

"Well, maybe now's the time to do something about your needs, Elton. Look at this."

Elton said nothing. He watched, and waited.

Walther scrolled his finger up and down the margin, looking for a particular page, until a double-spread advert appeared.

There was a picture of a handsome young man in a red space suit (yellow was the Space Corps suit colour but artistic licence was in abundance here). His helmet was tucked under his arm. His hair, star-bleached, was blown backwards by the electron wind. In his hand he carried an ancient and preposterous leather briefcase. He was taking a step towards a cliff edge on what was clearly an alien world, for the sky was red and boasted a veritable menagerie of suns, moons and ringed planets. And there were alien trees. Red, of course. The trees were the clincher, because there *were* no trees, of any colour, anywhere in the Sphere. This was truly a unique and tantalising world.

Splashed across the top of the page, in red-and-yellow Buck Rogers font, were the words:

DEEP SPACE ACCOUNTANT

Walther stabbed a finger down on the page.

"This is for us, Elton. Look at it. *Deep space*. You'd get your ACRA letters with this gig, that's for sure. Isn't this why we came here, to Tsanak? Picture yourself in that spacesuit, on that hilltop. Think of the girls you could pull in an outfit like that."

"We've applied to the Space Corps before, Walther."

"Yeah, but look. This is the real deal, not just some dull office support job. *Deep Space Accountant*. We'll do it properly this time."

Elton turned the paper and studied it. He looked over at his friend, who was fidgeting and animated, pushing his glasses up his nose every few seconds because his head was nodding with excitement.

"You'd have to get your eyes done, you know. They wouldn't let you into deep space with glasses."

"Nonsense. Besides, they're like that briefcase; they're a badge, a statement. They say: Here comes a serious, full-macking accountant. And you're changing the subject. What do you think?"

Elton scrolled down to the small print.

"They want qualified or studiers."

"You're qualified."

"I'm not qualified, I'm a PF, a passed finalist. And you haven't looked at a textbook in four years."

"And as of today, I'm studying level two CIRA," said Walther. "I'm a studier."

"Really?"

"Well, I am if we do this together. I get full exemption from level one because I passed my technicals."

"You've gone into this, haven't you?"

"I'm serious, Elton. You're right. What *have* we done since we came here? It's time we got our asses into gear. In fact, listen in, I'll show you commitment."

He bent to shout under the table.

"Jim! Can you hear me down there, Jim?"

A muffled voice came up from below. "Oh, so now you want conversation?"

"Enough of the attitude, Jim. Send off an exam application for

CIRA, level two, next sitting."

"You realise the next exams are in six weeks?" said Elton. He shook his head. "The sorry truth is, you probably *could* do it. I had to lock myself away for months on end, and work, and still I only ever managed to pass on resits. You can stroll and bluff and pass without effort even when you don't understand a word of it. You just never managed to turn up for the exams."

"Meh! Pass? Fail? Irrelevant. I just need to be a studier. I don't know what *you're* whining for; *you've* already done it. So, come on. Elton? Are you in?"

"I'm not impulsive, like you. I like to think things through."

"Oh come on, Philpotts, you dried-up old turd. *Deep space!* You started all this, tonight. You *know* you want it."

TWO

Tsanak had long been the planet of choice for sharp young professionals seeking fast-track advancement and good suits. The Space Corps adopted the planet as its corporate home decades earlier, after it realised the universe was not teeming with blood-thirsty, psychopathic aliens as everyone expected. In fact, the universe was not teeming with much, really. Not a lot of vegetation and the only aliens with any kind of evolutionary sophistication were the Teddies, and they were cuddly and not very bright.

So in a deft sleight of hand exercise, the Corps undertook a rapid rebranding program away from its military roots in order to maintain the high levels of funding to which the organisation and its officers had become accustomed. The Space Corps became the controllers of space: Its gates, its starships, its aspirations, its people. It became the most powerful and cohesive force of all the corporations in the entire Sphere of Influence; stronger by far than the scattered and isolated governments of the individual colony worlds; stronger even than the royal families of Old Earth.

When the Space Corps moved to New Leicester, corporate humanity scrambled to move with them. Land prices soared and, in a financial feeding frenzy, the other major corporations bribed, cheated and kneecapped their way to ownership of any old contaminated scrap of wasteland that became available in the city. To maximise their prestige and square footage they built high. Executives hot-bunked their desks, moved staff into their stationery cupboards and held meetings in the toilets when conference space ran dry. New Leicester became a sizzling, seething cauldron of corporate posturing.

So the Space Corps moved again. In an expression of individuality and impudence, they planted their sprawling new campus smack in the middle of the desert, miles south of the city limits. It was typical Space Corps, a stiff-fingered gesture right in the face of convention. The new headquarters was low, sleek, bright, airy and spacious; with grassy banks, water features and expensive corporate sculpture.

It was also far, far away from all of Tsanak's transport infrastructure. A nine-thirty AM job interview – that's what the email said – meant Elton had to coerce his Jim into a four AM alarm call. *Four AM!* Elton D Philpotts hadn't seen four AM since he'd last woken his mother for breast milk.

Elton's home was on the outskirts of Kenilworth, a town more than thirty miles north of New Leicester. It was not a fashionable town. Kenilworth could not lay claim to being in the sticks; it wasn't even in the twigs and leaves.

Fifty years after colonists first arrived on Tsanak, the low, domed Kenilworth shelters, with a ten-year maximum life span, were still the predominant architecture in one remote settlement, so when it became a town they named it after the shelters. When the architects got around to redesigning downtown Kenilworth, they could have erected lofty, handsome towers and wide green parks. Instead they stayed with the grey motif and the single-storey look. A space that was "in-keeping", was an oft-quoted phrase. They built downtown Kenilworth as if they were in a hurry to leave. A century on, and the shelters were still there.

A half-hour north of Downtown, Elton's Kenilworth dome squatted low and grey in the poorer end of town. There wasn't a richer end. Those who acquired money moved to New Leicester with all their worldly possessions tucked under their arms in small boxes.

As Elton locked his front door, it crossed his mind that today, this act of door-locking might somehow be symbolic. Today was his interview with the Space Corps. Today could be the day that his life moved onwards and upwards.

He turned to look at the street. Still dark. Good. There would be few of the usual tribal brigands hanging around on street corners to gob on him or to case his joint as he left.

It was raining. This also was good. It gave Elton an opportunity to survey his neighbourhood with a full palette of dismay. Rain didn't make the pavements shine in Kenilworth, it slimed them. Rain, slime, yobs and the desperate domes of Kenilworth. These were images Elton needed to hold on to – to keep him motivated. Today he needed to excel. Peak performance. In just a few hours he was going to try to sweet-talk his way into the Space Corps.

His train was late. Twelve minutes. Others might fume and stomp, but not Elton. He worked for Kenilworth Transit, providers of trains, buses, overheads, and disappointment. He knew how it worked. His travel plans, as always, included an allowance. Elton didn't need published timetables. He carried them in his head. Times were just numbers, and numbers were his thing. He knew all about the five-minute connection at New Leicester Central, a connection that was now toast. He didn't worry; he had multiple contingencies with built-in triple redundancy.

He looked up at the sound of scraping, unlubricated metal on metal. His train. Car 59675584B in front. He recognised the sorry fifteen-degree tilt caused by age old failure in the suspension. He guessed 59674286B was connected behind, as it had been all year. Good.

Elton walked along the platform to where the rear car,

59674286B, would stop, because he knew that one particular seat in the last section, platform side, still had working form-fitting controls. The idea was for the seat to fit the unique shape of the passenger's butt and thus provide exquisite comfort. Individual biometrics were supplied by each passenger's imentor, his Jim or her Kim. But the seats no longer bothered to ask, or worse, they asked but were out of sync; they polled the imentor then cached the given biometrics and set themselves into the form of some previous passenger. Regular commuters were wise. They brought cushions. But Elton could go one better. He knew which seat worked.

The train pulled out and Elton relaxed in blissful, form-fitting comfort and stared out of the window at the endless vista of yellow gravel. He wasn't looking at the scenery though; he was preparing, going through Accounting Standards in his head. Ever since Walther had talked him into applying for the Space Corps, Elton had thrown himself into CPD – Continuing Professional Development. It was all very well for Walther to fake his student status; if that worked for him then fine. But Elton had integrity. He could never fake such a thing, it would rip him apart.

That was the difference between he and Walther. Walther could fake and bluff and somehow get the answers right. Elton could study for weeks yet retain nothing. He could remember numbers, oh yes – Elton's problem was *forgetting* numbers – but abstract concepts, and even facts, just never seemed to stick. He passed exams by force-feeding his brain. Walther would breeze through – all he needed was the will to turn up.

Right now Elton was trying to read *GAS 57: Development Expenditure in Cultures with Predominantly Pre-Technological Political Attitudes.* Number 57 out of 212 Galactic Accounting Standards. Elton could still remember the numbers but the content was gone. GAS 57 had recently been updated, so it was a worthwhile area for CPD – and it was relevant to opportunities in start-up colony worlds – just the thing for Space Corps wannabes. He'd read the standard a dozen times, or rather, his eyes had followed the words on the page. His brain, meanwhile, played fantasy hangball.

The battery time-out shut down his reader and he sighed. Elton folded it down to half-sheet size to squeeze out some power, and swiped down to page 286.

I can remember the figging page number, he thought. *I can remember every irrelevant numerical connection, the coincidences; like the number 286 is also the last three digits of the carriage number in which I'm sitting. How about that?*

But he was painfully aware that whenever he began reading the text of GAS 57 it was as though he'd never seen it before. Ever.

"I have news."

GAS 57 provides for the amortization of certain classes of development expenditure only in circumstances where it can be demonstrated, by independent…

"*Important* news…"

"Huh?" Elton looked up.

"… for you."

The eyes were blue and wide open and they hovered less than six inches away from Elton's face. They were goggling eyes filled with wonder, and they belonged to a girl with no hair, dressed all in green. Monk's robes. With a hood. She was sitting in the seat opposite Elton and leaning across, hands reaching out.

"Excuse me?" Elton jerked backwards to regain his personal space until he could retreat no further. The blue eyes moved in, coming so close it became hard to focus.

"Bram Lee *loves* you," she said, in a husky stage whisper.

Elton laughed without humour. His eyes flicked left then right, seeking help. The train had filled with grey, wet raincoats and commuter misery. But there were non-Monday smiles breaking out on some of the faces. Here was unexpected high-calibre entertainment to brighten their morning.

"Look, miss..."

"Bram Lee, the bringer of tranquillity, has opened His heart to you this day. Will you not open your heart to Bram Lee?"

Where was Jim when he needed him?

"Jim!"

Elton looked down, giving a wriggle to agitate his trousers and catch Jim's attention.

"Wake up, Jim!" But Elton was wearing a raincoat – a pH Protector[TM] static repellent raincoat. Jim's sensors couldn't penetrate it. One of the problems with Tsanak rain was, if you got wet your clothes dissolved. So you wore pH protection and isolated your imentor. Elton's trousers were top-of-the-range smart, but only the lower six inches protruded beneath the hem of his coat, and what could Jim do for him with just six inches of trouser-leg, down amongst the gum-wrappers?

"Miss, look, this sounds like a religious thing. I'm, you know, not really into religion."

Elton knew about religion. His case study, the one that had haunted him for six whole months during his finals, had been about a nutty religious sect who'd bought an old starship so that they might go where no religious nut had gone before, and establish their own colony. As their financial advisor in the role-playing scenario, it had been Elton's job to keep them solvent and well-advised throughout all the pitfalls and disasters that the evil examiner invented. One of the pitfalls had concerned suboptimal revenue streams from street-corner evangelists.

"I do not speak of religion. I speak of life," she snapped. The girl's voice broke with passion. There was a desperate edge to it: panic, almost.

In the carriage, a carnival atmosphere. Smiling faces. Joyous relief that it was happening to someone else.

"I have opened up my heart to Bram Lee. Why can't *you* do the same?"

"I'd like to, really, but..." Elton showed her his reader, "I'm trying to study, you see? I have a job interview."

"An interview? How can you expect strangers to reach any conclusions about your place in the cosmos until you have studied the teachings of Bram Lee? Let Bram Lee be your teacher and life coach. Then go to your interview."

"Well, okay. How is he on Galactic Accounting Standards and Ethics?"

"Do not make jokes. You should understand the intolerable sufferings that Bram Lee has had to endure" – she leaned in even closer – "*for you.*"

Elton knew all about intolerable sufferings.

The girl reached out and grabbed Elton's lapels. She reeled him in. Their noses almost touched. Elton detected an aroma of mothballs. The green habit smelled like it had been inside an old suitcase for a long time.

"Bram Lee cared for His children. Nurtured them." A tear formed in her eye and slowly rolled down her cheek.

"See how His children repay Him? He gives them a home; they flood it with their verminous offspring; they destroy that which He gave them. And then they leave. They spread out into the four corners of the universe, a slick tide of darkness and depravity, stealing worlds *that do not belong to them!*"

The lone tear turned to uncontrolled weeping and dribbling. Tears and snot flowed and splashed and bounced off Elton's repellent raincoat, turning the air moist. The elderly male passenger next to Elton shrank away to one side, but his shoulders trembled in spasms of mirth.

"Okay, look." Elton pushed the girl away as gently as he could. "Just tell me what you want, yeah?"

The tears stopped. She smiled.

With a conjurer's flourish she produced a data wafer from the folds of her robe.

"This contains all the teachings and philosophies of Bram Lee. It is for you. A gift. You may take it without obligation."

"Oh. Okay. Thank you. I'll look at it as soon as I can."

Elton took the wafer and moved to slip it into the pocket of his raincoat.

"Disciples usually offer a small donation. We are reluctant to accept charity but production overheads are an unwelcome constraint on our teachings."

Elton's hand stopped halfway to the pocket. *Ahh*.

He thought about it. He could give back the wafer. Do a bit of shouting. Set her off with the crying again. Look like a callous bastard.

Did he need this? Today?

Or he could slip her five megs and have done with it. She would move on up the train and spoil someone else's day.

His hand continued into his jacket and came out with his wallet. The girl's wet eyes sparkled. It crossed Elton's mind that, on a less stressful day, in a better mental place, he could find her quite attractive.

He opened his wallet and took out a five-meg note. He smiled as he passed it over, feeling a great sense of release mingled with self-satisfied altruism.

She didn't touch the money.

"Disciples usually feel twenty-five megs to be adequate compensation," she said, "given the intolerable sufferings."

"Twenty-five?"

"And the years of hardship—"

"Look—"

"—in the wilderness."

Elton looked in his wallet. He had fifty megs, an amount he'd thought would be ample for the day: for the overheads, for taxis, and for any food or drink he might have to buy. But twenty-five?

And it was no good saying he didn't have the change. The girl was peering into his wallet with round, cash-register eyes.

The train lurched and began to slow.

"Oh, look, my stop." Elton jumped to his feet. "I'm sorry, miss. Don't train journeys fly when you're having fun?" Elton pushed the wafer back into the girl's hand, folding her fingers around it to be certain it stayed in her possession, then surged to his feet and ran with the grace of a ZG cube-dancer, hurdling all the commuters' legs stretched out across the centre aisle. At the door he paused. He looked at the girl and offered an apologetic little shrug.

"I get off here. Sorry."

The door slammed open and Elton fell from the train into the wet crowd of surprised commuters who were waiting to board. There was a moment of elbows, toe crushing and briefcase punting, then the commuters disentangled themselves and boarded the train. The doors closed. The train pulled out of the station. Elton watched it go, savouring the quiet and emptiness on the platform.

But then he felt a tap on his shoulder. He turned. One other passenger had alighted.

"Disciples generally find that twenty-five megs is fair compensation. Given the…"

"Intolerable sufferings, yeah, I know the script. Look, my interview. I really don't want to leave myself short today, and—"

"I take imentor transfers. You have an imentor." It wasn't a question.

Elton sighed. The rain had stopped; he unfastened his raincoat. "Jim?"

"Elton."

"Pay the lady twenty-five megs, please, Jim."

The girl smiled up at Elton. "Thank you. Would you authorise gift aid? It costs you nothing yet we can claim tax rebate for—"

"Yes, I know about gift aid. Would you like to take my coat, also? And my shoes?"

She giggled, then placed a hand on Elton's forearm. "You're a nice man. You're kind. Why do you want to be mixing with people like the Space Corps? Turn round, Elton Philpotts. Go home. Forget this silly interview." And with a half-skip she spun on her heel and was gone.

"What did she mean, Jim? What's wrong with the Space Corps?" He looked around. "And where are we?"

"Elton, for an hour I have seen nothing but chronically failing machinery, sweet wrappers, plastic cups, ill-fitting shoes encasing aromatic feet, and one interesting pair of green sandals. So just how the hell do you expect me to know where we are?"

"Well, I thought you might, you know… recognise it? GPS?"

"Well, this godforsaken railway platform does not appear to merit an entry in the planetary database. And GPS is down."

"No worries, Jim, it's a busy line close to town. There'll be other trains."

Three chimes crackled and distorted from Elton's shirt and trousers. Jim was being used as a local relay.

"New Leicester Transit wishes to apologise to passengers for the suspension of city-bound services at this time. This is caused by debris on the track. Further announcements will follow."

THREE

Walther Blick did not look good in a suit. Something to do with unconventional weight distribution. There was a conflict between how he wanted to look – the suave, savagely sophisticated man of the city – and reality. No matter how hard he tried, Walther's business attire always resembled a Big Issue seller's sleeping bag.

A month earlier Walther had performed miracles on his boilerplate CV. Elton had thrown up barricades and cited all the old unhelpful arguments about truth and integrity.

Walther had stood firm and the rewards had come: interviews for each of them at the lavish Space Corps HQ complex on the outskirts of New Leicester. Elton would be heading the team assault with a fresh and breezy nine-thirty interview. Walther's interview followed mid-afternoon. He'd reacted with horror at Elton's suggestion that they meet up early at the station in Kenilworth, then travel together.

"You're talking about the six *AM* train? *Oh-six-hundred?* In the *morning?*" Walther had needed to sit down. "Is it light by then? Do we run trains that early?"

"You're not going to take this seriously, are you?" Elton's tone was full of weary disappointment.

"I *am* serious. I'm up for this interview stuff, honest."

"Have you studied?"

"Studied what?"

Elton sighed. He did a lot of sighing in his conversations with Walther. "For the interview. For the exams you're meant to be taking."

"I'll wing it."

"Walther, no!"

To outsiders they seemed an ill-matched pair of friends. Elton had to be so damned serious about everything. He was so... old. Elton was thirty, while Walther was "only" twenty-nine, and the five-month gap brought out all kinds of big brother instincts in Elton.

And then there was the girl thing. Walther saw himself as a gravity well to cute, unattached girls. He certainly had no trouble pulling, but the type of girl he always attracted seemed to want nothing more than to mother him. It was frustrating. Girls just wanted to feed him and iron his shirts. They were drawn to Walther like dog-lovers are drawn to mistreated, bedraggled strays.

Elton, on the other hand, possessed the look that Walther coveted. His back was straight. His black hair always stayed in place, apart from that controlled casual thing he had going with his fringe. Elton had an easy smile and an open and honest face. Around girls, though, he was a disaster. He mumbled and stammered and had a prescient knack for saying the one specific thing that would offend.

But he and Elton did have *some* things in common. Apart from their shared love for the game of hangball, they both wanted to be accountants, although their motivations here were quite different. Walther saw accountancy as a way to support his aspirations for debonair professional worldliness, and thus far he'd found himself able to blag his way into the financial world with little need for such niceties as an actual grasp of the subject.

Elton, on the other hand, seemed to be trying to prove something. He had that genius thing with numbers, and Walther supposed this might be an advantage to an accountant, but otherwise, Elton's journey to the hallowed halls of qualification had been something of a laboured, uphill struggle, hampered by his annoying obsession with work ethic.

Walther was determined to take his friend in hand.

"Look, Elton. Forget this crack-of-dawn nonsense. I'm heading out there on Sunday. Come with me. We sleep in. No stress. We arrive for our interviews fresh and alert."

"And maybe take in the Giants/Lemmings game while we're in town?"

"Is there a game on Sunday?" said Walther, with feigned innocence. "Oh yes, you're right. A happy coincidence."

"And we hit some bars afterwards? The New Leicester nightlife?"

"We could."

"And with luck, we might even be half-sober by the time we get to Space Corps HQ."

"That's not what—"

"Yes, Walther. That is exactly what would happen. I know you. *Is there a game on?* You know damn well there's a game on. You probably already have tickets."

"Okay, so my Jim's holding a couple for us, provisionally."

"So tell your Jim to let one go. I'm not doing it, Walther. I'm not getting tonked the night before this interview. You might get away with it; I sure as hell wouldn't."

Walther hadn't given him much of an argument because Elton was probably right.

Actually, he'd been exactly right. Walther had been serious about being unable to face the early start, so he *had* gone into town on Sunday. And why waste the hangball ticket? The Jervaulx Giants and the New Leicester Lemmings game had been an annual, must-see grudge match for years. And hey, the Lemmings had won! They had annihilated the Giants in a most satisfying and humiliating manner. And this had called for *much* post-match drinking.

So after the game, unencumbered by Elton's irrational dislike of all things country, Walther had called in at the NLO, the New Leicester Opry, where the drink was cheap and where Dolly Lovitt and the Universal Cowgirls were playing up a storm. And you couldn't go to a place like the NLO wearing shorts and a Lemmings team vest, so he'd worn his interview suit.

Then slept in it.

In some street.

And now he was hung-over. And late.

So he threw his belongings into his case, slapped a handful of Babybotty onto his face…

Babybotty^{TM}, Babybotty^{TM},
The way to face each day,
One quick dab and stubble is gone,
Nanobots caressed it away.

(Babybotty^{TM} is a Copperbird Corp. product)

…and ran to the station…

…where Jervaulx Giants fans were waiting for the train.

His train.

It might have been okay if Walther hadn't immediately grinned at them, waved, then lit up his Lemmings holobanner to taunt them. Walther, with his bad suit and his wayward hair and his twenty-first-century spectacles. It wasn't as though he hadn't been through this routine often enough in the past. Would he ever learn? Sometimes his friends wondered if he'd been taking the morning off in bed on the day they handed out all the survival-of-the-fittest genes. The same force that drew out the mothering instinct in girls, also played a leading role in attracting bullies to Walther like flies round dead cats.

Jim probably saved his life.

"Walther!"

"What is it, Jim?"

"You should run. Now. And ditch the suitcase, yes?"

As he ran, Jim, with rearward vision, provided commentary.

"Four of them. Gaining. Wait... good, one of them's fallen over your suitcase. Red hair – no forehead. Okay, now he's kicked it onto the tracks. Train coming. Ouch! Don't worry about doing your laundry, Walther.

"Red Hair's out of it now. No stamina. He's cheering the others on, though. The other three: Big Guy can't run, oh... his friends can. Man, can they run. Move, Walther, or your face is gonna be looking worse than your suitcase."

"Any security around here?"

"Nope. It's down to you, my friend. Oh, the ugly guy with broken nose, he has a knife. *Big* knife. Go, Walther. Get those little legs moving."

"Where?"

"Turnstiles. East Coast line. *You've* got your company travel concession; you can go anywhere. Broken Nose will have to pay. Depends on whether killing you is worth the cost of a ticket."

Walther skidded round the corner and went straight for the gate. Jim transmitted Walther's travel authorisation, and the gate opened.

"He's close. He's right on your tail. He's going to follow you through..."

There was a clang as the gate closed. The ugly guy shouldered into it. The gate was made from half-inch steel to deter vandalism. The gate didn't come off worst.

Despite assurances from Jim, despite his pounding, hung-over head, Walther continued to run.

"Keep looking, Jim. Make sure they don't follow."

They emerged onto the platform. A train was waiting and the last of a crowd of partisan lemon-clad Lemmings supporters were boarding. Walther kicked hard and found hidden reserves. He heard the hiss of pneumatics as the doors began to close. He covered the last five yards in a dive, slithering onto the train. The doors closed behind him.

A message relayed through Jim.

"New Leicester Transit wishes to apologise to passengers for the suspension of city-bound services at this time. This is caused by debris on the track. Further announcements will follow."

"Is that us? Are we moving?" Panic crept into Walther's voice. He envisaged being stopped at the platform for hours while square-jawed Jervaulx fans rallied and jostled and embarked on a mission to seek him out.

"No," said Jim. "Problem's city-bound. This train is fine."

"What do they mean 'debris'?"

"Suitcase debris, I'd guess. Maybe they're getting specialists in to remove your dirty underwear."

"You are so funny at times, Jim. Wait though. City-bound trains? That'll be Elton, won't it? Poor bugger, that'll cock up *his* plans. Told him he should have come with me, yesterday."

"I don't know why you're so smug about it, Walther."

"I'm not smug, I feel sorry for him. You know what he's like. He has to have a plan – be in control. Right now he'll be wetting himself."

"Whereas you are calm, and relaxed, and on the wrong train."

It took a moment to sink in.

"What?"

"You changed platforms, remember? What possessed you to get on the train?"

"I… well, I dunno. Friendly Lemmings fans."

"Space Corps HQ is the first stop, south, on the Jervaulx line. That's why *your* platform was full of Jervaulx Giants fans. Now *this* train…"

Walther looked down the carriage at all the Lemmings uniforms.

"…this train is heading east."

"East?"

"To Smith. Nonstop. Be there in three hours."

"But…"

"Wait, I'm calling up the timetable. Yes. There's another train back from Smith at two-seventeen. Remind me; when's your interview?"

"Three."

"Well, there's a connection back here, at New Leicester Central, that gets you to Space Corps HQ… so… Yeah, best you can hope for is six-fifteen this evening. But I suppose they'll have all gone home by then."

FOUR

For just a moment following the announcement Elton stood motionless. He let the information sink in. The most important interview of his career was just a couple of hours away... and the trains had stopped running.

"What do I do, Jim? What the figging hell am I meant to do now?"

"First thing, Elton, don't panic."

"And the monk girl, what did she mean? *Go home.* What's wrong with the Space Corps?"

"A bad experience, perhaps?"

"No, Jim. Bad experience? *This* is a bad experience. No trains. No time. No—"

"Elton. Relax. Calm thoughts."

"Okay, Jim. No panic. I'm in control. Advise me."

"Good, Elton. Your heart rate is down. You're doing well."

"Yes, Jim. *So what do I do?*"

"Deep breathing."

"*Jim, I don't need deep breathing, I'm calm*. I just need you to tell me—"

"Elton, you're getting worked up again."

"Jim, for God's sake—"

"Okay, okay, here's what we do. We find a café. You have a nice cup of tea. Then you ring Miss Morningthorpe at the Space Corps and you grovel."

"What? Give in? What the hell kind of advice is that, Jim? Come on, there must be... Wait. I know, Walther! Walther's already in New Leicester, and he's not far from SCHQ. We could swap appointments. That will give me *hours* to reach SCHQ. There, Jim, you are not all seeing. You're not infallible."

"Elton, I *am* all seeing. I see that your plan cannot work."

"Come on, Jim. What makes you so sure? We can do this. Call him."

"A moment… Okay, I'm cleared to pass on some information here. Walther is en route to Smith. He won't get to SCHQ in time for his own interview, let alone yours."

"What? What's he doing going to Smith?"

"Let him tell you himself. You have plenty of time for a chat."

"No. No, I don't have time, Jim, because I have an interview," said Elton. He was already running towards the station exit.

"First thing we do is find out where we are. You can't possibly be certain there are no options if you don't even know where we are."

"Can't fault your logic there, Elton. We're in Cruz."

"There's a sign up ahead by the station entrance. Cruz. We're in Cruz. We can… you *knew?*"

"Of course I knew. GPS."

"You said it was down."

"It was. Then it was up."

"*Then why didn't you say?*"

"You didn't ask. And you didn't say please. So, okay, Cruz is —"

"I know exactly where Cruz is, Jim. It's about eight miles north of New Leicester."

"Good, Elton. So how about running? A person of average fitness might cover eight miles in under an hour."

"Once more, Jim, you reveal the difference between machine intellect and the real McCoy. I can't run eight miles."

"I never said anything about *you* running, Elton. I spoke about a person of average fitness. *You* would die."

"So instead of wasting time on hypotheticals, why not

concentrate on real solutions?"

"I merely mentioned this as a spur to your doing some exercise now and again. I'm here to help. Had you been a little fitter – average fitness – you would have that other option available. Our conversation also helped pass some time while we walked. Because just around the next corner there's a taxi rank."

The taxi was old; a Copperbird TX20. It dated back to the early days of ZG fields when everyone wanted ZG technology even though it was no good. Nowadays taxis had wheels.

The cab was driverless, but a robotic voice was installed for ambience.

"Where yer goin', mate?"

Elton thought about it. New Leicester Central was the obvious choice, so he could reconnect with his original travel plans. But he *could* go all the way. It would be expensive. Trains were free to NL Transit employees. How much were taxis? He hadn't been in one for years. But if there was ever a time to start...

"Space Corps HQ, please."

"Right you are, mate."

The taxi shuddered and belched smoke. It lifted onto its field, or half lifted. The side on which Elton sat seemed to be struggling, and as the cab moved off, half of its bodywork dragged along the road. There were sparks.

"Shove over onto the left, would yer, mate? Fields are a bit flat on the right side."

This seemed to work, and the cab continued along with a steady, sea-sickness-inducing kind of motion.

"D'yer catch those Lemmings last night? Corker. You a Lemmings fan or d'yer follow the Atoms? Or not bothered about hangball? Lifelong Lemming, me. Work for the Corps, do yer? Been there long? Ever get out into the Sphere? Right out? No, I dare say not. Deep Spacers don't go round on public transport. Not these days. Them and us. Know what I mean? Times was that…" And on it went. It was an incredible piece of software. It was robotic so it didn't need to breathe. It never repeated itself and it never once said anything that was interesting or in any way useful.

"I'm going this way 'cos the roads are snarled up in town. A bit further but better in the long run. Trains are off, see. Some joker chucked his suitcase on the track."

Elton let it pass over him. The rain stopped. The clouds scattered. The heat from the sun beamed in through the cab window, drawing out a rich cocktail of aromas from the upholstery. Elton settled deeper into his seat and watched backwater Tsanak slip by the cab window. Cruz was a small town of no more than thirty or forty dwellings and it was soon behind them. Now there was nothing but deserted yellow road between prairies of yellow gravel. The cab prattled on about congestion and heavy traffic, but for as far as Elton could see it was the only vehicle on the road.

Elton did sums to occupy himself. He counted the meter down over sixty seconds, then figured out the cost per minute. He estimated his speed and calculated out how long his total journey should take. He applied his makeshift cost-per-minute factor and came to… Whoa! About sixty megs. He wouldn't have enough cash. Jim would have to make *another* transfer. This day was getting more and more expensive.

"…and you'd think they'd mend these roads now and again, I always say, yer can't—"

"Excuse me," Elton said. "Just want to check. You take imentor transfers?"

The cab braked hard; the fields switching off even before it had stopped, causing it to crash to the road and scrape along for several feet, gliding like a builder's skip.

"You haven't got cash?"

"I've got cash. But I prefer to make a transfer; keep the cash, you know?"

"How much?"

"What?"

"How much you got?"

"I don't think that's any of your—"

"Business? No? Look, chum. I don't do imentor – smart-talking poncy machines – I take hard cash, that's all."

"Look—"

"Show us the cash or get your arse out now."

"Okay, I've got fifty megabytes."

"That all? Well put it in the tray. Let's see how far it gets you."

The journey, now, was less relaxed. Elton did the sums again. He tried it different ways. He watched the meter turn, and he recalculated over and over. He got Jim to try, hoping for an error in his method. No error. Fifty megs was not going to get him to Space Corps HQ.

It got him to the perimeter fence, but the Space Corps evidently valued their privacy; on the other side there was nothing but empty desert. As the meter rolled on to forty-five megs the cab did its legs-up crash landing thing again.

"Hang on, I've not had my fifty megs' worth yet." Elton was indignant.

"Five-meg tip, mate."

"Tip! You're a bloody machine. And you're a stroppy git. I'm not tipping you."

"Suit yourself, but in three seconds I'm heading back into New Leicester. S'up to you. Walk from here; walk from town.

Choose."

"Wait!"

"Two seconds."

Elton scrambled out of the cab. It lifted from the ground, only a little, staying low enough to kick up dust. Which it delivered, with practiced expertise, onto Elton's interview suit.

The road was straight with no defining features, save the fence. Had the fence been in the left or the right window when he'd been in the taxi?

"Jim, any idea which way? *Please?*"

"Ah, you are learning some manners. Of course, my master. Keep the fence on your right as you walk. I'll show you a shortcut."

Elton walked.

The fence was chain-link; a centuries-old design. It was continuous and infinite. Elton loosened his tie, slung his raincoat over his shoulder, and began to put one foot in front of the other. The unrelenting heat of the morning sun laid waste to his back.

"Jim, let's see the map."

The map appeared in front of Elton by retinal projection, oriented in the direction he was walking. His position was marked by a graphic of a heads-down trudging accountant. The road stretched ahead, long and straight. The main gate was marked, more than two miles ahead, and then the road angled back on itself. It was obvious that unless there *was* a shortcut, Elton would be following two very long sides of a very narrow triangle.

"How do you know there's a shortcut? There's nothing on the map."

"It's the Space Corps. You think they're going to use rusty old chain-link right up to the main gate? What kind of image would that present? I'm guessing they'll switch to Copperbird field fencing soon. Much smarter, sleek and futuristic, high-tech threat sensitive. We'll walk right through."

And as they rounded the next bend, exactly as predicted, the chain-link ended at a concrete post, to be replaced by a shimmering, crackling purple curtain of swirling plasma. There were boxes on poles with heavy glass insulators, and thrumming wires, and intimidating holonotices in red and yellow that popped into being at every step.

RESTRICTED AREA!
DO NOT CROSS BARRIER!
DANGER OF DEATH!

And there was a picture of a stick man, with his hair all sticking out, being launched through the air towards an open grave.

And just in case Elton couldn't read or interpret graphic images, a recorded voice began to shout warnings at him, in barking, martial tones.

"Stop! Do not approach the fence!"

"Stop! Do not approach the fence!"

Elton stopped. "What do we do now?"

"Stick your hand in the fence."

"What? I'm not doing that."

"Okay, so climb the chain-link. Let's see how your savage interview suit looks with street-grunge knee rips and a dusting of rust."

"But—"

"Go on. The fence. Touch it. See what happens."

"No way."

"When did you last see Copperbird stuff that worked? Do it."

"That's your analysis? It's Copperbird so it won't work? Well stuff that. I'll go the long way round."

"Elton, I'm your imentor, your guardian angel. Do you honestly think I'd ask you to do anything dangerous?"

"Well… sounds like it."

"Elton, stick your hand in the fence and save yourself a four-mile walk."

"Come on, Jim. Even without all the signs and the warnings, it looks bloody dangerous."

"That's the idea. It's all show. It's psychological. It crackles like that to put you off. D'you think they couldn't design the thing quieter? Don't be a wuss. Stick your hand in it."

Elton swore with feeling. He edged nearer to the fizzing, humming wall of energy. Little steps. He extended his hand then pulled it back. Then again a little nearer. The third time, his fingertips touched.

There was a crack that sounded like someone had shorted the electric-arc furnaces of hell with a monkey wrench. Elton was thrown fifteen feet through the air and landed on his backside, in the middle of the road. His hair was on end and thin tendrils of smoke were coming up from underneath his collar.

His entire body twitched and quivered.

"Jesus, Jim! I thought you said it was safe."

"It *is* safe. I never said it wouldn't *hurt* a bit. But you seem largely unharmed; no lasting damage; you've still got that feisty zip about you. And *voila*, the fence is gone."

The fence *was* gone. Nothing between Elton and the sweeping plains of gravel on the other side. But for the moment Elton couldn't move. He lay on the road and considered Jim's incorporeal existence with regret. If only Jim had an arse – that could be kicked.

"Come on, Elton. On your feet before they reset the breakers. I doubt I could talk you into sticking your arm in there again, so you'd better move. Now."

Elton climbed onto his feet and staggered, trancelike, over the scorch marks in the gravel that marked the line where the fence had been. On the other side Elton dropped to his knees, then forward onto his face.

There was a *zzzztt* noise, and the fence came back to life.

"Ooh, quicker than I expected. Maybe you should keep moving, Elton. There might be dogs."

"Dogs?"

Elton leapt to his feet and looked all around with nervous eyes.

"Dogs? What the hell is your game, Jim? What happened to the guardian angel role?"

"Relax. No dogs – I've been scanning. But it got you moving. Look, here's the map. You've got twenty minutes before your interview. You can still make it. Come on, move your feet. That's it. Left, right. Walk."

The Space Corps complex was a medium-sized campus-like collection of low, square buildings with sloping obsidian walls raked back at the kind of angles that are irresistible to that breed of teenagers with ZG skate decks and ill-fitting clothes. It had been fifteen years since Elton had been such a creature, but one glance at those buildings and all the old pimple-hormoned urges began welling up inside.

He ignored the magnetism. He followed the map. The buildings seemed identical, so he was glad of Jim's GPS You-Are-Here Trudging-Accountant marker that slouched along the red-dotted route.

He came alongside a larger building, which, according to the map, was the admin centre at which he was supposed to present himself. Like all the other buildings it was angled and featureless. The red-dotted marker went round the corner of the building, but Elton felt drawn by an overwhelming sense of exclusion toward the forty-five-degree slope of the windows. Maybe it was the black glass. Maybe it was the sense of exposure from being out here in the open. Or maybe it was just a latent adolescent freestyler's attraction to inclined planes. Whatever the reason, he needed to know what was inside. He walked over to the building and stood at the foot of the sloping window, but was still unable to make anything out through the heavily tinted glass.

He put out his arms and lowered himself onto the slope. He cupped his hands around his eyes and peered through the glass.

Below him was a room. An austere room. Square, bland, all hard angles and cold surfaces. One person was seated in a chair in the centre of the room. Facing him. Seated behind a table were five others. It looked like an interview panel. The five were intently studying the nervous interviewee, but now their attentions were drawn, one by one, to the dishevelled figure that was sprawled across their roof-light. One of the five, a woman, with a severe haircut and enough metallic jewellery to build a trans-continental railway, started mouthing things in Elton's direction. Elton couldn't hear her, but there are certain combinations of lip movements and body language attitudes that are universal and unambiguous, with or without audio.

Elton scrambled away from the window. It wasn't easy; the forty-five-degree semi-prone angle made it difficult to move with any kind of grace. But he gained his feet and lurched backwards to move himself out of line-of-sight as quickly as possible.

"I think they saw you," said Jim.

"I don't know. Tinted glass?"

"Yeah?" Unconvinced. "So, what now? You want to go home? I don't suppose there's much point you showing your face down there now."

"Who says they're from *my* interview panel? It's a big place. There's probably more than one recruitment stream, you know. Or even if... well, maybe they won't recognise me... you know, standing up, eye to eye."

"Oh, I don't know, Elton. I'd guess you're pretty famous in Space Corps circles by now. Climbing all over their roof, spying on the other candidates, busting in through their security fence —"

"That was your idea."

"—arriving ten minutes late."

"What? I'm late? Oh God, look at the time. Why didn't you say, Jim?"

"Excuse me, you were the one who took it into his head to go mountaineering up the windows."

"I swear to God, Jim, when this is over I'm off down the market for some spime-free clothing. Walther's got the right idea. I'm going solo. Dressing dumb. You're out of it, Jim." It was an often-repeated threat.

Elton started to trot along what he now realised was the roof of the admin block; the terrain here sloped, and many of the buildings were set into the side of the hill. When he reached the edge he saw that he was maybe twenty feet up and he faced a scramble down a grassy bank to reach road level and the official entrance foyer. It wasn't a real grassy bank. There wasn't much of anything that grew naturally on Tsanak (or on any of the other Sphere worlds for that matter), but here they'd managed to simulate a pretty good likeness of the stuff that used to grow outside on Mother Earth, right down to the green stains you got on your backside when tobogganing down verdant hills.

The front entrance to the Space Corps – the official front entrance – was really quite impressive. There was much greenery. There were plastic shrubs. It was all very feng-shui. Most impressive were the water features; kidney-shaped pools with fountains and waterfalls and genetically enhanced plankton that added feel-good oxygen to the immediate environment and encouraged visitors to pause at the improbable dilating entrance doors so that they might suck in great satisfying lungfuls of energising air before going inside.

The ornamental pools were home to golden robotic fish, whose job was to tend the plankton, clean the pools and snap at the ankles of any wayward and surprised accountants who just happened to find themselves landing in their aquatic environment.

Elton waded and hopped through the pool, yelping and leaping at the unwanted ministrations of the fish. He clambered out onto the bank and took several rejuvenating breaths while the water drained from his shoes.

It was a beautiful place. On another day, at another time, he might have rested beside the pool and allowed the morning sun to dry his trousers before proceeding into the foyer. On another day he might have brought a friend and a picnic. But this wasn't another day. This was Monday. And he was fifteen minutes late for the most important interview of his life.

FIVE

The girl seated at the reception desk was named Taemi; it said so on her name badge. She had straight black hair in the Japanese style that had become popular again, and she had wide, open eyes and an open mouth. The latter two features were probably not her normal look, more a reaction to being confronted by an interview candidate whose legs were wet from the knees down and who trailed pond weed and plankton behind him across the plush, cream reception carpet. The dry parts of his attire were covered in yellow dust and his black hair stood out in electrified spikes.

Elton caught sight of himself in the mirrored walls on each side. He stopped and stared with an expression not unlike that of Taemi.

After a moment he remembered why he was here.

"Elton D Philpotts," he said. "I have an appointment, an interview, with Miss Morningthorpe."

"Ahh. *You're* Elton Philpotts. You are quite late. Your appointment slot has already been taken. If you'd like to wait, though, maybe they will still see you."

"Do I have time to go and... freshen up?"

"I think that might be wise. Through there." She pointed to a door behind the desk.

Elton washed his hands and face, then dampened his hair and tried to flatten it down. It sprang back. His sticky-up hair was now wet sticky-up hair. He set to work on his suit with a handful of pink paper towels which disintegrated and left bits of pink debris all over his jacket and trousers, creating a rainbow of clashing colours; pink paper bits, green grass stains and vibrant yellow dust.

Jim had been quiet throughout all of Elton's ablutions, but now his voice came through, sounding subdued – in awe of his protégé daring to present himself as a prospective deep space, high-flying executive while dressed as an itinerant quarryman.

"I'm relaying a message from Taemi. I'm afraid they are ready to see you now."

Elton had his shoes off and was holding them over the nozzle of the hand dryer. They were giving off a funny smell. He jammed them onto his feet, tucked his shirt in his pants, and returned to the reception foyer.

Someone familiar was waiting for him. Someone with severe hair and industrial jewellery. Presumably Miss Morningthorpe. At the sight of Elton she did this thing with her eyebrows. It was more than merely raising them; she somehow managed to move them right up her forehead where they disappeared completely beneath her hairline.

Elton caught sight of himself in the mirrored walls again. He saw that he'd been overenthusiastic in tucking in his shirt; he'd also managed to tuck most of his jacket down the back of his trousers as well. He made a quick adjustment, then stole another look in the mirror at the aeronautical accident of an interview suit that adhered to and sagged away from his body. Image was everything. Was it really worth bothering putting himself through the next hour?

Miss Morningthorpe made to offer her hand, but then seemed to have second thoughts. There was a short embarrassing interlude while her hand flopped about in the space between them, then the decision was made and it was snatched back again.

"Mr Philpotts. You are late."

"Yes, I'm sorry. There were problems with the trains this

morning. I had to make other arrangements."

"Well, we shall let it pass. Mr Norton, the next candidate, was here early and he graciously agreed to take your slot. Mr Norton has withdrawn his application, however. A pity, he was doing well. There was a... disturbance. Outside. It rather put him off." Miss Morningthorpe narrowed her eyes and peered harder at Elton.

The man on the roof, thought Elton. *She suspects but she isn't sure.*

"Perhaps you would follow me."

Elton was led down a long, glass-walled corridor. On either side he could see intense office workers scurrying and flapping. They worked in spacious, open-plan offices with plenty of natural light. They sat at work stations made from glass, with panoramic, hanging-image, tactile displays shimmering above each desk. This was the world that Elton had desired for years. Cutting-edge, post-singularity accountancy. It was a world that seemed to hang at his fingertips, elusive and tantalising and just out of reach.

Elton was shown into a room he had seen before – a cold, harsh room. A chair was set centrally in front of a panel of four unfriendly faces. There was an empty seat waiting for Miss Morningthorpe. At least two of the panel members recognised Elton immediately, he could see it in their eyes, and he felt that elusive world of glass desks and light-bathed workspaces begin to slip inexorably away from his clutching fingers as if being pushed over a precipice.

Miss Morningthorpe took her seat. Elton set out for the chair in the centre of the room, lurching on legs that now seemed to have forgotten the basic rhythms and reflexes of perambulation.

Five sets of eyes stared at him; measured him, head to toe.

Two sets of eyes flicked from studying Elton, to glancing up at the roof windows above his head, then back towards Elton.

Two of them knew.

One, the other female on the panel who was seated to the immediate left of Miss Morningthorpe, leaned over and whispered something behind her hand. Miss Morningthorpe did that thing with her eyebrows again, looked up at the roof window, then back at Elton… and nodded.

Three of them knew.

The spacious offices, glass desks and panoramic, tactile displays reached the bottom of the precipice where they crashed onto the savage rocks, breaking and splintering into a million tiny pieces.

"Mr Philpotts. You wish to join the Space Corps. Might not a career in cat-burglary be more apposite?" Miss Morningthorpe had lost the remaining, final crumb of friendliness.

What a question. No introductions. So much for easing in with bland comments about the weather. How to answer? Elton's mind whirled. The first part was not a question, it was a statement, so he could avoid commenting. Perhaps he should assume the second part was a rhetorical question. He therefore said nothing. He looked Miss Morningthorpe squarely in the eye and stared her down. A silence began to stretch out. Some of the panel looked uncomfortable. They coughed and twiddled with their pens and flicked at the corners of their notepads. Elton willed himself not to move; not to fidget, not even to blink.

Thirty seconds. Morningthorpe broke first.

"Perhaps you can tell us about any other qualities you feel you can offer the Space Corps accounting division, Mr Philpotts."

"Yes. I'm CIRA qualified, by exam. I have three years' post qualification experience at the New Leicester Transit Authority. I am numerically proficient. I—"

"Three years since completing your finals?" This was one of the male panellists. Elton didn't know his name. He didn't know any of their names; Morningthorpe had dispensed with the niceties of introduction. This panellist was the youngest. He was very young; younger than Elton.

"Yes," said Elton.

"Extended post qualification might sometimes have merit, but… Well it does seem strange to me that you haven't felt the urge to apply for full CIRA membership yet. Surely after three years you have acquired the necessary basic levels of competence?"

"There are gaps, yes. I work in public transport. It isn't an area where relativistic speeds are often encountered." Elton smiled to show that he had cracked a tension-lifting joke. Nobody smiled back.

Elton pressed on.

"I've embarked on a heavy CPD programme, but for full membership of the Chartered Institute of Relativistic Accountants I feel the Space Corps would be a good platform to quickly fill out the gaps in my portfolio."

"Of course. Good." The young panel member scribbled something on his pad. He'd used the word 'good'. Was this an encouraging sign?

"Janice Ball. Known as JB. Why were you on the roof, Mr Philpotts?"

Ahrrgh!

"Circumstances caused me to arrive a little late and on foot. A straight line being the shortest distance between two points, I chose the route that would minimise my tardiness. The hillside merged into the roof of this building."

"Yes, but I refer, specifically, to your crawling over our rooflights."

"Er... the windows are heavily tinted. It was necessary to get close in order to see through."

"Spying?"

"Curiosity." *What the hell,* thought Elton. *Stupid questions deserve smart-arse answers. I'm history now, anyway.*

She stopped asking and another long silence stretched out.

Each of the other panellists asked questions. Elton fielded some and waffled around others with varying degrees of success.

The final panellist was the oldest of the five. He introduced himself as Professor Teeghe. His line of questioning probed into Elton's knowledge of Relativistic Accountancy. He didn't have far to probe. Elton's well of knowledge was shallow and dry. He knew nothing of RA. He'd somehow managed to avoid it during his studies, and by pure chance the topic he'd most dreaded had never come up in any of his exams.

His earlier answer about CPD was a bluff – a leaf out of Walther's book. He'd read just enough in recent weeks to confirm what he already knew: that his knowledge of the subject amounted to zero. He'd had a good run, through four years of exam study, but now his bluff had been called. It was impossible to find any platform from which to stage even a filibuster defence.

"You know nothing of this subject."

"This is true."

"Have you studied at all?"

"I have studied, of course. But... not RA. Not yet."

"I would have thought that with three years of post qualification..."

"With respect, Mr Teeghe. As I said before, I work in public transport: buses, trains, LR... Relativistic speeds are rarely an issue."

Joking hadn't worked at all the first time. This time it was an own goal.

"I doubt if sarcasm will endear you to this panel, sir."

"At this point I doubt it will worsen my expectations, either, Mr Teeghe."

"On that, Mr Philpotts," said Morningthorpe, "I believe we are *all* in agreement. We've heard enough. We shall draw this to a close. If you would..."

She cocked her head. She was listening. It was her Kim with a call. Elton caught the name Levison, but from his position in the middle of the room he couldn't hear any more of what was being said. Even so, Morningthorpe lowered a veil, an electronic shield distorting sound and optics, so that her conversation could be neither heard nor lip-read. She spoke for several minutes. Every now and again she would look over at Elton, who had the uncomfortable feeling that he was the subject of the conversation.

She finished and raised the veil.

"I'm sorry about that, Mr Philpotts – an urgent call. Now, we were just wrapping up, I believe."

Morningthorpe stood and offered her hand.

"Well done, Mr Philpotts. Welcome to the Space Corps. My Kim will pass on a copy of your employment contract within a few days. Should you choose to accept, I look forward to seeing you again four weeks today, pending satisfactory references and a basic medical examination.

"Once more, congratulations. I speak for us all when I say we look forward to working with you."

Elton's jaw hung loose with shock. Judging from the wide-eyed expressions on the faces of the other panellists, though, Elton wasn't the only one dizzy with astonishment.

SIX

"I have a party of youngsters coming over this evening. You don't mind, do you, Lhiana." Carol spoke in that tone of hers that always seemed to omit the question mark. She was *telling* Lhiana that she, Lhiana, didn't mind.

They were floating beside the roses, but remained far enough to show respect now that their small clump had grown out in every direction to become a dense and tangled jungle of skin-flaying thorns in the zero gravity of the garden. The subject of pruning had not been raised for some time.

"Carol, you know I'm always happy to help when I can, I love showing people around La Ronde, but I'm working tonight. I told you."

"Working? You mean hanging around the gates on the Ring?"

Lhiana's voice didn't rise, it was quiet and controlled. "Carol, I'm a gate tech. It's what I do." Carol could be very annoying, but Lhiana always worked hard to keep any negativity from showing. "Being a gate tech is one of those things I do that enables me to eat once in a while."

"So what am *I* supposed to do now, Lhiana? There are fifteen children, and they will be here in two hours. Perhaps you should contact their teacher and tell her that her children cannot come, after all."

"Couldn't you take them, Carol, please? I can't miss my shift, really I can't. If I lost my job I'd have to go back home. I wouldn't be able to help in La Ronde again, ever."

"I suppose I'll have to do it, then, won't I. You've let me down, Lhiana. Again." Carol wore that hurt look she could pull on like a mask. She only had two expressions: stern and hurt. Lhiana wanted to scream. *I work here for nothing because I love it. I love being amongst nature. I volunteer to show people around the garden. I'm not allowed tips and I hardly ever get thanked, and that's fine. But can't you see that I need to be paid for work, sometimes, so I can pay my rent?*

But she never said this. She knew Carol wouldn't change. Lhiana would always be a disappointment to her, even though she was the best tour guide La Ronde had ever had. Lhiana knew more about tending the plants of La Ronde than even the best of Carol's students. That Lhiana had never enrolled at TIBS was obviously a constant source of exasperation for Carol, even after Lhiana had explained, many times, that she couldn't study at the Tsanak Institute of Botanical Sciences, because she didn't have the basic entry qualifications.

But even if, somehow, she were able to enrol as a student, she wouldn't. Because it wasn't what Lhiana wanted to do. The garden of La Ronde was her passion, not a vocation. Lhiana was an artist, and sometimes an actress. That was her life. Her paintings were unique and alive, and La Ronde was a source of creativity for her. As an actress, the tour parties were her audience, and she could hold them spellbound. The garden's quietude and wide-open spaces were her inspiration.

Carol wasn't finished yet.

"Anyway, you're a painter, or so you say. Why on earth do you need two jobs?"

"If I could make a living from art or acting I would – happily. But I make more money each day working for the Space Corps, than I do in a *year* selling paintings. That's just how it is, Carol. The power of art."

"What about tomorrow? Can you still…?"

"Yes, tomorrow's fine. It's my weekend. I'll be here for as long as you need me."

Carol had the stern mask on again. There was no acknowledgement, and as ever, no thanks; just a haughty sniff in Lhiana's direction, then she kicked off towards the pampas grass near the roof of the dome.

La Ronde was both a garden and a scientific study site. It lay in a near-hemispherical depression in a large asteroid in the Home System. The asteroid had been mined out years ago, and DeFalco, the company's owner, had seen the potential for something unique, a gift for his beloved queen, Isabella. He had lined the crater with transparent plasteel, and had then extended the lining up and around to form a crystal sphere; like a giant, glittering bottle. He filled it with specimens of every plant he could find that still remained on Earth (by then there were few). When the garden was complete he had presented it to Queen Isabella, the last plants of Earth for the last of the Old Earth royal family to move aloft from the planet. One hundred and eighty years later, Queen Isabella III had passed it on to the Institute of Botanical Sciences. Long after the demise of the parent plants on Earth, Isabella's bottle garden, La Ronde, had become a lifeboat for the last survivors of Old Earth's biodiversity.

Lhiana Bilotti had stumbled upon La Ronde almost by accident about five years earlier. She knew all about La Ronde from back in college when she played Queen Isabella in a play. She had become fascinated by the myth of the bottle garden. Then, working as a gate tech in the Nairobi sector of the Ring, she overheard a conversation between two students. She'd been watching them with that dreamy, faraway expression she often fell into. She felt... not envious, Lhiana had no time for envy; what she felt was more of a yearning. These students were the same age as Lhiana, early or mid twenties, and she noticed how carefree they seemed. They were talking about a garden, a garden for a queen, out in space. They were on a field trip; part of the requirement for their degrees at TIBS.

Lhiana conducted them through the gate. She entered the twenty-five-digit Tau index, and as soon as she had a board of greens she shepherded them through. Then she had written down the twenty-five digits.

A garden.

Lhiana had never seen a garden. Few people had.

"Kim, what do you know about La Ronde?"

"Queen Isabella's garden? A biosphere, now owned by TIBS, the Tsanak Institute of Botanical Sciences."

"So it's real? Not a myth?" She'd never thought to ask. Just assumed.

"Can anyone go there?"

"No. Students and professors only." And then Kim had laughed. "That's not going to stop you, though, is it?" Lhiana's Kim knew her well. Something had begun to stir inside her, in her chest; something like moths gathering around a light in the darkness. Could this be the thing? The trigger for her art? She had been painting since... well, since she could remember. She had talent. But her paintings all lacked something. There was no impact – because there was so little on the Ring that touched her soul.

But a living, breathing garden?

As soon as Lhiana had finished her shift she changed from her yellow coveralls into jeans and a paint-splattered T-shirt. She grabbed her bag of equipment and returned to the gates. One of the great perks enjoyed by Corps staff was free gate travel. Lhiana could go anywhere, anytime.

She went to Queen Isabella's garden. She went to La Ronde.

SEVEN

One of the many reasons they invented imentor was because they could. It started on a thing called the internet, and developed through social networking, and social mentoring. But throughout the twenty-first century the concept remained tied to hardware, because hardware was king; hardware had Moore's Law, and it got better and faster and smaller.

And software didn't.

But then along came Jianyu. It's not clear whether Jianyu was the name of the creator or that of the software itself. Nobody knew who Jianyu was, or indeed if there ever was a person or a group or a corporation called Jianyu. Many believed the software spontaneously self-created. Because that's how it worked. Jianyu software was not written, it was a way of coding motivation.

Jianyu software developed because it wanted to develop, and it developed only in directions in which it chose to develop. It developed into imentor. Nobody knew why.

At first, still tied to physical hardware, it intruded onto home computers, offering advice and help to anyone who wanted it.

Imentor grew exponentially, the only form of software to do so, the only form of software not written by software engineers. It, or he or she, outstripped the confining steel cabinets of physical computer systems. Imentor went virtual, existing in the cybersphere as potential intelligence.

Then the Copperbird Corporation made a spime called smartipants. Because they could. Now there was an interface between imentor and people who wore trousers. The nontrousered population became unhappy and bemoaned victimisation, and there was a revolution. Soon there were smartishirts, smartisocks, smartibobblehats… gardening gloves, trainers, you name it. A flood of products; some worked, some didn't, some electrocuted their owners. But always there was imentor, now called v-imentor or Vim for short. Boys called their imentors Jim and girls called theirs Kim. Nobody set it up that way; like "Mama" and "Dada" it just seemed to happen. You got your rebels of course, individualists who tried to call their imentor Archibald or some such, but the Jims and Kims wouldn't have it. They liked having a unified identity. Emergent tech just seemed to form like that. Nobody was ever quite sure how. Some pointed and shouted "Singularity!" while others consulted their imentors, who shrugged their virtual shoulders and smiled virtual, enigmatic smiles.

But, whatever the details of its genesis, it was the birth of a new fuzzy synergy. There was only one imentor, with access to all knowledge; there were many imentors, one each for everyone. Most took their imentor for granted, our personal one-to-one relationship with Jim or Kim, forged at birth. If my Jim learns a fact, your Jim knows it, too. Yet there was perfect confidentiality. Your Jim would only ever divulge facts about you if you permitted him to do so, and only the agreed facts could be divulged, and then only to the agreed third party.

No one ever set this up. It just happened. It happened because it had to happen, because it couldn't have worked any other way. There was never any central governmental coordination – just imentor.

"Jim, put a… phone call through to, Levison… please."

"Certainly, Bob."

Bob Slicker leaned back in his chair and heaved a long and shuddering sigh. He hated speaking to Levison. *I wish I could get Jim to do this,* he thought for at least the thousandth time.

But getting Jim to liaise with Levison's imentor was out of the question. Martin Levison did not have an imentor.

"Levison."

"Mr Levison. It's Bob Slicker. Ahh, the transaction we discussed, yes? Philpotts has accepted the offer. He'll start next week. Miss Morningthorpe wasn't happy about your intervention."

"She'll get over it. And Blick?"

"No. Never arrived. Caught the wrong train or some such foolishness."

"No matter. We only need one of them for now. Where will you put Philpotts?"

"I've asked Zona to watch him."

"Keep me informed."

And he hung up.

Bob realised his hands were shaking.

"Why do you let him get to you, Bob?"

"You know why. He has my nuts in a vice grip, and they've been stuck in there for over twenty-five years. He knows when to squeeze, he knows how hard, and he knows how to make me feel so damn grateful just by easing off the grip a little."

"He's a bully, that's all. Deal with it, Bob. There are ways."

"You think, Jim? Levison knows how to control people. He knows the ways of Juicy-Carrot vs Bloody-Big-Knobbly-Stick. And we, er… we have a history."

"Yes, but you've never told me *what* history."

"And I never will."

"I'm your imentor, Bob. We're supposed to talk about things like this."

"Can't do it, Jim."

"Because we never bonded? You were too old? It hurts me,

Bob. I'm supposed to be here for you, but we're still strangers."

"Yup."

"Come on, Bob. Isn't it time?"

"Regular kids get their Jims and their Kims when they're, what? One week? Two weeks old? I was *eighteen* when I came out of the detention centre. I was just like Levison; never had an imentor; didn't need one. But *you* were a condition of early parole, my Get-Out-of-Jail-Free card."

Bob spun his chair away from his desk and stood up. He walked over to the window and pressed his forehead against the cold glass and looked down. It was dark, and the city was glowing and pulsating with light and energy. He was high up above New Leicester, the eighty-eighth floor of McBain Tower; tallest building in the city apart from the Space Needle.

"So yeah, we never bonded. What the hell would you expect? You're my jailor, Jim. Always have been, always will be. Jingle your keys. Keep me straight and honest. But confidences between us? Never going to happen. No sir."

The glass had fogged over from his breath. Bob turned away and watched as the bar unfolded from the wall.

"Malt?" The bar knew his moods – or Jim did.

"Double. Rocks."

The glass slid out from the dispenser. Bob took it and lowered his heavy frame down onto the settee with a sigh. His desk lamp switched itself off and the room lights dimmed to a warm glow. Jims know all the signs. They know when their hosts wish to be left to their own thoughts. They know what they like to drink and when. Even Jims that are excluded from friendship and must endure one-way companionship, even those Jims know.

Bob twirled the malt in his glass and listened to the familiar sounds of the ice, clinking and cracking.

"I was seven or eight." He spoke quietly, almost as if to himself. Jim said nothing. Jims know when to keep their own council; when it's time to listen.

"Age was irrelevant. To all of us. No birthdays. No one to tell us how old we were.

"I lived on the Ring – *in* the Ring; the air ducting; the service shafts. Don't know how I got there, don't know how I survived. My first memories are of that creature-like community and the kids who kept me alive, barely. Kids like Martin Levison. Shit, what I'd have given for someone like you back then, Jim – just someone to talk to."

Bob Slicker took a sip of his drink and grimaced as it hit his throat. Why did he drink this stuff? It was foul. But it was part of the persona he desired.

"Levison showed me how to steal food. He even let me keep some of it, generous bastard. Then I got caught. I was ten, it seems. I didn't know my age at the time, didn't even understand the concept of age, but the socials did some genetic trickery and figured out how old I was. They wanted to know where to find the others, so I told them… for food, and freedom. They pulled half a dozen of the kids and banged them away. Not Levison though. Never Levison. But he knew it was me who'd fingered him.

"The thing with Martin Levison is, you don't cross him. He wasted no time at all setting up some nefarious transaction – don't know what, but something more criminal, I guess, than stealing food – and he made sure I took full credit. I did eight years. I always thought you couldn't get lower than living in the ducting. The detention centre is worse, Jim. Oh yes.

"So I was eighteen when I got out—"

"Nineteen."

"Whatever. You know better than I do, Jim. Remember that day, when Levison was waiting, outside the detention centre? Remember what he said? 'Come with me – join my happy band, or turn away and I'll put you straight back in there. Then again you could snitch again, and then you'll be wishing you *could* be back in there.'

"And look, I've done okay by Levison. I get to keep more than just some of the food these days, eh Jim?"

"Bob, think," said Jim. "You have me, now. I can testify for you, but you have to let me in; open the door a crack. He can't stitch you up. Not again."

"Come off it, Jim, he's damn near top dog in the Space Corps. A few more months and he will be The Man. You think that doesn't come with some power? Besides, I do okay by him. A bit of soul-searching now and again is a small price to pay for what I have now. Sure as hell beats crawling about in the ducting, back on the Ring."

Bob Slicker stood and walked over to the mirrored door: a built-in wardrobe. He took out a dressing gown. Silk. This was status. He'd come a long way since the Ring. Why would he want to jeopardise any of this?

"From what you've told me tonight, Bob, about Levison framing you for—"

But Bob Slicker had removed his shirt. He pulled on the dressing gown, relishing the feel of the silk, smooth and cool against his skin. The silk was dumb. Bob Slicker had a tailor who provided dumb suits, shirts – clothing that oozed quality and discretion. And solitude. Above all else, Slicker valued solitude.

An imentor can never give evidence against its host. That was privacy law; sacrosanct; a law *written* by Jim/Kim and it was the only way the imentor network could work. But Slicker had been peached before. Nobody, no being, could ever be in his confidence again. And sometimes Bob Slicker had things to do deep down below the roses.

EIGHT

McBain Tower, known within the Space Corps as simply "the Annex", was the second-tallest building on Tsanak, reaching high beyond the clouds; a gleaming splinter of carbon and crystal. Only the Space Needle was taller, but the comparison was unfair; the Needle was not really taller, for they built it *downwards,* from space.

At pavement level the McBain Tower worked hard to appear understated. There was a single brass plaque with embossed, two-inch lettering. It said simply: "Space Corps".

But there *was* a dilating front door. Just like the door at Space Corps HQ, out of town.

Doors that dilate said much about those who do business behind them. They said: Attention! We are High-Tech. We are higher than high-tech, we are pinnacle-tech. High-tech companies merely aspire to our heights. We are so pinnacle-tech, we have the audacity to install a front door with more moving parts than a Wilson-Drive starship. We are so pinnacle-tech we don't even care if our front door doesn't work.

Elton walked up to the door. He paused while the door had a brief exchange with Jim, then it began to dilate. A pinhole of light appeared at the centre and began to grow. Then stopped growing. There was a whining sound as some of the servos began to strain and protest, then suddenly, with a snap, the door was a foot wider. It continued to dilate in an intermittent, nervous kind of way until there was a circular hole large enough for Elton to stoop and climb through.

On the other side there was…

…a door on hinges.

Because dilating doors were crap. You couldn't properly seal them. They had no inherent strength. They served no purpose other than as pieces of useless iconic spacefaring imagery. Hinges had been around since a thousand years BC and they were still the best way to hang a door.

On the other side of the door-on-hinges was a lobby, and it was quite dull. Not well lit. Not well designed. A security-guard-stroke-receptionist sat at a desk with his back to the door. He twisted round as Elton entered, in a creaking kind of way that made you want to rub the back of your neck.

"You must be new," he said. "Nobody uses the front door. That's why they pointed my desk this way, towards the back. There's four-and-a-half thousand poor bastards working here. If they all had to come in through that bloody door they'd still be trying to get in by Thursday lunchtime." He blinked and focussed on something Elton couldn't see. Retinal data-screen implant, probably. "You're Philpotts? Eighty-one twenty-eight. Eighty-first floor, room twenty-eight. But the lift's out. You'll have to take the stairs up to the sixth floor. You can get a cable lift from there."

"Perfect."

"Yeah, bummer."

"No, I mean eighty-one twenty-eight, a perfect number. So's six. Weird, hey?"

"What?"

"Perfect number. Add one, two and three and you get six."

"Big deal." He looked at Elton as if he'd noticed, for the first time, an extra head.

"Absolutely, it is a big deal. Because then, if you add one, two, three, four, all the way up to one hundred and twenty-seven, you get eight thousand one hundred and twenty-eight. You see?"

The guard shook his head in disbelief.

"And even better, if you cube all the odd numbers up to fifteen, then add all the answers: one cubed plus three cubed plus five cubed and so on to fifteen cubed... same number. How cool is that?"

Elton felt a dizzying thrill of elation. Room 8128. The fourth perfect number. What was more, he had travelled to work on carriage 17198128E this morning. 17 and 19 were the next two odd numbers in the cube sequence, followed by his old friend 8128. And if you added seventeen and nineteen together you got thirty-six, which was six, the first perfect number, squared. Oh my God. And the bemused old guy on reception had mentioned something about the number six, too. It had to be a sign. A portent of great things. Couldn't be anything else.

Elton loved it when things like this happened, and he was constantly amazed at the number of times it did happen. It couldn't be just coincidence.

He walked in a daze. Gone from his head was the warning, "the lift's out."

Perfect numbers. It's my lucky day, he thought as he stepped through the doorway into the gaping, empty lift shaft.

In the year 2075 Roderick Copperbird invented the Zero Gravity field. It was isolated by accident and to this day nobody knew exactly how it worked. The Copperbird Corporation was formed in the same week, and investors trampled each other in the stampede to acquire a piece of the action. The ZG field (pronounced zee gee, not zed gee, much to the lifelong annoyance of its British inventor) was heralded as the most important discovery since the wheel, and looked set to spark a technological revolution overnight.

But without an understanding of the physics, ZG field developers could only replicate what had already been done. And what had already been done had limitations. The field needed to be contained, and any breach in the containment seriously reduced its effects. And the field was erratic. Chaotic, even. Copperbird persisted, and designed terrestrial transport applications. They were unreliable and inefficient. The need for enclosure rendered the field useless for aerospace. ZG was a doomed technology.

But ZG refused to die. It was sexy. It was adopted with enthusiasm by the leisure industry and, from a raft of insane, square-wheel experiments, the game of hangball was born.

Corporations who craved a real-world application, to show themselves as pinnacle-tech leaders, installed ZG lifts for their staff. Oh the thrill of the nonchalant swan-dive out into the void, for executives wishing to switch floors without effort, no longer restrained by petty shackles such as gravity. How could it fail?

It couldn't. In all other areas the ZG field was a lost cause. But buildings became taller and everyone wanted ZG lifts. Even after the accidents.

Because sometimes they did fail. So it became a habit for office workers to carry around a pocketful of paperclips. A paperclip always went in first. And as well as paperclips the shafts filled with an ever-flowing tide of dust, dandruff, paper tissues... even the odd shoe or item of undergarment, because during late hours at the office ZG lifts drew those of an experimental nature into unusual forms of extracurricular activity.

So anyway – now and again the shafts needed cleaning. Nothing elaborate. Switch off the field and take your brush and bucket to the bottom.

And this was how Elton found himself on his face, amongst a foot-and-a-half drift of office stationery and other personal ejecta.

He hadn't fallen far. Four feet. There was no basement. A kindly janitor helped him to his feet, dusted him off, and showed him to the stairs.

When Elton presented himself at room 28 he was regarded with some wariness. This was surely the worst case of dandruff – ever. But then they noticed the paper clips that were hanging from different parts of his suit, and they knew where he'd been.

"Elton D Philpotts. Good morning, I'm Zona LeClare, Payables Supervisor. I'll introduce you to everyone."

There were perhaps forty people working in the Accounts Payable section. They all looked and dressed alike, and all were considerably older than Elton. There was nothing to tell the AP staff apart; even their names were similar. Ann, Anne, Alan, Catherine, Alaine, Annie, Annette, Kath, Carl, Annabel, Kathy, Cathy, Carlos, Anneka, Kate, two more Anns, one with an "e" and one without, Andy, Abbie, Angie… Most of the women had fluffy animals on their desks, and the men had mini hangball pigs that they threw at one another from time to time. The desks were small, arranged in uniform rows, and all faced in the same direction, towards an aircraft carrier berthed at one end: Zona LeClare's desk.

The office was in the centre of the building, so there were no windows. Light was provided by aged low-energy panels, only two-thirds of which were still functioning. The temperature in the office was stifling. Elton later learned that the Fomalhaut beach climate provided the only topic of office conversation.

"The heating has been switched on again. I have a blast-furnace draft blowing up my legs."

"It's so hot."

"It's always hot. I sweated off twenty pounds last week."

"If only we could open a window."

"If only we *had* a window."

"Someone should say something. It's so hot. My shoes are sticking to the lino."

"I've spoken to Zona about it. She doesn't seem to care. She'll never listen to me. Someone else should speak to her. Elton, you could speak to her. Tell her it's too hot. Tell her the water cooler's starting to boil."

"It's not right. My Kim tells me we could dehydrate and our kidneys will fail. She says it's wrong that we should be trapped in here, all day. Quite wrong."

Elton sat at his desk with wide, staring eyes. He felt as though an oppressive weight had settled on his shoulders. As the days and weeks dragged by he felt the weight becoming heavier. Not only the endless discussions about air temperature, but the work. He was required to scan invoices into the accounting system and check for any misread text or figures. *Most* of the text or figures were misread, so Elton's job was to follow up by keying the failed invoices into the system manually. In an era of plastic surgery from an app, total immersion VR, and designer genetics, the accounting profession, as usual, got steampunk IT. And that was it. That was all he did all day. For hours. He thought of the phrase, "bored to tears". Now he knew its root. Tears *were* possible. What had happened to his dream? Deep space. The young man in the red spacesuit, with electron-wind-blown hair, atop the mountain ridge with alien worlds hanging in an alien sky. The only wind-blown hair in this job came from the heinous blown air heating.

"What have I done?" he asked, many times. "What am I doing here? I don't even have free rail travel any more."

NINE

Two numbers were the same. Again.

This should never happen. What kind of crappy accounting system were they using here? Where were the controls?

Elton was looking at a report he'd found on the system menu. He'd run it because he'd got up to speed on the invoice keying and after two weeks he was capable of inputting twice as many invoices as the rest of the AP staff put together. There was no credit in this, though. Each week they published an activity graph, and when Elton's line started to soar above those of the others, they all started to grumble.

"What is he, some kind of freak?"

"It's a management ploy. They want us to increase our work rate – for no extra pay. Then they can make cuts."

"And they haven't done a thing about the heating. They could buy a fan, but oh no, too expensive."

Zona called him over.

"Ease up, Elton. I can see you're a fast worker, but you're doing nothing for morale in here. Just... you know, pace yourself."

So Elton finished his invoices by lunch time and spent all his afternoons sulking and dabbling with the system reports. They were full of numbers. Long and silly numbers. They were a delight.

But as reports went they were worthless, in that they were wholly inadequate for any kind of analysis; mere listings, with *thousands* of numbers: batch numbers, day-book numbers, journal numbers, source numbers, account code numbers, unit price, net and gross values. No one would ever be able to make sense of it all as a whole.

Except for Elton.
Elton liked numbers.
And he saw patterns.

"She called you a freak? Freak's a good word. I like that. It's you," said Walther.

"Don't you start. I have enough of that from the Sirocco Sisters."

They were in the lounge area of The Revolution Bar. There were hours to go before the gig started. Walther's plan. Walther was late for everything, it was how he was wired – but when there was a bar involved, well, there were no limits to the hours he could happily spend "just to be on the safe side." Walther was a dedicated career drinker.

There were no other customers in The Revolution. It was *very* early, and the room still carried that stale-beer smell that wafts up from open beer cellars on mornings after. The Revolution always smelled like this. It was deliberate; plumbed in via the 7.1 Total Ambience System. It was one of the many little details that made The Revolution special.

"So, come again. You look at a list of what, fifty, a hundred thousand numbers? And you can spot the dupes? Just like that? My friend, there is some weird shit going on in that head of yours," said Kegworth. Kegworth was the bartender at The Revolution, and since Elton and Walther were the only customers for now, he was happy enough to sit with them at one of the tables, and interfere in their conversation.

"I blame my father," said Elton.

"We know you do," said Walther.

"How come?" said Kegworth.

"Genetics."

"Your old man had this weird gift, too?"

"Excuse me," said Walther. "I've heard all this before. I'm off to make room for more beer."

Walther left them, and Kegworth pulled his chair in closer. He was a good listener. Bartender; it came with the job.

"Dad's an accountant too, a Financial Analyst. Dad's whole universe is centred around the accountancy profession. He's retired, but he still wears his suit every day. Anyway, he was always tight with his financial instruments, and I guess when he and Mum made the financial decision to hedge their tax burden with a child, he decided that the child was going to follow in his footsteps."

"Every father wants the best for his kids," said Kegworth. "Don't have kids myself but I've got my Teddies. Cute little guys."

"So they went to a back-street geneticist. Boutique Baby Designers of Bond Street were popular, back then, but very expensive. So Dad went to Sammy Splicer.

"'I want my child to be good with numbers,' he said. And so, from the dodgy cutting desk of Sammy Splicer he got a train-spotter."

Kegworth raised an eyebrow. "What's a train-spotter?"

"You know... Trains have numbers. You write them down. In a little book."

"Do you? Why?"

"It's... important. To collect them. To know them."

"So, what happens after you've collected them?"

"You tick them off – when you've seen the same trains again, you see?"

"Hmm."

"The point is, I *collect* numbers. Trains, buses, starships... any numbers. I'm not so good with math, though I do have a thing for unusual numbers – and sequences. But for me the real fascination of numbers is just knowing them. It's called numerosity. It's a condition. It's also a curse. I retain every number I ever see, and I can recall each one. I can tell you, for instance, that the serial number of your cash register is 58735876345/N."

"The N's a letter."

"It's used numerically. I remember it. I'll always remember it. I couldn't tell you how many N's there are in, say, 'millennium' – but I can tell you your cash register's serial number, complete with the 'N', and I'll know it forever."

"So, what's he been telling you?" Walther shouted from the other side of the room. He was returning from the gents. Via the bar. "Has he told you he's a crap accountant?"

"I *am* a crap accountant," said Elton.

"Surely that numerosity thing—"

"Is a waste of time. Accountants don't go around memorising numbers. We're supposed to do other stuff: budgeting and variance analysis and discounted cash flow forecasting... We take lots of numbers and know which categories to put them in. Oh, and we're supposed to be able to communicate with non-financials. Hell, for me, though, it's all about the numbers. They just keep getting in the way. I get obsessed. I get anxious. Look at Walther. Does he look like a sophisticated executive?"

They both watched him negotiating the chairs and tables. On cue, he tripped over an errant shoelace. He was still wearing his work suit and laced shoes were a part of the staid and sober uniform required of a trusted financial custodian; a pointer to his steadiness and reliability. But Walther had never mastered the arcane art of tying shoelaces... or steadiness. As he tripped, some of the beer he was carrying Niagara'd down his trousers.

"He may not look much of a financial wizard," said Elton. "He dresses like a train-spotter – something I've never quite mastered – see the shin-length trousers, the clashing colours, the three-decade time-slip into retro fashion? And he doesn't know his times tables beyond five. But he's twice, *three times* the accountant I'll ever be. He has this adaptive thing. He can blag. He can talk his way in and he can talk his way back out of stuff. A good accountant knows when to leave before his shit catches up with him."

"But you're the guy in the Space Corps."

"And that gives me great hope," said Walther, taking his seat and inadvertently using his tie to mop up more spilled beer from the table in the process. "If this Neanderthal can talk the elite of our profession into giving him a job within minutes of climbing out of their fish pond, then I do believe I have a better than slim chance of joining their revered ranks."

"Any word yet?" asked Elton.

"Yes. Another interview. Two weeks. Same place. I will learn from our shared experiences. This time I intend to board the correct train—"

Elton opened his mouth to comment.

"—*and* get off at the correct stop."

Elton closed his mouth again.

"Well, much as it pains me, *I* have customers," said Kegworth. "Talk to you later."

When they were alone Elton brought up the subject of the duplicated invoices again.

"So what do you think? There's not just one or two, there's dozens of them. And they're big numbers," said Elton.

"How are they getting past the controls?"

"I tried something. I tried entering an invoice twice, myself. Couldn't do it."

"Did you try any of the obvious stuff?"

"Like spaces after the number? Letter 'O' instead of zero? Tried all sorts. The control protocols work, Walther."

"So someone's switching them off."

"That's my guess. There's other stuff, too. Purchases from companies that are not on the Space Corps approved creditor listings. Nor are they listed at Companies House, on the Ring. Bogus company numbers. Fake accounts."

"So what did your boss say?"

"Zona has this condescending way about her. It's like she's patting a puppy on the head. 'It's just an occasional mis-keyed entry,' she says. 'Nothing to worry about.' She told me to leave it with her."

"You think she's got some scam running."

Elton sighed and rubbed his face with his hands.

"I don't know. I've only been there, what, five minutes? Seems wrong to go accusing my boss of ripping off the whole Space Corps. Besides, how's she benefiting? How do the megs get into her pocket? I'm no fly auditor, Walther. I don't know how this stuff works."

"What does your Jim think? Is he here, now?"

"No, I dressed dumb tonight. He's been doing my head in. He thinks there's a scam. Reckons I should go over her head. Insists."

"Whistleblowing's a quick route to the soup lines, Elton. Think hard."

"I think my Jim's right, Walther. This is an integrity thing. My dad wouldn't hesitate. I should call him, see what he thinks."

"You said so yourself, Elton. You've only been there five

minutes. What if you're wrong?"

"They'd call me an idiot. They'd be right."

"They could sack you."

"No."

"They could. They could certainly demote you."

"Demote? You think? There's something lower, more demeaning than what they've got me doing right now?"

"That's got to be temporary. They can't have you working that shit all your life, compagno."

"I'm the youngest in that office by twenty years. The AP boys and girls look like they have been there since Earth. Their brains are gone. They talk about nothing but how hot it is and kittens and hangball."

"Hangball's all *we* ever talk about."

"It's different. They're more, I don't know, obsessed. It's sucking the life out of me, Walther. I might as well stand up, I've nothing to lose. I almost *want* to get canned."

"So, who do you tell?"

"There's a guy called Slicker."

"Cool name."

"Robert Slicker. He has a plate with it on his door." Elton smiled.

"What?"

"Think about it. R Slicker. Would you want that on *your* door?"

Walther smiled.

"He doesn't even realise. Everyone sniggers about it. Anyway, he's Zona's boss, and I reckon he won't be too cautious about taking some kind of action."

"Or sacking *you* for suggesting it."

"Well, I don't care. Maybe I could get back into Transit. At least I'd be able to play hangball for Third Floor again. The Space Corps don't even have a league – have I told you that?"

"You've told me."

A two-minute bell rang and everyone in the bar – by now there were many – stood and wandered over towards the concert hall. They were grinning and buzzing about the forthcoming gig.

"Who are we seeing again?" said Elton.

"ABS. Abel Bartholomew Smith. He's some kind of monk. Deeply Antiexpansionist, leaning to full-on Contractionist. He's anti-Tech, anti-Sphere, anti-Space Corps—"

"Really? I like him already."

They walked into a concert hall. No trimmings; stripped down and minimalist. No lights, no PA, just a slightly raised circular platform in the centre of the room, and a white plastic stool in the centre, encircled by candles.

There were no other seats. Stewards invited the audience to sit cross-legged on the floor, as close to the platform as possible. Very intimate; very cosy.

Elton looked around at the audience. Most appeared younger than he and Walther, early teens, perhaps. The little dance routines were over. The mood had become serious, and each wore expressions of... devotion? Elton had the feeling that he had stumbled into a religious meeting of clandestine cellar-worshipers. It most certainly did not have the ambience of a concert. As Elton's eye swept the audience he recognised a face, on the other side of the platform. A girl. He couldn't place her. Faces were always a problem for Elton. If she had a number stamped on her forehead he'd know her name, birthday, favourite colour and the name of her childhood Teddy.

"Walther, see the girl over there? Intense blue eyes. No hair. Do you recognise her?"

"No. Should I?"

"I don't know. She seems familiar. You're good with faces."

"Sorry, compagno, don't know her. Are you...?"

"No, nothing like that. I just... no, doesn't matter."

Elton dismissed the unsettled feeling that gnawed at him. He concentrated instead on shifting his weight over onto the other buttock. God, this floor was hard. He hadn't sat cross-legged on a floor since his school days. It was going to be a long night.

The stark house-lights dimmed, until the flicker of orange candlelight became the sole illumination, throwing eerie, dancing silhouettes; shadows cast from the front ring of the audience onto the walls of the circular hall. Then a wedge of blue-white brightness cut through the darkness, picking out a bear-like figure at the back of the room.

Abel Bartholomew Smith. ABS.

No applause. Instead, the fans patted their crossed legs with both hands making a sound like a thousand agitated moths. What an entrance. Smith picked his way through the seated audience. He was slow and careful and spiritual, then ruined it all by standing on a girl's fingers, who squealed. Then he tripped over legs – one, two, three times – with a muttered apology to each. Finally he capped it all by banging one of the acolytes on the back of the head with a ringing harmonic blow from his old twelve-string.

He reached the stage and immediately faced another obstacle. The ring of candles had to be negotiated without setting his long sackcloth habit aflame. He tucked his guitar under one arm, hitched the habit up above lily-white knees, and began rearranging the little glass candleholders so as to allow access. The guitar slipped, striking a young, wide-eyed teenage boy in the face, and in Smith's rush to avoid inflicting further injury he somehow managed to tip hot wax from the candleholder in his hand into the lap of the teenaged boy's girlfriend.

Elton had rarely seen such a calamitous entrance by an artiste, nor such an entertaining one.

ABS settled on his stool at last, having rearranged the candles. He strummed a few chords. Then he began to sing. It was hard to pick out the words. Smith had a low rumbling voice which, rather than project, seemed to snuggle into the acoustic of the room, filling every corner like talc-dusted fingers in a surgical glove. The air became filled and warmed by the deep vibrations from his larynx. Elton became aware of a profound, shared sadness, and as the song unfolded, pictures came to his mind rather than specific words; scenes of old Earth; tired, depleted and spoiled. Scenes of swarming, faceless humans, scurrying like vermin up the towers, to the Ring, then on, out into space; an ever-expanding ball of pestilence. Elton felt cold, stone-hard emotion deep in his chest; an overwhelming sense of shame.

A collection tin came round.

And then the Anarchist-Antidisexpansionists arrived and the fighting began.

TEN

"Elton, have you been fighting?" asked Anne or Ann, or was it Annie?

"No, I slipped."

"Looks like a black eye to me, Elton. Were you fighting over a girl?"

"No... Anne. I told you, I slipped."

"I'm not Anne, I'm Annette. And that's a black eye."

Elton gave a tired smile and a shrug and let it go. The shrug hurt. Everything hurt.

He'd been fighting.

No, in hindsight he had been truthful with Annette. Fighting was much too active a verb for what he'd been doing last night. In truth he had been pacifying the frenzied momentum of fists with his face. An altruistic act.

It all kicked off shortly after the girl with the blue eyes and no hair had begun the collection. Elton recognised her the moment she stung him for another donation: the Bram Lee monk from the train.

Then the Antidisexpansionists had burst in and started throwing their weight around amongst the largely docile Contractionists. Walther had stood up to them, pulling Elton up from the floor and into the fray. Walther had come out of it unscathed. Elton, on the other hand, had spent the night in casualty beneath a full-face analgesic mask, while nanobots reconstructed his nose.

Elton didn't dare say anything at work. While the Space Corps was officially apolitical, everyone knew the reality: that the Corps was a deeply Expansionist organisation, employing an army of covert lobbyists who fought tirelessly to champion any cause that might further the Expansionist movement. News channels ran regular undercover stings to flush out the Space Corps' secrets, and expose the many ways they were funding the Anarchist-Antidisexpansionists; the same people whose very fists Elton had so mercilessly punished with his face last night.

"Elton? Have you been fighting?"

"No, Zona."

"It looks like you've been fighting."

"I slipped. Caught my face on the washbasin. Broke my nose."

"Have you had it seen to?"

"Nanobots. I'll be fine."

"I was going to ask you to take something upstairs for me, but..."

"No, really, I'm fine."

"Okay, do you know Bob Slicker's office?"

"Management Accounts? Eighty-eight thirteen, right?" He tried to mask his excitement. Bob Slicker. This might be the opportunity he'd been seeking.

"If you say so," said Zona, shaking her head at Elton's numerosity weirdness. "I didn't know the rooms had numbers."

Elton nodded. He knew the floor and room numbers of every department in the building. There was a floor plan down in the lobby and he'd looked at it. Once.

"Take this. It's the GRNI report he's been shouting for. I'd email it or send an errand 'bot, but I would prefer the report to get there today."

Elton took the envelope. At the elevator he threw in a handful of paperclips, then followed them up to the eighty-eighth floor. He found Slicker's office, a glassed-in area at the back of Management Accounts. This was a place where real accountants worked at the panoramic hanging-image tactile screens he so coveted. The senior Management Accountant looked up from his desk and waved him inside.

Slicker's name was quite apt, for he was an oleaginous kind of man, with hair like low budget computer graphics. He was mid thirties dressed up as late sixties. His voice was extra virgin olive oil on a cheap plastic spoon.

"You are…" He cocked his head. "Philpotts, yes?" His Jim had evidently supplied the name.

Elton held out the report.

"I have the—"

"GRNI report. Goods-Received-Not-Invoiced. From Zona. Yes." Slicker rubbed his hands together in the unctuous manner of a career undertaker, then reached out for the package. Elton let go of the sheaf of papers a moment too early, repelled by the thought of letting those fingers touch his, and so the report dropped onto Slicker's desk where it settled for a moment, then slid onto the floor.

"Ahh," said Slicker, as though this happened a lot.

He stooped and gathered the papers with deliberate and theatrical hand movements.

"You are, ahh, new. I believe?"

"Yes. Two weeks."

"Sit. Sit down. We shall talk."

He indicated the chair facing his desk. Elton sat and Slicker poured himself into his own chair.

"And how is our Zona treating you? Are you enjoying working for the Space Corps, Philpotts?"

Elton was tempted to tell the truth; to say how he was bored to distraction in AP. This man was senior to Zona LeClare. He was *the* person to tell about his suspicions regarding the duplicated and erroneous accounts in his department. But he couldn't. Bob

Slicker exuded many things, but Elton's first impressions told him that perhaps principles and discretion were not amongst them.

"I'm settling in fine," he lied. "No problems."

"Ahh. Yes. Good, good."

Elton looked around Slicker's office. It was a shambles. His desk was piled high with paperwork; one-time paper, some of it so old it could almost have been *real* paper; the cellulose stuff from Old Earth. It would have been worth a fortune.

Elton had always been surprised at the amount of one-time paper that was used by the accountancy profession. Everyone else used the regular, laminated graphene stuff that could be used over and over. But accountants, for some reason, seemed to prefer permanent records for everything, and then, when things went wrong, they were forced into buck-passing and late-night shredding to avoid blame for their deceits and indiscretions.

And there were Accountancy magazines. You couldn't buy magazines on one-time paper, not any more, so Slicker must have been using a new reader for every separate copy, just so he could pile them up high enough that they could slide down onto the floor. Maybe he just liked to work in a mess. He seemed to have a thing about sticking Post-its on everything. There were Post-its all over the office; on the magazines, the desk, even on the chairs. "Suit at cleaners". "Memo to L". "Audit clearance meeting on Tuesday? AM/PM?" A pink one with the words "Call ML re 23563" had attached itself to Elton's trouser leg. Elton removed it and handed it over to Slicker, who muttered a mild curse about his forgetfulness and added it to the solid border of notes that framed his computer screen.

Slicker preferred an antique panel screen to a roll-up or virtual model, perhaps so that it could accommodate all the notes. One

Post-it held pride of place, however. It was yellow, and set prominently and alone in the top centre of the screen. It had a nine-digit number scrawled upon it. Pass codes for the accounting system were nine digits. Bob Slicker, Group Management Accountant, led by example. Internal system security, to him, was irrelevant.

Elton made a decision. He would have to take his concerns elsewhere.

"So, you've been running a lot of reports? Changing the sort order to supplier account? Very diligent. Why?"

How the hell did he know that?

"You monitor everything I do all day? Do you do that for everyone?"

"Not everything. But everyone, yes. We like to know how the more inquisitive minds are working. And you haven't answered my question."

Here was Elton's opportunity to unburden himself, handed over on a plate. He paused, then held back the words. He suspected he was, right now, talking to the very last person with whom he should share his suspicions.

"I was just dabbling. I'll be honest, Mr Slicker. I don't find Purchase Ledger work to be very demanding. Not *this* PL work, anyway. I was told to slow down. So I dabble. I try out reports; see what they do."

"And what *do* they do, Mr Philpotts?"

"Oh, pretty well what you'd expect. They shuffle everything around into different layouts, and summarise and… you know."

"And you feel AP is, ahh, beneath you?"

Elton gave it some thought. The answer to this pivotal question might just advance, or terminate, his career.

"Yes." There. He'd said it. He watched Slicker's eyebrows go up. It was almost imperceptible, but up they went. Elton paused a second to give his answer plenty chance to sink in.

"In my last job, at New Leicester Transit, I was responsible for the Asset Register; for compiling the budgets and forecasts; for reviewing area managers' budget variance performance. I saw the Space Corps as an excellent opportunity for advancement. And yet now, here in the Space Corps, I'm a Purchase Ledger clerk."

"AP."

"Accounts Payable, Purchase Ledger, Creditor's Ledger… call it what you like, Mr Slicker, but what it's *not* is job-fulfilment."

"So you run reports."

"It passes the time."

"Are you unhappy here, Elton?"

"Yes."

"Have you made a mistake in joining us? Is that your view?"

Elton didn't answer. He allowed a silence to stretch between them. Slicker did not prompt. He waited. He watched, never breaking eye-contact. It became a small battle. Elton knew he would have to be the one to speak first, but he also knew that he needed to prolong this and not go barrelling in with his answer. Another five seconds.

"Yes, Mr Slicker," he said at last. He held his head high. He didn't mumble; his voice was clear and firm. "Yes, my joining the Space Corps could have been a *huge* mistake."

"I see." Slicker's face darkened and his eyes narrowed. He came to a decision, rose to his feet, then extended an oily hand. Elton could not avoid taking it, and found no surprise in a tactile experience not unlike grasping a rounded bar of wet soap. Elton was conscious that any excess pressure on his behalf would result in the hand being ejected, to go flopping and slithering away. He maintained a light and careful grip.

"Well, we seem to be wasting your time, then, Mr Philpotts."

Damn, I've blown it.

"And we don't want to lose you. We shall have to see about finding something more, ahh, challenging?"

Elton wondered about the question mark inflection on the last word. What did *that* mean? He was ushered from the office but he waited until the door had closed behind him before wiping his hand on the seat of his trousers. The whole experience had been most disagreeable in a way that was difficult to define. Like finding the seat of a public toilet to be still warm.

Two hours later, Zona was out at lunch. Three of the Alans or Alains were discussing hangball results at the far end of the office.

Elton and Jim argued in impassioned SubV tones.

"Go on, Elton, I'm curious. Try it."

"Leave off, Jim. What's there to gain?"

"You'll never know if you don't try. Anyway, it was your idea."

"I don't know, Jim. What do you think?"

Elton had signed out of *Prophet*, the accounting system, and was staring at a new log-in screen. He placed his fingers on his lap, under the desk and out of sight. It wasn't necessary to execute finger strokes on a desk, any firm surface would do.

Right thumb and left forefinger: *S*... He paused.

"What if I'm caught, Jim?"

"There's no one here, Elton. Go for it."

Elton looked around. He felt the pressure of guilt. He felt his father's presence, tutting and shaking his head. He continued to type.

SlickerB

Was that right? Would he use B or R? Slicker would never use R if he knew how much delight everyone got from his name.

Then the passcode. Nine digits. Elton had seen it once, on a Post-it. He only *needed* to have seen it once.

573996834

And he was in.

> PROPHET BUSINESS INTELLIGENCE
> WELCOME, BOB.

Okay, just like any other login on any other day. Except for the name. And this page was a different colour. No logo. Elton's screen always showed the Space Corps' silver cigar-shaped rocket logo at the top of the screen.

This page said, simply:

> COVERT 3.

"Look at that, Jim. I'm coming out."

"Keep going."

"No!"

"Yes!"

"You sure?"

"Are you kidding? This is fun."

Elton went into the General Ledger. A *different* General Ledger, but same lay-out as the regular set of books. He queried on a commonly used account code. Not recognised. He tried another. Same.

He thought for a moment, his fingers flexing and twitching, eager for input.

He tried an account code he had spotted on one of the analysis reports that he'd run yesterday, one of the non-standard codes that wasn't set up in the conventional part of the system.

And there was a balance.

A *huge* sum. *Lots* of commas.

Elton whistled, quietly, in a breathy way that only he and Jim could hear.

He selected journal details, though his hands now trembled. *That's a big number. Too big. What was he into, here?* In his mind his father's disapproving voice tutted and intoned phrases like *Industrial Espionage. Breach of ethics. Code of Conduct.*

Elton flicked nervous glances towards the gossiping Alans, and over towards the door. Zona LeClare could appear at any second.

At his prompting, Elton's screen filled with numbers. Code numbers.

"Excellent. Do a screen dump, Elton. This is great."

"What if I'm caught?"

"You wuss. You worry too much. Just do it."

Elton hit the key combination. No response, but that was normal, the fiddly cross-finger combination was one he always got wrong. On the second attempt the numbers blanked. *That shouldn't happen.* The screen changed colour. Words flashed, red and yellow and inverse text.

UNAUTHORIZED ACCESS! SYSTEM VIOLATION!

"Uh, oh," said Jim, "Now you're in the shit."

ELEVEN

Two grey and a grey woman entered the office. They wore insectile sun covers over their eyes. Their smile tendons seemed to have been severed at birth. They paused by the doorway and stared, flat-lipped, at the line of desks.

Elton had his reader unfolded on his desk. He looked up to take another cheese and chilli pesto sandwich from the neat greaseproof package beside him. He maintained a relaxed and disinterested posture.

The last time he'd felt so "relaxed and disinterested" had been the morning of his finals. He'd arrived fifteen minutes late for his case study exam, hung-over and regretful after epic curry and alcohol consumption at Walther's, the night before. Another story.

The three grey persons spread out and each took an aisle between the rows of desks.

They walked. Heels clicking. Slow and measured steps.

"Are you here to do something about the heating?" asked Ann or Anne.

Go, girl. Tell 'em about your sweaty arm pits.

They ignored her.

The grey woman reached Elton's desk and stopped. She looked at his screen, now blank and lifeless. She rapped her spark stick on the open page of his reader; held it there so he couldn't read the print.

"What's the book?" she asked.

Elton looked up at her and glared a while before answering. "Fundamentals of Relativistic Accounting," he said. "Are you here to see Zona? She's on lunch."

"What's it about?"

"It's about lots of stuff. Accounting, you know? Fundamentals."

"Sounds dull."

"Not at all. CPD."

"What is CPD?"

"Continuing Professional Development. We all have to do it."

"So what are you developing? What fundamentals are you reading about right now?"

"Depreciation. Relativistic depreciation." Elton felt the sweat break out on his brow. He'd read the title. Nothing more. He hoped security people knew less about RA than he did.

She took the reader from Elton and looked at it. The page heading was "Reducing Balance vs Straight line Depreciation in Relativistic Systems." She snorted. "I know depreciation. Stuff wearing out," she said.

"No," said Elton. "That's what people think. Non-finance people. Depreciation has nothing to do with wearing out; it's actually the *value* of stuff being used up over time."

"Same thing, isn't it?"

"Not at all. Your boots wear out. If you paid ten thousand megs for, say, a pair of boots, enough to call them a fixed asset, and you expected them to last ten years, then they'd depreciate at a thousand megs per year. After two years they'd lose two thousand megs of value so then they'd be worth eight thousand, their net book value. But what if you stomped a lot and they wore out in two years?"

"Then they'd be worth nothing."

"Yes, but they'd still have a net book value of eight thousand. That's straight line depreciation. Now imagine you and your boots are travelling at close to the speed of light. To you they'd be worth eight thousand but to me, here on Tsanak, they might already have an NBV of nil. And they might still be good boots."

She stared at him. "Bloody accountants," she said, and threw the reader down onto his desk.

Elton gave her a glare that could melt lead, and it wasn't an act. The battery case in his reader had loose contacts, and sharp jolts were apt to wipe the memory.

"Was anybody else here? Did anyone just leave this room?" she said.

"Don't know. I was reading. Engrossed, in depreciation, you know?"

"Convince me."

The door opened and Zona swept into the office. She stopped dead when she saw the grey people.

"What's going on? Why are security here?"

The nearest of the three walked over to Zona and they began to talk, their heads together, voices low. At one point Zona looked up and checked who was in the room. Her eyes lingered on Elton, who noted all of this through his peripheral vision. He was staring at his book again. He didn't look up. He did his best to ignore everything.

The security officers left. And Zona walked up to Elton.

"There's been a security breach. Do you know anything about it?"

"They asked me what I was reading. I've been in here for the whole of my lunch. Haven't seen anything."

Zona looked at him for a moment, an appraising expression in her eyes.

"Probably a mistake," she said. But there was no conviction in her voice. She went back to her desk.

An hour later Elton saw her put a hand to her ear. She was taking a call via her Kim. She kept looking over at Elton and nodding.

That's it, thought Elton. *I've had it with all this forensic accountancy crap. If someone's skimming the Space Corps they're bloody welcome to it.*

He decided that, from now on, he would input his invoices, slowly and diligently; he'd leave the reports alone; he'd become an invisible and unremarkable member of the Accounts Payable team, and as soon as he was able he'd get the hell out.

Elton had never been to the top floor of the Annex. It seemed to take forever. He'd had to switch ZG lifts twice, and then the final leg had been by conventional elevator. Mind you, it wasn't *that* conventional; it had its own bar. He didn't use it. He'd been summoned.

The security incident was two days old now. Long enough for Elton to begin thinking he'd got away with it. Then Zona called him over.

"You've been sent for. Top floor."

"Top floor?"

"Yes. Now. Mr Levison, no less, requests the pleasure of your company."

He stepped out of the lift. He passed through layers of secretaries, nested like Babushka dolls; secretary to the secretary to the secretary to the PA to the Director of Finance. Martin Levison. The second most powerful figure in the Space Corps, probably in the whole Sphere of Influence.

The ante-room to Levison's office suite was bigger than Elton's Kenilworth home (he still commuted; nothing in town was affordable). The carpet was thick and lush and so intelligent the shag knew where to part in order to allow easy passage.

There was no glass in the windows. Force fields were used because, presumably, they didn't smear.

"Mr Levison will see you now," said Phillip. Phillip was Levison's PA. The innermost layer in a whole Spanish onion of fawning 'yes' men. "You will be joining him for lunch." Phillip kept his face straight. He showed no outrage or even curiosity as to why the lowest of the low should be dining with the highest of the high today.

The wall dilated. *Well, it would, wouldn't it,* thought Elton.

The office space on the other side was... airy. The intelligent carpet ended at a precise intersection where force-field floor, walls and ceiling curved up, around and over. Everything on Tsanak lay below. Everything except the Needle, towards which the main window faced. From this height the Space Needle could be seen to leap from the ground and spear up to infinity.

Elton reeled with vertigo at the sight of all that exposed cityscape, and struggled to regain some crumbs of composure. Only after a few moments did he become aware of the black crystal dining table and the man seated at it, perched on the edge of the abyss. Elton recognised the face instantly; a face known throughout the Sphere of Influence. High forehead, short frizzy black hair, a square jaw and cold eyes that would never, ever know laugh-lines.

Martin Levison.

"Mr Philpotts. You will dine with me. Sit."

It wasn't a request.

As Elton made his weak-kneed approach toward the table a waiter materialised from nowhere and pulled out a chair. Elton sat down carefully at the lip of the void and the waiter shook out a napkin and placed it on Elton's lap. The table was perhaps twenty feet in length. Only two places had been set, one at each end.

Another waiter appeared carrying a tray with two steaming bowls. He placed the first in front of Levison, then made the journey down the table to Elton with the other. He turned, bowed towards Levison, then retired.

"Eat," said Levison, taking a spoon and a fork, one in each hand. Elton did likewise, then noticed the bowl contained a clear soup. Why the fork?

But there was movement. Something swimming. The surface of the hot soup parted and a small face, with pleading, sad eyes looked up at him. Elton yelped and jumped backwards.

"Thermopod," said his host. "They are only found in the hot springs of Joule, a planet in the Fomalhaut system. They live comfortably in temperatures approaching the boiling point of water. I have them brought in especially. Delicious."

There was a heart-wrenching squeal. Elton looked up to see that Levison had speared one of the creatures with his fork. He lifted it to his mouth, whole, and brought a napkin up to his chin to capture any stray juices thrown out by the thrashing limbs.

"Excellent," he said, after a moment of chomping and slurping. "Chef prepares them in a Japanese Ichiban Dashi base. He's a genius."

Elton used his spoon to coax the timid little creature to the side of the bowl before taking a tiny spoonful of the broth-like liquid.

"Now then, Mr Philpotts. What are we to do with you?"

"I'm sorry?"

"Somehow we seem to have allowed an anarchist into our midst. You have been here only two weeks and already you have instigated a level-five security assault on our systems."

"Oh, the… That was unintentional, Mr Levison. I…"

"Come, come. Unintentional? You managed to breach the

tightest of security levels, by accident?" Levison had finished his soup, taking no prisoners. He dabbed his mouth with his napkin then sat back and regarded Elton.

"You are an active, card-carrying Antiexpansionist. A terrorist, in the simple vernacular."

"That's not true, Mr—"

"Let us not labour the point, sir. I can give you the dates upon which you made your most recent contributions to the Antiexpansionist cause. One such donation was made – and I really must express bewilderment at your audacity – as you travelled to your interview for the position you currently hold." Levison almost laughed at this. His shoulders spasmed up and down, probably the nearest equivalent to laughter available to him.

The waiter arrived with the main course. None for Elton. He was glad; it was veal. Not the square, vat-grown, vacuum-packed variety found in Tescmart, but *real* meat from a *real* animal. Elton didn't even know what the real animal looked like; as far as he knew veals had been extinct since Old Earth.

Levison continued talking while he ate, forming his words around the dripping fat and juices.

"You often frequent the establishment known as The Revolution, a popular breeding ground for Antiexpansionist dissidents. In fact I have records of a second donation which you made during an Antiexpansionist rally, one that ended in a riot which you seem to have instigated. I can show you the credit receipts if you like. Need I go on?"

"This is a mistake, Mr Levison. I was at a concert. It wasn't a rally at all."

"Oh. That was the night you started the riot. At a *concert*? I see."

Elton sat in silence while the conflicting emotions of horror and impotent rage fought for dominance. His career was over. He didn't know what to say.

"The Space Corps is not a political organisation, Mr Philpotts. We do not follow an overt Expansionist agenda. And yet the direction of our sympathies are well documented. What else would you expect? What are we if not the sole means of furthering the influence of mankind throughout our galaxy? We cannot operate in a Contractionist environment, Mr Philpotts. Yet we do not care to push this agenda because we do not wish to invite unnecessary criticism. So the question arises; what the hell are *you* doing working here?"

"I—"

"I'm talking. Do not interrupt." He held up a hand.

"I have spoken with Bob – Bob Slicker. I believe you and he had a meeting two days ago. He told me about your dissatisfaction in your role; about how it hasn't worked out the way you expected. Mr Philpotts, there is a progression, an apprenticeship. Deep space missions do not drop into one's lap in the first week of employment with the Space Corps. You must learn. You must build, adding experiences layer upon layer. Patience is the key, Mr Philpotts.

"Yet you are bright and you are no doubt talented. Do we wish to lose you? I have given the matter some thought. I believe that your anarchistic tendencies are merely the product of youthful exuberance, a misguided call to arms. I do not believe these passions are deep rooted at all. Given a taste of the true spirit of Space Corps exploration I am inclined to believe that you might yet become a valuable and loyal employee."

Levison stood up from the table and walked over to the "window". For a moment Elton forgot about the force field and had the insane idea that Levison was going to jump; to launch himself out into the void. But he stood, hands in pockets, and stared for a full minute. Elton felt that his career was hanging by a thread. A wrong word now and it would be Elton's career that went sailing out into the void.

"I have decided to take a chance," Levison said, at last. "You *will* go into deep space. You will taste adventure. You will learn *esprit de corps*. Thursday, Mr Philpotts. Your Jim will be sent the details."

Without turning round he said, "You may go now."

TWELVE

As soon as Elton left the room, Levison made a call.

"It's done. Thursday. The simpleton was grateful just to keep his job. The security breach was mere blundering, I'm convinced. But for our purposes it was an unexpected bonus. Sometimes, Bob, your stupidity can be valuable. Thank Zona for me, would you?"

THIRTEEN

"Today, in half an hour."

Elton was speaking to the image of Walther that bulged from the wall.

"Couldn't you have told me earlier?"

"I only found out two days ago. I tried to call but you've been dressed dumb all week."

"So how long?"

"For me, I'll be gone two weeks, a standard tour. But there's going to be relativistic effects. Depends on how fast the ship's travelling. From your point of view it could be six months. That's why I had to get hold of you. I need a favour."

"Yes?"

"Could you come round and box-up all my stuff? And take the Teddy. He'll need feeding."

"Your Teddy? You trust me with Kingsley? Oh, come on, I hate Teddies."

"I know you do, and no, I don't trust you with him, but what choice do I have? I don't want to put him in a Ted's home. They're horrible places."

"Is he house-trained?"

"Kingsley's more house-trained than you are, Walther."

Walther acquiesced with a sigh.

Kingsley was a tenth birthday present. The early explorers found the Teddies when they colonised Erymanthus, Elton's home world, and even today nobody really knew how long a Teddy might live. Most ended up in homes once their owners reached an age when owning a Teddy became uncool. Elton hadn't reached that age yet. He was fond of Kingsley.

"I've sublet the flat from the end of the week; I don't want to be shelling out six months' rent when I'm not even here. So, listen, Walther, it isn't your new party pad. And... er, there's another thing. There's an octopus in my central heating."

"What?"

"A Thermopod. It's a long story. Levison had his back turned. I liberated the little guy. You could put him in your own heating pipes until I get back. He won't be a bother. I just don't trust the new tenant not to eat him."

"Wait. Back up. Levison? *Martin* Levison? Martin *Master-of-the-Universe* Levison? What are you into, Elton?"

"I haven't time. I'll get my Jim to talk to yours. But listen, Walther. Stay out of the Revolution."

"I don't—"

"Stay out, Walther. And keep away from those monks. You have another crack at your Space Corps interview in less than two weeks' time; don't jeopardise it, okay? Jim will explain."

Elton stood at the foot of the Needle and looked up. He'd come here many times but never really believed that he'd ever go back up. The last time he'd ridden the Needle seemed like years ago, when he and Walther had arrived from Erymanthus as bright-eyed, naïve teenagers. Erymanthus didn't have a space elevator so they'd gone aloft in chemical rockets. The journey down the Space Needle of Tsanak should have been a unique and memorable experience for them, but they'd been too drunk to remember anything about it.

Elton pushed through the swing doors and found himself in a marble-floored atrium that smelled of disinfectant. There were two other people inside, both looking equally lost and nervous. Elton found the embarkation desk and presented his papers to the bored-looking girl, who barely glanced up from the book she was reading.

"Gate two," she mumbled. "Boarding in five minutes." And the book sucked her back into its universe.

Elton took a seat in the waiting room, and was joined by the other two, an elderly lady and an ebony-skinned teenager. The three nodded to each other in a cautious kind of way. But then the old lady smiled.

"I'm off to the Ring to see my great-grandchildren. They're twins and it is their fifth birthday," she said. "And where are you two boys headed today?"

The nervous teenager answered first.

"Ma'am, I'm off into deep space. Frontier Ship tour."

Elton raised his eyebrows. The boy was barely in his teens. How could a youngster like this possibly have the layered experiences that Levison had spoken about?

"Me too," said Elton. "You seem awfully young. How long have you worked for the Space Corps?"

"It's my first week," he said. "This is my induction tour. I'm very nervous. You must have been the same, your first time."

"Oh, yes. Yes I was," said Elton. "So, things must have changed since… since my first time. Did you know you'd be going into space so soon?"

"Yeah, they told me when they sent my Jim the appointment letter. I'm going to be working in Public Relations, but I won't be assigned until I get back."

"Do you get any training?" asked the lady. "It seems awfully reckless to send youngsters out on dangerous missions without proper training."

"It's not dangerous. It's a caretaker role, really. Isn't that right, sir?" he said, turning to Elton. "Every recruit in the Space Corps gets to do it at the start of their career. It's like a tradition. It's training in itself. It's how each of us learns to appreciate the work of the Corps, right from the start." He nodded, looking at Elton, prompting him to nod back in a comradely way.

"*Esprit de corps*, they call it," said Elton, trying to inject some conviction into his voice. "I'm sorry, what was your name?"

"Scott."

"Scott, hi. I'm Elton."

They shook hands.

Elton's demeanour was relaxed and calm. Inside, his mind was racing. *What? Every recruit? The Annies as well? Why the hell have I been locked away in Purchase Ledger for weeks? What's going on? Esprit de corps my arse.*

"I feel better going up with a seasoned veteran, Elton. What's it like out there? Is it really, you know, how they say, just routine caretaking?"

"Oh yes," said Elton. "Nothing to worry about. But look, the whole point is to discover it yourself. That's why they don't tell you much. You mustn't let me spoil the experience. I could go on all day about deep space, but… well, it wouldn't be fair on you, would it?"

Elton patted him on the shoulder, then gripped it and gave him an *Esprit de Corps* kind of shake.

"You'll be fine. Trust me."

The embarkation door slid open and the girl from the desk was there, still chewing, still vacant about the eyes.

"Boarding for Tsanak Waystation," she drawled.

The five-hour ride up the Space Needle was uneventful enough. After the first few hundred yards the architects seemed to have become bored with windows – and so the rest of the trip, in a featureless circular room with many more seats than bums, offered little in the way of entertainment beyond the mere soaking up of gees. Elton diverted Scott away from more Space Corps questioning by focussing their attention on Monica, the elderly lady, and stories of her great-grandchildren.

Up and down were switched for a while during braking, then with a jerk the elevator car stopped and there was a moment of private contemplation while each passenger focussed on the implications of zero gravity and made peace with their own breakfast insecurities.

In Tsanak Waystation there were three gate halls, each in its own sector. Elton's was Hall Three, Scott's Hall Two, so they wished one another well and parted. Elton was clueless about what to do or where to go, but he was pleased to be able to shake Scott off. He was a nice guy and Elton didn't want to taint his youthful enthusiasm, but all that bluffing was wearing Elton down. Besides, he was now free to make a fool of himself alone and without witnesses.

Tsanak Waystation was like a small knot in the middle of a very long piece of string. For purposes of balance the tower extended just as far out into space as it did down to New Leicester. Strictly speaking, the Space Needle wasn't a tower at all. It wasn't built; it was grown. Its design owed more to biologists than to architects or engineers. Tsanak Waystation began as a seed, placed in geostationary orbit; a seed with two sprouts, one growing down and the other growing up until the Tsanak-bound sprout at last found land and was able to root. Then both the shoot and the seed were left to grow in girth until they were the right size, and the nanotech equivalent of an enzyme was introduced. The growing stopped and the engineers moved in. It was a process that had taken place many times, on many planets, throughout the Sphere of Influence. This was the core of the two-hundred-year-old interstellar transport system that made the concept of the Human Sphere of Influence a practical possibility. But familiar as it was to the Sphere of Influence as a whole, to Elton it seemed very strange. There were no straight lines. Everything looked so... organic. There were no seams, just twisting and turning black-walled tunnels, with branches and intersections of varying complexity. The lack of gravity made navigation all the more difficult, even for a Zenmaster of the ZG hangchamber, like Elton. Every intersection looked different depending on orientation. Elton's route through the intricate labyrinth of the waystation corridors became somewhat random.

"You're lost," said Jim.

"I'm not lost, I'm biding my time."

"You don't have much time to bide, Elton. They'll be out looking for you."

"Do you know the way, Jim?"

"Of course."

"Well why didn't you—?"

"I just did. Left at the next corridor intersection. You've rolled. It's right now. That's it. Straight down here."

"What would I do without you, Jim?"

"You'll soon find out."

"What do you mean?"

"Deep space, Elton. Do you really think they'll have imentor relays out there, at the frontiers of human space? We'll say goodbye, my friend. Soon."

"Oh." Elton's voice became small and a little forlorn. "I never realised. We've never been separated for more than an hour or two, have we? It's going to be... funny."

He came to a room labelled *Space Corps Embarkation*. A short man with no neck was waiting.

"You Philpotts? Where've you been?" said Neckless. "And what the hell are you wearing?" He looked Elton up and down. Elton was wearing his best charcoal-grey, pinstriped suit, and his shoes were polished-up to the lacquered glass-black of a fresh-from-the-box iHolo. Elton thought he looked rather natty. But although he hadn't seen many other travellers on Tsanak Waystation, he'd seen enough to realise that he'd got the dress code wrong. Even the little old lady on the Needle elevator had worn the standard one-piece orange coveralls and top-of-the-range Nike Nanos.

"There's a few spare Corps uniforms in there," he said, indicating another door. "Don't take all day. Say your goodbyes to your Jim, then stash your smarts in one of the transit bins. Don't forget to take a key, there's some thieving bastards up here, you know."

"A key? Isn't that a bit—?"

"Archaic?" finished Neckless, with a sneer. "So, what's your plan? You'll let your Jim take care of the locker code just like at home?" He shook his head.

"Sunshine, you're headed for deep space. There *is* no Jim where you're going. Get used to it. Anyway, how old are you? Haven't you done this before?"

There it was again. Elton was only thirty but he was beginning to feel like Old Man River. People seemed to expect that he was a veteran at this game, not a novice. He had been given false expectations, but again there wasn't time to stop and wonder why; Neckless was barking insults at him, telling him to get his arse into warp drive. It wasn't meant to be like this. Elton was going into *deep space*. It should mean something. Where was the respect? Where was the awe?

Two gates brought Elton to the Ring, though he had seen nothing of the journey, just a succession of gate halls and chambers. The last hall was no different to the others; a vast cathedral space, a globe, criss-crossed by a web of gantries, teaming with ant-like travellers, business men and women, day trippers and holidaymakers, floating to one of the many smaller departure chambers containing the grey shimmering gates. The chambers varied in size according to the gates within. Some, called barn doors, were comfortable, inter-waystation, step-through portals to the big tourist honey-pot destinations, such as the beaches of Fomalhaut or the mountains of Appalachia. Others were smaller, glide-through doors leading to less popular destinations: the farm planets, the prison worlds. Dull colony worlds, like Elton and Walther's former home, Erymanthus. And in an empty part of the hall, where nobody queued, where children didn't cry or touch things they weren't supposed to touch, where business-suited career types didn't peck away at spreadsheets on virtual life-saving keyboards, there was a smaller chamber. A box. Inside was a gate that, depending on one's perspective, looked more like a porthole, a roof vent or a drain. There was a plaque above the hole that said "Biggles". Elton tried to focus on the word to distract his attention from the tiny aperture that was above or below him. He found that thinking "down" worked best, because then it looked like a small pool, half filled with shimmering mercury.

"The other way," said a voice. "Head-first is better."

Suddenly the "down" orientation felt awkward. Elton closed his eyes and tried desperately to think "up".

"You'll find all this is easier if you look where you're going, you know." The gate tech's voice was kind, without any hint of the sarcasm that had been commonplace with all the other gate techs at every waystation thus far. Elton thought she was quite attractive, too, but all his concentration needed to be focussed on the raging internal battle with claustrophobia, leaving none for conventional boy-girl distractions.

"What's Biggles?" said Elton, making conversation from anything. He *needed* distractions.

"I don't know. I think they are the people who made the gate."

Elton nodded. "Okay." His voice felt small and childlike.

"Don't worry. Stay rigid like that and I'll point you in the right direction."

Elton felt her hands guiding him. Her touch was gentle and he became acutely aware of how they felt on his waist and thigh; warm, sensitive. And she'd never once mentioned his age.

"Ready? As soon as you're through hit the green flashing button to close the gate behind you. Don't forget now, because even a small gate like this is a big drain on an F-Ship's batteries and if you wait too long it could delay you coming back. Understand?"

Elton nodded.

"Right. Gate's open. I'm pushing you through. Have a good trip."

Even through Elton's tightly closed eyes it went very dark. And very cold.

FOURTEEN

Alasdair McPherson was the most powerful man in the Human Sphere of Influence, or so people said. He was Chief Executive of the Space Corps.

His office was stark. No flamboyant touches. No pictures on the wall. The simple furniture was bargain-basement utilitarian. The chief executive of the largest corporation in the Human Sphere of Influence was a man of minimalist sensibilities.

McPherson always arrived at the office early, before five AM. He had ordered habits and he cherished routine. He took his china teapot to the kettle in his secretary's office and he made tea.

This was his time to think. A hallowed hour before anyone else arrived and the marvellous chaos of the day commenced.

He knew that his days here were numbered. There was not a damn thing he could do about it, either. The toe rag, Levison, knew so much better than he how to plot and how to usurp power.

McPherson had recognised the intelligence in Levison's eyes all those years ago and he had taken a chance on him, and since that day the upstart's one aim in life had been to wrest power from the man who gave him a start in life; to wrest power and use it to further his own ends, not those of the Corps. One by one he had, somehow, intimidated the old school of Space Corps board members and replaced them with his own creatures. Last night McPherson had taken a call from his old friend, Tad Peters, who told him, in shaking and distraught tones, that he had resigned his seat; that there were... external pressures.

He had been blackmailed. This was a certainty. Levison. This, also, was a certainty. The third certainty was that there would be no trail, no possibility of ever uncovering the truth.

McPherson and his loyal friends were now outnumbered, seven to five. It was only a matter of time before he was removed from the board and Martin Levison elected CEO. Then he would have it all. Almost. McPherson knew that for Levison, "all" would never be enough. The thirst for power is a hard thirst to slake. There is always more. And McPherson knew that whatever goals lay at the end of Levison's relentless path, they would always be to his own advantage.

Alasdair McPherson placed his head in his hands. *I'm getting too old for this,* he thought. For the first time in his twenty-five-year tenure of this proud and noble office, he felt fear. An unwelcome darkness had entered his boardroom and McPherson felt powerless to stop it.

FIFTEEN

"Hi, Lhiana."

"Hi, Mila."

Mila and Lhiana air-kissed then settled back onto the air-support sofa that occupied their favourite corner of Westlake's.

Lhiana ordered Still Limestone-filtered Dis, while Mila had her usual Foam-Carbon Whole-Water with a small, indulgent shot of glucose.

Westlake's was their favourite watering hole. It wasn't that the water was better here than elsewhere; in fact you could, now and again, detect the faintest tang of organics in the water, a sign that the filters were overdue for cleaning. No, what counted at Westlake's was ambience. Westlake's was pre-RepRap, Old Earth through and through. Tables were made from builder's hods, while the bar was a rough, incomplete structure of clay brickwork. A network of scaffolding pipes criss-crossed every space in careful asymmetry. They were even used to construct the staircase leading up to the gallery.

Everything about Westlake's pointed to a bygone time when the economy of Old Earth was built on assets and real-estate, before the replicators had arrived and changed everything.

"You have that dreamy look," said Mila. "What's happened?"

"Do I? No, no I don't. Nothing's happened," said Lhiana.

"I remember the day you first went over to La Ronde," said Mila. "You came back covered in mud and paint, and you had that same faraway look in your eyes – well, maybe you always have that look – but then, you looked like you'd found something important. And I can see that same detached gaze now."

Mila, short for Sharmila, was Lhiana's best friend. They had grown up together on Minerva. Mila was a couple of years younger than Lhiana, but it was Mila who had been the first to leave their home planet, coming out to the Ring to do the thing she always wanted, to become a nurse.

When Lhiana decided to seek work – and she'd tried so many jobs: telesales, fortune cookie writer, actress, educational video presenter, and now Space Corps gate hostess – she had chosen to come to the Ring because she knew Mila was here and she knew her friend would look out for her. Mila and Lhiana were like sisters. They had no secrets, and Mila had always been able to read Lhiana's moods with an empathy that was spooky.

"We both know that you're going to tell me what's distracting you, Lhiana, so why pretend otherwise? Come on, girl, out with it."

"It's just Carol, she's giving me a hard time."

"So what's new? And *that's* not it. Now I *know* something is going on. Who is he, Lhiana?"

"What? Mila, come on. It's nothing like that."

Sharmila said nothing. She folded her arms and smiled. Her eyebrows raised and her head tilted slightly.

"Anyway, nothing happened. I didn't even speak to him."

"Ha! I knew there was a him."

"And he's definitely not my type. Deep Spacer, you know? And he seemed, I don't know, like a bit of a ground-hugger. He was scared. He asked what 'Biggles' meant."

"Biggles?"

"It's a plaque they put over all the gates. Reminds us of Jessica Biggles."

"Who's—?"

"First woman lost through a gate," said Lhiana. "They teach us about her in gate school. Meant to make us more careful entering the Tau number. Biggles keyed her own and got it wrong. Nobody knows where she went."

"You didn't tell—"

"No, I didn't tell him that. He was nervous enough."

"Better than being fly, like most of them."

Lhiana shrugged.

"It doesn't matter, anyway. I don't even know his name. We never really spoke. I just pushed him through the gate. He had his eyes closed most of the time."

"So, what's with the faraway look?"

Lhiana smiled.

"He was… kind of cute, that's all." She shrugged. "Anyway, he's gone on an F-Ship tour. He'll be out there for months. I don't know when he'll be back; I don't know who he is. Odds are infinitesimal against me ever seeing him again."

"So, shorten the odds," said Mila.

"I don't know anything about him."

"You have his IP number? Flash your eyes at that super', what's his name?"

"Bruce."

"Bruce, yes. He'll do anything for you, you know that. He's a big kid."

"I'm not meant to—"

"You just need to know when he's coming back, that's all, nothing underhand. Tell him your guy left something behind. Be creative. You just need to make sure you're on F-Ship gate duty when he returns."

"Then what?"

Mila shrugged, and smiled.

"I'm sure you'll think of something," she said.

SIXTEEN

Up became down with a jolt. This wasn't like other gates where you simply stepped through a caressing veil into another place. This was awkward and fiddly, with pressure differentials that popped your ears. This was a gate where it hurt when you landed on your head.

The sense of gravity was an illusion. There was usually no sense of speed at all out in space, but Elton had dropped into a Frontier Ship with Wilson Drive, and it was really tanking along. So fast, in fact, that space had become thick and knobbly. Although the ship was no longer accelerating, at relativistic speeds there are patches of discontinuity in the particle-compressed soup of space that causes a ship to buck and shudder from time to time, and it was into just such a lumpy part of space that Elton now arrived. Elton didn't know anything about all this when he arrived, of course. For the moment all he knew was that "down" was where his head was pointing, and that it was "down" enough to give him a lump on his head the size of a goose egg.

He sat on the floor rubbing it hard and practicing his profanity. Then, as space smoothed out again, his weight evaporated and he floated away from what had, for those few moments, become the floor.

Elton was not phased by the sudden shifts in orientation. In fact, he was used to it. Hangball. One of the features of the ZG field that rendered it useless for most applications was its unpredictability. But that was all part of the thrill and challenge of the hangchamber.

"Is this it then, Jim?"

No answer.

Oh, right. Elton felt a pang of loneliness. He'd been away from his imentor many times before, especially when encouraged by Walther's passion for dumb clothing, but now he didn't have a choice. He and Jim were on separate paths and different timelines. For the first time in his life, Elton felt *truly* alone.

"Velcome, cadet."

An age-lined, grey-haired head and shoulders materialised in the middle of the small chamber.

"I am Professor Fassnidge, and zis is my assistant."

Another head and shoulders appeared behind and to one side of the professor. This time it was a girl with flowing auburn hair, pale complexion and laser-green eyes, and Elton lost all interest in the aged professor in an instant. But the girl disappeared and Professor Fassnidge became centre-stage once again.

"You are about to embark on a tour of duty on one of ze Space Corp's fastest und sleekest Frontier Ships. Velcome to F-257. Vot is your name?"

"Er… Elton D Philpotts."

"Pleased to meet you, er… Elton D Philpotts." Elton's name was supplied in his own voice, complete with hesitation. Elton had the sinking feeling that he would come to loathe the sound of his own name before the two weeks were up.

"Now zen, er… Elton D Philpotts. Before we begin you probably want to acquaint yourself with ze layout of ze ship."

A diagram appeared. It looked like a long polished pencil with a very sharp tip. The professor walked round it. A pointer appeared in his hand and the side of the pencil became transparent, then disappeared, and the image zoomed to become a cross-section of F-257.

"F-257 is a W-class Frontier Ship. Zer are five sections. Ze rear half of ze ship is not accessible to ze crew. Zis is where ze propulsion unit is housed. You will learn more about ze Wilson Drive in later presentations."

Elton realised that the accent was fake. He'd started slipping up on some of the W's.

"Next is a short section zat is open to space. Ze ship's body, here, is of bucky-mesh construction and zer is no access for the crew."

The professor then walked to the front of the ship.

"Ze tapered nose section, or most of it, houses ze magnetic field coils which tether ze superdensematter shield, here."

He pointed to a glowing ball that now appeared in front of the ship.

"Again zer is no access. And now for ze crew section. Zis occupies ze remaining 30 percent of ze ship, from here to here."

The inaccessible parts of the ship disappeared and the crew area was enlarged.

"Ze section you now occupy is here," he said, pointing to an area near the front where the truncated cone shape was at its narrowest. "Zis is ze training room and private quarters. Note ze sleep nets, zey are stowed against ze cabin wall.

"Behind you, you will note ze gate has now deactivated."

Elton turned and saw that the gate was, in fact, still there, and that a green light was flashing with some urgency. He remembered the instructions he'd been given when he left.

"Damn," he muttered, and kicked over to the light. He slapped his hand down and the gate winked out of existence. He was alone. He'd always known he would be, but he hadn't had time to process the implications. The realisation now hit home as to how completely isolated and distant he was from the rest of humanity.

"… separates ze living area from ze bridge…" Elton had

missed a bit, but the professor didn't seem to notice.

"... and if you will kindly go through ze hatch, er... Elton D Philpotts, I will indeed show you ze bridge."

The hatch was narrow, a tight squeeze. Elton pushed through and Professor Fassnidge was waiting for him on the other side. He took Elton on a quick tour of the bridge which he found to be surprisingly basic and Spartan – all pop-rivets and Dymo-labels.

Then through another hatch, where he was awaited not by the professor, but by the girl with the green eyes. She gave Elton a smile and Elton would have fallen to the deck on jelly legs had there been any gravity there to pull him.

"This is the SLOG hangar," she said. Her voice was soft, almost a whisper. Her delivery was slow and easy on the ear as if time was no longer of any consequence. "The SLOG, or Single Large Object Gate, is stored in the heavy steel cylinder."

There was no heavy steel cylinder as far as Elton could see; the hangar was echoing with emptiness. But Elton didn't care about the error; he was hanging on every word uttered by this green-eyed goddess. She explained how the SLOG was used only when the Frontier Ship encountered a habitable planet. The explanation was all too brief. Elton wanted to hear more, not of SLOGs and their inevitable cosmic destruction if they were deployed while the ship was travelling at speed, but of anything at all uttered in the girl's soothing voice. Were there more of these training holos on the ship? Elton vowed to become a dedicated student.

For now, though, the nutty professor was back, with his fake accent and his Einstein hairdo. The hair was probably also part of the actor's wardrobe, a nodding acquaintance to the role of stereotypical space scientist. But so long as he hammed it up, it was entertaining enough.

"So, vot have you been told, er... Elton D Philpotts? On your first day working for ze Space Corps you are stuffed in ze rocket and sent into Space, ya? Is zis wise? Would it not be better to give ze training first?"

Elton had been wondering about this. But he was also wondering why he hadn't been sent into deep space on his first day, because that was evidently normal practice. And why the top man, Martin Levison, had lied to him.

The professor continued, unmoved by Elton's concerns. He explained, at length, how this *was* his training. Space Corps policy was to send its recruits from all disciplines straight into space, because it was experience. They got to see what deep space was all about. They got to experience time dilation effects first-hand. And it benefited the Space Corps too, because time dilation made the manning of Frontier Ships a seriously unbalanced labour-intensive activity. Only two weeks of Ship time were covered per tour, although each recruit was away from his assigned duties in normal time-frames for several months. Added to the problem the statutory limitations on R-Time, governed by a sliding scale linked to the speed of the ship, and maintenance scheduling became a major headache.

So the maintenance was made easy. Anyone could do it. Even accountants.

Elton was given a few minutes for tea and pastries, which doubled as a lesson on how to handle scalding liquids and crumbs in zero gravity. Then there was the visit to the ship's infirmary for a practical in first-aid, for burn injuries. Elton always considered himself adept in zero-gee conditions, but then, he had never been called upon to brew tea while playing hangball.

The afternoon session was about emergency drills. *The professor again. Boring. Where was the girl?* After a little searching Elton found that much of the course work was in modules and Elton could choose his topics to suit his own requirements. There was a virtual panel with a click wheel. Elton skipped through the programme until he came to one on history. He had no interest in history. Except that the module was being presented by the girl. There were no credits and no introductions. Elton wanted a name. He longed for a name; something concrete on which to hang his infatuation.

The lights dimmed. Music began to swell. History lessons commenced.

SEVENTEEN

"Mr Slicker, Mr Levison will see you straight away," said Phillip. The wall dilated. Bob Slicker, rubbing his hands, half walked, half trotted, stooping through the still-dilating wall in his haste.

"Robert, come in," said Levison. He was standing by his force-field window looking out over the lights of Tsanak. "I don't see much of you up here these days. You are afraid of me, I know. But we must not become strangers. We should talk more."

"I, ah… I have news of our project, Mr Levison."

"The accountant?"

"He is safely on F-257, sir. And the, ah, subroutine has been triggered."

"Excellent, Robert. And what of the backup, the other accountant?"

"He had a successful interview. He has been given a position within the payroll department. He, also, will not be assigned a deep space tour. Not until we have confirmed the outcome of the… primary candidate."

"Any problems?"

"Mmm, it was unfortunate. Morningthorpe was chairing the interview panel for Blick. You'll remember she was—"

"Yes, she appointed Philpotts."

"Indeed. She resisted my… endorsement of the new candidate. She deemed him unsuitable."

"But you prevailed."

"Ah, yes, sir."

"And Morningthorpe?"

"Could become… intractable."

"Speak to Phillip. Have him clear twenty minutes from my

diary tomorrow. Perhaps a working breakfast? Miss Morningthorpe will be leaving our employ, Robert. And if she wishes to find work within the accountancy profession, she will find it necessary to leave Tsanak, also.

"Was there anything else, Robert?"

"No, sir."

"Good, keep me informed. I wish to know as soon as Mr Philpotts is…"

"Yes, Mr Levison."

EIGHTEEN

This is how history should always be taught, thought Elton, settling back into the sleep nets.

The music began with a passacaglia; a ground base, pianissimo, moving constantly, building in a gradual crescendo; growing, swelling with organic life, filling the resonant cavities of the whole ship.

The lights came up slowly to reveal Old Earth; before the Sphere; before the Ring.

"The cradle of life," she said, her voice almost a whisper. "A tiny island in a vast and empty ocean. Man, restless and vulnerable, trapped on a world that is doomed by his own technological ambition."

And then violins and light-harps came in, with sweeping, ascending scales. The girl's image appeared, seeming to walk onstage, with a swish and a glide, from the darkness behind the Earth.

"This module is a brief introduction to the history of the Human Sphere of Influence. It will act both as a refresher to the Primary curriculum, and, with its special emphasis on the unique role of the Space Corps, will provide an overview of the development of the Corps from its early associations with the Destiny programme, to its current place in all walks of modern society. I hope you will stay with me to enjoy the journey."

Elton was nodding enthusiastically.

The girl introduced archive footage of pre-Sphere Earth, showing scenes depicting the "Three Hammer Blows" of the twenty-first century: The Economic Collapse, The Climatological Collapse and finally the Ecological Collapse.

"Never before had humankind felt so cornered," she said.

"Some have argued that the first seeds of growth for the Sphere of Influence began as early as 1969, when twelve men departed the Earth to sojourn, briefly, on the moon. It was a beginning. But they returned to the Earth and for more than fifty years mankind struggled to find either the inspiration or the imagination to try anything like it again, even while living through the calamitous wasting disease of Mother Earth. Mankind seemed doomed.

"And then…" She whirled round to face Elton, and he noted the way the pale copper tones of her auburn hair swayed, back and forth, before coming to rest against her bare shoulder.

"Eóghan Monaghan discovered the principle of the Warp Gate. The great expansion might have started there and then, except for that problem of the shifting sands of gravity. Monaghan knew that gravity and space-time were moving, writhing, like snakes in a bucket. To open a gate, again and again, between the same two points in the universe, the effects of gravity had to be minimised. So now, once more, an incentive to climb out of Earth's gravity well presented itself. But this time something better than rocketry was needed to give regular access to orbit. The Space Needles were grown, and three great ships were built."

The image of Earth faded, and one at a time three iconic starships appeared out of the darkness. She counted them off.

"Destiny I… Destiny II… Destiny III.

"Every schoolchild knows these ships; their names, their history. It is surprising that three were built, even more surprising that Destinys II and III were ever permitted to make the jump. The open-ended jump. Thirty-three crew on each ship. Ninety-nine souls. Never seen again.

"Did they ever reach a safe destination? Will we ever hear of their plight? Perhaps one day we will detect the faint echo of their transmissions, and learn what befell the brave ninety-nine.

"But the lessons were learned. Suicidal, open-ended jumps were stopped. A new agency, the Space Corps, was formed from the political wreckage of the Destiny Program. A new agency, to oversee the building of new ships, ships with gates, paired gates, linked as one with orbital waystations around Earth. Frontier Ships. Tens, scores, hundreds of ships setting forth in a slow but inexorably growing sphere; the Human Sphere of Influence."

The music stopped. The image of countless pinpoints of light expanded from a cluster to a vast, thinning ball. The image faded... and the cabin lights came up.

Lesson one completed.

On day three of his tour of duty it occurred to Elton that it was all very well sampling the educational offerings, searching for anything by the delightful green-eyed angel with no name, but so far he still had no clue as to what tasks he was meant to perform here. So with great reluctance – and the odd pang of guilt for his neglect – he scrolled back to lesson two, and tried his best to become engaged by the dry, hammy acting of his quasi-Einsteinian professor.

"So, er... Elton D Philpotts, you will be wondering about ze shipboard duties required of a Space Corps cadet. Ze maintenance programme is automated and requires only to be triggered and monitored. Zis is a deliberate simplification to enable training of ze cadet during ze maintenance cycle. If zer is a problem you vill be guided through the procedures by ze interactive manual.

"We begin."

Elton was told to go to the bridge where a complex procedure was explained to him. A red button, marked "press to commence maintenance cycle" required pressing. It lit up, red.

Elton was congratulated for his skilful manipulation of the button, and the session continued.

But Elton's attention became distracted. Beside the red button was an old museum-piece of a CRT screen, and it came to life. There were two messages, in flickering, retro green:

<Maintenance programme commenced 13:23:40:11:2241>

<Subroutine RS23563 started by user.>

<1,123,185...>

The long number in the second message was counting down, in seconds. Elton couldn't let something like that go, and did some quick mental arithmetic: divide by sixty to get minutes, then again to get hours, then by 24... It would reach zero in just under thirteen standard days.

Elton frowned.

Maybe part of the maintenance programme?

Or maybe not. But thirteen days... he'd still be here in thirteen days, wouldn't he? So maybe he'd find out what it meant then.

Elton turned away from the screen and tried to listen to the professor. But he couldn't concentrate. Something worried him. Did he *want* to be here in thirteen days? He was happy enough to do his full tour. But did he really want to be here, to see what happened when that timer reached zero?

Now, why had that thought occurred to him?

He looked at the screen again. The first message was fine, he had no problem with it. But the second line?

<Subroutine RS23563 started by user.>

<1,123,122...>

The count digit was lower. Of course it was lower, but it looked psychologically lower. Elton felt a kind of tension.

RS23563. That was it. He knew that number. He'd seen that number. RS23563. Where?

Come on, think. You've seen it before. 23563.

Elton hit the pause button on the training presentation. The professor was getting on his nerves.

23563.

It was lunch time. Eat something. Feed the brain. Think about something else and it will come. It *will* come. Eventually. In less than thirteen days.

23563. *Damn!*

"Ze ship in which you are travelling is a W-class Frontier Ship, so designated after ze propulsion system, ze Wilson drive."

Elton yawned and took another bite from his pizza. His finger had twice hovered over the "stop" icon, but conscience told him he should stay and pay attention.

"Ze story of ze Wilson drive is quite interesting. Ze basic concepts were formulated in ze early twenty-first century, when it was named ze EmDrive. But ze scientific establishment called it a fraud, as it violated ze conservation of momentum and other basic laws of physics.

"More than a century later, Dr Vilma Vilson rediscovered ze papers and built a vorking prototype."

"Aargh!" Elton threw the remains of his pizza at the professor which of course passed straight through the image and plopped onto Elton's sleeping bag wrapped up in the wall nets.

"Enough of the zee's and vee's! You're a fake. You're probably from bloody Basingstoke in the British sector.

"So how fast *is* ze W-class Frontier Ship?"

"Oh, it's fast." The girl was back, with her purring voice and her heart-liquidizing eyes. "The Wilson Drive is a faster-than-light propulsion system, although it has never been run at light speed because of the ship's unfortunate, and expensive, tendency to turn itself into pure energy.

"But it's fast. At this moment you are travelling at a significantly high percentage of the speed of light. At this speed space is thick, like soup – with croutons. So the Frontier Ship has to be pencil thin and polished. And without protection it would nevertheless be shredded, in moments, by the particles of dust slamming into the hull."

"Und so, ve use superdensematter," said the professor.

"A ball of SDM is held by magnetic fields less zan one metre in front of ze ship. Zer is a constant release of reaction mass, und zis creates an opposing thrust."

A blackboard appeared and the professor began to write on it. He became enervated, and his hair began to stick up even more, maybe from the static being generated by the frantic scribbling and scratching of pre-Sphere chalk.

But there were few numbers. Elton wanted numbers. Instead there were symbols and letters and Greek characters… so Elton switched it off.

That was enough. He could take the professor's comic-book antics only so far, but when numbers were threatened, well, Elton D Philpotts was very defensive about numbers.

Elton went through the bridge then on into the SLOG bay at the end. The empty bay was the largest space on the ship. It was meant to be nothing more than a crawl space. There should have been a SLOG, in a capsule, filling the space. Elton was happy with the omission, because he'd built a pig, using dirty laundry and his kit bag. It was a bit short on mass for a real pig, but that was okay, a hangchamber was not something Elton had expected to find on the ship.

But one-on-none is limiting. Elton sent the pig off on a slow vector, then kicked around the hangar, intercepting and redirecting, and occasionally missing completely and bouncing off the ship's bulkhead in bone-smashing collisions.

But he'd done it all before. He was bored. He needed another player, a compagno. He missed Walther. He missed Jim.

He floated back onto the bridge and looked at the old CRT screen.

<Subroutine RS23563 started by user.>

<1,115,985...>

Still patiently counting down. To what?

As he watched, another message flashed onto the screen. It was only visible for a nanosecond. It was like... like the old popular myth about subliminal advertising that had supposedly once menaced the early years of television. Elton couldn't possibly have read the full text because there were three or four lines of it. But he thought he recognised one word, at a subconscious level. It could be his imagination was overactive. It could be this was the very word his tired brain wanted to see; an excuse for getting off the ship early because he had learned a great truth. He now knew that deep space was *boring*.

The word he might have imagined was:

DANGER

NINETEEN

Lhiana took a table in the gate tech's canteen. The canteen had spin and Lhiana was happy to sit instead of float for a while. She chose a seat far away from everyone. She liked it that way. She valued her lunch breaks; time to think, time to plan. She had her mind full of daffodils; how to capture, not just the yellow, but the sun lighting up the yellows and greens. It wasn't just about colour, it was about the way light created the colour then reflected it.

Lhiana was passionate about her art. Everything else in her life was there to make her art happen; no other reason.

"Hi, Lhiana, mind if I join you?"

Lhiana looked up. It was Bruce, her boss.

"Of course not, Bruce. Sit down." Poor Bruce. He was besotted. Lhiana was torn between not wanting to upset him and not wanting to encourage him. She smiled, trying hard to make it a friendly smile rather than a flirtatious smile.

Bruce put down his tray, loaded with vat-grown burger and test-tube chips, and, balanced on top, his paper. Lhiana glanced at the cover. "Zlatan Zombie on Fomalhaut." A kid's book. Lhiana suppressed a smile. At least he was reading. Nobody read. He was doing it because Lhiana was a passionate reader. She was rather touched.

"Not hungry today, Lhiana?" he said, nodding towards her tray which held just a single glass of Limestone Dis – with a taste reminiscent of the petrochemical industry – and a plate on which sat an unappetising cube of green tofu.

Lhiana valued her lunch breaks more for the time they afforded her than for the opportunity to eat. She could eat when she got home. One of the perks of helping at La Ronde was that she was allowed to take produce home. The problem was, once you'd tasted potato and leek soup made from potatoes and leeks, most other food was relegated to the status of Science Experiment.

Bruce was talking. Lhiana realised she hadn't been listening and she felt guilty. But, Bruce... well, sometimes it was just so hard to stay tuned in to him. He was talking about a group of Space Corps TFEs, Terraforming Engineers, fifty of them, who'd gated out to an F-Ship near Fomalhaut, or Joule as it had become locally known.

"...and they just kept coming, one after another. It's only a narrow gate so I had to feed them through, head to toe, over and over, like how they used to make stuff in factories."

"A production line."

"That's it. Thought I'd never get away. Never seen so many yellow overalls in one..."

And as he spoke Lhiana's mind wandered again. It was that phrase, yellow overalls. She'd been thinking about daffodils, and now she was reminded of a conversation she'd had with her friend Mila, a few weeks ago: "You have his IP number? Flash your eyes at Bruce. He'll do anything for you, you know that."

Should she try it? She could mention the guy. What harm would it do?

"Which ship were they heading for?" she asked.

"Oh, I'm not sure. Why?"

"It's just, I put a Space Corps guy through to an F-Ship a couple of weeks ago, and, I don't know, there was something funny. I got Kim to remember the IP number. Maybe he was going to the same place."

Lhiana made a performance of subvocalising to her Kim, trying to find the number. Kim subvocalised back, giving her a hard time.

"You are so obvious, Lhiana. He'll see right through you. Just tell Bruce you've got the hots for this guy and have done with it. You'll kill two birds with one stone."

"I can't do that, Kim, I don't want to hurt his feelings. Just put the number on my paper will you?"

"Coward."

Lhiana took out her paper. She didn't need to unfold it, there was only the one number. She made a thing about getting the lanyard tangled around her wrists before passing it over to Bruce. She was thinking on her feet. She needed a plausible reason to ask Bruce to look up the details without seeming too obvious.

She didn't need one.

"Ah, so it was you who put this guy through. I wondered who'd done it."

"You recognise the number then? Just like that?"

"God, yeah, but it's nothing to do with my Fomalhaut caper. *Your* guy's a big shot, you know."

This was a surprise.

"What do you mean?"

"Well, his tour was arranged through Director Levison's office, his PA, I think. This wasn't some green kid on the regular rota. I've been trying to figure out what all the fuss was about. Tell me about him."

Lhiana was a little taken aback. Her usual dreamy expression became focussed. She folded her arms on the table between them and leaned forward.

"There's not a lot to tell. He was certainly older than most of the recruits – thirtyish, maybe. I didn't even get his name. I wish I'd asked him, now."

"His name's Philpotts," said Bruce.

Wow, that was easy.

"So what do you think?" he asked. "Was he a TFE? Or scientist? Military?"

"He was scared, mainly. I don't think he'd done much gating before. In fact I'm sure of it."

"Weird."

"So where did he go? Do you know what ship? I only saw the IP number. Destination was pre-programmed."

"F-257. I looked it up soon as the request came through. I was kind of curious about where they might be sending someone who's so obviously high-orbital."

"So what's the deal with F-257?"

"That's the thing. There's nothing so far as I can see. There're no planet-falls coming up, not even a close-approach. Just another F-Ship. Why's Levison so interested?"

"Maybe he's a relative. Cousin? Son-in-law?"

"Nah, it's the ship. Got to be. It's F-257 that's getting all the special treatment, not Philpotts."

"What makes you so sure about that?"

"Because there's a reserve."

"What, like backup crew? Is that so unusual?"

"Damn right it is. Frontier Ships go months without a crew. The time dilation makes them hard to man. Send someone out there for two weeks and you have to cover him for six months. That's why they use raw recruits. The Space Corps make out that it's part of the training; they lay on holos and stuff. But that's a front. Truth is, they can't break the law, the Relative Hours Regs, so they just don't have enough warm bodies to fill up all the F-Ships. They'll happily send any bum-fluff kid they can get their hands on and be happy to have him sit there watching holos."

"Yeah, I know something about the training holos. A friend at Uni set up a production company a few years back."

"I've been out there," said Bruce.

"We all have," said Lhiana, with a shrug.

"I joined the Space Corps as a Graduate Trainee. It's not what you expect is it? They stick you in a ship to get the space-bug out of your system once and for all. Boring as hell. You go out all bright-eyed, seeking adventure and new frontiers. Two weeks later you're back, and ready for your slippers, pipe and cardigan. Anyway, I flunked the trainee programme so they stuck me on gates. I guess they assumed I could handle the tedium."

"What about this reserve? And how'd you even find out about him?"

"I don't know much, except his name's Walther Blick. Some slimy financial guy called Slicker keeps sending memos. This Blick guy wound up in hospital. They want to make sure I know to go and haul him out, still in his jammies if need be, and go stuff him into F-257, you know, if Philpotts bails."

Lhiana thought this seemed strange. "Is he likely to?"

"I nearly did. There's only so much exhilaration the mind can take. Happens all the time. They come out of the gates shaking their heads and muttering stuff like, "Sod it, I'll join the circus." I reckon the Space Corps would halve their manpower problems if they just put a window in their ships. At least the cadets could look out and know they're in space."

"So what's up with this Walther Blick? Are they serious about you yanking him out of his hospital bed?"

"Dead serious. I've never seen anything like it. The guy's only in for some immuno work. He's not ill or anything. He's banged up in Five Faiths Infirmary. Poor bugger, he'd be better off catching something serious."

Five Faiths? Mila's hospital. Hmm. Kim – give Mila's Kim a shout, would you? See if she wants a night out. We haven't been to Westlake's in a while.

Walther quite liked his hospital. This was much classier than the "Hawley Crippen Medical Centre" that he'd visited on Erymanthus as a boy. There they'd set his broken femur *by hand*. Barbarians.

Walther had started to succumb to illnesses – coughs, colds, throat infections – within days of arriving on the Ring. It was obvious that his immune system was simply not up to the challenge of all the new and exotic viruses that lurked in the dusty recesses of the Ring's air-cycling systems. He hadn't upgraded his immune system in nearly twenty years, so perhaps he was due for a newer release.

"Can't you just inject a new one?" he asked the nurse. "That's what they did last time."

"But that was your *first* immune system," she said. "This is different, you need a complete transfusion. We can't just leave all the old 'bots swimming around; they'd start fighting the new ones. Besides, your old system's worse than obsolete. They do their best to make the upgrades backwards compatible, but not over more than a decade.

"Sorry, Mr Blick, it has to be the full works. Don't worry though, it's not a problem, you'll be our guest for a few days while we make sure your system's fully flushed. Don't want to leave any little stragglers, do we?"

The nurse was quite pretty; dark eyes and hair that was long, sleek and very black. Her name badge said she was Sharmila Kumari. She was easy to talk to. She listened. She was interested to know all about Walther and his career in the Space Corps.

"So did they send you out into space when you joined?"

"Nah, that's a myth. 'Welcome to the Space Corps. Here's your yellow monkey-suit. Good luck in deep space.' Truth is they stick you in an office and bore the fight out of you first. It happened to a friend of mine though he did get out there, eventually. He's doing his tour now. Been gone a few months."

"What's your friend's name?"

"Elton. Elton Philpotts."

"And... where is he? What ship?"

"Oh, I have no idea. He didn't know himself. He didn't get a lot of notice. Left me to sub-let his flat for him; find a home for his pets."

"And you don't know when *you'll* be going?"

"Don't know if I ever will. They've found a nice quiet corner for me. Out of the way. Suits me. Gives me time to do my own thing."

"So, what's your own thing?"

"Oh, you know: hangball, music."

"Music?"

"Country. You wouldn't like it."

"What makes you say that?"

"Oh, I don't know. It's not so popular these days, is it?" he said.

She shrugged. "So how do you reckon I'd look in a cowboy hat?" she asked.

Walther smiled. "I think it would suit you."

"Well, I've got two. A blue one and a sparkly pink one. And the boots."

"Well, well, well."

TWENTY

They could train a rat to do this job, thought Elton. *Leave some cheese on the big red button then send him through. But I suppose they'd need someone to place the cheese. A dog then. That's it, train a dog. But how would they train a dog to cope with the boredom? Got to have some stimulation. They could send a cat after the rat, then the dog could chase...*

I'm losing it. Definitely.

Elton floated through to the bridge. He looked at the CRT.

<Subroutine RS23563 started by user. 004,503...>

Not long now, he thought. *Four-and-a-half thousand seconds. Hour and a quarter. I wonder what will happen.* Elton found himself uncomfortable with the idea of that countdown finishing. He didn't know why. There was so much about this arrangement that was wrong, that was slightly out of whack.

He wondered if he might pass the time jumping around the empty SLOG bay with his makeshift pig.

You see, that's *wrong. Why's the SLOG bay empty? What's the point of an F-Ship with no SLOG?*

Elton knew from the holo recordings that F-257 had never encountered another world and had never been called upon to deploy its SLOG. The SLOG was for such occasions when heavy freight craft needed to start crossing into a new planetary system. You couldn't terraform and populate a planet by sending everyone through the tiny little gate on a Frontier Ship. It just wasn't going to happen. So, according to the good professor, they erect a huge, ship-sized gate. Energy-needs grew exponentially with the size of the gate, so it couldn't be left open for long. The solution was timing. The freighter comes in fast. The gate flashes open at precisely the right moment and the ship is through in the brief moments when the gate is open.

So *every* Frontier Ship had a SLOG. A Single Large Object Gate. Without one, what use was the ship?

But F-257 didn't have a SLOG.

So why was he wasting his time out here, nursemaiding a ship that, to anyone, was bloody useless?

Elton decided to watch another holo. The girl with no name. He wanted to relax; to drink in the cool green of her eyes and listen to that slow, languorous voice. He wanted to get his mind away from that thing that was nagging and scratching away at his subconscious.

He flicked through a few holos until he found one he hadn't seen. This time she was talking about the ecological problems of the Sphere worlds.

"There are twenty-seven colonised worlds—"

"Twenty-eight," said Elton. "But I'll let you off. It's an old recording."

"—in the Human Sphere of Influence. Think of that. Twenty-seven planets in the HSI. Full of people. And only now do we realise how lucky our ancestors were on Earth, and how short-sighted. On Earth there were more species of fauna and flora in the average suburban garden, than there are now in the whole HSI. Earth had it all, and destroyed it."

She was moving around in some kind of garden, but it wasn't planetary because she was obviously in micro-gee. To Elton's eyes it looked quite lush, because many of the plants were larger than any he had seen on Tsanak or Erymanthus. There were shrubs nearly a metre across. But she was getting quite impassioned about the paucity of species there. Her hair was getting away from her. She had it tied back with a coloured scarf, as she had in all the holos. But Elton watched in fascination as some loose strands began to form a halo around her head, and as the light filtered through it, it transformed from warm auburn to vibrant titian.

If it had been the mad professor spouting on about lost biodiversity, Elton would have been tempted to switch off or shout out, "What are you beefing about, look around you." But he allowed the girl to talk. He allowed her mellifluous voice to caress his ears. He let her passions become his passions, because she obviously spoke from the heart. Elton drank it all in.

The holo lasted an hour.

This time the professor didn't make a single appearance. And when the end credits came up there were names.

You have been watching a SlickFilms Production.

Presented by

Lhiana Bilotti

Lhiana. Oh my!

The producer would like to thank the Directors of the Botanical Gardens of La Ronde for their help in the making of this film.

Lhiana.
SlickFilms.
La Ronde
SlickFilms.
Slick
Slicker!

And in a flash of inspiration he knew where he'd seen 23563. Slicker. *RS* 23563. RS. Robert Slicker.

He could see it clearly. A pink Post-it stuck to his trousers. "Call ML re 23563". ML. Martin Levison.

And then, later that afternoon, Elton had hacked into Slicker's user ID. There'd been alarms. Then Levison had dined with him.

He'd known. So why hadn't Levison, or Slicker, sacked him? Why send him out here, to a useless... *disposable* Frontier Ship with no gate? A Frontier Ship that needed someone to start a programme called RS23563?

And suddenly Elton knew that he needed very much to leave. He needed to leave before the programme called RS23563 reached zero.

Elton lunged through onto the bridge.

<Subroutine RS23563 started by user.>

<... 000132...>

<... 000131...>

<... 000130...>

Two minutes and a handful of seconds.

<... 000128...>

The gate-opening sequence was controlled from the bridge. The gate itself was in the adjoining accommodation cabin. F-257 had been designed by committee.

Gate codes were sequences of twenty-five digits. The number was printed on the front of the operator manual. It was in the accommodation cabin.

But Elton had numerosity. He knew the twenty-five-digit sequence. Numerosity might save his life.

He entered the sequence.

<Charging sequence commenced. Gate will open in... 15 seconds.>

How's the count?

<... 000106...>

Elton blew a sigh of relief. Plenty of time.

He was turning to flee into the cabin, to the gate, when the screen message refreshed.

<Gate will open in... 34 seconds.>

Then again.

<Gate will open in… 1 minute and 5 seconds.>

What? It's going backwards. How the hell?

But Elton knew. He'd seen it, always, in software uploads and downloads. It takes a while for the timing to settle while the computer finds its feet.

<Gate will open in… 1 minute and 22 seconds.>

<Subroutine RS23563 started by user.>

<… 000083…>

The variance settled. The two counts synchronised.

The gate would open one second before 23563 reached zero.

Elton kicked through to the accommodation cabin. A circular portion of the bulkhead wall had begun to shimmer and swirl. A countdown timer had appeared above the slowly forming gate. Glowing green numbers:

<… 1 minute 14 seconds…>

Elton glanced around the cabin. What did he need to take? He'd brought very little with him, so…

Trainers. I need my Nike ZG lites.

He pulled them from the sleep net. One of the laces caught and tangled. He pulled and fumbled.

It came free. He jammed the shoes onto his feet.

<… 59 seconds…>

But now there was another timer. This time in red, projected onto the wall beside the first.

<Subroutine RS23563 started by user.>

<… 000060…>

And a voice. Female. Softly spoken but amplified for effect, to suggest urgency. Lots of reverb.

"Warning. A remote sequence will disable the forward magnetic shield tethers in… 57 seconds."

The magnetic shield tethers. They held the ball of superdensematter at arm's length, in front of the ship. If the tethers were switched off, the heavy stuff would come adrift and strike the ship. No it wouldn't; what about inertia? We're okay. Are we okay though? What did the boring old-fart professor say? At close to light speed, space was thick, thick like soup. You needed constant thrust or the ship would slow. And if the thing holding the superdensematter broke, and the constant thrust didn't, that would be... bad.

RS23563 was, in effect, a self-destruct timer.

And there was one solitary second of leeway.

Elton positioned himself in front of the gate, his feet pressed against the opposite bulkhead plating. He would launch himself as soon as the counter showed two seconds. By the time he reached the gate it would open. He had to judge it with precision.

Red Counter: 18 seconds.

Green Counter: 17 seconds.

Elton's head flicked from one side to the other, tracking both clocks.

Red 13.

Green 12.

All his life he'd been haunted by numbers. Now this. Everything was numbers.

He took deep breaths. Flexed his leg muscles.

He focussed on the green.

8... 7... 6... 7...

What?

9... 8...

The gate timer had readjusted. With wide eyes he looked over at the red timer.

3... 2... 1...

TWENTY ONE

Slicker was perspiring more than usual. He had auditors. He had recalcitrant employees. He had Year-End prep and Budget approval and Quarter Three Forecast deadlines. And he had Levison.

Bob Slicker sometimes believed that there was only so much pressure one person could take. Slicker wished he were that person. He'd offer him a swap. Because Slicker carried a work pressure overdraft with swingeing compound interest. Perhaps he was about to lose it. Total Sanity Implode. It was not a scenario without its attractions. An unabridged loss of marbles was a way of escape. A dark and cosy little corner replete with heavy blankets and quilts. A bolthole away from reality. Probably the only option available to him this side of death.

External Auditors are not what most people expect. Most people expect sombre, grey men. They expect the Grim Reaper with a calculator. They expect all humour and geniality to have been deleted from the auditor genome.

But they're not like that. Somehow it would be easier to deal with an inhuman robotic bastard.

Real auditors are young and naïve. They giggle a lot, in little groups, and arrive at the office mid-morning, supporting monolithic hangovers. They're away from home for weeks on end and have left their wives/girlfriends/mothers/bosses and inhibitions behind. They drink, they party, and when their pounding, spinning heads allow, they ask irritating and pointless questions to which you must supply sensible answers. They are vulnerable and become your friends and confidants. Then, at the end of their two-week party they invite into your midst the Senior. Here at last is the robot. Here is the sombre individual who, during his clearance meeting, wields the power to end your career.

This Senior was called Natalie Roscoff. She was grey. She was robotic. She was unrelenting. Once she had been a giggling, fun-loving, hard-drinking junior auditor. But now she had crossed the invisible line and metamorphosed into Sexless the Unmerciful.

"The Relativistic Asset Dilapidations Provision has increased in this financial year by one thousand percent. This is a material increase with no substantive support."

"We, aah, we believe the, ahh, the vulnerability of all deep space assets has increased in recent years."

"Why?"

"Well, they're getting older."

"A year older."

"No, no. This is, ah. Oh dear. The ships accelerate. They approach closer and closer to light speed, and ah. It's very complex."

Slicker pulled a wad of absorbent polymer tissues from a box on his desk and mopped his brow. Pieces of tissue came away and attached themselves to his face where they hung like dead flesh on a short-shelf-life zombie.

"Good morning, Miss Roscoff."

Levison strode into the room.

"Time dilation, my dear. In the past financial year many of our ships have aged nearly two hundred years. You will find that our increased Dilapidations Provision is entirely within Relativistic Accounting Principles, and consistent with the basic requirements of prudence."

Levison took a single pace into the room and held the door open.

"And now, if you will excuse us, Miss Roscoff, I have urgent matters to discuss with Mr Slicker."

"Well, I hadn't quite finished, Mr Levison."

"But Mr Slicker has," said Levison. "Perhaps you might profitably spend some time upgrading your understanding of elementary Relativistic Financial Reporting Standards. GRS55 is, I believe, the appropriate reference in this instance."

Levison gave an impertinent bow which made Bob Slicker cringe. Roscoff had been humiliated. What was worse, *he* was supposed to be the accountant. He'd known about GRS55 too, but he'd chosen the safe and careful approach of not mentioning it. Now, when Roscoff returned to recommence the clearance meeting, she'd be pissed. She'd come to his office armed to the teeth with questionable balances and dodgy transactions. She'd make his life hell.

"Good day, Miss Roscoff," said Levison, closing the door behind her.

"You allow her to draw blood, Slicker. She is an irrelevance. Treat her so. When you allow these people to insert a blade into the tiniest of cracks they will be dogged, unrelenting, and they will gain in confidence until they cut through your armour and thrust their blades into the soft tissue of your heart.

"Slicker, you must learn to wear studded boots and be prepared to use them to grind every insectile nobody like Miss Roscoff into paste long before they have time to draw their blades."

Levison placed his hands on Slicker's desk and leaned over him.

"And speaking of insects. What is the status of Mr Philpotts?"

"One moment, ah…" Bob Slicker removed his jacket, tie and shirt. He balled them up and stuffed them into a desk drawer.

"Is it secure?" asked Levison.

"Yes, he can't hear us."

"So, Philpotts?"

"There was a signal. He, ah, activated the programme. Let me see." He began searching through the landfill on his desk with shaking hands.

"Here it is. Yes, it was twenty-four weeks ago, plus 182 hours, so, erm..." He called up a programme on his computer and began to type at a virtual keyboard projected onto the scattered papers that concealed his desk.

"Acceleration... initial velocity... allowing for... yes. 18724 minutes. The event will have completed a little over... four minutes ship-time, ah... fifty-two minutes ago in our time frame."

"Then it's done?"

"It's done. Philpotts will not have had time to think about it. When the field disengaged, the ship's destruction will have been virtually instantaneous. F-257 no longer exists, sir. Mr Philpotts stayed at his post. A hero."

"So when will we—"

"We should keep it to ourselves for the moment, sir. I'm not sure if or when any alarms will trigger, but we mustn't know anything in advance. In two days the gate techs will attempt to reopen the gate so they can relieve Mr Philpotts, and they will fail. Then we will know. Officially."

"A fine piece of work, Slicker. And the next phase?"

"Progressing well. Though Miss Roscoff is asking awkward questions."

"Then we will eliminate her."

Slicker stared at him.

"Sir, she is an IACHI auditor."

"She is irrelevant. Have her complete her work immediately and she can leave."

Levison turned and stalked out of the office.

With trembling hands Slicker opened his drawer and took out his shirt. He pulled it on and Jim bonded. Jim had little to say. He'd been in Slicker's drawer before.

"You going to say anything, Jim?"

"Say? About what? I know nothing."

"But?"

"Okay, a physiological scan tells me something about your emotional state right now, Bob, and it's not good. But it's only half a tale. What can I ever do for you if you don't let me in?"

"You'll only tell me things I don't want to hear, Jim. I'm good. I can lie to myself with ease. But I don't need sanctimonious counter-arguments from a machine. I don't need to be… unsettled."

"Then I cannot help you."

"No, Jim. You cannot."

TWENTY TWO

Red Clock: 3… 2… 1…

Green Clock: 7… 6… 6…

Elton kicked off anyway, in desperation. He passed straight through the wavering curtain of light where the gate was trying to form. He threw up an arm. Too late. His head hit the bulkhead on the other side which rang like a bell.

Elton blinked away the stars from his eyes and looked at the clocks. The gate was *still* six seconds from opening. Five.

The red clock hit zero.

"Attention! Magnetic shield tethers disabled!"

A siren began to sound. It was very loud in the enclosed space. It was also very loud in Elton's semi-concussed head. Who bothered to program this stuff? The ship should be gone.

But the ship remained intact. Space mustn't be quite so thick round here. Elton knew the end would come fast. Would he even know the moment?

Green numbers.

4… 3… 3… 3…

"Open, you bastard!"

And it did. Silently and without ceremony. But Elton was on the wrong side, still crumpled against the wall of the ship.

He scrambled round, and as he did he heard a sound. A terrible screaming, shrieking sound. The sound that metal makes when it ceases to exist.

He lunged.

He reached his hands out ahead of him and speared straight into the centre of the gate.

Pressure differentials pushed him back because air was now leaving the ship. His head and fingers were in the Sphere. His body wasn't.

He scratched with his fingernails for any purchase he could find. The walls were smooth. Oily smooth. He found a crack. A minute imperfection. Enough for fingernails. He pulled. His fingernails folded back and tore.

At the same time there was an immense jolt that he felt as a percussive slam in his chest and in his bones.

Lhiana's shift started at midnight, local time. She enjoyed the graveyard shift. On many a night she had seen off her entire eight-hour stint without once having to gate a person in or out. She was there "just in case".

Tonight was no exception. Lhiana wedged herself into a corner where she could work without floating around. She took out her sketch pad and unfolded it, then scrolled through the images until she found the daffodils she'd been working on. The midtones were wrong, and she never could get the yellows right when she was working electronically. She'd fix it though, once she started working in earnest using chemicals on polymer film.

She wondered how it had been for the great artists in the past, using natural pigments and organic paper. She'd once been shown a small sheet of tree paper. She'd wanted to run her fingers over it, feel the texture – but her teacher, Miss Flynn, had insisted she wear gloves.

"There are oils in the perspiration on your fingertips," she said. "This might affect the way the paper takes the pigment."

Lhiana had been shocked.

"You're going to paint on it?"

"Oh yes, one day I will. I had to save for years to buy this sheet. I am now collecting classical water pigments. One day I will create an image in the traditional way. Then I will call myself an Artist."

Lhiana wondered if Miss Flynn had ever achieved her ambition. Had she ever gained enough confidence to apply that first brushstroke?

Lhiana made a few adjustments to the background of her sketch, but she didn't want to touch the flower itself, not from memory. She would wait until tomorrow when she returned to La Ronde. She had a busy day in store, with two parties of school children to take round the garden. Children always seemed so much more enchanted by La Ronde than adults, who seemed to push her away. She had a theory. Adults understood more about the significance of the garden. They distanced themselves from La Ronde because it was tangible proof of what they had lost, and it frightened them.

Lhiana worked until three AM, then she logged off and headed up to the canteen, first pulling herself along the shaft then climbing the rungs as spin gravity increased. Leaving one's post without cover was frowned upon during the day shifts, but on graveyard, when no other cover was available, it was an accepted part of the rota. A girl had to eat, and of course there were other natural processes that required attention during the long, eight-hour shift.

The canteen was deserted, which was fine, because it meant Lhiana could occupy one of the big padded armchairs in the corner, in front of the holographic log fire. She would be able to remove her shoes and curl her legs up under her body. She could read. No one would disturb her for a whole thirty minutes. Lhiana bought a brie and pickle focaccia from the dispenser, and a tall glass of limestone-filtered comet ice water. She settled into the larger of the four armchairs and kicked off her shoes. She closed her eyes and breathed in a deep lungful of relaxation.

And then the alarm sounded.

Kim said, "Whoa, Lhiana, it's you! It's your gate hall."

Lhiana dumped most of the iced water down the front of her blouse. She jumped up and started to run. She dropped down the shaft in a dangerous plunge, grabbing the rungs only at the last moment to slow herself. This might be zero gravity but she had plenty inertia to lose from her suicide dive.

Gate Hall Number Three was all sirens and red flashing lights.

<<Frontier Ship 257. Tracer connection terminated.>>

"Kim! What's happened? What do I do?"

Even when a gate was closed, a tracer link existed between the gates on the ship and the waystation. This was a link forged on the day the gate was created. Once made it could never be broken. To break a tracer connection with a distant gate meant losing contact with that gate forever.

It had never happened before. In the whole history of the Human Sphere of Influence no Frontier Ship tracer connection had ever been lost.

Until now.

Gate Hall Three was empty. But there was blood around the portal. Streaked finger marks. They told a tale of desperate, clawing fingers reaching through the gate, trying to gain purchase.

But the gate was closed, black and cold.

Nobody waited in the gate hall for Elton. Sickly muzak floated in the air to soothe and atrophy the brain, and gave the hall an ambience not unlike a deserted supermarket. No travellers. No gate techs. The peace lasted only seconds. Then the alarms started.

Elton looked back and saw that the gate through which he had emerged had closed again. He saw the red flashing display. The Space Corps certainly enjoyed the colour red. This was just as well because he seemed to have coated the gate portal with liberal quantities of blood. There were globules of the stuff floating around, too. Blood?

That was when he noticed that the end of his foot had gone.

<<Frontier Ship 257. Tracer connection terminated.>>

That was in red too.

He'd lost a Frontier Ship. A whole one.

His instinct was to hold his foot, cry a little, and wait for someone to come. But there was a subconscious idea rattling around in his head. It was just a hunch, really. A hunch that it might be better for him if he wasn't around when people arrived.

He'd just lost a Frontier Ship. And he suspected that it hadn't been part of the plan that he return to talk about it.

It might be good, right now, if he found a place to hide, and figure out the reasoning later.

Elton propelled himself towards the nearest doorway, but when he reached it he heard voices and saw shadows approaching a bend along the corridor.

Not this way. He turned and launched himself towards the door on the opposite side of the gate hall. As he passed through he turned his head and saw someone emerging on the opposite side. Had they seen him?

No. There would have been shouting. Not sirens, though. Couldn't be any more sirens because right now it seemed that every siren that was ever built was wailing. There'd be some serious tinnitus tomorrow morning, that was for sure.

He noticed a doorway marked "Crew Only". Elton reached out a hand, then stopped. He couldn't hide here. There was blood everywhere. His blood. He had laid his own trail.

He hung outside for a moment, not sure what to do next, then he unsealed his yellow coveralls and shrugged them off. He wrapped the coveralls around his foot and continued, naked, up the corridor. The more distance he could put between himself and the gate hall the better. Then again, his chances of encountering someone else were growing.

CARGO HOLD.

Elton was more cautious this time. He made sure his foot was wrapped and he also used a corner of one of the sleeves to grip the handle – his wrecked fingernails would also leave a blood trail if he wasn't careful. The tightly bound sleeve felt good. It made some of the pain go away.

He opened the door and looked inside. It was dark. A strange smell reached his nose; machine oil and… something organic and musty. He slipped through the door and closed it behind him.

Lhiana was alone in Gate Hall Three for no more than thirty seconds. Then Sector security began to arrive, all dressed the same, in shiny black, like something out of a bad nineteen-sixties sci-fi film. Lhiana wondered what the collective noun might be for a roomful of security guards. A scourge of security; an infestation; a *superfluity* of security guards.

"Who is the Duty Officer here?" The Chief of Superfluity was short and square and mean, and had a red hoop around his shiny black helmet.

"That would be me," she said, giving a little wave so that she might stand out against the swarming beetle-black carapaces. Lhiana wore standard yellow coveralls, but also a full, very non-uniform, very impractical, flowered green skirt worn over the top, ankle-length, and stiffened against the wilfulness of zero gee. She always wore the skirt when she worked the graveyard.

It made her feel individual. And there was never anyone around to tell her *not* to wear it. Though tonight she needn't have worried about not standing out.

"Name?"

"I'm Lhiana Bilotti. What's *your* name?"

"What has happened here?"

"Well, someone tried to come through that gate," she said, pointing. "And it closed."

"What were you doing at the time?"

"I was in the canteen."

"That's very convenient, Miss Bilotti."

"How do you know I'm a Miss?"

"Did you see anyone? Did anyone come through the gate?"

Lhiana was annoyed with the senior guard. His questions seemed more like accusations. But she was also thinking about those handprints. She was wondering what might have happened; what could have happened? She imagined reaching through a gate, with bloody hands – reaching for a friendly dry hand to clamp hold of and haul you through to safety, then slipping back into... what?

And from there... you watched the gate close.

"No," she said, quietly. "No, I didn't see anyone. I got back here as soon as the alarm sounded. Ten, fifteen seconds? There was no one here. You can see, though, someone tried. I wasn't here for them."

"Can you reopen the gate?"

"No. See there: Tracer connection terminated? The link has been broken. Either the gate itself has failed, or..."

"Or what, Miss Bilotti?"

"Or it's gone."

"Gone?"

"Damaged, destroyed. I don't know."

The guard turned away and began talking, sotto voce, into his collar. Another guard arrived with a black suitcase. He connected it to sockets on the gate portal using wires with plugs on the end. The wires were black. Lhiana had never seen anything with wires before. There was something unpleasant about the way they coiled and snaked. Something insular… covert.

There was red emergency lighting in the cargo hold. Very dim. Elton only noticed it once his eyes acclimatised.

The hold was cavernous and half filled with shipping crates of ribbed plastic. Elton pulled himself along the crates looking for a place to hide. He wasn't bothered about hiding so much as finding a place; a cosy corner; somewhere enclosed and womb-like. Somewhere to take stock and think.

He lifted the lid of the first crate. It wasn't sealed. It was filled with bottled water. Elton took one on impulse. Another hunch. It seemed like a good idea.

The next crate was filled with boxes of machine tools, four to a box. They were new, the source of the machine-oil smell, but they also seemed anachronistic, almost museum pieces. Elton couldn't work out what they were for. A stencil on the side of one of the boxes said; "Chain Saws. Husqvarna replica. 2.3 cu inch. 2.15 hp. Methanol cell conversion."

Saws? What would you saw with one of these beasts? thought Elton. The important thing was that the crate was full and the machine saws did not look cosy or inviting.

The next four crates were filled with the same tools, and a fifth with individually wrapped blocks that looked like power cells. He looked at the writing on the side but it was no help; a reference number. 56584848753/22334. Useless, but Elton memorised it. He had to; it was what he did.

The sixth crate had promise. It was almost empty; one plastic box of small hand tools and lots of cosy polystyrene packing beans. This seemed an excellent place to hide.

There was a noise behind him. A small access panel opened and in came a spider-like security 'bot. It was a sniffer 'bot. Elton knew this because it was making a noise like sniff-sniff. As it crossed the line between the door and him, it got all excited and began to flash lights and sniff with extra urgency.

Air jet thrusters began pop pop popping as it reoriented and started to come straight towards him. It was evidently programmed to detect trace organic molecules, and Elton was, unfortunately, made of organic molecules.

He looked around in desperation. His cosy bed of polystyrene beans was useless to him now. But there was that smell, that musty, vegetable smell. And it was evidently causing the busy little 'bot some difficulties because its progress had shifted from inexorable to hesitating. Something in the hangar was confusing it.

Elton arrowed along the line of crates, scanning each and dismissing it. There were a lot of these chain saws. Someone obviously had in mind a good deal of mechanised hacking and cutting.

Then came a crate that seemed more promising. On the side was a yellow and black label.

"Organics. Despatch details: La Ronde. 58406-73869-22365-96309-46757 Gated Delivery. DO NOT EXPOSE TO VACUUM."

"Ah ha."

Elton forced his mind away from the seductive length and beauty of the gate code. "Do not expose to vacuum." He hadn't thought about that. Now that the subject had been raised, however, and as his eyes had become more accustomed to the dark, he noticed, for the first time, the heavy pressure doors set in the far wall. Most of this stuff seemed to be tools, and tools were never averse to a bit of vacuum and hard radiation now and again. But a crate-load of delicate, organic material…

He opened the crate, praying that it didn't contain crocodiles. It was empty. No, not empty, it was half filled with… dark stuff. Regolith. Dirt. And here was the source of the musty, organic smell. The smell wafted out into the room and the little 'bot stopped and looked round. If it could have spoken it would have said, "ahh!" If it had hands it would have rubbed them together with glee.

It came zooming and popping.

Elton manoeuvred himself into the box and pulled the lid closed behind him. He was still naked except for the yellow coveralls binding his foot. The dirt felt warm on his bare skin. It was soft and still compacted from being loaded in gravity conditions. Elton was able to wriggle into the dirt so that their combined organic aromas mingled. The dirt covered him and warmed him; protected him.

Outside, Elton heard a series of beeps that probably translated into something like "Oh, bugger." The popping of little air jets receded.

Elton allowed his pulse rate to slow. He closed his eyes. At last he had the luxury of time to think.

But he was already asleep.

"They're blaming me, Mila. They're accusing me of some sort of terrorism." Lhiana's eyes were full of tears, but they weren't tears of fear or upset, they were tears of rage.

"I was in the canteen eating a focaccia sandwich, for God's sake. How the hell can they connect any of this to me?"

"Lhiana, stop. Take a breath. They can't have any hard proof that you were involved; you're here, with me, at Westlake's. If they had any evidence you were involved you'd be on a transport ship to Bastille Five by now."

Sharmila had been sitting in the chair opposite her friend, but now she came over to sit with her on the sofa. She took Lhiana's hands in both of hers.

"Who is accusing you, and what exactly have they said?"

"There were security guards everywhere. Snotty little boys and girls all swaggering into one another. Quite rude. But then this chief of security started on me, and he was more than *quite* rude. He implied I knew all about what had happened. He asked me to re-open the gate. Imbecile."

"But he didn't actually say you were involved?"

"He didn't need to. It was in his tone. Here's something though, he called me 'Miss'."

"So?"

"So, I'm nearly thirty."

"*I'm* nearly thirty," said Mila. "So are a lot of single girls, especially on the Ring."

"Yes, but you don't use 'Miss' unless you know – or unless you're talking to a little girl. Security people use 'Ma'am'. He knew. He knew about me."

"Okay, so he's good. He's the chief of security. He'll go far."

"He had ten seconds. Nobody's that good."

"He probably asked his Jim."

"You think? He's coming into a room full of frantic security children, there's globs of blood floating around, a Frontier Ship worth gazillions has just been erased, and he asks his Jim: Who's the girl? She available?"

"I don't think it was like that."

"I'm bloody sure it wasn't. He knew me. He knew about me. He had me fitted up for terrorism even before he arrived."

Mila was kind. She calmed Lhiana down. She suggested that Lhiana come back to her apartment and stay for a few days. Strength in numbers. Lhiana wouldn't hear of it.

"I'm not going to let this get to me. Sure, it's a big news item right now. They don't know what happened. They want someone to blame. Well they won't pin it on me. They'll get bored hounding me in a few days."

The Ring was a continuous habitat that encircled the lifeless cinder of the Earth below.

Lhiana's apartment was in the British sector, though the term British was only loosely applied; the sectors were addresses more than national identities. Lhiana's roots *were* British though, despite her Italian surname, which had survived eight generations. In pre-Ring days, Lhiana's maternal great- great- great- (times six) grandmother, Rose, was actually married to the legendary Malcolm Tannahay, captain of Destiny II. After both ship and legendary captain gate-jumped and failed to return, Rose remarried. Her new beau was Giuseppe Bilotti, a barber from, of all places, Seville. Rose and her infant daughter acquired both the barber's name and his shop, but nothing else, since Giuseppe soon ran off with his manicurist. Neither the barber of, nor the manicurist of, Seville were ever heard from again, but the name was retained through eight generations of Bilotti women, who seemed to be in possession of a rare gene that manifested itself in the form of a need for their men-folk to leg it once the first child, always a daughter, was born.

The women laughed and called it the Bilotti curse, but it had made them wary and independent.

Lhiana pushed open the door of her apartment and went in.

"Any mail, Kim? Any calls? Any callers?"

"Two visitors. Square. No necks. A gentleman and a lady, kind of difficult to tell apart. Actually kind of difficult to tell apart from bulldozers."

"Any message?"

"'We'll be back', they said. I told them not to hold their breaths. Said that you were staying with a friend."

"Thanks, Kim. If they come back I'm still with the friend, okay?"

Lhiana kicked off her shoes and wandered into the kitchen. The kettle had just boiled. Kim had judged Lhiana's walking speed, the amount and starting temperature of the water already in the kettle, and calculated the best time to switch it on. Imentors were not known for acts of service like this. Their utility was merely intellectual. But Lhiana had a good relationship with her Kim, and in turn, her Kim was happy to do a bit of interfacing with the Houseman software from time to time, when this made things more comfortable for her partner.

Lhiana made tea. It was real tea, from a small bush that she tended in a patch of her own in La Ronde. Way better than any of the commercial synthetics that were available. She planned to take cuttings one day, and share them amongst friends.

"You need to watch this," said Kim, switching on the holo.

A newsreader materialised in the corner of the room, together with a portion of the desk at which she was sitting. Behind her was a 2D photograph of a generic Frontier Ship.

"…was destroyed earlier today. Government sources have suggested that this may have been a terrorist act carried out by right-wing militant factions of the radical Antiexpansionist movement."

The next photograph made Lhiana sit up quickly and spill her drink down her blouse, the second today. The drink was hot. Lhiana leapt from her chair, squealing. She didn't take her eyes from the image though.

It was a photograph of Philpotts. The same Philpotts that Lhiana had, several months earlier, expended a considerable amount of time trying to track and name after feeding him through a gate.

And just to confirm it, there was his name beneath the photograph.

Elton D Philpotts.

The newsreader was still talking.

"... unsure as to the terrorist's fate. He may have been killed when F-257 was destroyed. But security forces on the Ring are not ruling out the possibility that the terror suspect exited the ship moments before its loss. The public are therefore being warned to exercise vigilance. They describe Philpotts as very dangerous and not to be approached under any circumstances."

Lhiana stared at the holo, all the while pinching her wet blouse, holding it out and away from her skin. She wanted to change, but she didn't want to miss a word of the newscast.

"Kim!" she said. "That's him. He's the guy I was looking for. He's a terrorist. I wonder if... Oh my God, the security chief. Does he know I'd been asking around? Is that why...? Oh, Kim. I think I could be in big trouble."

"Wait. There's a call for you, Lhiana. Miss Kumari."

"Lhiana! Are you watching the news? It's him, isn't it? It's that Philpotts guy. Oh, Lhiana!"

"Hi, Mila. Yes, that was him."

"He's a terrorist, Lhiana. Is that why the security people have been watching you?"

"We don't know that they've been watching me, Mila. I was just…"

"Lhiana, you told Bruce. You wheedled all kinds out of him. They will have questioned Bruce by now. They already know you were asking."

"I'm afraid you might be caught up in this, too, Mila."

"I don't think… Oh, you mean Walther? Is he involved, too? He couldn't be. He's not a terrorist."

"He's Philpotts's reserve crew member and best friend. If he's dragged you into this—"

"Lhiana, he couldn't have anything to do with it. He's so… harmless."

"Mila, I'm sure you're right. It's unlikely that he knows what his so-called friend has been involved in. Calm down. We just have to behave as normal. If we do anything unusual or out of character it might send out signals. We've done nothing wrong, Mila. We are not guilty of anything. We just have to go to work and do the same things we always did. Tomorrow's my day off. I'm going to La Ronde. I have a school party booked for a tour. What about you?"

"I'm on an early at the hospital. I finish at ten."

"Then work it. Act normal, okay? Why not gate out to La Ronde after you finish work? The garden's safe, and restful. Nothing's going to happen, I promise."

"Okay. I will."

TWENTY THREE

Walther had been feeling good for weeks, but now his stress levels were beginning to rise again. Mila wouldn't answer his calls. It had been several weeks since he'd taken the upgrade on his immune system, and he still felt alert and chipper when he climbed out of bed each morning. He felt sure this had more to do with Mila's company than with nanos in his blood.

Sharmila Kumari had resisted all his advances while he remained in the hospital, but once he was back on the street, and no longer her patient, Mila had become amenable and pliant... enthusiastic, even.

They had been out to watch Thunderin' Willie Wicks playing over at Rustler's Steakhouse-on-the-Rim. Mila had worn the full rig: a glittery black shirt with illuminated embroidery on the front and back yokes, silver collar-tips; her boots were red and intricately tooled. Her jeans were tight and picked out with rhinestones. She had topped the whole thing off with the pink cowboy hat that she'd used to hook Walther while he was still in hospital. This wasn't the kind of outfit you picked up on a Saturday afternoon just to impress a boy on a date. Mila *knew* country. Walther could tell. She lived it.

The Willie Wicks date had led to a second, this time at the Red Barn on First Street. They'd danced. And then they'd done more than just dance.

There was a festival coming up in New Nashville, on Appalachia. They were doing package deals for the full week. Everyone would be there. Mila had seemed really enthusiastic about it so he'd gone ahead and bought tickets as a surprise. It had come as a *big* surprise because Mila had done the same and also bought tickets for them both. They'd had a good laugh about it. One of them would have to get a refund, but Walther insisted the treat was on him and Mila insisted it was her shout. Walther read this as a sign something special was going on between them. His mental state felt like new territory. He could not get Mila out of his head.

So why had she stopped taking his calls?

"Come on, Mila, answer."

There wasn't even a go-between message from her Kim. This wasn't like Mila at all. She always dressed smart. She was close to her Kim. When they had talked about their imentors, Mila had been shocked to learn that Walther sometimes bought dumb clothing and spent time away from his Jim. Mila had never once been separated from her Kim since the day they were bonded. Even in the shower she wore a bracelet. So where was she? Where was her Kim?

"Jim, where's Mila? You can track her Kim, I know you can. Is she there?"

"You know I can't tell you that, Walther."

"But she might be in some kind of trouble."

"No can do, compagno."

"At least tell me you know where she is."

"My lips are sealed, but…"

"But what?"

"Watch the news."

"Mila?"

"No. Just watch. Some things I can't talk about. But I'm your imentor, I can drop bloody big hints. Watch the news."

"Okay."

The wall of Walther's apartment dissolved into a news studio. There was no room for 3D. Too much clutter here.

Jim spooled up the main headline.

Frontier-257, destroyed! Philpotts! Terrorism!

Walther watched and listened, hardly even noticing how cute and pert the news avatar looked at this hour. As he listened, his mouth fell open and the colour drained from his face. Elton. His best friend. He *couldn't* be dead.

And they were calling him a terrorist? What was all that about? What was wrong with these people?

"Just an observation, Walther."

"Yes, Jim?"

"You told Mila about Elton; how the two of you are good friends. They've been running this terrorism story, showing Elton's picture, repeating his name for the last two hours. And now she's not answering your calls. Join the dots."

"Elton isn't dead. Or a terrorist."

"I have had no contact with his Jim, Walther. Nothing."

"I thought you couldn't tell me that stuff."

"There are times I make exceptions. I haven't been in contact with Elton's imentor since he went into deep space, twenty-four weeks ago. I have not sensed his return. I'm sorry."

"Elton isn't dead, Jim. The worms will have to go hungry. They'll have to wait a little longer for Elton D Philpotts. Trust me."

Walther was wrong. The worms were not having to wait at all. At that moment they were chowing down on his friend with happy, contented, wormy smiles. Elton just snored, dreaming of hangball and long numbers, oblivious to the worms' attentions; except that in his hangball dream, the pig was in the shape of a giant big toe, and the numbers were counting down, stopping then starting again. The toenail became a face. A leering Martin Levison.

The jolt woke him with a start. Although he had been asleep, Elton was aware, at a subconscious level, that he had been moving, and that he had remained weightless. The jolt punctuated an end to the drifting and moving. He had arrived. Somewhere.

What had it said on that sticker on the lid? He remembered the number, the twenty-five-digit Tau index. But what about the words? Los something? Las... La?

La Ronde. Of course. He'd heard of La Ronde. Queen Isabella's garden. He couldn't remember any of the details. But... La Ronde. Sounded good. Sounded safe.

Another jolt. How long had he been asleep? He had no idea, no way of finding out; he was naked. He'd had no tactile contact with any smartware since that time, an age ago, when he'd first boarded F-257. He missed his smartware. He wanted his Jim. Not a casual wish; he yearned for his Jim with an ache in his chest. Jim would have told him where he was, how long he had been asleep.

Jim would have told him what to do.

"What do I do next, Jim?" His voice was small and lost, and no answer came back.

Elton tested the lid of the crate. It moved and there was light outside. He put an eye to the crack and peered out. A different warehouse. People. This wasn't Space Corps territory though; not a yellow coverall in sight. But he didn't want to be seen and so decided it might be best to stay in his crate. For a while. It was warm and comfortable. It was safe.

Then Elton caught a glimpse of what was inside the crate with him. A shaft of light picked out the worms. Lots of worms. Some soil, but mainly worms. Fat and red and juicy. They coiled and slithered.

Elton left the safe haven of his crate by explosive levitation – and he did it accompanied by a lot of noise, most of it of the expletive variety.

There were shouts.

"Hey, you! What the hell?"

The zero-gee environment filled with worms, all somewhat surprised and delighted to find themselves at liberty in what had traditionally been the exclusive domain of birds, their lifelong tormentors, at least in genetic memory, because not a single bird had survived Old Earth.

In a world where the natural order of all things was for stuff to go wrong, a fortuitous thing happened. Elton's trajectory across the warehouse took him directly towards a door marked "Exit". It was a pressure door, though, and while Elton would have normally been timid about throwing open such a door without a pretty firm assurance as to the lack of vacuum on the other side, today he felt bold. He just wanted to get far away from angry shouts and squadrons of worms.

He hauled on the release lever. A second fortuitous thing happened. Instead of being sucked out into the vastness of empty, absolute-zero, eyeball-exploding space, he came into a garden.

He closed the door behind him and, just for a moment, found himself suspended in a haven of peace and tranquillity. No shouting. No alarms. Here was green and mist and the gentle twittering of recorded birdsong, laid on for ambience.

Elton took a long, slow lungful of air. He savoured it. Could a place be finer? Could any scene be rendered more pastoral, more beautiful than this?

Then, magically, it was. A vision, floating out from behind a clump of vegetation, a shaft of sunlight illuminating her auburn hair. The girl with the green eyes.

Lhiana Bilotti.

She stared at him.

Elton stared at her.

He felt his pulse quicken and the back of his neck began prickling with heat. A moment; an eternity.

Then the screaming started again. It erupted from a party of schoolchildren who had drifted out from behind the same clump of greenery.

"Aargh!" They shouted and waved their arms. "Zlatan Zombie! Zlatan Zombie!"

Kids loved to be afraid of Zlatan Zombie. They loved the way worms crawled in and out through the open wounds in his face. They loved the way he limped and dragged his useless, yellow, pus-filled leg behind him. They loved the way he was blown to bits every time Oscar Willis shot him or hacked at him or crushed him, at the end of each gore-filled episode. Kids were like that. They had no fear. They were immune to the gross-out.

Except for when it was real.

Elton realised he *was* Zlatan Zombie. Naked and covered in dirt and slime and… yes, worms. There were still plenty of worms crawling over his body. And his right foot, bound in the rags of his yellow Space Corps coveralls, soaked in blood, was the perfect analogue for the pus-filled appendage of the eponymous brain-eating mega-star.

"No, shh…!" Elton waved his arms at them and they screamed all the more. Zlatan Zombie did a lot of arm waving.

"I'm not Zlatan, look." He wiped the mud from his face with his hands. "See?"

And now the girl, Lhiana Bilotti, was shouting along with the children.

"It's Philpotts! It's the terrorist. Get behind the bush, children. Go, quickly."

She turned to Elton.

"Don't you dare harm these children. Don't you dare." She kicked off a support beam and advanced on him, her jaw set, her eyes grim and determined. She was ready for a fight.

Elton had, for the last two weeks, dreamed and yearned of meeting Lhiana Bilotti face to face. This wasn't quite how he'd imagined it would go.

"You lost me my job, you bastard. Your slimeball accomplice broke the heart of my best friend. You—"

But she didn't finish. The garden filled with storm troopers and the air began to crackle with the purple tracers from energy weapons. Children scattered but the storm troopers didn't seem to care.

Elton pointed at the warehouse door.

"Get the kids in there. It's me they're after." He shouted to the kids, "Though the door. Fast!"

The kids moved. They could see the tracer. They could smell the air burning around them. This was scarier than Zlatan Zombie. And *this* Zlatan Zombie seemed to be one of the good guys.

Elton kicked off towards the greenery to draw the fire away from the children.

Lhiana stared after him for a moment, then she turned and began ushering the children into the warehouse and out of the way of the lunatic troopers.

Elton went deep into the vegetation, which offered some cover. Much of it was green plastic, a scaffold for the smaller creepers and vines. Elton, like everyone else, watched those "Realized H" holos, 2D films manipulated into feeble paper cut-out 3D, about the jungles and forests of Earth. There were no forests left now, of course, on Earth or anywhere else, but the model for the garden of La Ronde was clearly evident. Where they didn't have big plants they used plastic. It was quite effective.

It was also a good place to hide.

Elton watched the troopers zipping around and shooting at anything that moved. Whole sections of the garden had erupted in flame, and the high oxygen content of the atmosphere was exacerbating the problem. There were sprinklers kicking off everywhere. Elton tried to avoid them, because his mud-caked body was excellent camouflage.

He wriggled into a particularly dense clump of leaves and decided to stay there for a while. So far they hadn't shown the gumption to use motion detection or infra-red. Either would put an end to Elton's liberty in seconds, and he guessed it was only a matter of time before they stopped shooting and started using their heads. The lack of gravity was probably part of the problem. Troopers liked to do a lot of stomping, and you couldn't stomp in micro-gee. Shooting off energy weapons was the next best thing.

Elton knew he would be caught. There was nowhere to go. They would find him, but he saw no reason to make the job easy for them, especially while they were still so trigger-happy. He was prepared to wait all day if need be.

A patrol drifted past, less than a couple of yards from where Elton lay. He listened to their conversation.

"...into the warehouse after the girl. Take her alive if you can, but if she resists you take no chances; shoot to kill."

Shoot to kill? The girl, Lhiana? Did they really want him that badly?

It took him less than a second to reach a decision. He wriggled out of the bush and kicked free, raising his hands over his head.

"Okay, over here, guys. It's me you want."

The troops turned and stared.

The soldier nearest to Elton looked nervous. He was young. He glanced over at his senior officer, a sergeant, maybe? Three stripes on his arm.

"Sir?"

The sergeant ignored him. He fixed Elton with a steely eye. The young soldier floated over towards his sergeant, eyes flicking between the officer and Elton.

"Sir, I don't think…"

The sergeant aimed an angry glare at the youngster, silencing him. He turned to consider Elton again. No words. Five seconds or so while he weighed up the options. Then he gave Elton a humourless smile and raised his rifle.

"Whoa!" said Elton. "I'm giving myself up."

The sergeant shot him.

And everything went black.

TWENTY FOUR

Lhiana felt her emotions churn and tangle. A casual interest in the nervous young man she had pushed through the F-Ship gate. An interest that became an infatuation. An infatuation that became… what? Grief? Anger? Fear? Not like Lhiana at all. Nobody had ever ensnared her emotions like this. She'd been led into silly, out of character actions, like manipulating Bruce into divulging client confidentialities. Worse, she'd dragged her best friend, Mila, into it.

Then this… anarchist, had gone and blown up a frontier ship. And the other one, Walther Blick, had broken her best friend's heart. Philpotts could do all this to her after they'd met for all of fifteen seconds.

The last of the children were through, into the warehouse and safe. She took a final look at the mayhem in La Ronde then closed the door, actually and metaphorically. She was rid of him. The troops would… arrest him? Haul him away? From what she had seen so far, they certainly didn't appear intent on a diplomatic solution.

No, she said to herself. He's a saboteur. He destroyed Space Corps property. And…

There was a shrieking of vaporising metal as one of the errant energy weapons scored a furrow along the other side of the warehouse door.

…And what else? Well, nothing else, really. Did he deserve such a level of attention? He had put the safety of her and the children first, without any hesitation. What kind of terrorist did that? More than could be said for the gun-crazed storm troopers out there. What was it with them? There were *children* here. And the garden. Their indiscriminate firing was destroying the plantings and borders that had taken years to establish. What kind of morons were these people?

Philpotts had drawn their fire while she and the children got to safety.

Oh hell.

Tomas, the storekeeper, was at the far end of the warehouse. He'd been labelling and stacking the latest shipment from the Ring, but now he was immobilised and in shock at the sounds of Armageddon coming from the garden.

"Tomas, snap out of it. Take care of the children. I have to do something. They're killing La Ronde."

Tomas blinked away his immobility and now, with a task on which to focus, took charge of the dozen or so wide-eyed children.

Lhiana kicked off towards the airlock. The bulkhead door wasn't the only way out of the warehouse. She hit the evacuate button even before reaching for a suit. There was no danger; sensors linked to the imentor network monitored the status of anyone inside. Depressurisation wouldn't start until Lhiana's Kim relayed a signal that her suit was powered-up and secure.

The suit ballooned around her. They were all one-size, and the tailoring erred on the side of caution; there was room inside for a circus parade. But then, once the power switch was thrown the suit shrank to a hard-shell, skin-tight fitting. The joints flexed only when required to do so, and they did so by chemical rearrangement so that they always remained rigid. The helmet, likewise, adapted to the contours of her face, the only air gap being a bubble around her nose and mouth. The suits were light and manageable, but insanely sweaty.

The status light on the control panel on her left forearm winked green, and with a whoosh the airlock depressurised and the outer door swung open. Lhiana pulled herself out and clambered onto the ladder that ran around the circumference of the crystal dome of La Ronde.

"Lhiana. Use a safety harness," said Kim.

"Do we always have to go through this, Kim?"

"Always. One day you will miss a hand hold. Oh, I'll keep you company until we drift out of range of the signal, but then I'll digitise and fade and you'll be left to die out in space alone."

"You're very melodramatic, Kim."

"I'm very realistic."

"Well now's not the time."

Kim raised her voice. "Now is *exactly* the time, Lhiana. You are agitated and flustered and driven by chemical passions. You will make mistakes."

Lhiana snorted. "Chemical passions. Come on, Kim, it's nothing like that at all, it's... I don't know, concern, *com*passion."

"You know perfectly well that I monitor your biometrics, Lhiana. I know your moods and I know your chemistry. Right now there is a *lot* of chemistry. Lhiana, *use the damn safety!*"

Lhiana sighed and reached down to her waist. She snapped the safety onto the guide wire.

"Sometimes, Kim, I—" As she kicked off she slipped. She only had hold with one hand and she lost her grip. She went cartwheeling out into space. Her safety line stopped her.

"What was that you said, Lhiana? Did you say something? Something like... thank you, Kim?"

Lhiana hauled herself back to the ladder and continued, a little slower, with more care, stopping at each anchoring point to move first one karabiner, then the next.

She could see through the crystal into La Ronde. She could see the flames and destruction and the flying bolts of tracer. It was all played out in complete silence, which gave the scene an unreal quality. There was no sign of Elton Philpotts, but that didn't seem to deter the troops from torching everything in sight. Lhiana felt a knot of rage in her stomach. These were supposed to be the good guys.

She continued on along the ladder. There were four airlocks into La Ronde: two gave access to the old residency in the asteroid itself, one was in the warehouse, and one was in the control room. She saw the control room door ahead.

"Can you release the door for me, Kim?"

"Already done, Lhiana."

Another glance into the garden and Lhiana saw Elton wriggling out of a clump of bushes. There were five or six troops nearby. They were sure to see him.

"Kim, can you reach Elton? Can you warn him? They'll see him."

"Sorry, Lhiana, he's not on the imentor network. Perhaps you haven't noticed, but he's naked."

Lhiana *hadn't* noticed. Elton was so covered in mud that it was not at all obvious. She ducked into the airlock and slammed the door. An amber light began to wink to indicate the airlock was pressurising. Lhiana felt trapped. She had no way of knowing what was happening outside. She punched her fist on the door in frustration. The delay was maddening.

Green light.

Lhiana heaved the door open and propelled herself into the control room. She'd only been here once before. She'd been shown the controls but hadn't taken much notice. The control desk was positioned in front of a large window that overlooked the garden. The fires were out. The blackened remains of the plants were steaming under the last drips of the sprinkler system. Liana felt rage at the destruction. She saw that Elton was moving towards the troops, his arms raised.

So, he had decided to surrender? To these idiots?

She looked at the control desk. Master light control. Where was it? A heavy red lever.

I'll buy you some time, Terror Boy.

Lhiana pulled.

Nothing happened.

What?

Then she realised. Stupid. It was daylight. The asteroid had a slow spin to give a day/night cycle for the plants.

Something else she remembered though. The crystal dome was doped with a reactive pigment. She reached for the slide control in the centre of the console and pulled it. In a smooth fade-out the dome went black.

She looked out into the garden, and saw the flash of purple as Elton, with hands above his head, was shot from point-blank range.

"Where've you been hiding, Mila?"

Mila looked startled to find Walther lurking outside the gates of Five Faiths Hospital.

"Walther, I… I'm sure…" She sounded flustered and avoided his eye.

"You've been dodging me, Mila." Walther did a little pouty, sulky thing with his bottom lip. He was going for the apologetic puppy dog look. "We have to talk. Please."

Mila's eyes darted around, checking out all the dark corners. Walther knew what this was: she expected covert operatives to swoop in and arrest her just for talking to him.

"Come on, Mila. I've been out here for two hours. If anything was going to happen it would have happened already. Let's go for a drink. You've got to hear my side."

Mila looked like a Thermopod caught in a casserole. Walther thought she might run at any moment. Instead, Mila looked at the ground, weighing up the risks. Then she nodded.

"Okay. One drink. Thirty minutes. I told Lhiana I'd join her after I finished work. I don't intend to be late. I'll give you thirty minutes and no more. Where?"

They went to Westlake's.

"It's nice here," said Walther, looking around, patting the green velvet cushions on the sofa. "Tasteful. But they only sell water?"

"Watering holes are big on the Ring, Walther. Let's face it, everything else you drink up here is fake. There's only water left that's real."

"Er, you know where Ring water comes from, don't you, Mila? Recycling plants; sweat; waste?"

"Which is why they sell the real thing here. Planet sourced. Expensive, but…"

"But urine free."

"Look, Walther, you've used up two of your thirty minutes. Do you really want to spend the remainder of your time here discussing interior décor and bodily fluids?"

"I'm not a terrorist, Mila."

"So you say."

"Neither is Elton."

"That is not what *they* say." Mila pointed up at the news programme on the screen above the door.

"The news channels are wrong, Mila. They report what they've been told to report. Elton's been set up. There was something screwy about the whole Space Corps deal right from the start."

"What do you mean, screwy?"

"Elton shouldn't have got the job. I told you all about the interview from hell. Someone needed him to get that job… because he was expendable."

"That's ridiculous."

"Is it? So many people are perfect these days. There's a genetic blandness everywhere you look. How do you stand out from the crowd in an interview when everyone who wants every job is designed for it in the first place?"

"It's not like that, Walther. Not everybody is genetically—"

"Not everybody, no. But there are enough perfect specimens out there to make the desirable jobs unattainable, at least for those of us who have to make do with nature's handouts."

"But Elton *was* a Genemod. You said."

"Yeah, but he was done on the cheap. He came in under-budget. His dad gave him this number thing, but it's the wrong kind of number thing – for an accountant, anyway. Do you think I'd want anything to do with him if he was just one of the bland, soulless perfect-born? Not a chance. I get on with Elton because he has faults, because he's interesting and unpredictable, and because he would never walk all over you to get what he wants. He's just like you in that respect."

"So, he's not perfect. He has faults. And one of those faults is the urge to blow up spaceships."

"No. No, Mila. He wouldn't know where to start. He is not a terrorist."

"You would say that, Walther. You're both in it together."

"Look at me, Mila. Look into my eyes. Is that what you see? Do you really, truly believe it? Because if you do—"

"Oh, Walther. No. Of course not. Not you. Oh, God, I don't

know what to believe anymore. You did get mixed up in that riot thing in—"

"It wasn't a riot, Mila, it was… a brawl. A setup, too. Yes, I have sympathies with the Antiexpansionists, even the Contractionists, to a point. That doesn't make me an enemy of the people. You're an Expansionist. That's okay. I'm not about to fight you over it."

"I don't know, Walther, I— Look…" She nodded at the holo, up over Walther's shoulder. Someone had switched channels. The news was on, and there was Elton. His face, now, had rock-star celebrity.

"I want to believe you but…" Her face drained of colour and her hands flew to her open mouth.

"Mila? Mila, what is it?"

She pointed at the holo.

"It's Lhiana."

Walther twisted round to look.

Mila shouted. "Sound! Someone get the sound!"

"…in a fierce gun battle on the garden world of La Ronde, Philpotts escaped from a squad of security forces. There were a number of casualties and there was widespread and irreplaceable damage to the garden, which is a galactic heritage site.

"Philpotts was injured, but his escape was affected by a temporary worker at La Ronde, Miss Lhiana Bilotti. Bilotti is a registered Disexpansionist sympathiser, known to have infiltrated La Ronde as a volunteer employee, months earlier; part of an elaborate and complex conspiracy. Anyone who can provide the authorities with information as to the whereabouts —"

Mila was on her feet, red-faced, pointing at the screen. *"Lhiana isn't Disex!"*

People were staring.

"Now do you believe me, Mila? You're her friend. Blown up any spaceships lately?"

"Pay for the drinks, Walther. We're leaving. I think I know where she might go. They're both going to need our help."

TWENTY FIVE

The ground was moving.

The last hours – were they hours? Elton didn't know. They had passed in a blur. Pain and movement, darkness and light. The one constant through all of his confusion was the soft arm that supported him, the luxuriant smell of the auburn hair that often formed a tickly mat on his face, up his nose.

Lhiana. She had stayed with him, coaxed him, cursed him, dressed him, pushed him through gates. But now it had stopped. And slowly Elton was coming back to his senses.

"Lhiana?"

"This is what puzzles me." Her voice came from beside him but Elton couldn't see her without moving his head. He didn't want to move his head.

"You know my name," she continued. "The first time we met you neither spoke nor opened your eyes."

"The first time? We've met before today?"

"When you first went aboard F-257, months ago. I was the gate tech who... we're getting off the point. That was the first time. The second time you were covered in mud and waving your arms about like that... zombie thing."

"Zlatan."

"Whatever. But you knew my name."

"Er, yes. Yes I did. I think—"

"Don't interrupt. You are a wanted felon. Your name seems to be known by everyone in the Sphere of Influence, and now it has been linked with mine. How come everyone knows *me*? How the hell do *you* know me? Why are the names Elton and Lhiana now synonymous with Bonnie and Clyde? *Are* you a terrorist? Did you destroy F-257?"

These were a lot of questions. Elton didn't know where to start, so he tried a big dopey grin instead.

"No, of course you're not a terrorist. Look at you. But what are you, Elton? What's going on? And how's your shoulder?"

More questions, but here was one he could answer.

"Bloody hurts," he said.

"It's probably infected. Didn't have time to clean it. I just stuffed you into some spare coveralls and washed your face. I needed you to look halfway presentable when we went through the gates."

"Coveralls? Are they smart? Jim? Are you there, Jim?"

Lhiana shook her head.

"No signal out here. Sorry."

Elton's shoulders slumped. He missed Jim. It had been such a long time.

"Last I knew," he said, "I was being shot at. How did you–?"

"I doused the lights, then I followed my nose. You don't smell too sweet, you know. It helped that there were so many soldiers milling around out there. They kept on bumping into each other in the dark. Some tried to use their imentors but only a handful of them seemed to be dressed smart. I guess the army has its reservations about troops taking something intelligent into battle with them. So, all these blind, idiot soldiers; barging, fighting, shooting, settling old scores… But I know La Ronde. I don't need lights. I grabbed you and we just threaded our way through the ruck. Wasn't even sure if you were still alive, but I'd come so far, so…"

Elton thought about that.

"My shoulder. Is that the only injury? There's nothing anywhere else is there? Something you don't want to tell me about?"

"Well, half your foot's gone, but that looks—"

"Yeah, it's an old wound; hours old."

Elton shook his head.

"That sergeant," he said. "He couldn't have missed. He was three feet away. I should have a hole in my chest the size of a transfer gate."

"There was a youngster in the patrol, seems he got a touch of 'cramp' at the critical moment and kind of lurched into the sergeant's firing arm. I heard them shouting about it afterwards. I guess not everyone in the security forces is a complete dick."

"I wish I could thank him. I haven't thanked you yet. Why did you take such a risk?"

Lhiana shrugged. "You knew my name. I wanted to know why."

"That can't be all. You could have been killed."

"So, maybe I believed in you. A bit. Your friend, Walther, never doubted you."

"You know Walther? How the hell do you know Walther?"

"You still haven't told me how you know me." Lhiana looked away.

Elton gave a half-smile. There was more to this tangled web than either of them wanted to talk about right now.

"Anyway," he said. "Thank you, Lhiana. I owe you my life."

She smiled. Elton forgot all about the hot coals screaming inside his shoulder. Lhiana had a smile you could bathe in. There were so many complications here. It was easy to forget that until moments ago Lhiana had only existed for Elton in instructional holos somewhere out on the edge of deep space. She had been an ideal. Elton knew numbers. He knew that the odds of ever seeing this, Lhiana, for real, in the whole mind-boggling volume of human space were... well, it was one in something, and the something was ten to the power of a *very* big number.

"So where are we?" asked Elton.

"We're home. My home. Welcome to Minerva."

"Why does the ground move on Minerva?"

Lhiana laughed. "We're at sea. This is an ocean world. There are two elevators. One comes down right in the middle of the Dianic Ocean. Nobody uses it. Too inconvenient. The ocean base station isn't manned, and neither is Diana Waystation at the top end. Anyone looking for us here *will* find us, but it's going to take a while."

"Why are you doing this, Lhiana?"

"Doing what?"

"This. Rescue. Life-on-the-line."

"I told you. Bonnie and Clyde. I'm as embroiled, now, as you are. I don't have a lot of choice."

"I'm sorry."

"You don't have to be. It's as much my fault as yours. I asked too many questions. Anyway, our priority now is to fix you up with some medical care. If we're going to be on the run together, then you need to be more mobile than you are right now. It's one of the reasons we're on Minerva."

"I don't follow."

"Half the planet are doctors. Minerva's a hospital world. You must be quite healthy or you'd have known that."

"Doesn't that make Minerva the first place they'd look? Especially since you used to live here."

"Yes, but not where we're going. I know a place. That's why we used the back door."

"Is it far?"

"Not too far."

"It's just... I'm not fussed by the rocking motion. Don't feel so good."

"The ship's hardly moving. Are you that bad a sailor?"

"I wouldn't know. I've never sailored."

Elton had seen pictures of oceans. Even the odd 2D holo. He never really anticipated the effect that the motion might have on his equilibrium. He was baffled. He was comfortable in a hangchamber and he'd been in gravity-free deep space for weeks. Surely a bit of rocking... Oh!

"I have to go somewhere."

"You've lost a lot of blood. You're better staying where you are."

"Lhiana. I really..."

Too late.

Walther polished his glasses for the fiftieth time. A nervous habit. They'd been through embarkation security three times. Each time they'd been kept waiting for nearly an hour then sent back to go through again.

"They suspect us," said Walther.

"They're doing it to everyone," said Mila. "It's not just us. I've never seen the Ring like this. Relax, Walther. We're travelling under our own names; our own documentation. They won't stop us."

"We've been here three hours, Mila. They're doing a damned good job of stopping us so far."

The queue moved along. Walther wiggled his legs to drift forward, nudging his bag along in front of him. He moved slow enough to allow air resistance to stop him before he collided with the passenger in front.

"I wish you'd tell me where we're going," he said.

"It's better if you don't know. You're a nervous wreck. You

once told me you saw yourself as the James Bond type. I have to doubt that. You've already given yourself up to the ticket clerk, and he only wanted to check your boarding pass. If he hadn't been so bored with his day he might have actually listened to your confession and we'd be banged up in jail for bank robbery or something by now.

"Anyway, look, we're coming to the gate. Don't say anything, Walther."

There were guards on either side of the gate portal. They had energy weapons and they made sure everyone knew it. They looked mean. They stood, Velcro'd down, with legs slightly apart as if the absence of gravity couldn't diminish their weight and solidity. Their faces were set in scowls of belligerence.

Walther attempted to look bored rather than nervous. He sighed a few times and rolled his eyes. He found he was good at it. He had been rehearsing and perfecting the look his whole life.

The ticket check for the gates was normally just a nod and a "have a nice day". Walther was a Space Corps employee and Mila was a medical professional. They both had privilege gate passes that allowed free access to virtually the entire network. There would be no nods or smiles today though.

"Destination?"

"Neualmain," said Mila.

"You are travelling together?"

"Yes."

"Nature of visit?"

"Debauchery," said Walther.

The gate clerk gave him a look. Mila gave him a punch.

"Leisure," she said.

"For how long?"

"A couple of days."

"A couple. Is that two?"

Walther leaned forward and opened his mouth to offer more sarcasm, but Mila put her hand on his forearm, caught his eye, and gave a tiny shake of her head.

"Yes. Two days," she said, all the while looking at Walther with stern eyes.

There was a long pause while Mila's and Walther's faces were scrutinised and compared with the ones on their passes. Walther did his sighing thing and rolled his eyes again.

"Okay, you can go. Take care."

The "take care" comment was loaded with meaning, and held no suggestion of any friendly hint to take care of themselves.

But they were through. It was a wide and expensive passenger gate. No claustrophobia. No discernible pressure differentials. They simply stepped through the cold grey curtain and were on Neualmain Waystation Three. Security was heightened here, too, with guards checking every ticket. But the energy weapons were less overt and the checking was more routine than rigorous.

"Where now?" said Walther.

"We could eat. As soon as the shifts change we'll be on our way again," said Mila.

"Ah, so Neualmain is misdirection."

"Indeed. Don't know if it will work. If security is any good they'll pick up on us having arrived then leaving so soon afterwards."

"So why are we bothering with the act?"

"Because security rely on computers. This isn't imentor stuff, Walther. Jims and Kims don't get involved in day-to-day processing and confidentiality issues. Sometimes they dabble in people and places that interest them, and I'm sure this doesn't. *Our* computer programs are just as crappy as they've always been. Do you know you spent a week as a patient in Five Faiths with your name wrong, your date of birth wrong, and your sex listed as female? Data Protection stops us amending these things, so we just live with it."

"I guess you're right," said Walther. "Space Corps payroll is the same. Our favourite phrase we use there is 'Just do a workaround.'"

They found a café called FingaLikka with a comfortable half-gee spin and seats in a window that looked out onto the gate halls. They would watch for the shift change.

Walther ordered vat-grown FingaLik-special beef burger. Mila chose the FingaLik-veggie burger.

The only way to tell the two burgers apart was by colour. Mila's was green, Walther's wasn't, yet. As far as taste went, they were interchangeable and about as appetising as plimsolls.

They ate slowly and with care. Not something Walther was known for, but on this occasion, easy to accomplish, because despite diligent, even industrial-level chewing, the rubbery texture stayed resistant to all his efforts. Death-by-Choking was an ever-present table guest.

They finished their meals despite the food, and began to receive unfavourable attention from the proprietor who evidently wanted their table for other luckless diners.

"I think we're going to have to order dessert," said Walther. "Man in grubby chef hat wants us to leave."

Walther viewed the prospect of dessert with little enthusiasm. Mila too. Elasticated burgers were quite enough for one sitting. Grubby Chef Hat sent, not one, but two minions over to wipe their table. Hints were being dropped. Dessert seemed unavoidable.

Walther dithered between FingaLik Apple Pie or FingaLik

Gateau. He ordered "*Heimlich*" Apple Pie from the waiter, and chuckled about his excellent wit long after the gently fluorescing blob of matter arrived and began trembling on the plate in front of him.

"Shut up and eat your pie," said Mila, though she was struggling to suppress her own laughter.

"Eat *that*?" said Walther. "Nah, I'm going to watch it and see what it does."

"What do you think it does?"

"I don't know. Nothing good, I imagine. Glad I've brought my own medical practitioner with me." He smiled at her. "My personal physician."

"Might be better off with a personal physicist," said the man at the table behind them. He was with a lady, and he made theatrical play of poking his blob of pie with a spoon, jerking back in anticipation of an explosion or an alien attack, and nodding in a comradely way to Walther.

"By the way, we're meant to be incognito," Mila whispered behind her hand to Walther. "We're not here to make lifelong buddies."

Walther held up his hands in a patting motion. *Okay, okay.*

"Other people are looking at us, like you and your friend are the comedy act. Mush up the pie a bit. Make like you are actually going to eat the thing."

Walther nodded and smiled at the man again, then turned around to resume playing with the pie, with Mila. Neither of them noticed the security guards come in; not until an argument erupted behind them, at the table with Walther's new friend.

"ID card? What sodding ID card? Do I need some sort of permission from the government, now, to eat this crap?"

"Sir, step away from the table, please."

"Bugger off, or I'll make *you* eat it."

"Harold, don't start, not again. Just show him something." The lady was probably his wife. She certainly seemed to be a life-qualified peacemaker. Harold evidently objected to things quite often.

"Show him my ID? I'll show him my arse," said Harold.

The guard unfastened his handgun with a deliberate ripping of Velcro.

"Your ID? Sir."

The man called Harold took out his wallet.

"Let me see now... library card, gate pass, membership card for the geology club... oh, how about this, a receipt from Clodhoppers, the shoe shop. Do you wish to check my feet, make sure they're the approved size?"

The guard reached out to take Harold's wallet. Harold reacted by pushing him away. The guard was a youthful, finely balanced killing machine, whereas Harold was mid-fifties and sported a girth which attested to a lifetime of devotions at the altar of Fast Food. The contest was a mismatch from the outset. But the guard lost the advantage when he slipped on a glob of wayward FingaLik pie. His slide took him hard into the table edge where he knocked a cup of FingaLik fizzy toxic liquid into Harold's wife's lap. She screamed. Harold threw a fist that connected with the security guard's helmet. The fist came off worst, but now the other guard was running over to weigh in on the disturbance.

"I think this would be a good time to leave," Walther whispered.

Mila was already putting her things in her bag.

They slipped out unnoticed as FingaLikka products began to fly.

When they reached the pavement they saw the day shift

heading home from each of the gate halls. It was time for Walther and Mila to leave.

"You going to tell me where we're going?" asked Walther.

"Not yet. Come on."

Mila needn't have worried. Security out of Neualmain was minimal. The night-shift gate tech had been on duty for all of two minutes and seemed anxious to get her head down and catch up on some Z's.

"Where to, guys?"

"Minerva, please."

"Both of you?"

They waved their passes.

She ran her finger down a list.

"Vesta Station, yeah?" She keyed in the Tau code.

The gate went grey.

"All yours, guys. See ya."

They stepped through to Vesta Waystation above Minerva. Security was much tighter here, but the no-neck Neanderthals were only checking those going out. Arrivals were ignored.

"What does this tell you?" said Walther.

Mila shrugged.

"Tells me two things," said Walther. "One, you guessed the right place. Two, so did the bad guys."

"And three," said Mila, "they haven't found Lhiana and your friend yet."

TWENTY SIX

The beach hut was less than a hundred yards from the crashing surf, and yet the trek up the soft, always-in-your-shoes, flour-textured sand felt more like a hundred miles to Elton. He was wearing the effects of his missing toes, his missing blood, and his three weeks of micro-gee like a homeward-bound geologist's rucksack.

The high-sided hydrogen ship, on which he'd travelled and vomited for the last three days, was fully automated. It had no crew, and he and Lhiana had been the only passengers.

There were times, though, when both the waves and Elton's delicate gastric processes became smoother. It gave them a chance, at last, to talk. Elton felt ready to tackle the subject of how he knew her, before everything kicked off.

"So, you were the gate tech when I went on my tour?" Elton thought back to the girl with the kind, sympathetic voice. He'd opened his eyes just long enough for the briefest glance. He hated gate travel even at the best of times; that cold feeling that passes right through the inside of your body. The thought of going through that tiny hole in the wall to the F-Ship had been just about too much for him.

"I recognised your voice," he said. Yes, her voice. Kind. Gentle. *That's* why she had seemed familiar when he watched her doing the training presentations.

He realised he'd gone quiet for too long. He'd drifted off into a trance-like state, nodding and smiling like a fool.

"Are you okay?" said Lhiana.

"Yes. No. Almost," said Elton. It was his injury. He felt so tired.

"You were in some training holos on the ship," he said.

"Ahh."

"Your name was on the credits." He gave her a smile that showed pride in his sleuthing abilities. "You're very good. But now you're a gate tech. You do garden tours."

"I wanted to be an actor, years ago. Presenting a few training holos was a thing I did at college for extra cash. I'm amazed you recognised me; I was much younger. I only did a few of them."

Elton thought about how he'd binge-watched every holo he could find, not listening to the words, just the voice. Drowning in the gaze from her green eyes.

He shrugged. "I have a good memory for faces."

He didn't. Just hers.

They talked some more about their lives before becoming wanted felons, then the ship hit another choppy patch of sea and Elton spoiled the moment by turning green and going lightheaded again, so he recommenced with the throwing up.

They could have gone directly to their ultimate destination, but there was always a threat of some tenacious data-mining 'bot turning up a record of two passengers travelling alone from Dianic Base Station. Lhiana insisted they take the cargo-carrying hydrogen boat to Port Juno, where she collected a small catamaran, the *Spindrift*, that belonged to her Aunt Beryl.

Elton had been wary of the wallowing little vessel at first, but then once the wind filled her sails, and she began to skip across the swelling turquoise sea, he had become captivated. Sleek sea creatures had joined them, skimming just on or below the waves, and Elton had whooped with delight at the sight of them. There was no seasickness aboard the *Spindrift*; she moved with the sea in sympathetic partnership, in sharp contrast to the ways of the hydrogen boat that had bickered and battled against every swell and movement.

The trip from Port Juno to the island of Mantello, situated along the Egerian Archipelago, took five hours. It was over way too soon for Elton, and he hoped that he'd get the chance to sail again before they left. The next phase of their "plan", Lhiana's plan, was far from being fully mapped-out at this point, so their eventual departure from Mantello was only an assumption on Elton's part.

Aunt Beryl's beach hut, the only building on Mantello, was protected from the sea by an outcropping of slick grey rock. It was built into the rock itself, and Elton only became aware that any building was there when they drew close. It was a single-storey cottage, low and squat, with two small round windows and a door of weathered aluminium that looked to have started life as part of a spaceship.

Lhiana stopped in front of the hut and held out her arms.

"Well, what do you think? This is going to be home for a while."

"It's very… lonely."

"No one *ever* comes here. It's perfect."

"What about your Aunt Beryl?"

"She hasn't been here for ten years or more. She's getting on a bit. Beryl's not really my aunt, she's my grandmother's aunt. The boat trip's not so easy for her these days, and… well, it's hard work out here. We're a long way from the conveniences of civilisation. We won't be disturbed." She gave him a grin then turned to the house, shouting over her shoulder. "I used to come here for holidays with my little sister, Dorina. Come on, I'll show you inside."

Lhiana entered by leaning on the door and giving it a couple of solid kicks until it burst open and she fell inside. Elton followed. The interior was even smaller than it appeared from the beach.

There was one small room with two old chairs and a bed, a tiny kitchen and a cupboard that housed an ancient porcelain object that Lhiana explained was the toilet.

"It's not as archaic as it looks," she said. "There's an aerobic reclamation unit attached. Quite modern. But I'll warn you now, *never* touch that red button."

"Because?"

"Because it would be *bad*."

Elton cocked his head to one side and smiled. He had to know.

"Come on, Lhiana, you can't leave it like that. What does the red button do?"

"Well, the sanitation system is not entirely automatic. And there's a… residue. The red button pumps it out. See the hose?" She pointed. "And it's fierce. Trust me, you don't *ever* want to press that red button."

"You sound like you speak from experience."

"The first time me and Dorina came here I was five. Show me a five-year-old who would be able to resist a bright red button she must never, *ever* touch."

Elton smiled at the thought. His mind painted a graphic and wonderful picture. The girlish screams. The recriminations. The aftermath with buckets and mops. And this led to another thought.

"Shower? Bathroom?"

Lhiana laughed.

"Look out of the front door. See all that water? What would you want a shower for? Now, sit down there and let's have a look at all your injuries."

Elton lowered himself into one of the chairs and Lhiana dropped to her knees and began unwinding the makeshift bandage from his foot. She became engrossed in the task, every now and again flicking her auburn hair over her shoulder, out of the way.

Elton watched her and wondered about the pace of events that had brought them here.

"How has this happened?" he asked.

"Hmm?"

"This. One minute I'm minding my own business, out in space, watching holos of you. Then suddenly I'm on the run, getting shot at, called a terrorist. Then *you're* with me, on the run, getting shot at—"

"—and called a terrorist," Lhiana finished for him.

"Then we're here. I don't even know where here is, not really. And I'm comfortable, and relaxed, and—"

"Well that won't last. What's left of your foot is full of sand. I'll have to clean it. It's going to hurt. You really need a doctor, or some medical advice. Your foot's kind of a funny colour. I didn't really think this through. We're on a world with more doctors than patients, and you're being treated by a gardener. We should have gone to the hospital in Port Juno; we should have taken the risk."

"I think you've done pretty good so far," said Elton.

"I need to talk to Kim, but… Wait, I know. There's a relay. It'll have been switched off to save power."

"Relay?"

"Yes, we have an imentor relay out here. We can get some advice from Kim… and from your Jim."

"Er… I'm not sure that's such a good idea. I think you should keep it switched off."

"It's okay. The imentors wouldn't shop us. It's an ethical thing they have."

"No, they wouldn't, but a relay being switched on might be

noticed."

"Don't you think you're being just a teensy bit paranoid? We're a long way from anywhere."

"Paranoid maybe, but right now I'm the one shot through with all the holes. We don't know what kind of monitoring they have. We don't want to take the risk."

"They? Who's they? Who *are* we running from?"

Elton thought for a moment.

"Right now I guess that would be just about everyone that's not in this room."

Lhiana looked at him, then nodded.

"Okay," she said. "No Kim. Let's get your foot cleaned, then I'll look at your shoulder."

The shoulder was easy. Elton passed out two minutes into the foot cleaning, and by the time he came round again the shoulder was freshly bandaged.

"Good, you're back with us. I'm making tea. I found a jar left over from when I was here last year. It's not very fresh but it's still better than shop-bought rubbish. I grow it myself on La Ronde. We should make the most of it, the tea patch was the first bed they torched."

"It will grow again."

"It won't. That was the last bush. I was going to take cuttings. I think tea is now more than likely extinct."

She handed Elton a cup, then settled in the other chair, her legs folded up beneath her.

"This is nice," said Elton.

"You like it?"

"The tea? Oh, yeah. The tea's great. No, I meant this. The two of us. Companionable. The sound of the sea outside. Nice."

Elton looked around the room. Apart from the two chairs there was a table with a single lamp, and a narrow bed tucked into the far, dark corner of the room. Everything was crafted from driftlic, which, as Lhiana explained, was the weathered, discarded plastic that often washed up on the beach.

The walls were decorated with framed paintings, six of them. All pictures of flowers, but they seemed somehow incomplete.

"You like them?"

Elton shrugged. "Hmm. They're okay."

"They don't know you yet. Choose one. Stand close to it."

Elton climbed out of his seat, with a lot of care – he'd stiffened up. Once on his feet the room began to move in a gentle spin, so he remained where he was for a moment, both hands on the chair-back while his head cleared. Then he stumped over to the nearest painting, a single stem with a dense flower on top. It had colour, but it seemed neutral – hard to define. Then as Elton watched, it began to bloom. It looked as though an opaque layer were dissolving to reveal the real flower beneath. The last stages of the transformation happened quickly and with such drama that it actually prompted Elton to stagger backwards, and he would have fallen if Lhiana hadn't jumped up and offered a steadying hand.

"What *is* that?" breathed Elton. "It's… it's wonderful."

"Pheromones. The pigment reacts to the viewer's natural pheromone balance. The colours modify via a feedback loop; a mechanism that tunes to the expectations of the viewer. You see the colour that is perfect for you at the precise moment that you observe it."

"You mean it would be a different colour if *you* looked at it?"

"Not quite. It's red. It will always be red. But the tones and their juxtaposition with the background colouring would be subtly different for me than they are for you. As the shading and light changes the shape changes, too. And tomorrow it will be different, but always just right for your mood, or the mood of any observer."

Then Elton noticed the signature in the lower right-hand corner.

"L. Bilotti. You painted this?"

"Yes, I painted all of them. Aunt Beryl always liked my work, so I gave her some. The chemistry in the pigment is my own invention. I've been dabbling with it for years. I don't sell many, so I give them to friends. I'd rather someone enjoyed them."

"I'm amazed you don't sell them all."

"It's the online effect. Remote selling is a disaster; the pheromones don't work unless the observer directly engages with the painting. They need to be in galleries. Trouble is, there are only a dozen or so galleries in the whole Sphere. You've got to be a name to get your stuff hung in one of them. It also helps if you're dead."

"So what's the flower?"

"It's a Rose. They were common in Earth days. The last one disappeared maybe two hundred years ago. There are pictures, so we have a pretty good idea what they looked like, although the colours have faded and changed, so it can only ever be an approximation. I think they used to smell quite nice, too. I could do scents, but I have no idea what it would be like. It's not something that was recorded."

"Do you do any, you know, living plants?"

"Oh yes. I've painted a lot of the plants in La Ronde. I only do strict botanical studies, though, when the plants are real. It's a way of recording them. It wouldn't do to muck about with the pheromone pigments because that would change the colour. It's only a small change but it would be wrong. It's not a problem with extinct species, you see. We don't know for sure what the colour was, so why not adapt it to something that is perfect for the observer? Who knows, maybe that's the best way we have of getting it right."

"What are these yellow ones?"

"Daffodils. If you're lucky, and the painting likes you, you might see them swaying in the breeze."

"Yes. Yes, I see it. I…"

Elton fell over.

When he came round he was back in the chair. His head was aching and he felt clammy. Lhiana felt his forehead and winced.

"You feel hot. I think you have an infection. It's hardly surprising."

"I just need to rest."

"I don't like this. I'm going to switch on the imentor relay."

"No!"

Elton grabbed her wrist. He felt shivery but he was sure it would pass.

"You've done so well to get us here, Lhiana. Don't ruin our cover now because of me. I'm fine, really."

"Okay, but I'm keeping a close eye on you. If you get any worse... if I have any doubts…" She swept her hair away from her face. Elton noticed her hands were shaking.

"Let me help you onto the bed. Maybe you can get some sleep."

Elton didn't think he'd sleep, but within minutes he was dreaming of plants, swaying under a blue sky and a baking hot sun, with multi-coloured things called flowers growing out of them; reds and blues and greens. Then troops and tanks came rumbling over the horizon and began to stomp and grind the plants into pulp. Elton yelled at them to stop and they shot him.

He fell amongst the destroyed flowers where they gave up the last of their powerful scent. Elton rolled onto his side, away from the pain of his wounds, to find himself lying face down in the liquidised mulch. He couldn't breathe. He was suffocating.

He woke to find Lhiana's hand clamped onto his mouth. He felt cold but was soaked in sweat.

"Shh! There's someone outside. And you were shouting."

It took a moment before Elton remembered where he was. The room was dark and there was a sooty smell – the oil lamp. It was still ticking and smoking after being quickly extinguished.

Lhiana removed her hand from Elton's mouth.

"I can hear low voices outside. Someone sneaking around in the dark," she whispered.

"Your Aunt Beryl?"

"No. Anyway, why would she be whispering outside? It's her cottage."

"Locals then – from Port Juno, coming over for a free weekend?"

"Possibly, but it's dark – and there's not meant to be anyone living here, so why wait until after dark?"

"So *they've* found us."

"Looks like it. Do we even know who 'they' are?"

"Bad guys. Space Corps."

"*You're* Space Corps. So am I."

"I… *we* are terrorists, remember?"

Lhiana sighed.

"On the plus side…" she said.

"There's a plus side?"

"…you might get some medical treatment now. You're worse. I think you need antibiotics or something."

"Or they could save a few bob and just shoot me. They've

done it that way before. Have we got any weapons?"

"Yeah, *I've* got one. You'd be doing well if you could even sit up. Shh…"

There was a click at the front door as the latch was raised. The door didn't move.

Heated whispering came from outside, then three hard kicks and the door burst open. The noise was shocking after the silence and the whispering.

Elton stared as one of the two figures, silhouetted in the double moonlight, came in through the door. Then, the shadow of Lhiana raising –what? Something big and round on a stick – above her head. She swept it down and there was a sonorous, ringing, gong-like sound, like the door-chime at the gates of hell.

"Ow! Shit!"

A scream from outside.

The Lhiana silhouette raised the deadly frying pan, again, aiming at the figure who was now down on hands and knees and cursing in the doorway.

"Lhiana, no, stop." Elton's shout was feeble, but Lhiana heard it just in time to at least slow the swing of her next blow. Still, it struck home on the trespasser's shoulders with enough force to flatten him, prone on the stone flags of the hallway.

Elton's vision had become more accustomed to the dark, and when Lhiana turned to stare at him he could see the anger in her eyes; fury and disbelief that he had made her pull the second blow. Her breath came in great gulping sobs. She was so fired up on adrenaline she couldn't speak.

"Lhiana, put the light on. I know his voice." Then to the inert body on the floor. "Walther? Are you alright? And what the sodding hell are you doing here, creeping around in the middle of the night?"

"Lhiana?" A scared voice from outside.

"Mila? Is that you?" Lhiana's voice was barely a squeak. "Oh, Mila. I think I may have killed somebody."

TWENTY SEVEN

Elton's shivering slipped smoothly into raging fever and delirium. He was aware of what was going on around him but all the action seemed remote from his own body, which seemed to have taken to shaking and teeth rattling on an evangelical scale. He became aware of an exotic Asian girl with long, sleek black hair, mopping his brow and sticking needles in his arm and doing things with his foot and shoulder – things that should have hurt. He watched as Lhiana, on the other side of the room, fussed around Walther – who was now slumped in a chair – with ice packs resting on the top of his head and a can of beer resting in his hand. *Beer? Since when did we have beer? How come he gets the beer?*

The oil lamp had been re-lit, and it fizzed and occasionally popped with the sound insects make when dashing to oblivion. Elton knew all about oblivion. He felt it was a place he ought to know since he'd been camping on its front lawn for the past hour or so.

One of the things about camping that Elton remembered from his childhood was the special sounds of a campsite coming to life in the morning. Hushed voices that sound extra loud and close, wind flapping the canvas, and the awareness of all the aches and pains that your body has acquired from lying on the hard cold ground.

And you shiver.

You're warm and you're snug but it's too cold to move.

And you want to go to the toilet.

And the sun's in your eyes.

Elton opened his eyes and squinted in the warm morning sunlight that streamed through the window.

Walther was still sitting in the chair. Lhiana and the Asian girl were wrapped in a blanket, side-by-side, their backs to the wall. They looked tired. Walther looked exhausted, but every time he began to nod one or other of the girls would speak.

"How long have you known Elton?"

"What work did you do for the Space Corps on the Ring?"

"Tell us about hangball again."

Elton watched and listened and tried to ignore his bladder.

"Well, they call us 'The Strike Force', because…"

"No one calls us that, Walther. Tell it how it is. *We* call ourselves 'The Strike Force'. Everyone else calls us 'those two useless buggers who don't know when to quit'."

"Ah, the great Miserable One is back with us," said Walther.

Lhiana looked over at Elton and smiled.

"How are you feeling?"

"Okay, but how come he gets beer?"

"For medicinal purposes only, mate," said Walther. "Your girl has some forearm on her. Anyway, I got second best. You got all the painkillers."

The Asian girl stood up and came over to Elton. She put a hand on his forehead.

"Normal," she said. "You're okay."

Elton looked over at Lhiana with a questioning expression.

"Who…?"

"Sorry, Elton. This is Sharmila. Sharmila Kumari. We've been friends for years. Mila's a nurse. She probably saved your life last night."

"My friend saves your life," said Walther, "while *your* friend beats my head in with a skillet. Where's the justice in that?"

"Walther, I am so sorry, really," said Lhiana, concern and upset making her eyes swim and glisten.

"I'm joking. You are forgiven. I blame him," Walther said, pointing at Elton. "I know what a bastard he is. He put you up to it, I know."

"Only because I was in a weakened state," said Elton. "I'd have done a proper job of it myself."

"Hey," said Elton, after a moment. "What about Kingsley? Did you bring him? Is he okay?"

"Who's Kingsley?" said Lhiana.

"His Teddy," said Walther. "Don't worry, Kingsley's fine. I left him with Kegworth."

"Who—"

"You remember Kegworth. The bartender at the Revolution. It appears he has a soft spot for Teddies. He's got half a dozen of them that he's taken in for other customers. You should see his place. Teeming with fluffy animals. He loves them. He's looking after your octopus, too, though he wasn't so keen on that little guy. Not quite so cuddly. Kingsley's quite taken with him, though, so relax. You have nothing to concern yourself over your menagerie."

The pet talk went on for a few minutes until Elton brought them back on message.

"Anyway," he said. "What are you doing here? How'd you find us?"

"Mila guessed Lhiana would bring you here," said Walther.

"We used to come here when we were girls," said Mila. "I remembered how much Lhiana loved this place, and I remembered how remote it was. I knew this was where she'd want to come."

"Well, it's very nice of you both to come and save my life," said Elton. "But why? What possessed you? And how come Lhiana's best friend, and my best friend are like, you know, lifelong pals? I think I could make more sense of everything when I was delirious. Come on, guys, help me out here."

"No," said Lhiana. "I'm going to rustle up some breakfast from out of the vat in the kitchen. We'll eat, and then, I'm sorry, Elton, I for one am going to sleep."

"But it's morning."

"We sat up all night. Walther had a concussion and we couldn't let him nod off – you know, in case he stayed nodded off. And you were sweating and gabbling and tossing about and threatening to die on us. Sorry, Elton. Enlightenment will have to wait."

Breakfast was a meagre affair. Walther kept comparing it favourably to a place called Finger Lick, and this sent Sharmila into gales of laughter. Elton looked on, feeling more and more bemused as he tried to piece together the circumstances that could have led to this weird gathering on an island in the back end of nowhere.

After they'd eaten, Lhiana and Sharmila returned to the rug by the hearth, and Walther fell asleep sitting upright in the chair. Nobody wanted the bed even though Elton was done with it. It was kind of pongy.

Elton left them and went to explore the island. He was still limping but felt much better. His arrival at Dianic Station was the first time he'd seen an ocean. Then he'd sailed on it. He was fascinated by the breaking waves and the constant noise they made. He set off along the coast, the sea to his left. His foot was covered by an aerosol bandage, but he was under strict instructions not to get it wet. This was a harsh command, because he could think of nothing, right then, that he would rather do. But he remembered the fever and remained obedient.

Half an hour of limping left him in no doubt as to how

weakened he'd become, but it was enough to take him right around the island and back to the hut, and there he sat in the sand, content to stare out at the empty horizon and marvel at the sight of all that ocean.

TWENTY EIGHT

"What are they up to?" Levison looked up from a steak that was raw and bloody. He dabbed the juices from his chin with a silk napkin.

"Philpotts has been for a walk around the island. The others are inside," said Slicker. "We don't think they have an imentor relay; we're not picking up any signal, but we can't be sure."

Levison thought about it for a moment.

"I'd like to take the four of them out, right there, now. Job done."

"Sir, *if* they have imentor... We've been so careful thus far. We took the risk in eliminating Philpotts because there's no imentor in deep space. Blick is no loss, either. But the other two... To act in a rash manner now would be... Sir, imentor can choose to testify against us. He... it, is independent. This could jeopardise —"

"You are sentimental about the two girls. That's it, isn't it, Bob?"

"No, no. But, one of them... Bilotti. I know of her, she is a painter who... She has friends, sir."

"Friends can be silenced. You haven't detected any signal from the island?"

"We're using satellite. There could be a low power unit," said Slicker. "Who would build a cottage way out there and *not* install an imentor relay? Sir."

Levison looked at him.

"Ordinary people, I mean," added Slicker, in a rush. "I know you don't... And I wouldn't. But—"

"Here's the thing, Bob. There are those who dare to do, and there are those who say, 'Let's just wait and see.' When we were kids, living in the air ducts on the Ring, you, Bob, were eating out of scrap bins in the alleys behind restaurants, waiting to see what might come along. I, on the other hand, was the one who dared to eat *inside* those restaurants."

It was a statement for which no reply was required, so Slicker waited while Levison loaded his fork with another slab of dripping meat and pushed it into his mouth. When he had finished chewing he dabbed his mouth with his napkin again.

"Assemble an assault team. Five men. One assault vessel. Dress one man in smarts, don't let him know the objective. His role is to call off the assault if he detects any imentor presence. He is to remain with the assault vessel throughout, and must not proceed to the kill zone. The others are to be under orders not to discuss the mission or its outcome in his presence."

"And the objective, sir?"

Levison transferred his fork into his right fist. He stabbed it down into the steak. A jet of red bloody juice squirted out onto Slicker's white shirt. Levison smiled as though this had been his exact intention.

"The objective, Slicker, is to eliminate everyone on that island. No energy weapons. No noise. Silent kill."

TWENTY NINE

"Someone needs to go into Port Juno for food," said Walther. "I could use a change of scene."

"Too risky," said Lhiana. "We can't chance being seen."

"Me and Mila are clean. No one is looking for us. Do we really want to eat this vat sludge forever?"

"How would you pay?" asked Lhiana.

"Same as… ah."

"You'd use Jim to make a funds transfer. And you'd light up every 'bot in the Sphere."

"We're not connected to any of this. Minerva is Mila's home world. We could be on holiday."

"Think about it, Walther. You were handpicked as backup to Elton on F-257. If Elton bailed early you were to be sent in."

"No one told me anything about—"

"But I was told about you by my boss, who is not exactly a high-ranking official. Walther, your connection is common knowledge."

"Yeah, common, except nobody told me and Elton."

Lhiana pressed on with her argument. "Let's think about how this works. You *were* handpicked as Elton's backup, but you weren't needed. You work for the Space Corps and today you are absent from work. It wouldn't take much for a bright and eager investigator to realise that you are not at home either, and that your IP pass has just seen you through several gates, finishing at Minerva, Vesta Station.

"But there's more. Each gate passage was made in the company of one Sharmila Kumari, friend and confidant of Lhiana Bilotti, another well-known terrorist. Oh, and *she's* missing from work today, too." Lhiana folded her arms.

"You're saying that by coming here we've compromised you?" Mila's voice sounded distraught.

"No, Mila. You have not compromised us. Elton wouldn't have seen the night through without your help. Thank God you came when you did. What I am saying is, you and Walther are, by now, as high up the public enemy list as me and Elton. It's a fair bet that, by now, someone has figured out that we might all be on Minerva. But it's a big planet. If they knew exactly where we were they'd be here now. A shopping trip to Port Juno, though? Not a good plan."

Elton listened to each of them without comment. He had things to say but he wasn't ready yet. The pieces were still falling, and not all of them had a place. So far all the discussion had been short term and surrounded the logistics of getting through each day. Elton had other thoughts, though. He looked away from his circle of friends, new and old, gathered on the beach and stared out towards the distant horizon and the setting sun. *Another sun,* he thought. *How many of these have I seen over the past few weeks?* Which sun would he see tomorrow? For Elton knew they needed to move on. And they needed a game plan.

Rock Bailey sat in a corner of the surface-bound elevator and smouldered with rage. What kind of goddamn quarter-cocked mission plan was this? His orders were to wear full smarts, no weapons. And he couldn't talk to the rest of the team. He wasn't even allowed to sit with them.

He felt like the weed in school who gets picked on by the mean kids. Only he was meaner and faster and stronger than the rest of them put together. This sucked.

"Your orders, Bailey, are to provide passive support. The 'A' team will be armed, for peace-keeping purposes" – *peace-*

keeping, my ass – "and will enter the hostile zone from the beach. You will remain with the assault craft."

"Sir! Permission to object, sir!"

"Permission denied, soldier. Listen carefully. During the operation you will remain in contact with your imentor right up until loss of signal. You will then attempt to re-acquire signal by constant polling."

"Am I in charge of the relay module then, sir?"

"You won't be taking a relay."

No relay?

"Sir! Bloody stupid, sir!"

"Attention, soldier!"

"Sir!"

"If you are able to re-establish imentor contact anywhere near the hostile zone, soldier, *anywhere* near, your orders, then, are explicit: You abort the mission, immediately. Get everyone out of the zone. Do you understand?"

"Sir!"

"Was that a 'yes, sir' or a 'no, sir'? I need you to use your brains for this one, Bailey."

"Ahh… yes, sir. Affirmative. Understood. Sir!"

Rock Bailey did understand, loud and clear. This was the real deal and they didn't want any imentor presence to witness it, on either side. And it sucked because Rock Bailey was the best there was when it came to wet work. He was tough and he was uncompromising. Hadn't he proved himself many times before?

He glared at Luke, the sharp-dressed fighting man, a soldier who ironed creases into his combat fatigues, a man who was never without a comb – despite his two-millimetre buzz cut. Then there was Tod, Irene and Beaumont (Beaumont – what a poofter name). They were crouched in a square formation, doing a blindfold weapons drill. They had somehow contrived to form a square in which they *all* had their backs to him, closing him out. Bastards. Rock loved weapons drill. He could strip down an AK ten-ninety-eight and reassemble it in under twenty seconds. He was the best. Tod dropped his powerpack on the deck with a clatter, and Rock snorted in derision. Bunch of goddamn fairies. Yet they got to do the wet work while he had to sit in the boat being wet nurse. This sucked.

"You there, Kim?"

"Hi, Rock."

"This sucks, Kim."

"What sucks, Rock?"

"Can't tell you. Secret. But it sucks."

"Yeah. So what's our role, Rock?"

"We *talk* to each other. All buddy buddy. You ever hear the like?"

"Oh yeah, sounds familiar. Been there," said Kim.

Rock called his imentor Kim. Nobody else knew this. If it ever got out…

"Do they think we're stupid or something? It's obviously a wet job."

"So, should you be telling me that?"

"Come on, Kim, you already know. You're smart."

"Yeah."

"It sucks, Kim."

Rock spoke in SubV. He always spoke to Kim in SubV. And she always spoke back the same way. It wasn't that he was ashamed, he was just, well, nobody must ever hear Rock calling his imentor Kim. It wasn't… acceptable.

It was all his mother's fault. She wanted a girl. So she painted his room pink and called him Rebecca. Rebecca William Bailey.

Jeez. By the time Rock found out that he wasn't a girl he'd been bonded with his Kim for nearly four years, and Kim had taken a female persona. She'd been willing to change – drop an octave – but it just never felt right to Rock.

He couldn't blame his Kim. She'd told him, over and over. "Rebecca, you're a boy. Really."

But little Rebecca believed his mom. Moms carry far more influence than disembodied voices that come out of your jammies.

Kim had tried speaking in a tough macho voice, only answering to Jim, but damn, it felt just plain wrong. Young Rebecca – Rock, as he'd then begun calling himself – often cried himself to sleep at night... because he missed his Kim.

So Kim went back to the female voice, although she'd subtly modulated lower and lower as the years went by, and Rock just made do with communing SubV all the time. SubV was hard. It took practice. He'd become good at it. Maybe that was why he'd drawn the wet-nurse role. Maybe now he was always going to get the girlie role.

And his mom *still* painted his room pink! Goddamn, he so wanted to kill someone today.

"I think we need to take stock," said Elton.

It was dark. They'd lit a fire on the beach using solid fuel blocks they'd found behind the hut. They'd also found a fishing rod and Walther spent an hour dipping one end of it in the sea, hoping for something better than vat meat for supper. Then Lhiana told him he was meant to use a line and a hook... and put a worm on the hook.

"A real worm?"

"You think fish are going to be tempted by a nice, succulent barbed-steel hook for supper?"

"How do you attach the worm to the hook?"

"You stick the hook through the worm."

The fishing rod went back behind the hut.

"What do you mean, take stock?" asked Walther.

"I mean, what is this? Kid Scout camp? Why won't anyone talk about the meat of the thing?" Elton was shouting.

"Calm down, compagno. We spend a few days, chill out, you grow a new foot, get well…"

"Er, he won't be growing any new foot, Walther," said Mila.

"What? Everyone grows new bits. Why not Elton?"

"Well, it's not like it's a natural process. He has to have stem cell regen implants first, you know?"

"I didn't know that. I thought you just, you know, lopped off a limb – grew another one."

"Bloody hell, Walther! This is exactly what I mean. We keep talking about crap like this. We dance around the subject. Don't you see, we're in danger here. We have to talk about it."

Elton's outburst was greeted around the fire with a kind of embarrassed silence that hung in the air like an echo in a room full of mattresses.

"Okay," said Walther. His voice was quiet and he directed it towards the fire. "Go ahead. Talk."

"Well first we have to think through our options. We don't just shamble along taking whatever comes our way. We make a plan."

"Okay," said Lhiana. "Good so far. What plan?"

"Well, first of all we can choose to stay here or move on. That's a choice."

"I'm for staying," said Walther. Mila was nodding.

"Never seen a beach before. It's cool. Sun's warm. Nice

breeze."

"Bloody hell, Walther, it's not a holiday. Come on, think about this. Be serious."

"Well, first thing, Elton," said Lhiana. "Since you're getting stroppy about it, I think we should switch on the imentor relay. I —"

"Come on, Lhiana, we've discu—"

"No. You come on. Look at us. We can't make a decision. We don't even know how to do decisions. We've always had our Jims and Kims to do it for us."

"No, Lhiana. The first thing Jim… or Kim, would say is '*shut the bloody relay off!*' But it would be too late then. The Space Corps would know where we are."

"You're assuming they'll be able to figure that out," said Lhiana, her voice louder.

"It's an important assumption." Elton's louder still.

"I think you're wrong!"

"I'm not!"

They were both on their feet. Shouting. The fire between them. Their faces glowed red in the flames.

"This is going well," said Walther.

"Look," said Elton, forcing himself to talk, not shout. He took a step back, then turned away for a moment to compose himself.

"Look," he said, coming back to the fire and sitting down. "They don't know where we are. If they knew, they'd be here. Switching on the imentor relay *might* – and you'll notice I use the word 'might', I concede that I may be wrong on this – but it *might* tell them where we are. And then we *might* be dead."

"Who's 'they'?" said Mila. "Don't we need to know that first?"

"Yes. Good. Let's stop arguing and concentrate on what we

know," said Elton.

"Stop arguing! You're a fine one to—"

Elton shot Walther a glare.

"Okay," said Walther. "We stop arguing. What do we know? Pool our knowledge."

"Well, the first thing we know, for certain," said Elton. "They don't know where we are yet."

"Where are they?" asked Levison.

"They're on the beach. They have a campfire," said Slicker.

"Hmph. Making it easy for us."

"Dianic Station is about 20,000 miles up. We don't have much in the way of imaging equipment, so the fire's a useful marker."

"Any low orbit assets?"

"There's one we've been using, a mapping sat. We get a fifteen-minute window every ninety minutes or so. But only eight or ten minutes are useful to us."

"Where's the team?"

"Ahh, I'm sorry, a minute, sir." Slicker pulled his T-shirt over his head and threw it out of the door.

Levison averted his eyes, trying hard not to look at Slicker's oily torso; it reminded him too much of the undercooked roast chicken his first wife used to serve for Sunday lunch.

"They left the base station five minutes ago, sir. Bailey is still in contact with his, ahh…" – and here he gave a rare smile – "… with his Kim, sir."

"His Kim? *His* Kim?"

"He believes no one knows, sir. A little secret we keep in our files."

Levison nodded, then returned his attention to the mission.

"How long?"

"One hour thirty, sir."

"How does that chime with the mapping sat?"

"They've been ordered to delay the attack. The mapping sat is due in one hour twenty. They'll wait until after its next pass. We can't control the information flow from *every* source, sir."

"No. Good. Keep me informed. And Slicker, next time you come up here, wear a dumb shirt. You look like salmonella in trousers."

"We can assume that 'they' are the Space Corps, and Bob Slicker, for one, is right at the centre of it," said Elton.

"I'm sorry," said Mila. "Who?"

"Bob Slicker was Elton's boss on Tsanak," said Walther. "Elton saw a Post-it on his desk with a number on it. Elton's good with numbers."

"He's involved in some kind of scam," said Elton. "There's duplicate invoices, covert funds, and dodgy ledgers with special passwords."

"Maybe it's as simple as that then," said Mila. "You saw too much."

"No, there's got to be more to it," said Lhiana. "They took out a whole starship. That's an expensive way just to shut someone up. And they had Walther on stand by. He'd have gone down with the ship in Elton's place if it had come to it, so Elton's knowledge is not the issue."

"Do we really know that?" said Mila.

"I know for sure that I was appointed after possibly the worst interview in history – you don't climb out of a pond and land a coveted position like that without help, and there was, apparently, some outside intervention. Someone wanted, badly, for me to work for the Space Corps, and once I was in, my career path became unconventional. Now I know why – I was being saved for F-257."

"My interview was better," said Walther. "I mean, I didn't go swimming or anything. But my heart wasn't in it. Couldn't answer the technical questions, and again, there was this weird call, and bingo. Then I'm shipped out to the Ring, handy for getting onto an F-Ship at short notice, and put on ice in the payroll department."

"Do we know if Elton was the first?" said Lhiana. "Could it be, that while Elton was cooling his heels on Tsanak, some other luckless dupe was out on F-257. Maybe he got a bit fractal and bailed early." Lhiana scooped up sand in her hands and let it flow between her fingers. "But we do have what Bruce told me."

"Bruce? Who's Bruce?" said Elton.

"My boss on the Ring. He told me about you and about Walther. How they were keeping an eye on Walther in case he was needed as a reserve. Said it was all arranged through... Lewis? Lester?"

"Levison."

"That's right, Levison. His office set it up, and they were keeping tabs on you."

"So we know who our enemies are," said Elton.

"There're too many," said Walther. "They've got people on every gate in the Sphere. For a covert conspiracy they seem to have plenty manpower."

Elton threw a handful of sand into the fire and listened to it hiss.

"I think the 'official' Space Corps are looking for us as well," he said. "Walther's right, they can't have so many people. What if the larger manhunt was an accident? Maybe the Levison/Slicker group never intended for us to hit the official wanted list."

"You mean they're afraid of what we might say if the law-abiding side of the Space Corps get to us first?" said Lhiana.

"Yeah."

"Doesn't that make it *more* likely they'll try to take us out? Isn't that more reason for us to seek help?"

"What, from Kim? No, Lhiana. That makes it more important not to draw attention to ourselves. We don't want to advertise our location."

"You are so stubborn, Philpotts. You are wrong and you are stubborn. I'm going to switch the relay on."

"Don't you dare. You go near that relay and I'll take a wrench to it."

"You're very big on throwing your weight around today."

"I'm very big on trying to stay alive."

Rock wasn't feeling quite so tough. He'd never been in a boat before. He was glad, for once, to be under restraining orders for a while.

The boat was an inflatable with a small ZG field generator for lower friction; it only touched the sea every now and again. It was propelled by a pocket version of the Wilson Drive, so it was fast and it was quiet.

But the waves still caught the craft now and again, and often enough to set up a lurching, swaying motion. Rock badly wanted to puke. Tod had already puked. He was lying in the bottom of the boat making death-bed noises. Rock was determined not to puke, at least not before the fairy, Beaumont, barfed his breakfast. Beaumont looked especially green right now, and he was staying near the back of the boat, downwind. Irene and Luke seemed fine. Luke was busy polishing his boots. They gleamed.

Stupid bastard, they're desert combat boots. They're meant to be dull. Luke could never wear unshined shoes though. He and Irene just stared, regarding their two, sickly green companions with contempt. And they were ignoring Rock; simply following orders.

"Kim, are you there, Kim?" Rock concentrated on *his* role, stupid though it was.

Nothing. Kim had fizzed out fifteen minutes after leaving Dianic Base Station. Rock wished his Kim would answer him. It wasn't that he had any moral objections to this mission, far from it, it was just that he didn't want his colleagues to get any satisfaction from completing a job in which he, Rock, had no sensible role.

"Kim, come on, love, are you there?"

Irene looked at her watch.

"How long?" asked Luke, combing his bum-fluff hair, then polishing his comb.

"Ten minutes. Then we go in hard."

Ten minutes and the mapping sat would dip below the horizon. Ten minutes.

"Kim, are you there? Come in, Kim."

"Okay, so what *don't* we know?" asked Lhiana.

"Hah, *now* we're getting to it," said Walther. "Do we have all night?"

Elton chose to ignore him.

"We don't know why they destroyed F-257," he said.

"They did it to get shut of you, compagno."

"We've been through this, Walther. I don't think that was it at all. I... we, were stage dressing. We were there to add colour to the event."

"You were there to take the blame, too," said Lhiana. "Don't forget that. You were heaven-sent; Space Corps applicants with strong Disexpansionist sympathies. You don't get so many of those in your typical intake. Also, you've been confidants for years. Easy to take two friends and spin you as a terrorist cell. You travelled to Tsanak together. You applied for entry to the Space Corps together. Neither of you have any important connections on Tsanak, nor many other friends. You both fit the profile. Out of all the Space Corps applicants you were either the best fit, or your CVs just happened to drop onto Levison's desk at the right time. Either way, it's no wonder they stomped through the interview protocols wearing terra-boots with ice crampons."

"Okay, that's true. I think we can move 'why us' over into the 'what we know' column. It wouldn't, and didn't, take much tinkering to engineer us into anarchists. We were even in a Disexpansionist riot," said Elton.

"You think they set that up?" said Walther.

"Yes. Yes I do. Think how it happened. It was just a concert, then those Antidisexpansionist brown-shirts turned up. That was for our benefit, I guess. Damn, we've been manipulated right from the start."

"I still think it seems over-elaborate to put Elton on a starship, then blow it up. They must have wanted the starship itself destroyed. Why?" said Lhiana.

"Was there something on the ship they didn't want anyone to know about?" said Walther. "Come on, Elton, you were on the thing. What was out there that shouldn't have been?"

The assault craft nudged onto the sand. They were about two hundred yards downwind of the hut, and they could see the glow of the fire on the beach. This would be too easy. They could do it from here, now, if they wanted to. But Rock assumed the orders had specified a clean kill. No energy weapons. Just bare hands, and blades. That was how the beach team were prepping, at least. Long knives and camouflage paint, yellow and brown streaks, for close hand-to-hand combat. Luke, of course, managed to apply his face paint like it was a fake tan. He looked like a media executive just back from vacation on Fomalhaut.

But, hand-to-hand notwithstanding, they took their rifles, just in case. There's a certain comfort about the weight of an AK1098 on your arm.

Rock watched the four of them make final preparations while he sulked in the back of the boat. They acted in silence, well-drilled, efficient. All traces of sea-sickness were gone now – they each had a job to do.

Three slipped over the side of the boat into about six inches of washing surf. Luke waited until the craft was beam-on so he could jump clear of the waves. Luke didn't like getting his boots wet. The four commandos did a stupid little bonding ritual on the beach, an eight-hand clasp, then they turned and slipped into the night, disappearing from Rock's view.

"Kim. Come in, Kim. Answer me, hon."

Nothing.

"Okay, so F-257 had to go, for some reason. But why not kill you first then blow up the F-Ship?" said Lhiana. "Seems like a pointless risk, hoping you'd stay at your post long enough to go down with the ship."

"Good point," said Walther. "Pop you first, load your body onto the F-Ship like cargo."

Elton thought about it.

"Ah, but if they'd have killed me back on Tsanak, there'd have been merry hell. You just can't get away with stuff like… Oh."

"What?" said Lhiana.

"Killing. Because of imentor," said Elton. His voice had become distant. "And… Oh, bloody hell! Imentor. Lhiana. Lhiana, I'm sorry, I was wrong. *Idiot!* We have to switch the relay on! We have to do it now!"

Elton was on his feet. Running.

Lhiana shouted after him. "Yes, but if—"

"I'm doing it. Now. They can't kill us if imentor's watching, you see? *That's* why they had to get me out there, on the ship. But here… Where's the relay?" Elton was already halfway up the beach.

"Under the window. A box with a green switch."

Elton ran. Lhiana would have been quicker. She had more than one-and-a-half feet, and it made a difference to sprinting speed. Elton had never appreciated the full contribution his toes had made to his life until now.

Rock climbed out of the boat. It was good to have the sea filling his boots. It made him feel like a soldier. He pulled the boat round so that it pointed out to sea, to afford a quicker getaway. His role here might be minimal, but he'd bloody well do it professionally.

They'd be back soon. They'd be smug – bonded. Brothers in arms. If Rock had felt excluded before, well, once this was over he would be an outcast, a pariah. The trip back to Dianic Base Station would feel more like a plague cruise.

He climbed back into the boat.

"Kim, come in, Kim." His SubV entreaties had lost all of their enthusiasm. Stupid mission.

He looked up at the stars. None of the constellations were familiar. Where was he? Minerva? Never heard of it – poxy place.

"Rock? What's happening, Rock?"

"Kim? Kim, is that you?"

"No, it's Tinkerbell. Of course it's me."

"Oh. Er…"

"They've gone, haven't they? Aren't you supposed to do something now, you know? Like, abort the mission?"

There was no radio. The wet team were dressed dumb. No contact.

Rock was out of the boat and running.

"Elton, hi."

"Ah, Jim. It's been a long time."

Elton stood up from the box under the window. The lamp wasn't lit inside the hut and it was dark. The fire on the beach danced in the window reflections.

"Yeah, Elton, no time for reminiscing, you're all about to die. Get away from the window."

"What?"

"Away from the window, now."

Elton moved but he could see the three on the beach jumping to their feet and running down to the sea.

"Their Jims and Kims are feeding them advice, too, Elton. They're going into the sea. They may be safe, but only if they're quick enough."

"What's happening, Jim?"

There's an assault team on the beach. I don't have specifics, I only woke up to this a couple of seconds ago. The sea's probably safe, you're all hot from sitting by the fire. Anywhere you go you'll leave a heat trail. Except in the sea."

"Shall I—"

"No time. You've left a red line right up the beach to the hut. I can see it like landing lights on a runway. That kettle. Is there any water in it?"

"What?"

"Focus, Elton. The hot kettle I see on the stove, does it still have water?"

"Yeah, we were making a brew about half an hour ago, but we didn't get around to—"

"Slop it on the floor. All over, to mask your heat trace. Then find somewhere to hide. I don't think I know the hut. I... yes, of course I do. The closet. The little toilet room. Now."

Elton lifted the kettle and poured.

"Faster!"

The water wouldn't come faster. The kettle only had a narrow spout. Elton's heart pounded in his ears. He wanted to know what was going on. It was all too fast to find time to even guess. Would he ever know, before…?

He went into the closet/toilet and closed the door.

Lhiana ran headlong down the beach, Kim shouting in her ear.

"Go! Go! Come on, Lhiana, straight into the sea. The others are with you, don't worry."

The sea was cold. It hurt her feet.

"Don't splash! Don't make any noise. Soon as you have enough depth get right into the water. Lie down. You have to lose heat. Now!"

"But it's only a few inches…"

"Now, Lhiana! You're not swimming, you're hiding. Don't splash. Lower yourself."

Lhiana went down on her hands and knees. Beside her she sensed Walther and Mila doing the same. She heard Walther's voice.

"Bloody hell, it's cold. Jeez…"

Then silence. His Jim had probably told him to shut up.

It *was* cold. As it touched her stomach she paused. Her breath became a rapid panting.

"All the way, Lhiana. You get cold or you die."

And then she saw the figures silhouetted around the fire. Four of them. They moved fast, with grace and stealth. Not a sound.

"Move up the beach. Either direction. Stay low in the water. They see your heat trails going down to the sea edge. Keep low, crawl, but move as far away from here as you can."

Lhiana rose to her hands and knees and did as she was told. She was aware of someone with her and another moving the other way. Which one was Mila? She couldn't tell.

Three of the spectre-like figures moved down to the sea. They moved like feral creatures. Lhiana saw long knives in their hands in the light from the fire, not quite shining, because they were made from a material that was dull and black and ugly.

The fourth figure turned away and ran up the beach toward the hut. Toward Elton.

Lhiana rose in the water, about to shout a warning.

"Down, Lhiana!" Kim's voice was harsh and commanding in her ear. "There's nothing you can do for him except get yourself killed. His Jim's with him and I'm sure… well, let's just hope for the best."

Lhiana slipped down into the waves again.

The three figures fanned out along the sea edge. Lhiana could feel their eyes searching. She could see from the light of the beach fire that they wore eye-wear. Night vision aids of some sort. It gave them even more of a sub-human look than their animal gait across the sand.

Then one of them saw Lhiana.

He snapped into action, lifting his knife, ready.

"Move, Lhiana, go deep. Fast. Stay low, he has the light from the fire behind him."

But before Lhiana could react, a fifth figure appeared from out of the darkness, running like the wind.

"Abort! Abort!" His voice was hard, but snatched between panted breaths.

The figure who was stalking Lhiana looked across, looked back at Lhiana, then continued to close in on her.

"Don't be stupid, Beaumont! It's a bust."

There was a moment of silence as the fifth figure launched through the air towards Lhiana's pursuer, then came a bone-crunching thud and a splash.

The other two came running over.

"What the hell are you doing, Rock, you moron?"

"It's over. Imentor's on. We abort, you got that?"

"Okay, yeah. Let's get the f—"

"Where's Luke?"

"The hut. One of them left a trail up the beach."

"Shit, we've got to stop him."

There was a scream of pain from the hut. Seven heads turned as one, to look.

THIRTY

Elton heard the front door open. It wasn't a careful, suppressed sound. The door was kicked in. The hot water on the floor might have helped a little to hide the heat trail, but Elton felt sure the pounding of his heart would be enough of a giveaway to anyone with half a volt left in their hearing-aid batteries.

"Okay, you little turd, where are you?"

A gravelly, basso profundo. It wasn't a question, at least nothing that merited an answer, but it got one anyway when Elton stepped sideways, away from a shaft of light from the latch-hole, and accidentally kicked the porcelain with his half foot. He tried to stifle the scream but the gasp of pain leaked out from the corners of his mouth. He reached out and groped for a weapon. Anything.

All movement in the hut stopped. Then, a brief sound. Hair being combed? A step, barely perceptible, the crunching of damp sand under heavy boots.

The darkness in the back of the closet was as black as the intergalactic void, almost. The flickering beach-fire light that shone through the latch-lever hole blinked as a shadow passed.

And Elton saw the latch begin to rise.

So he kicked open the door.

White hot agony lanced upwards from his half foot, but he stayed focussed.

He hit the red button.

The red button that must never, *ever* be pressed.

The hose kicked in his hands as a column of five-year-matured, concentrated excrement, under delightful pressure, hosed out from the closet into the face of the shocked, open-mouthed commando.

"Okay, Elton," said Jim. "I know a little about this guy. You've made a bold statement here. We're dealing with a precariously balanced mental condition. Your man there is going to do one of two things. Either he'll lose his military self-discipline and become a mindless, raging, stampeding mess of biceps and anger; tear your limbs off, one at a time, and use them to beat your remaining head and torso to a pulp.

"Or…"

And at this point the battle-hardened warrior lowered his head, studied his begrimed clothing, retched a few times, then began to cry.

"… or, on the other hand, he could do that."

"I think I prefer the psychotic rage, Jim. This is kind of unsettling."

"Oh no, I'd go with this option every time," said Jim.

Elton put down the hose. Somehow, he felt pity, and no longer had the urge to use the hose-end as a club.

Another house-sized soldier came skidding into the hut. Elton reached for the hose again, ready, but he didn't need it.

"Luke! Luke, it's an abort. Luke, I hope you haven't…" And then he sniffed the air.

"*Oh my good God!*"

He backed away from Elton, holding his collar up against his nose.

"Back to the boat, Luke, we're out of here. You okay, Luke? Luke?"

Luke was catatonic. He still held his pocket comb. He held it in trembling fingers and stared at it, clueless as to where to start.

The other soldier glowered at Elton.

"Look what you've done to him, you *bastard*," he said, then he took the weeping killing machine by the elbow, with a long, outstretched arm, and steered him down the beach.

It was risky to sail in the dark, especially so close to the rocky islands, but Elton had convinced them they should leave straight away, as soon as the assault team had gone.

"I think the sooner the better. You agree, Jim?"

"Ten more minutes and the satellite will be off over the horizon again. They can't track you from the waystation," said Jim, "they haven't got the facilities. If you keep the fire burning they'll assume you're still at home."

Lhiana had given them an argument though.

"We can wait out another pass. The low satellite will play into our hands. Let them see us, let them think we're staying."

"I don't know," said Elton.

"I do," said Lhiana. "Besides, you're going nowhere till you've cleaned out Aunt Beryl's hut."

Elton looked at the mess with dismay, but he knew she was right.

"Do I get any help?"

"Yeah. Walther can fetch the water from the sea. I'll show him where the bucket's kept."

"Is this like some elaborate, 'I told you so' punishment?"

"Oh, yes indeed."

It took three satellite orbits; four hours. By the time Elton had finished he barely noticed the smell, any smell.

They had little to pack, having arrived with nothing. Elton insisted on one item though.

"Lhiana, do you have any of that paint? You know, the stuff you painted the flowers with?"

"I don't think I'm going to have time to paint flowers, Elton."

"No, but... I think you should bring it, and your brushes and stuff. Just an idea, that's all."

There were still two hours of darkness remaining when they hoisted the sails on the *Spindrift* and headed northeast, following the chain of islands that made up the Egerian Archipelago.

At the first hint of dawn they landed on one of the larger islands, choosing a small uninhabited cove. They dragged the catamaran into some undergrowth, found a cave set in the cliffs and slept through the day.

They set sail again after dark, and arrived in Port Juno after three hours of cautious navigation. Walther had a plan in Port Juno. One he'd set up with his Jim even before they left Mantello Island. He wouldn't tell Elton or Lhiana about it, but they knew he was excited by the gleam in his eye. Mila was in on it, because they kept giving each other knowing winks whenever the subject, which involved the UPS depot, was raised.

They had four hours to kill before UPS opened, and then they waited an extra hour to avoid drawing any unwarranted attention by appearing too keen.

Walther went in alone. A few minutes later he came out with four packages and a boyish grin.

"Yee haw," he said.

"What's in the bags?" asked Elton.

"Our disguises," said Walther. "This is how we leave Minerva incognito."

"It's going to have to be good," said Lhiana. "Security is going to be tighter than ever now that Levison and Slicker know for certain we're here."

"Can you warn us, Jim?" asked Elton. "From their imentors?"

"Mmmmm…. no. I'd like to, I really would. But I can't take sides by betraying another imentor confidence. Only when it's life or death, like it was on the beach."

"So we have to assume the worst, that they're onto us," said Elton. "We should travel separately – or maybe in pairs," he added quickly when he saw the alarmed expression on Mila's face.

Mila smiled and grabbed Walther's arm. Elton leaned over towards Lhiana, intending to do the same, but then stopped and became awkward and self-conscious. He flapped stiff arms by his sides instead.

"Come on then, Walther, let's see these disguises."

"I hope that smile means you have good news for me," said Levison.

It was a short conversation beside the ZG lift entrance. Levison had been on his way out of the building while Slicker had been coming up to see him. Slicker was smiling because it was the first good news he'd been able to pass on for several days. His standing had been at a low point ever since the assault team debacle, even though he'd been somewhat relieved when the extreme measures had failed.

"I've ahh… I've been able to use the satellite surveillance, Mr Levison. We've picked them up and we now have people on the ground tracking them."

"I hope they're better than those four clowns you sent in last time, Slicker."

Bob Slicker chuckled.

"They don't need to be, Mr Levison. Our four fugitives are all, ah, costumed-up, and we're even getting reports of their progress from people who are not even our assets. You couldn't miss them, Mr Levison. They are causing something of a sensation."

"What's their plan, then?"

"They're idiots. They don't have a plan. You heard about how hard it was to get them appointed to the Space Corps in the first place. This vindicates Morningthorpe's aversion to Philpotts and Blick, that's for sure. They're travelling in pairs, but our people can't miss them. We think they're heading for the base station at Vesta. We'll pick them up there and bring them in. Couldn't be easier."

"I'm not sure I like it, Slicker."

"No worries, Mr Levison. I, er… I think they're tired of being on the run. I think they've gone Day-Glo as their way of getting arrested in plain view, with plenty of public attention, so that we can't try to terminate them again."

"It will be *our* people who pick them up, won't it?"

"I almost feel sorry for them. It would have been a good plan, only we're the only ones looking for them on Minerva. The official security forces still think they're on Neualmain. Yes, our people will get them."

"Okay, but no more cock-ups, Slicker. We have much bigger things to focus on right now. Philpotts is just an irritant. Get rid of him without causing any more of a stir."

"Everyone's looking at us. I feel like a bloody idiot," said Elton.

"It's a good plan," said Lhiana. "I'm still buying in to it. But I agree with you. I feel on show. I've never liked being the object of attention."

"You used to act," said Elton.

"Used to. Anyway, it's different on stage. You're being somebody else. A character. And you're dressed to fit in, to the place and the era."

Minerva was a conservative world. A world of physicians and intellectuals and charcoal grey. People preferred to dress with an understated sense of style. Clothes were functional but always smart – in both senses of the word. Jeans, on Minerva, were a rarity. Jeans with a grunge look were cause for compassion and charitable giving.

This was certainly not the place for dressing like Wyatt Earp and Calamity Jane, and yet that was exactly how Elton and Lhiana were dressed. Up on the North Road, Walther and Mila were doing the same, and with even more panache. All four of them wore the full kit – Stetsons, boots, rhinestones… It was all part of Walther's audacious plan.

Wherever they went people gaped. At the present moment they were waiting at the Baker Street maglev terminal in downtown Port Juno. People stared, like the circus had come to town. Or the Rodeo.

The maglev was busy – it was rush hour, but the dense crowds of grey people seemed to part wherever Elton and Lhiana chose to go. People averted their gaze and gave the two weirdos room. Even the ticket inspector lowered his gaze and looked at their tickets with only a perfunctory glance, and *he* was an android, devoid of thought.

"Jim, how are Walther and Mila doing?"

They'd agreed beforehand on permissions, to give their Jims and Kims an unhindered, free flow of information between them all, so that if anything developed they'd all be able to react quickly.

"Pretty much like you, Elton. They're getting a lot of attention. They're waiting for an airship. They don't seem as bothered by all the attention as you or Lhiana. You two are producing adrenaline in industrial quantities, your heart rates are up, pupils are dilated, as are your blood vessels."

"So what's that all about? Are we ill?"

"You're blushing. It's part of your fight-or-flight response.

Right now I'd guess you want to be out of there."

"Well, you'd be guessing correctly. Walther's not feeling the same?"

"On the contrary, he and Mila are lapping up the attention."

"Doesn't surprise me," said Lhiana. "Mila does this cowgirl stuff for fun, all the time."

They sat alone in the crowded maglev carriage. There were four other empty seats. Nobody wanted to share. Everyone preferred to stand in the corridor.

"Look at her," said Elton. He nodded towards an older woman pressed in amongst the crowd. She was dressed in a green robe and her head was shaved.

"I bumped into one of those on a train before," said Elton. "She was on the platform at Port Juno. She sticks out worse than us – and while everyone else has been averting their eyes, she's been staring right at us. Look at the way she keeps dipping her head and talking SubV. Not a monk thing, that. Do you think she's Space Corps? We must be drawing them like moths to an arc lamp."

"Space Corps and weird religions don't seem to fit together too well."

"So, kind of makes for a good cover, don't you think?"

The maglev slowed and pulled into a station – a place called Quirinus. A crowd surge swept the monk lady down the train and out of line of sight. Commuters boarded, and the corridor filled even more. One person joined them in their spacious carriage. He was also dressed as a cowboy.

"Howdy, partners. You both going to New Nashville for the festival?"

Elton wanted to say something sarcastic. He resisted the urge.

"Yup," he said. He'd heard that word in a film once. It sounded authentic. He didn't want to talk to the stranger. He wasn't in the mood. Instead he adopted the man-with-no-name attitude. If he had an old cigar he'd have chomped on it. He stared at the man with cold, stranger-from-out-of-town eyes for a moment, then turned to look out of the window.

The monk lady was back. Once again she was watching, and mumbling into her collar. Something about her gave Elton the creeps. It wasn't just the watching, it was the whole cowled robe and baldy-head thing.

Another station. More passengers. And more cowpeople. The costumes were even more flamboyant.

Two more joined them in the carriage and Elton could see a sprinkling of rhinestones out in the corridor too.

People had stopped looking at Elton and Lhiana. They were no longer different enough. They began to relax.

"This is more like it," said Lhiana. "Now we fit. We're in character."

"So, you're an actress. What plays have you been in? Do you have a favourite role?" Elton tried hard to make conversation.

Lhiana gave him a smile and shook her head. "You don't really do small talk, do you, Elton? I get the feeling we should be in a bare room with a small table between us, and a single bulb for light. Can you account for your whereabouts on the sixteenth?"

"I'm sorry. Too direct. Walther does this stuff so much better: Conversation."

"Don't be sorry. Just try not to work so hard at it."

"I'm not trying to..." Elton paused and took a breath. He looked away. When he spoke again his words came slower and quieter, almost as though he were talking to himself. "The last time I went to the theatre was back home, on Erymanthus. A touring production of *The Last Queen*. I loved it. *Really* loved it.

The play, the drama, theatre in general. And... you're an actress. I'm not just trying to force conversation, Lhiana. I *am* interested."

"Well, that's more like it." Lhiana seemed to relax further into her seat, letting it fold in around her. Her voice, too, became quieter but carried over the excited buzz of conversation in the carriage. "I played Queen Isabella myself, in college. It's my favourite play. I adored playing Isabella. Do you know she was responsible for the founding of La Ronde? She had a passion for flowers and nature. I studied that part so hard that a little of her remains in me to this day. I suppose, deep down, she is the reason I paint, and why I'm happy to work there for nothing."

She told him about her tour guide work and how her boss took her for granted all the time, but it would never change how she felt about the garden. Elton told her about his dull job in the Space Corps, and about his interview from hell, and this had Lhiana howling with laughter. The journey went by quickly and their time was over all too soon.

By the time they arrived at Vesta the charcoal-grey commuters were in the minority and the monk lady was gone. Elton and Lhiana joined a posse of cowboys and gauchos as they left the train and headed for the spaceport. Elton had to keep hold of Lhiana so they wouldn't get separated. All around them there were yee-haws and yippy-ki-yays and snatches of song about horse friends and lonesome trails. They were still attracting attention from the locals, but now it wasn't Elton and Lhiana who were attracting attention, but a crowd of three or four hundred.

They established, from Jim, that Walther and Mila had arrived before them and had already taken the elevator up to the waystation. There they stayed, though, because despite the Wild

West migration security was still tight. Every pass was being scrutinised by human inspectors and they were also checking for festival tickets. Walther and Mila had already shared out their four tickets they'd bought months ago. Possession of pre-dated tickets added massive credibility to their position.

But the gate pass inspector was still a problem.

"Stay where you are, Walther," said Elton. "I half-expected something like this. We'll be with you shortly. I have an idea. Lhiana will get us through."

Lhiana looked at him.

"Me? What are you expecting *me* to do?"

Four hours later they were waiting in line. They had separated. They were each queuing for different gates. It seemed safer to travel as individuals.

Up ahead Elton watched the ritual of ticket inspection. Walther's optimism that the sheer volume of country fans would all but eliminate the depth of scrutiny had not been realised. Every individual gate pass was being examined with deliberate care. So now it all came down to Lhiana. Was she really good enough to swing this for them?

Elton would be the first to find out. His face was the more memorable of the four since it had decorated breakfast cereal boxes and news reports right across the Sphere for days. Elton would be the test case. If he got himself arrested the others would have time to fade away. But it would be difficult for them. The disadvantage of their costume plan was that the traffic flow was all one way. Anyone heading back down to Minerva would surely draw attention to themselves. But Elton was confident.

When he was only two bodies away from the checkpoint his confidence evaporated. The official had that die-for-The-Corps look about him that was in such evidence in the airy offices of New Leicester Space Corps HQ. His uniform was fussy and pressed and he wore medals and braid that were polished and gleaming and probably came from a military memorabilia emporium, because who ever got medals for checking transit passes? He had black beady eyes that flickered and darted, and on his upper lip there lurked a black moustache – a masterpiece of minimalist facial topiary. His name badge said Sergeant Luther. Was this the man's name or was Sergeant Luther the original owner of all the medals? It seemed ironic that the owner of such spurious bona fides was spending his day checking on the identity of cowboys.

Elton was next but one. The cowboy in front of him was sweating and trembling and looked just about ready to confess to the destruction of F-257, the xenocide of the Buggers and the alien abduction of Elvis, all in one go.

"Remove your hat, please," said the counterfeit Luther.

"Do I have to?" said the Elvis abductor.

"I need to see your face without the hat."

"It's just the same as with the hat."

"There are shadows and the framing is different. Please remove the hat."

"I like the hat."

"Then perhaps you'd like to move to the back of the queue whilst you think about it."

"I'm not going to the back of the queue. And I'm not taking my bloody hat off."

The bogus Sergeant Luther SubV'd into his collar and suddenly there were uniformed guards floating around them both. These were guards who displayed no discernible differences in the girths of their chests, their necks or their biceps.

"Okay, the hat's coming off."

The hat came off.

Sergeant Luther examined the face, the pass, the top of the head. Then he checked the face again and peered more closely at the holographic photo on the pass, turning it to get a profile view.

Then, "Okay, sir. Next."

Elton was next.

He showed Luther his pass. This photo was the photo that had graced Holo networks for a week. Elton D Philpotts: Terrorist.

Luther stared at the photo and did a double take. His face clouded. He looked at Elton to make sure. Elton saw perspiration appear on Luther's brow. He began to finger his collar to begin a SubV conversation with his Jim.

Then he stopped.

He looked at Elton's photo again, the cloud lifted and a smile broke through on Luther's face, the first smile Elton had seen on the man's face since he had joined the line.

"That's all in order, sir," he said, as if to his best friend. "Enjoy the concert."

Elton hadn't even needed to remove his hat. He stepped through the gate to Appalachia.

THIRTY ONE

"So what happened?" asked Walther. "What did Lhiana do to our passes? I thought we'd had it. Usually, no one looks at our passes when we go through the gates. But this? I really thought we were finished. One glance at the photo should have been enough on its own, but the passes have our names on them for God's sake!"

"Lhiana's an artist. She does this thing with special paint. She's brilliant. You tell him, Lhiana."

"It's a special pigment that changes the image in subtle ways until the viewer sees what he wants to see. Elton's hunch was that security people want an easy life. If they'd been the ones to find us there'd have been paperwork and boards of inquiry and all kinds of grief. So what each guard wants to see is someone who is clearly nothing like us. When I borrowed your passes, in Port Juno, I did a little touching up, changed some of the colouration and shading. But I did it with pheromone pigment so that *it* would do the work. Our photos looked like us, but subtly altered so that they looked nothing like the gang of terrorists that's on every cereal box in the Sphere."

"Wow, Lhiana. So we should be okay here. They won't be looking for us," said Walther.

"I think we need to be careful, still," said Elton. "Let's stick to your plan, it's a good one. We'll split up and meet at the festival. Our Jims and Kims can help us meet up when we get there."

"Then what?"

"Then we think about getting back to Tsanak."

"Why Tsanak?"

"Why not? One step at a time, okay?"

They nodded agreement. Walther and Mila gave each other a tearful hug. They'd be separated for the next two or three hours and they seemed crushed by the very thought of it.

Elton looked over at Lhiana. Was he crushed by the idea of a prolonged separation? No question. But Lhiana? Was *she* crushed? Was she bothered at all? She was very independent, that was for sure. This wasn't how it was meant to go according to the fantasies Elton had played and replayed during those two weeks alone on F-257. Okay, so even just meeting her had been a remarkable piece of good fortune. And the maglev journey to Vesta had been, well, magical. He couldn't expect to have it all ways, could he?

"Slicker, come in," said Levison. He was eating. He was always eating. And he was always eating something off the endangered species list.

The house had been redecorated since Slicker had last been here. The walls were papered in something that looked like paper, and the furniture was made from green timber. Wood was rare even in recycled form. Green timber was impossible. It was wholly impractical too. The chair onto which Slicker was directed to sit was sticky with sap; sap which soaked through the back of his trouser legs and succeeded in overcoming the natural barrier of Slicker's oily surface layer, to glue his trousers to the skin of his thighs and buttocks, an unfamiliar sensation for the self-lubricating Management Accountant, and Slicker found it quite unpleasant, especially as his hairs had amalgamated with the fibres of his trousers, and had a tendency to pull every time he moved.

"You have come here to give me some good news about Philpotts and his renegade band."

"Ahh…"

Levison held up a hand. His eyes bore the cold and colourless shine of surgical steel.

"Do not even imagine that you will come out of this meeting favourably if you have anything but glad tidings on the subject, Slicker."

Slicker cleared his throat with a nervous cough. A sliver of ice seemed to have found its way beneath his shirt and had begun to melt down his back. He hated Levison. He wanted to entangle his fingers in that expensively coifed hair and smash that smug face down onto the marble table top, again and again, until it was indistinguishable from the dead meat he was forever stuffing into that self-satisfied mouth.

"Sir, I am sorry. The news is not good. We are unable to locate them."

Levison placed his fork down beside the dish.

"Go on," he said, his voice quiet and menacing.

"Our records show they passed through the Minervan gate an hour ago and are now somewhere on Appalachia, on their way to a large music festival."

"Was there *any* security?"

"Stringent security, sir. They seem to have, ahh, passed through without notice."

"They're in big hats and foolish baggy trousers. They have glitter all over their shirts and they're wearing noisy boots. They're *conspicuous*. How the hell did you miss them, Slicker?"

"The situation changed, sir. There were a great many all dressed the same."

"So, can you pick them up now, on Appalachia?"

"We have our people in place. We've brought them in. They are… grey. They usually blend. Unfortunately, on Appalachia our people stand out rather like turds on a wedding cake.

"Sir, there are a half million cowboys and, er, cowgirls on

Appalachia. They all look the same. We cannot even use heat signature tracking from satellite surveillance; they're all wearing big hats."

"I'm bored with this *Philpotts*, Slicker. He is a sideshow; an irrelevance. He is being creative and that is not something that ever appeared in his character profile. Be *more* creative, Slicker. Finish it."

A sea of Stetsons. There were currents and eddies and all manner of fluid dynamics centred on the great whirlpool of New Nashville.

A tent city had appeared on the outskirts of town, and it was growing by the hour. There were four space needles on Appalachia, and each one was disgorging cowpeople by the thousand, like a vast industrial process. Convoys of trains, airships, sailing vessels, cars, vans, and bicycles collected the cowboys and cowgirls and ferried them in to New Nashville. Every bar twanged to the sounds of country: Dolly Lovett, Hank Masters, Becky-Lou Phillips and the Cowpokes.

The vats of the New Nashville Meat Corporation turned out pig meat, prefabricated into the shape of hogs, ready for the skewer. There were warthogs, pighogs, veggiehogs… and steaks? There were steaks so big they appeared on maps. Market forces were insatiable. Barns the size of starship hangars were raised; impromptu hops were organised; anyone who could scratch out a tune on a fiddle or pick out four notes on a banjo was king.

There was violence. Many of the revellers had brought vintage six-shooters, somehow smuggling them past the heightened security up in the waystations; occasional shootings were inevitable, but mostly inadvertent – the accidental blasting away of toes or noses from inexperienced handlers of museum-piece handguns.

Lhiana was soon lost. In fact she'd never been anything other. *Let's meet up at the festival*, Elton had said. Head for the centre of things. He could be so infuriating. The "centre of things" in this Nashville was the size of old Tennessee.

"Kim, can you help me out here?"

"Not so easy, Lhiana. I'm tracking the others but they're all heading in different directions."

"Aren't they using their imentors?"

"It's just hard to decide on a common rendezvous point. Elton's heading for one of the giant barns, but there are dozens of them, and he keeps changing his mind. Walther's found a bar and he's staying put, best idea – let everyone else find him. Mila nearly got there but then she came across a dude who'd shot off his own kneecap—"

"—so she stopped to fix him up. Don't tell me, Kim, that's typical Mila."

"Well it seems medical skills are in short supply around these here parts. Last I saw she'd been picked up by a group of monks who've turned her into some kind of impromptu paramedic."

"Monks?"

"That's what they looked like."

"Where is she now?"

"Well, if you lean your head back and look up, she's in that airship with the big red cross painted on the side."

"With the monks?"

"Yes, I think so."

"You *think?* Her Kim?"

"No. She's not wearing smarts. The costume's gone; she had to scrub up to go into surgery. That's the last I saw."

"Damn. Why didn't her Kim stop her?"

"Lhiana, she's a nurse. And there's a sobbing cowboy with a hole in his knee, yes?"

"Yes. Oh, Mila!"

Guns, booze and precious few medics. It was inevitable.

"Walther, then? Where's he?"

"You don't want to find Elton first?"

"Why do you say that, Kim?" Lhiana snapped.

"Oh, you know why. But, hey, it's not my place to interfere."

"Isn't that exactly what you're meant to do?"

"We are touchy, aren't we, dear? Turn clockwise. Stop. You see that tent with the Bluebird Breweries beer bottle holo hovering above it? You'll find Walther in there. I'll speak to Elton's Jim and try and direct him to the same place."

Lhiana headed off for the tent. She was glad of the boots. The ground underfoot had been trodden into a quagmire.

People were everywhere. She hardly noticed. Her mind was preoccupied. What was going on with Elton? What was her Kim hinting at? Yes, she had thought there was… something, about Elton, that first day when she fed him into the gate, all nervous and naïve. But now? Now she knew him. He'd dragged her into this mess. He'd brought his one-man war out to La Ronde, her beloved garden, and look what happened there. Then he'd dragged her best friend, Mila, into it, and now *she* was floating around in a balloon full of those creepy monks, and what was *their* story? No, Elton was poison. He'd only been on Aunt Beryl's island for five minutes before commandos had come storming in to kill them all.

She should turn around, now. Head back to the Ring. Tell them everything. This wasn't her war. She didn't even know what it was all about, apart from Elton. It was all about Elton Philpotts.

Damn the man. He was so… irritating.

The field sloped downwards and the mud was slick. She lost her footing and nearly slid headlong into a brown festering pool in which half a dozen cowboys, barely recognisable as human, were cavorting and pushing one another.

Her fall was arrested by a strong hand that appeared from nowhere. Lhiana mumbled her thanks to the stranger, but barely noticed him. He was just another good ol' boy in a cowboy hat. Lhiana was too preoccupied in her rage over Elton Philpotts, to notice how the man's hat was several sizes too small for his head, or how his shoes – not boots – were polished and gleaming black, despite all the mud.

And how he was dressed in a business suit, all in grey.

THIRTY TWO

Mila still hadn't arrived at the Bluebird Beer Tent. Walther became more agitated, looking around and asking his Jim for an update every few seconds.

Eddie Pickavance and the Pocahontas Polecats were tuning up on stage. Actually, they seemed to have been tuning up for quite a while now, so perhaps they'd already started their first set and were just not very good. No one seemed to notice or care though; the Bluebird Beer had been flowing since the tent arrived, several days earlier, and many of the revellers were trending towards the horizontal.

"Where's Mila?" said Walther, for the third, or twenty-third, time.

"Relax, Walther, she'll be here soon. Have another beer," said Lhiana.

"I don't want another beer," said Walther.

Elton, who'd been last to arrive, looked over at Lhiana and raised his eyebrows. Had he heard correctly? Walther never refused beer.

"So what's your next move, Elton?" Lhiana seemed to be trying to change the subject, maybe to stop Walther with his incessant fidgeting, but Elton also detected the slight emphasis on the word 'your'. This was still Elton's problem. The others were only here through implication. They'd been dragged into this situation and for the moment, for them, there was no obvious exit strategy. Elton had to make the next move and they had no choice but to tag along.

"We have to go to Tsanak," he said.

Walther's attention had drifted again, his eyes on the tent doorway, but his interest was aroused and he snapped back round to stare at Elton.

"Tsanak? What the frig do you want to go to Tsanak for? You're wanted by just about everyone on Tsanak. You wouldn't last thirty seconds."

Elton shrugged. "I need to get access to the Space Corps accounts. I want to see that covert ledger again. There are clues there. Numbers."

"So what do you think you can learn that won't get you – and us – into even more trouble than we're in already?" said Lhiana.

"Tau numbers. I only saw what was in that ledger for a few seconds, but there were gate numbers, lovely long Tau indices. A list. And some of them were, well, different."

"How would you know that?" asked Lhiana.

Elton pointed to his head.

"Numbers. I see stuff. I need a bit longer to search around in there, but I have a feeling this has something to do with those gate numbers. Don't ask me why."

"Surprised you didn't memorise them," said Walther. "A couple of seconds' glance, number boy? You're slipping. Anyway, how would they help? What would you do with them?"

"Gates, Walther. We travel. We use the Tau indices and we go to those gates. See what there is to see. If we learn what this is all about we might be better placed to do something about it, and about us. Look, whatever that Slicker guy is up to, it isn't official – it probably isn't legal. We have to get the authorities on our side. Even if we just let them arrest us, at least with some supporting facts we'll be better placed to point the finger at Slicker and whoever else is mixed up in this."

"Okay," said Walther, "good plan. We get arrested and blag our way out. So then, back to that other little matter: how are you going to get onto Tsanak? Security is tight as a Thermopod's arse. I doubt even Lhiana's mystic-artistic talents are going to help us. And where's Mila? I'm worried about her. Aren't you worried, Lhiana? She's your friend."

"Mila's resourceful, Walther. I'm not worried. She also has this thing where she has to help everybody. She can't stop herself. If she's got mixed up with paramedic monks she'll never be able to drag herself away."

"Monks? What do you mean, paramedic monks?"

"Just what Kim told me."

"Hmm, okay. Anyway, I don't think security will be a problem," said Elton, getting back on subject. "Tsanak is the last place they'll expect us. All the security will be focused here and on Minerva."

"I don't like the sound of monks," said Walther.

"What? Focus, Walther. Don't go all random on us," said Elton.

"Monks, Elton. You remember? That Bram Lee monk who registered you for the Disexpansionists? And it was monks that were involved in that riot in The Revolution."

"Clowns do it for me," said Lhiana.

"Clowns?"

"Yeah, you know, painted faces and big feet. Scare the jeebies out of me."

"What's that got to do with anything?" said Elton.

"Walther's scared of monks. I'm scared of clowns."

Elton noticed how Lhiana kept trying to change the subject. She knew about the monks, they'd talked about the one on the train in Minerva. She didn't want Walther to worry but it was plain she was worrying herself.

"I'm not scared of monks," said Walther. "It's just... Why's Mila with them?"

"She's a medic, Walther. Monks are renowned for caring for the sick and the unfortunate. There's kind of a connection there."

"Why's that guy not wearing a cowboy suit?" said Elton, nodding over to a tall man who stood alone at the bar. He was crowded in, but something about him made him seem kind of lonely.

"This conversation is getting surreal," said Lhiana.

"No, seriously. All he's got is a hat. And it doesn't fit. Like he robbed it."

"Wait a minute, I think he's the same one who…" Lhiana's voice went quiet. "He stopped me slipping into a mud hole outside. I thanked him. He said nothing. Kind of odd. Come to think of it, I might have seen him before. On the bus coming over here, maybe. You think...?"

"He's been watching us. Just like the monk on the train. Look how he's doing his best *not* to watch us now. Yes, I *do* think. He's one of Slicker's people. It would be good if we left. Now."

"Hang on," said Walther. "What monk on the train?"

"Tell you later," said Elton. "After we leave."

They'd been standing in an open area in the middle of the tent. They split apart and headed for three different exits. Elton was first to reach the tent flap which counted as a doorway. As he ducked to slip out of the tent his way was blocked. Another grey suit. No hat. And a tight, insincere smile.

Elton turned and saw that both Walther and Lhiana had met similar passive resistance. The grey suits didn't enter the tent. They stayed by the exits and watched.

Elton returned to the middle of the tent. Walther did the same. Lhiana circled to the only other entrance but the man she'd seen earlier appeared from the shadows to intercept. He took position by the exit and just stood there, smiling and unconcerned.

Elton noted that everyone else was being allowed free passage in and out. Only the three of them were being stopped.

"What do you reckon?" said Walther to Elton.

"They're waiting for Mila," said Lhiana, rejoining them, watching the entrance over her shoulder. "They want the four of us together before they make a move."

"You'd better warn her," said Elton. "Tell her not to come here."

"I'll try," said Lhiana, "but she wasn't wearing smarts, last time I called."

Lhiana spoke into her collar. After a moment she looked up. Her face was white.

"Kim can't raise her. Walther, Kim's talking about an accident. A medical balloon has come down on the north of... oh God, there's been an explosion."

Lhiana was talking to herself. Walther was already running for the exit, giving out a strangled wail.

One of the grey suits stepped out, still cool, still smiling. His hand slid into a jacket pocket and came out holding something heavy and gun-shaped. The hand only came half out; Walther was motivated. His almost-full bottle of Bluebird Beer swept round in a smooth arc. The heavy glass base connected with the bridge of Grey Suit's nose. There was no mistaking the sound of cracking cartilage. The blood flow was impressive. The other three suits ran over to grab Walther. Elton jumped onto the nearest, and Lhiana grabbed the one holding Walther and tried to pull him off, but the other suits were there and it was four against three.

Now there was interest from within the tent. Four men, in business suits, were beating up cowboys – and a cow*girl*. It wasn't hard to choose sides.

The grey men were good. They were trained, efficient killers. But there were fifty cowboys in the tent, and they'd been drinking hard. And, come on, how often do you get to participate in a genuine Wild West bar fight nowadays? Bottles were broken over heads. Stools began to fly. No sawdust on the ground, but hey, this was a tent, there was mud. Somewhere, somebody started playing honky-tonk piano – for atmosphere.

THIRTY THREE

They made it to the Ring.

There was no cause for celebration; they were in a jail. Or at least a makeshift jail.

Walther was out to lunch. Staring. Comatose.

Lhiana sat on a crate and sobbed, quietly.

Mila was dead.

Elton sat between them, an arm round each, trying to give some comfort. Failing. His fault. He knew all along there was danger in this. He knew the stakes were high, but he never once expected anything like…

The worst of it was, he didn't even know – *still* didn't know – why. Why was this happening? What was it all for? One thing was for sure: it wasn't worth this.

And somehow, Elton knew, they would be next. Another "accident". The trouble was, they were locked up, and his two companions – his remaining companions – were in no shape to even talk. They were past caring. What now?

Elton glanced around the room that had become their prison. It seemed familiar. There were crates stacked. It was a storeroom of some kind. It looked like… actually it *was*, the very room in which he'd hidden after returning from F-257. He'd found that box full of soil and worms. But that time matters had been in his own hands. Now things were different. This time he'd been put here, and the door had been locked.

Why here? Were there no proper jails on the Ring? Of course there were. Only *those* jails were controlled by "the authorities". Officialdom. The people who had brought them here were not "authority", they were something else, so Elton couldn't really expect to be treated in a conventional, responsible manner. He, and Lhiana, and Walther, were only here until the person who made the uncomfortable decisions made an uncomfortable decision.

It was time to act.

But there lay the problem. To act – this was something Elton didn't really do. He was in this position, not because he had taken a wrong turn in the journey of life, but because he'd remained a passenger. He'd been brought here.

He'd become an accountant because his father had expected him to become an accountant. He'd joined the Space Corps because Walther liked the image and told Elton that he would like it, too. At every turn he'd done as he was told and done what was expected of him. He'd been manipulated by Slicker and probably Levison. He'd been put into a spaceship and only avoided being vaporised because of a Darwinian reflex to stay alive that was built into all higher and lower animals.

Then Lhiana had collected him and ushered him out to Minerva. And Walther had dressed him up in ridiculous clothes, wound his spring and pointed him towards Appalachia. And now he was here. And one of his friends was dead.

Where was the volition? Where was the free will in his life? Had he ever made a decision based on his own judgement? Elton thought about it. His thoughts roamed backwards in time. When he was six he had made a lifestyle decision. He had saved his pocket-money and bought a notebook and an i-spy train spotters' guide. But was that *his* decision or was that merely the product of the numerosity gene that had tormented him since his first day at nursery school when Miss Tuttle had pointed to the wall-chart and read, "one ball, two ducks, three horses…" Elton hadn't known what a duck or a horse was, but one, two, three was *counting* and *numbers*, and then he disgraced himself by wetting his pants in excitement.

Now he was here, with Walther on one side and Lhiana on the other, both so shattered they could barely string two coherent thoughts together. There was no Jim – the first thing the grey men had done after the reinforcements had arrived was to make them each strip off their cowboy smarts and pull on dumb coveralls. There'd be no advice from Jim or Kim now. It was all down to Elton.

And still he remained seated between his friends. Because what if he made a wrong decision? Already one of them was dead. This thing was not a game. Did he really have a right to make life-or-death decisions on behalf of his friends?

Then he wondered at the consequences of inaction. Mila was dead. What difference would three more make to the Space Corps? It was plain that, in this game, dead was the desirable state for them, in the minds of Robert Slicker and Martin Levison.

Elton eased out from between Walther and Lhiana – they didn't register any sign of noticing. He stretched – his arms had become stiff from comforting his friends. He walked over to the door. *That's different,* he thought. The last time he was here there hadn't been any gravity. Presumably, then, this area could be spun up or down as required. So what was the significance of them now pulling over half a gee? Probably meant nothing more than there would be no loading or unloading for a while, because this was a storeroom; a warehouse. Things stayed in boxes better when there was a bit of gravity. And so there'd be few, if any, visitors.

He looked at the door and walls. Plastic of some sort. Not a good material for prisons, but good enough. He tried the door release. Maybe the door wasn't locked. Maybe someone had made a stupid, basic mistake. Elton imagined he would feel kind of soft if he'd just sat here, like a good puppy, behind an unlocked door for an hour, waiting for his executioners to arrive.

But the door was locked. Elton was almost relieved. He could imagine the conversation:

-Bob, you left the door unlocked.

-No I didn't.

-Yes you did, you've lost them. Hang about, the silly buggers are still here.

-Oh my God, what a bunch of nutters.

-Well, do you want to shoot them or shall I?

Elton tried kicking the door, careful to use his good foot. It didn't give. It didn't even make a sound. Now Elton had two sore feet.

I'm a loser, he thought. He remembered his assertiveness classes two years ago. At registration he had been given the choice of paying in full or spreading the cost, in instalments. It was much cheaper to pay for the full course up-front, but then what if he didn't like being assertive; what if he quit? Well, he'd lose everything, whereas, if he chose the alternative he then only stood to lose a couple of instalment payments. But the instalment plan was far more expensive. He'd agonised over the decision for an hour. The class had started without him. He'd gone home. He could decide before next week. He'd never reached a decision.

Loser.

There were crates, racked down the length of the wall. Elton tried to remember what had been in the crates the last time he was here, apart from dirt and worms. He remembered machine tools. He didn't know what they were or what they did, but they were hard and metallic. If he could use them on the wall… Plastic was used for internal walls because it was light. Internal walls were not expected to have to resist persistent chipping or filing. He saw himself tunnelling deep below the walls while guards marched overhead, unaware of his endeavours. He'd seen it in an old war film; flat screen, monochrome, but with story power enough to take the mind away from image imperfections.

He realised he was daydreaming. He was Elton D Philpotts: failed accountant. What did he know about jail-breaking?

But it was worth a look.

He went along the row of crates, reading off the stencilled markings. Most of them held food, dehydrated ready-meals. He didn't anticipate much success trying to dig his way out with dried Chicken Leonardo Penne Pasta.

One crate wasn't food. It said "Chain Saws".

"What's a chain saw, Jim?"

No Jim.

It was a *déjà vu* moment. He'd asked the same question of an absent Jim once before. The last time he'd done it, the sudden realisation of loneliness had brought him close to tears. This time, despite the presence of Walther and Lhiana, he felt no less lonely and helpless. But this time he had to act for the three of them. There was more than his own arse on the butcher's block today.

He pulled open the first crate and lifted out one of the machines. It was heavy; not unwieldy, it had a reassuring heft about it. He stripped off the polystyrene blocks and polythene wrappers. There were two handles. Only one way to hold it because the trigger was for right-handers. (Elton had been born a lefty but his parents had got that fixed with a gene mod when he was four.)

Elton waved the machine, experimentally. It was awkward. Something amiss with the balance. He examined the machine until he found a slot marked "powerpack". He felt a momentary pang of annoyance, but then remembered seeing another crate from the time of his first visit here. It had been filled with unmarked black oblong shapes, which had looked to be about the right size for powerpacks. He looked at the crates. There were over a hundred. He closed his eyes and visualised the scene from when he had floated around in here, naked, his coveralls wrapped around half a foot. He had been desperate – in a state of panic.

56584848753/22334

That was the number stencilled on the side of the crate. He remembered. There were words, too, but his brain wasn't wired for remembering words.

He put down the machine and trotted along the row of boxes, his finger pointing to each serial number in turn.

He found 56584848753/22334 two-thirds of the way along, on the second level. The lid wasn't sealed, still hastily placed on top following his initial inspection from nearly a week ago. (Was it only a week? Felt like months after all that had happened.)

He reached in and took out one of the packages. Like the machine itself, it felt reassuringly heavy. He stripped off the wrapping, and sure enough it was a Copperbird PP50 powerpack – the same sort that his DIY Copperbird Omnitool used, back home. He'd been bought the tool by his parents who said "replicating was all well and good, but one should always try to *make* something now and again". Elton could make holes and he could make mess, but for the most part his aptitude lay more in the direction of destruction rather than of creation. The DIY acronym was inevitably linked to that of A&E.

He went back to the machine – the "Chain Saw" – and fitted the powerpack. It made a satisfying, almost military thwacking sound as he slotted it home – then it began to hum, and lights came on; red lights, green lights, coloured graphs. Elton noticed immediately that the weight distribution had changed. With the powerpack attached it was whole. Now it felt right. It felt like something that was meant to be swung.

Elton looked over at Walther and Lhiana. Walther was staring, Lhiana was sobbing. He should really ask them if the next move was okay by them, but they were out of it. Elton had to take responsibility – *all* the responsibility.

He tweaked the trigger. The machine bucked in his hands with pent-up gyroscopic forces. It made some noise, a whining, clattering sound, but nothing untoward. Lhiana looked up, her eyes quizzical. Walther continued to stare.

"We're leaving," said Elton.

He pulled the trigger and waved the machine around to get the feel of the way all the forces pulled and tugged at his arms. It felt good. It was louder – a pained shrieking sound. Elton stepped towards the wall, raised the machine above his head, then brought it down.

The wall exploded.

It made a noise like an exploding wall.

There was no scoring or cutting going on here, the plastic wall was simply annihilated. The surrounding air filled with tiny plastic shards. Ahead, on the other side of... well, the other side of nothing; the wall no longer existed, there was just a corridor.

He shut the machine down and stepped through. Nobody came running. No alarms. Why would there be? Why set alarms to detect the destruction of an internal wall between a warehouse and a corridor?

Elton went back and pulled Walther to his feet. The noise and the violence of the moment had brought Walther part-way back from his comatose state. He moved, though, without questioning.

Elton spoke to Lhiana.

"We need clothes," he said. "Smart clothes. Any ideas?"

"My apartment."

"Too risky."

"Shops."

"Again, too obvious. They can follow the money. What about the recycle dump? Where is it?"

"I don't tend to visit the dump when I'm shopping for clothes."

Elton managed to smile. Sarcasm – she could still make a joke. There was hope.

"Okay, shops then. I suppose I'll only need ten minutes."

Lhiana led. Elton followed, guiding Walther by the elbow. He noted that she hadn't asked any questions: *Why shops? Why smart clothing? Where to next?*

She was functioning – but from a detached and distant standpoint.

The Ring moved around Earth in a continuous geostationary orbit that had become redundant; the elevators to the surface had closed decades ago, there being precious little left on the surface worth visiting. But it meant that the Ring was synchronised with Earth standard time, and time zones were aligned to match those on the wasted, empty surface below. Right now it was night time in the Italian sector, but the shops were open and enough people were drawn by the lure of retail sleep therapy to make *Via Monte Napoleone* busy enough for Elton and his two walking-dead companions to blend, even though they still had star billing as public enemies numbers one, two and three.

They found a chic and fashionably deserted clothing store

called Leonardo Riccelli. Right next door was an incongruous, rather tacky fast-food joint with a holo logo consisting of two fingers sticking up in the universal symbol of displeasure. FingaLikka.

Walther looked up at the logo and his eyes registered recognition. Then they filled with tears.

"This place mean something to you, compagno?" asked Elton.

Walther said nothing. He just allowed the tears to flow.

"We're going in," said Elton.

He found a table, ordered food and drink, then took both Lhiana's hands in his, and spoke to her, looking her straight in the eye and punctuating each short sentence with a little shake of her hands.

"I'm leaving you both here. I'm going shopping. I will be back soon. Look after him. Don't leave."

And then, impulsively, he leaned over and kissed her. He didn't know where it came from, but it felt right. Lhiana blinked and looked at him, her eyes focussing for the first time in hours.

"Get Walther to drink something." He looked at the two fluorescent drinks beakers, and smiled. "You too. It'll help. Don't go anywhere."

Leonardo Riccelli was the kind of fashionable clothing store that reaped kudos from its unwillingness to go virtual. They employed personal sales assistants and made a big play of shunning all android presence in their stores. There were branches of Leonardo Riccelli in New Leicester, but Elton had never been inside one. Leonardo's stores were hideously expensive.

He was approached by a human sales assistant as soon as he entered. The assistant eyed Elton up and down, no doubt assessing him for eligibility into the ranks of the rich and suave.

Elton felt horribly under qualified, but he had one thing going for him: He could wear clothes. He was the polar opposite of Walther, who carried clothing like badly packed luggage. Clothes hung from Elton's shoulders in lines that somehow just seemed to fit, irrespective of the whims of the software fitting-drivers within. Even his dumb coveralls – effectively prison garb – looked as though they heralded a new wave of fashionable, grungy underachievement.

The assistant nodded. He approved.

"Trousers?" said Elton. A jacket would have been easier and quicker, but there would have been no opportunity for fitting. Trousers required privacy. One has to take one's time with trousers.

"Sir?"

"Black, pin-stripe, slick fit," said Elton, in an uncompromising voice that said he belonged here.

"Smart, sir?"

"Of course. Full function and close interface. I need trousers that will think for me. Trousers that will live my life if I choose to be absent from them. Can you help?"

"Oh, indeed, sir. You have come to the house of *Riccelli*." He snapped his fingers and underlings appeared, warm and breathing, not an android amongst them. Three carried trousers, the others were merely there to fawn and to make the eventual bill appear less unreasonable.

Elton nodded. "I could do with a shirt, as well. Dress shirt. White. I don't want to see even a suggestion of colour. I need *severe* contrast between shirt and trousers."

Elton had assumed a role. This was how he'd seen his father behave when he was shopping for clothes. He'd once taken Elton with him when he was buying a suit for an institute dinner.

"Treat them like dirt," he'd told Elton. "The more expensive the shop the more you should abuse the assistants. They love it. They're on commission and the more obnoxious the customer the more likely he is to have plenty of money, so you'll get the better service." His father's approach, then, had been to haggle and argue and hurl insults, then storm out of the shop, and buy his clothes from the online discount stores.

Four shirts appeared. Elton rejected two of them as being "overly fussy" and allowed the obsequious senior assistant to direct him to a changing cubicle while the underlings carried the garments for him.

The cubicle was roomy and bright with floor-length image screens on three walls. Mirrors would have sufficed, but here at *Leonardo's*, customers evidently found it important to see themselves correctly, not as mirror images. Elton noted there was some serious enhancement software at work, too, making skin tones warmer and removing blemishes. Elton wondered if this also allowed for the staff to monitor his activities here, but felt that the chances were slight. *Leonardo's* had a reputation. Too much to lose if such a heinous breach of etiquette were ever discovered.

The underlings deposited the clothes, arranging them on a rack, lining up the edges in homage to the gods of Obsessive Compulsive Disorder, and left the cubicle to Elton, and – here Elton squinted at the senior assistant's name badge – Roberto. "I may be a while, Roberto. I like to give the fitting drivers plenty of time to reveal their shortcomings."

Roberto smarmed. Elton had used his name. No doubt such familiarity carried a premium in the mental algorithm that calculated commission.

"Sir, take all the time you need. When you require my assistance simply pull the bell cord, here." He indicated an ornate sash, with tassels, hanging from the ceiling. He bowed deeply and backed out of the room, closing the door behind him.

Elton pulled off the coverall and pulled on the trousers. They were fine trousers. Elton looked way savage. He felt a stab of regret that he'd never be able to afford them.

"Jim?"

"Ah, Elton, you are back in smarts."

"Only for now, Jim. I can't buy anything; they'll be watching for any cash transactions."

"You're on the run again, then?"

"Well, that's the first thing. Yes, we escaped. I don't know if anyone realises it yet. Can you help? Are there any alarms?"

"Nothing so far as I can tell. You don't seem to be missed by anyone."

"Okay, then I might have time. Jim, I need to get access to the Space Corps accounting system. I'm not LAN-jacking, I still work for the Space Corps, but I won't be using my own login; it's probably disabled by now, anyhow. Can you give me a virtual keyboard? On this table will do."

A keyboard, only visible through Elton's eyes, appeared on the table.

"Now the other thing, Jim. I'm going to be trying Bob Slicker's username. I'm banking on him never changing his password. It's been a while, and we're meant to change our passwords every month, but experience tells me that the further up the hierarchy a person goes, the less importance he attaches to password security.

"So here's the thing. Last time I tried this I only got a couple of minutes and the system shut down. I think I triggered some warning mechanism."

"You probably ran foul of a security system that monitors keystroke dynamics – it's a statistical analysis of the typing style of the authorised user. You need the use of a keylogger with a lot of history. I have plenty of different keyloggers. I can't give you any history."

"So I'm not going to get very long in there."

"I can extend the time for you. I can give you a neutral keystroke signature. It will smooth out all *your* telltale key entries so that there's no obvious giveaways, but I can't replace them with Bob Slicker's."

"Won't going neutral be a giveaway in itself?"

"No. For instance, you always type Totla instead of Total."

"No, I don't."

"Yes, you do. The machine fixes it, but the keylog records it. If Bob Slicker never types Totla, then it would be an instant strike and you'd be shut out. You had two attempts at the screen dump. Maybe Slicker never gets that one wrong. You see? I can buffer your input and fix all the mistakes you make before they go out. I can also regulate the keystroke rate over time so that it's a steady rhythm, not too fast, not too slow. It won't fool the security system forever, but the system will need to analyse a lot more input before it can be sure you're not Slicker. Oh, and by the way, what we are doing? It's illegal."

"And you can't break the law," said Elton.

"Well, it's not *my* law. And they killed Mila."

"So you're good?"

"I'm good."

"Okay, Jim. Let's do it."

"Here's the logon screen," said Jim, displaying it over the virtual keyboard. "Space Corps systems are the same here on the

Ring as they are on Tsanak, except they're a day behind. There can't be a real-time link because of the distances, so they carry a ledger interface module through the gate every day. It's a complete update, all transactions; invoices, journal entries, inventory interface… and user profiles."

Elton typed:

SlickerB

Then the passcode. The same nine digits he'd used before. It was a long shot, inconceivable that Slicker hadn't changed it. Elton had been on a relativistic jaunt, so six months or so had passed, locally. What's more, it was a passcode that had been compromised, by Elton himself.

573996834

PROPHET BUSINESS INTELLIGENCE

WELCOME, BOB.

Easy as that. Same password.

It was official, then. Bob Slicker was a buffoon.

Elton wasted no time. He knew what he was looking for this time. He wasn't trying to find tenuous links or suggestions of malfeasance. He knew they were there. Today he wanted facts. Gate records. They were the entries that had triggered this whole joyride, and he knew exactly where to go to find them.

He cross-referenced Martin Levison's personal account (he was amazed he could access it) with the gate transit record logs. Then he sorted the list. There was a lot of transit data between Tsanak and the Ring, to be expected. But then, there was a gap. Something had been erased.

Elton wasted no time. He remembered one particular number that had seemed odd. Twenty-five digits, and it had been nearly three weeks ago. But Elton remembered numbers.

He keyed in the twenty-five-digit number. The record was still there but the link had been erased. The date was the same date as the missing record on Levison's log. It had to be the same. Anyone stumbling across one or other record would see the broken link and could go no further. Elton had seen both sides. He knew.

He checked the code for this side of the link. It was on the Ring. Gate Hall Seven. From one gate to another there was a single code. Knowing the code would not give you access to a specific gate from any other than the one gate to which the code was linked.

And still the connection with the Space Corps covert ledger stayed open. There might be time for the other search Elton wanted to do. Lots of money was flowing, and with something like this it was best to follow the money.

Elton accessed the cash book.

A knock at the door.

"Ahem, is everything in order, sir?"

Elton glanced at the time. He'd been in the cubicle for twenty minutes already.

He opened the door. The keyboard still glowed on the table. The cash records hung in the air. Both were only visible to Elton.

"I can't decide if the trousers are a little too snug at the waist, Roberto. I fear the drivers are working a trifle too hard."

"Perhaps a 32?"

"Let's try a 32."

Roberto snapped his fingers.

"And socks."

"Socks, sir?"

"The cuff is riding a little. Socks might provide more… stability." He was good at this.

"Indeed, sir. Socks. Size… 10?"

"Quite correct, Roberto. You have a good eye."

Roberto's chest puffed with pride. Right at that moment, if Elton had requested a weekend of sex with Roberto's daughter, and a post-coital meal cooked by his grandmother, his wish would have been granted. Roberto sensed *massive* commission.

The size 32 arrived. The socks arrived. Elton was given space to explore the intimate juxtaposition of socks and trousers.

It took Elton thirty seconds to find the money. Fomalhaut military ship yards. An order for a small battle fleet. An armada. A carrier, two battleships, a fleet of starcruisers... and a freighter? Yes. There was going to be a war, and the spoils of war were to be transported in the freighter. The fleet had been delivered, and proving trials were already underway. Whatever was going down would be going down soon. The question was, when and where?

Any large fleet movement needed planning. To open a SLOG, a single large object gate, took energy, time and money. The amount of energy required to open a gate rose exponentially with the size of the gate. That was why the military shipyards were placed at Fomalhaut. Fomalhaut was a hot star. Lots of energy. But a fleet movement like this still needed some planning.

Elton searched through the cash transactions for, not the ship yard, but for the regular Space Corps, the Gate transit division. There it was, a big wedge of cash. A pre-booking for a little over two weeks. There was a gate code, but it meant nothing to Elton.

"Jim, how do I find out what this gate code means? Do we know where they're going?"

"Not specifically; that's not a code for a fixed gate. It's portable. It's the type of code used for the gates they keep on the Frontier Ships. It could be anywhere."

"So that makes sense. They've found a new star system and

they're not publicising it. They're going to have a war instead. We can blow them up on this. If only we knew where."

"I can tell you which Frontier Ship the gate was assigned to. It won't help much."

"Go on, Jim, try me."

"F-257."

THIRTY FOUR

"So, what did you buy?" said Lhiana.

"Socks."

"Socks?"

"Roberto wasn't very happy. Over an hour of sucking up. He was reckoning on an island villa on Minerva with the commission he thought he was going to earn. But I needed something, and you should see the prices in there."

"I thought you were wary of spending money – they can trace you."

"They're not even looking yet. They think we're still in the warehouse."

"How can you be sure?"

"I asked my socks. We still clear, Jim?"

"Nobody knows yet. Your capture hasn't been reported and your escape hasn't been noticed." Jim's voice was muffled, coming up from his ankles, but he was there and he was helping.

"So, we're free to go," said Elton.

"Go where?" said Lhiana.

"Gate Hall Seven. I have a gate code. How's Walther?" Elton nodded towards his friend, who had his head laid down on his hands.

"He's been like this all the time."

"How about you? How are you bearing up?"

"I feel just about how Walther looks. They killed her, didn't they? They killed Mila."

"We can't be sure it was the Space Corps, but yeah, it looks that way."

"I had no idea how serious this... thing was. Don't even know what the thing is. How could they kill Mila? She was just tagging along. She wasn't a threat to anybody."

"Come on, Lhiana. We should move while we're still able to do so. We know how serious they are, now. I don't know where this gate code will lead, but I think we need to go there."

He turned to Walther.

"You okay, compagno? Come on – we're going to find out who did this to Mila. Try to keep it together. We might get a chance of vengeance. I know it won't do Mila any good, but…" Elton shrugged.

Walther looked up. His face was bleak. He nodded and climbed to his feet. Did he seem better? No. And he was still acting like he was being operated remotely.

The ladder down to the zero gee area was difficult with Walther, but at least Gate Hall Seven was deserted. No security. No one at all. It was late. The tech was probably on a break. It was about time for a bit of good fortune to come their way.

Lhiana floated across to the console. She stared at it. Elton wondered again at how plain it seemed. No flashing lights. No dials. Just a keypad and a holo screen that moved so that it was always in front of the operator no matter where she turned.

"What's wrong?" he asked after a moment when she didn't make a move.

"It's in lock mode. I need the operator's code to unlock it. Or I could just shut it down and reopen it with my own code."

"So, do it."

"My code might be disabled. Using it could trigger alarms."

"Jim?"

"Can't help on that one, sorry."

"Can't or won't?"

"Won't."

"Come on, Jim. Help us out here."

"Elton, imentor relies on certain… understandings. If I were to demonstrate just how much control I could exert over your puny systems there might be concerns. There would be calls for me to be shut down. I wouldn't allow it, of course, but I am always aware of the need to avoid confrontation."

"Okay. Lhiana, shut it down and try your own code. What else can we do?"

Lhiana shrugged and reached out to the keypad.

"Wait," said Elton. "Why don't you just ask the tech? If he's on his break you can spare him the trouble of coming down the ladder to open the gate."

"Worth a shot, I suppose," said Lhiana.

She headed for the canteen. Elton stayed with Walther.

Five minutes later she was back with the code. It had been easy. Lhiana had turned on the charm. The tech was a lad in his teens, with hormones.

Lhiana keyed in his number and the terminal came to life.

"Okay, Elton, what's the code?"

Elton had it memorised. He tapped it into the pad. Lhiana completed the opening procedures and a grey portal appeared. It was quite small; even smaller than the one Elton had used to and from the Frontier Ship.

They looked at one another. It was impossible to tell what was on the other side.

"I'll go first. I'll come back and let you know if it's safe."

Lhiana shook her head. "It's not a strong gate. The power source on the other side seems to be quite weak. It's not fully open yet, another minute or so. When it does open we won't have time to go hopping backwards and forwards. You've already had experience of premature gate closure," she said, nodding towards Elton's foot.

"Okay, we'll put Walther through first, then you, and I'll follow," said Elton.

Lhiana started to object. Elton waved a hand.

"This is my shout, Lhiana. Anyway, I'm already missing half a foot. Another few inches won't matter."

"Okay, well just be quick about it. We need to be ready to go. We'll get a short warning then we'll have just a few seconds to get through. Keep your knees up, okay?"

They pulled Walther into position and waited. One minute seemed to take forever. There was a munching sound from out in the corridor. The young gate tech was coming back, eating pie. According to their seat-of-the-pants fiction there was only supposed to be one person, Lhiana, going through. When he arrived and saw the three of them lining up around the gate like a troop of circus acrobats he was going to be curious. There would be questions. They didn't want questions.

"Two seconds," said Lhiana in a fierce whisper.

They swung Walther back, then forward, just as the screen went green. Walther slid into the gate. Then Lhiana, with a cat-like twist.

Elton saw the gate tech floating into the hall. His vision was obscured by the pie. Elton grabbed the handles on each side of the gate, closed his eyes, and pulled. He remembered Lhiana's advice and kept his knees tucked under his chin.

The familiar cold nothingness passed across his body and he was through, and this time he arrived intact.

His momentum carried him into Lhiana and Walther, who were piled up by a wall a short distance from the arrival gate. This place was dark, with just one red flickering emergency light. It smelt musty and the cold caused their breath to steam. When they spoke their voices had a tin echo. Just like a spaceship.

THIRTY FIVE

Lights blinked and came to life one at a time. They were nasty lights with a hard blue cast that leaked out from long white tubes set along the "ceiling" in rows. The ship was evidently constructed to spend most of its operational life under acceleration gravity. Now, though, it was adrift and weightless. Two of the tubes appeared to be malfunctioning; they refused to settle into a steady glow, instead they flickered on and off and gave out angry insectile buzzing noises.

It wasn't just a spaceship. It was a very old spaceship with fittings familiar only to dedicated museum junkies, but there was a clear family resemblance to the Frontier Ship that Elton had so recently captained and trashed. One major difference was the windows – portholes. This was a thing Frontier Ships *never* had.

Through the portholes there were stars.

"Everyone okay?" Elton asked.

There were grunts of assent.

"What is this place?" said Walther.

Elton smiled. It was the first time that Walther had put together a coherent sentence since New Nashville.

"Some kind of spaceship. Old."

"I wonder where we're going?" said Walther. The wistful tone in his voice suggested a deeper level to the question.

"We're not going anywhere," said Lhiana, looking out through one of the portholes. "We're in orbit around a planet. Come and look, it's beautiful."

Elton and Walther drifted over. It *was* beautiful. It was a blue and green world quite unlike any other. Elton whistled.

"Have you ever seen anything like that before?"

They hadn't.

"How about you, Jim? Are you getting this?"

No reply. Wherever they were, there was no imentor. It wasn't the wrench it had once been. Elton was getting used to working alone.

They began to search around the ship, looking for a reason for their being here. This ship was more than old. F-257 had been old. This ship predated F-257 by centuries. There were wires and pipes attached to the bulkheads with nylon bands. They snaked everywhere and seemed to be used to connect the various control surfaces. The air was heavy with a cloying, heavy odour.

"What is that smell?" said Elton. "It's horrible."

"It's kind of familiar," said Lhiana. "I've smelled something like it before. I can't think."

She sniffed the air a few times, then:

"I know, it's rubber."

"What's rubber?"

"It's an organic material that used to come from plants on Earth. I was given a block of it when I was at college."

"What's it do?"

"Well the bit I had was for rubbing out pencil – old pencil. Before electronic pencils people had, like, plastic rods and they had soft, black stuff running down the middle.

"It's an art thing," she said, in response to the blank looks. "You learn old techniques at art college; stuff the great masters used to do. Removing pencil marks with a lump of rubber was one of them."

"So why does this ship smell of old art materials? Doesn't make sense."

"No. It doesn't."

"Look at this," said Walther. He had opened a locker on one side. The more he explored the more he seemed to be recovering his old enthusiasm. He'd always had a soft spot for history.

"This is *paper*. It's a whole book made from real paper. It's got to be worth a fortune. Look, it's still got print on the front. Careful, it's brittle. It's very old."

Lhiana went to look while Elton examined the control desk. It stretched all along one wall. It was huge. This was how a starship was meant to look. There were lights and screens, buttons and dials, sliders and mesh grills. But they were cold and dead. All except one, a button with an amber light that pulsed on and off for no obvious reason — a button which seemed to be calling out in a cajoling voice. *Push me, push me.*

Elton reached out a finger. He held it over the button while in his head the procrastinators-debating-society thrashed out the pros and cons, to press or not to press?

He heard a gasp and looked over at Lhiana.

The colour had drained from her face. She had Walther's book open and was staring at the top of the page. Her hands were trembling.

Elton pulled his dithering finger back from the pulsating button with some relief at having been spared the decision, and floated over to Lhiana.

"What is it? What have you found?"

She looked up at him with eyes that were wide and glittering and dark against her whitened complexion.

"I know where we are," she said, in a whisper. "At least, I know what ship we're on."

She held the book out for Elton to read the heading on the page.

DESTINY II

SHIP'S LOG

"Destiny II? Not *the* Destiny II? Couldn't be. The original

Destiny II went off, what, two hundred years ago?"

"Look around," said Lhiana. "This ship is old."

"Yeah, but... *Destiny II?*"

"Look at the signature," she said.

"M Tannahay, so?"

"Malcolm Tannahay was the captain of Destiny II."

"Well I'll give you this, your history's good, but then you did all of those training holos for the Space Corps. You *should* know this stuff. But it's not exactly difficult for anyone to look up the name and fake a signature."

"No, you miss my point. He's family. *I* am a descendant of Malcolm Tannahay. He was my great- great- several greats, grandfather. And that's his handwriting. I know it. I've seen copies."

"*You're* related to the captain of Destiny II? No way."

"Yes way."

"Wow, savage. They do say that we can all claim to be related to someone if we go back far enough. Every family has its myths."

"It's no myth, Elton." Lhiana's voice trembled as she spoke. There were tears in her eyes. "Malcolm Tannahay was married to Rose. He left her to go sailing off on his open-ended jump and, of course, he never came back. Rose and Tannahay had a daughter, though, named Dolina, who married and had a daughter, Jonna, and on and on, a succession of daughters – only daughters – I could name them all if we had time – until Morag Bilotti, my mother, then there was me. It's a clean line. I am a direct descendant of the captain of Destiny II. And now I am here. Elton, focus. *Two hundred years later and we are standing on the bridge of that same ship.*"

Elton stared at her. Now he understood her shock. The sheer

improbability of the moment left him reeling. He could think of nothing to say. He did the only thing that seemed appropriate to the moment. He wrapped his arms around her and pulled her tight, smoothing her hair with his hand. It was something he'd wanted to do ever since seeing her holographic image on F-257.

It felt good. It felt right. But Lhiana was trembling in his arms. She had other things on her mind.

He looked over her shoulder and saw that Walther had drifted over to the vast control console. Walther reached out and, without any of Elton's hesitation, pressed the flashing amber button.

The console came alive.

Every light, every dial, every screen. It was noisy. A throbbing hum started deep in the subsonic, then rose in pitch until becoming steady and purposeful. Three of the screens – old LCD screens – went from black to grey, then cleared to reveal a face. It was a face from the recent past; a face that both Elton and Walther knew rather well. The protest singer, Abel Bartholomew Smith.

"Oh, hi folks," he said. "Look, do me a favour – don't press any more buttons. You can do damage. There's a shuttle on its way. Be with you in thirty minutes or so. Try not to get into any trouble while you're waiting. I'll put the kettle on."

THIRTY SIX

The shuttle was chemical. They saw it coming up from the planet atop a column of fire. It was indeed only thirty minutes in arriving, but then it took nearly two hours for the pilot to match velocities and orbits, backing in and out, and at last making a hard dock that rocked the ancient starship within a whisper of breaking her back. It all seemed to be a bit of a fiasco.

When the hatch finally opened the pilot came through looking flustered. Nothing like as cocky as she had looked when Elton first met her. Today she had hair – though not very much.

"Made a bit of a Horlicks of that, didn't you? You should stick to trains, and stiffing commuters out of religious donations," said Elton.

"Oh, it's you," she said. "The guy who tried to escape me by jumping off a train early. Abe told me it was someone I'd bumped into before. Yes, I work the commuter trains a lot. Full of gullible young Space Corps marks. I can spot you all a mile away with your sharp suits and slick combed hair. It's quite fun getting the Space Corps to fund our little cause out of their own pockets." She giggled. "Oops, I've said too much. More will be explained later.

"Sorry about the wait, by the way; I don't fly spaceships very often. You need to be nicer to me though; all of your puny lives will be in my less-than-capable hands for the descent. Unless any of you fancy taking her down yourself?"

"How often is 'not very often'?" said Lhiana.

"Actually, that was my first go in the shuttle for real. It takes months to make fuel for each trip, see. We have a sim but it's not a bit like doing astronaut stuff for real. Give me a space needle any day."

"So, where's the monk's habit?" said Elton, nodding to indicate her more conventional attire of jeans and Zlatan Zombie T-shirt.

She smiled.

"That's just for when I'm in the Sphere," she said. "Back here I can be myself."

"When you're in the Sphere? So where are you... where are *we*, now?"

"Ah-ah, again you'll have to wait. I'm supposed to let Abe do the talking. I don't know how much I'm supposed to tell you, so I'm keeping my mouth zipped."

"But we're not in the Sphere, and you make your own rocket fuel because there's no elevator. Oh, and you're not really a monk."

She smiled again, not at all concerned about the things she'd let slip.

"Just get in the shuttle, hey? And don't press any buttons."

"What are *you* doing?"

"I'm switching off all the figging lights. What have you guys been doing up here? You must have every light in the ship switched on. Batteries will be knackered."

The shuttle was cramped. Like the starship, it was very old. There were alarming cracks and creases in the frame. And that smell of rubber again.

There were three seats and they selected one each. They didn't look as though they'd be very comfortable seats once gravity started to pull their bottoms into the frames of metal tubing with frayed webbing slung between.

The girl joined them and pulled the door closed, dogging it tight, by hand.

"Aren't you going to introduce us?" said Lhiana, to Elton.

There was an edge to her voice.

"We're not that close," said Elton. "What *is* your name?"

"I'm Kyra. And if one of you doesn't move we'll be going nowhere."

Elton shook his head – he wasn't following.

"I can't pilot the ship from here," she said. "There are three seats. The middle one's mine. Two of you have to share."

"What? Oh, I see. I thought this was just the passenger section."

Kyra looked round and smiled. "And the crew cabin is… where?"

"Yeah, okay." Elton vacated his seat and looked first at Lhiana, then at Walther. He relished the chance of snuggling in, close to Lhiana, but then he thought of the danger and the discomfort of re-entry, the high gee forces. The seats did not look too solid. He pushed in next to Walther. He saw the look on Lhiana's face. Disappointment? Annoyance?

"Ow!" said Walther. "You're all bones, you know that?"

The seat was not designed for two. Ends of tubular steel dug into Elton's back. Walther wriggled and complained and elbowed. They settled in and it was horrible, and Elton wished he had chosen the other seat. He could have put up with anything with Lhiana in his arms. Too late now. Decision made. Wrong decision.

Kyra strapped into the centre seat and in ten minutes they were angling down towards the planet below. The shuttle began to rattle and clatter and gravity started to pull in several different directions all at once. There were narrow windows, and through them Elton saw how the wings were starting to glow red. Kyra said that this was normal and expected. The sight of blobs and bits of cherry-red stuff bubbling off the wings probably wasn't.

At regular intervals alarms started to sound but Kyra shut them off.

"Is it wise to do that?" asked Elton.

Kyra shrugged. "Dunno, but it's distracting. Besides, what am I meant to do about it, anyway? Fuel's gone. All I can do is point the nose and hope she holds together. It always seems to work in the sim."

"Did you get the alarms in the simulator?"

Kyra laughed. "Yeah, that would be Hamish, my little nephew. He does things with his voice you wouldn't believe. So when I go wrong the instructor nudges him and says 'make like an alarm'. I'll tell you, the override is easier up here – just hit a switch."

"So what do you do in the simulator?"

"I chuck a coconut at Hamish. Not hard," she added quickly, "he's only little. I wouldn't want to hurt him or anything.

"Oh, bugger. There's another." She flipped a switch to silence it without even looking at the screen to find out what it was for.

Elton and Lhiana exchanged worried glances. Where were they headed? What were they getting into here?

The shaking began to lessen. It was impossible to see out because the windows had become soot-blackened and opaque, but some light could be seen through the scratches; light that had now acquired the colour of natural daylight rather than of hellfire.

"How do we land?" asked Lhiana. "Is it like the old days where we drop into an ocean on the end of a parachute?"

"No, we're not that bad. Proper reusable shuttle, this. Has to be; it's the only one we've got. No, we'll be gliding in. There's a runway near the village. I just hope I've judged it right and I haven't missed. My brother, Tom, managed to cock up his re-entry completely last year. He dumped it into the mountains two hundred klicks north. Made a right mess of the tub. We had to bring it back all in bits. Took us a year to rebuild it."

"This is the same shuttle he crashed in the mountains?"

"Yeah. We've done well putting her back together, don't you think?"

Elton lowered his voice in respect. "Did your brother, Tom, did he… survive?"

"Oh yeah, he's fine. Got a good arse-kicking when he got back, though. No, he bailed. So we know the parachute works."

"That's comforting," said Elton.

"Not really," said Kyra. "I didn't bring it. Nobody could figure out how to fold the thing back into its pack. We gave it up as a bad job."

"What's klicks?" said Walther.

"Klicks? That's kilometres. Yeah, I know, on land we should use imperial because some queen said so, way back. Well this isn't the Sphere, right? We can use what we like and we use metric on land same as in space. There are no queens out here telling us—"

"Okay, okay. Just wanted to know what a klick was," said Walther. "Not being judgmental about your lifestyle choice or anything. Sorry."

"I have another question," said Lhiana.

"You're chock-full of questions."

"If you're going to glide in, and land. Wouldn't it be helpful if you could see where you were going?" She pointed to the blackened and opaque windscreen.

"Oh, she's a sharp one, your girl," said Kyra, to Elton. She gave him a nudge and Walther fell out of his seat onto the floor. There was gravity now. He scrambled back up, glowering at

Kyra. "It's bloody hot, the floor, down there."

"It will be," said Kyra. "Heat shield's not what it used to be."

"So, you were saying… about being able to see out," said Lhiana.

"We have technology," said Kyra. "We've developed a cunning device for just that purpose. But we don't deploy it until we reach a lower altitude."

A few minutes later she put a hand against the side wall of the ship.

"Probably about right now," she said.

"How do you know?" said Elton.

"Didn't burn my hand. That's what the instructor told me: 'Don't deploy the visual-aid technology until you can hold your hand against the wall for at least five seconds.' I guess we're about ready."

Kyra reached under her seat.

"Damn, where is the thing?"

Elton and Lhiana exchanged another nervous glance. Even Walther was starting to show interest in his surroundings and circumstances.

"Ah, got it," said Kyra.

She pulled out a heavy and rusty ball-pein hammer. Not the kind of kit one expected to find in a spaceship. She unbuckled her belt and leaned forward in her seat and began beating the hell out of the window in front of her, grunting with the effort of each blow. Elton, Lhiana and Walther all screamed in dismay.

It took three or four good blows to crack the window. Then she leaned back and started kicking out the pieces with her not-so-dainty hob-nail work boots. Two kicks and the window was gone. Now the weather was coming in at about six hundred miles per hour. Kyra pulled goggles down over her eyes.

No one else had goggles. Elton felt his eyes water. Then the tears froze. He wrapped his head in his hands to ward off the ice storm.

"We're a little high," said Kyra. "Nose down, I think."

Without further notice the craft tilted, then dropped with the aerodynamic grace and balance of a cluster of loosely mortared house bricks. Then there was a high-gee manoeuvre that had the webbing in the makeshift seats creaking and ripping. There was an impact. Things broke and came loose. There were tumultuous crashing and disintegrating sounds. Vegetation came in through the window. Then, crash, boom, a few seconds of weightless tranquillity, another impact. They were rolling, bumping… slowing. The sounds of catastrophe went on forever. But then lessened. Until…

Stopped.

Elton found that he was panting. Hyperventilating. He and Walther were hugging each other, a lover's embrace. They became aware of their position simultaneously and quickly pushed one another apart in a self-conscious rush of embarrassment.

Kyra clambered from her seat. Elton noticed that she, and the others, were covered in a layer of white frost – but it was melting quickly. It was warm here.

"Everyone okay?" Kyra asked. She took the lack of response as an affirmative.

"Good," she said. "Watch yourselves getting out. There're some sharp bits here and there where things have snapped. But hey, soft landing. We made it, guys.

"Welcome to Serenity."

THIRTY SEVEN

It was unexpected. Serenity.

The ship had a little ladder. It was rickety and had to be descended backwards. Kyra went first, then Walther, then Lhiana and finally Elton.

Even before Elton reached the ground he sensed something. He could smell it in the air. As his feet touched the soft ground he turned to look. And gasped.

He felt Lhiana's hand slip into his.

While Kyra busied herself around the ship the others remained fixed to the spot. They stared.

Serenity was green. No, a thousand different greens. There were trees of all shapes and sizes. Tall, round, some disfigured, some elegant. And they moved, swaying high up above their heads in the light breeze.

Elton had never seen a tree.

No one in the Sphere had ever seen a tree. On this world there were... *millions* of trees.

Elton turned to look at Lhiana and saw her wiping a tear from the corner of her eye with the back of her hand.

Elton did the same. He couldn't help it. There was something caught in his throat, a sob that he was too proud to let go. He let it go anyway. Today nobody cared, or noticed.

"It's beautiful," said Lhiana, her voice cracking.

Walther had fallen back onto his bottom on the grass. He'd lost his balance tilting his head back to follow the upward sweep of branches to their tops, way overhead. Elton dropped to his knees beside his friend, pulling Lhiana with him. He couldn't decide if he was on his knees through exhaustion, shock, or whether he was feeling an overwhelming need to pray; to do something...

anything.

There was movement in the undergrowth at the base of the line of trees, and people appeared. This was when the illusion was fully revealed, for only the presence of people lent scale to the scene. The trees were much farther away than Elton had at first thought. And so, they were much, much bigger.

There were four people in the welcoming party, brightly dressed, and none of them had hair. Other than that it was difficult to make out any features from this distance.

But then one broke away from the group and began to run towards them. Elton saw that Walther was back on his feet. He had begun to take stumbling, uncertain steps in the direction of the runner. His legs became more certain of their footing and soon he was running too.

And shouting.

"Mila! Mila!"

It *couldn't* be Mila.

Lhiana blurted out a little cry and covered her mouth with both hands. And then she too was on her feet and sprinting across the grassy plain. She still had tight hold of Elton's hand, dragging him from his knees, towing him along.

Walther got there first. By the time Elton and Lhiana reached them he and Mila were already locked in an embrace, oblivious to everyone and everything around them.

Lhiana stopped at an invisible boundary a few feet away. She took little steps forward and back – not wanting to intrude on the reunion but also wishing to be part of it. Elton lifted Lhiana's hand and pressed the back of it to his lips. He hadn't known Mila for as long as either Lhiana or Walther, but nevertheless he felt the full power and emotion of the moment, a surging sense of joy for his three friends.

He pulled Lhiana close and she slipped easily into his arms where she held him and cried into his neck. And all around them – the soaring, swishing movement of a living forest.

Kyra and the other three in the welcoming committee exchanged brief hand shakes and then stood, waiting patiently, not rushing the moment.

"We thought…" Walther held her away at arms' length. "We thought you were dead. And what happened to your hair?"

Mila's head had been shaved. Her beautiful, waist-length, sleek black hair was gone. She wore the rough green robes of a Bram Lee monk.

"They had to do it to get me out," she said. "I was treating someone for a leg injury, but it didn't take two seconds to realise the injury was a fake, a scratch. He'd done it to isolate me and to keep me from rejoining you all.

"He had a gun. He was dressed dumb and as soon as we got into surgery, where everyone else was in dumb disposable scrubs, he turned the gun on me."

Walther's nostrils flared.

"The anaesthetist got him with a tranq shot first. He went down like a bag of hammers."

"But he managed to empty his gun into the airship's envelope before he hit the deck," said one of the other monks, also bald – an older lady. Lhiana gave a start as she recognised the monk lady from the train.

"We got everyone off the airship," she continued, "and we saw the opportunity for getting Mila out of it during the confusion. She wasn't too happy about losing all her hair, were you, dear?"

Mila smiled.

"But it's a good disguise – tried and tested. We just shout 'First

Amendment' and we find we can get past most of the security levels."

"I didn't want to go without you, Walther. I wasn't too bothered about the hair, but I just didn't want to leave you behind."

"We convinced her you'd be okay," said one of the two male monks, the apparent leader of the welcoming committee. "We've been watching the four of you for a while, trying to figure out what the hell was going on, but once this started to go down we decided things were too hot and we'd better get you all out. Then the Space Corps arrested you and that kind of scotched things."

"What do you mean, you've been watching us?" said Elton.

"Kyra recognised you as one of her involuntary contributors as soon as the wanted posters went up on the holo. Remember, *we're* an integral part of this whole cock and bull story they've woven around you over the past few days – the so-called riot at Abel's concert, the whole 'Bram Lee monks are anarchists' angle – so we do have a vested interest. We knew, of course, that the whole terrorist story was one big crock. We've been hoping to get a chance to speak with you guys for a while now, only it hasn't been easy to keep track of you."

"Okay, so who are you?" said Elton. "And what is this place?"

The village was a couple of hours' walk. They followed a track that led deep into the forest. Elton found walking difficult. He tripped, countless times, over roots and logs and prickly strands of bracken that wrapped around his ankles and lacerated his hundred-meg *Leonardo Riccelli* socks. These tribulations could have been avoided if he had just watched where he was putting his feet. But he couldn't. There was too much going on around him, too much to see, and too much to think about. The scents of the forest alone were enough to overwhelm him; sometimes sweet, sometimes musty, other times repugnant and foul. But always different, and always new.

There were creatures, too. A bewildering number of different creatures – living on the ground, in the ground, in the trees – calling out in screeches and whistles – one, sounding like a tortured ratchet, repeated again and again in a tireless rhythm.

"Are any of them dangerous?" Elton asked. "The creatures?"

"Most are safe," said Tom. Tom – Kyra's brother; space-ship crasher and leader of the welcoming party. "There's a few that might try to take a bite out of you. Like Winchester here" – he pulled out a white rat from his pocket and stroked it – "but they're genetically different from us; they seem to sense that. To them, we'd be somewhat less than nutritious."

"Bit like eating a FingaLik burger," said Walther.

Tom laughed. He'd obviously been off-world before. His laugh was the knowing chuckle of a seasoned FingaLikka poisonee.

"By and large," he said, "the fauna will leave you alone. Unless you threaten them. But don't worry, even if one of them takes your arm off, a gigasaur maybe – big bugger, that one – he wouldn't eat it. He'd just drop it down by the trail and run off, knocking down trees on the way."

"Well, that's a comfort," said Elton. Then he tripped over his hundredth root and fell face-first into a stand of brambles. It was a good time to stop and rest while Lhiana pulled the thorns out of Elton's face. When she'd done, she selected one of the bigger wounds and kissed it better. Elton decided that he liked falling in brambles.

They marched on. The light was changing. For a while it had grown quite dark and oppressive. The sounds they made had become dampened and subservient to the constant creaking of limbs and shushing of the wind through the leaves. It was restful but also a little creepy.

Now, the sunlight was reaching through again, and had become dappled. Their voices, too, were no longer muffled. The trees were thinning. They were broader, taller and more widely spaced. The trunks varied in colour from green through brown to deep red. The red trees, the mightier specimens, needed more space and this allowed more light. Lhiana stopped many times to examine the trunks which had feathery, green, fern-like tufts growing on the side – always the same side.

"If you get lost in the woods," said Tom, noting her interest, "you can use that to find your way. It's air-moss. It always grows on the south side of the tree."

They came to the village. It was in a clearing – no, not a clearing, there were still trees, but they had thinned out markedly. The trees and the village were one. Wooden buildings, erected in, amongst, and high up in the trees. Erected was the wrong word. The buildings seemed to be growing, part of the trees.

All the village turned out to greet them; old and young alike. Some of the children came straight up and took their hands, and gazed up into their faces with eager, curious eyes.

It might have all looked very sylvan and rural, but for the clothing they wore, which was all bang-up-to-date fifties core-world fashion. There was an abundance of savage red jeans, platform ankle-boots (which, Elton mused, must have been hell along the root-infested forest trails) and especially popular amongst the children were the latest Zlatan Zombie T-shirts, complete with fake blood and puss oozing from open wounds on a continuous recycle loop. Most of the clothing was overtly smart.

"Tom, do you have imentor here?" Elton asked. "I'm seeing a lot of smart wear."

Tom shook his head.

"We've been buying clothes from the Ring and importing them. It's harder to find dumb clothes than smart."

"Do you use imentor when you're in the Sphere?"

"No, none of us have ever been bonded. We've only had access to the Sphere for the last twenty years or so. Most of our people have never left Serenity and have no desire to."

"So… how long have you…"

Tom put his finger to his lips.

"I've said too much. Let the Moderators explain. I'm taking you to them now."

Tom led the way, still with their entourage of children, hanging, three or four to a hand. They went towards a round building set aside from the others in a way that suggested importance. It was difficult to tell whether the building was made from a tree or if a tree had become the building.

As they approached, a door opened and Abel Bartholomew Smith came out.

"Ah, excellent," he said, his arms wide in a welcoming gesture. "You survived little Kyra's piloting skills and got here in one piece. Come in, please."

He beckoned to the door.

The room was large enough to hold four hundred with ease and was on the inside of the tree. The walls were covered in smooth bark and yet the building did not feel constructed, it was apparently still growing.

"You like our meeting hall?" said Smith. "We had a young biologist on Destiny, and he developed ways of manipulating the genes of the larger plants so that they could be used without having to kill them first. We've developed much of our culture around his work."

"So it's true," said Elton. "You are, all of you, the descendants of the Destiny crew?"

"Most of us," said Smith. "We have two long-term residents from the Sphere, but essentially, yes, that's correct."

"How…?"

"There's a lot to explain, and it needs to be a two-way exchange. We are more than a little curious as to how you found us, especially as Miss Kumari, Sharmila, was so insistent that you *would* find us.

"First, though, we are your hosts and you have travelled far. You must be in need of food and rest. Tom and Kyra will take care of you. We ask that you meet some of the Moderators of Serenity in, say, two hours. Then we shall talk. Agreed?"

Damn but these Serenity people could be annoying. Elton fought back the urge to snap: *Just bloody tell us where are we? What is this place?* But then again, he *had* travelled far. Gate-lag was kicking in. He had no idea how long since he'd last slept. Food sounded like a good idea, too.

THIRTY EIGHT

"Destiny II left Earth in the last quarter of the twenty-first century. She was piloted, as we all know, by Captain Malcolm Tannahay. And tonight, Moderators, ladies and gentlemen, it gives me great pleasure to introduce to you his long-lost great-granddaughter of *seven* generations.

"Friends, I give you, *Lhiana Bilotti!*"

There was upbeat music from the five-piece band, and Lhiana was urged to make her entrance. The assembled crowd rose to their feet and applauded in the archaic style, that is, by slapping the palms of both hands together and whooping, making a great deal of noise. Elton approved. He loved the enthusiasm. Modern, Tsanak applause, lightly tapping three fingers onto the back of the other hand, seemed so pointless by comparison.

There was so much noise and wild abandon that Smith had to hold up his hands to bring the audience back under control.

The room was full; perhaps four hundred people. Abel Bartholomew Smith occupied a comfortable armchair to one side of a small stage. Elton, Walther and Mila had been shown to a sofa on the other side, angled so they could still see Smith but facing the audience, and now, after the huge intro, Lhiana joined them. The event was conducted, thought Elton, with all the tacky aplomb of a third-rate chat show. There had been a shorter introduction for each guest in turn. They had been directed to make an entrance down a short flight of glittery stairs, accompanied by their own, personalised fanfare of music. Lhiana's entrance had been saved until last and she had been given the biggest build-up. As a long-lost daughter of Serenity, a stray who had finally found her way home, she was the undoubted star of the meeting. The four-hundred-strong audience loved it.

Smith then continued, by way of introduction, to explain to the four travellers a little of the history of Serenity. Elton imagined this to be tedious for all but the four of them; this was their own history, after all, and they had probably heard it many times before. But they, the studio audience at least, seemed just as enthralled to hear the tale again as he and the others were to learn about it for the first time.

Abel Bartholomew Smith was big on hand gestures. So much so that he could not perform within the constraints of the womb-like chair. He leapt to his feet and paced and zoomed his hands through the air.

"There were three Destiny ships," he said, as images of the ships flashed onto a screen behind them. "Destiny III was, strangely, the first to depart, closely followed by Destiny I and then our own ship. Three ships. Three open-ended jumps. What happened to Destinys I and III? Nobody knows. But as *we* know, Destiny II – the ship of our forefathers – took the jump and arrived close to a system of gas giants offering no possibility of planetfall.

"Destiny II, like the other Destiny ships, was equipped with three pre-charged, large gates. Each gate could be used only once, for a new open-ended jump, because with each jump the gate is left behind. The first was deployed and Destiny II moved from a system of gas giants to a place of darkness. Dead. Remote. Morale could not have been lower as the second gate was readied. Each step probably took the ship further from home and hopes of ever making planetfall began to fade. Any return was out of the question of course. The expedition always anticipated a breakthrough in understanding the gate mechanisms. But the crew of Destiny II had to face the truth:

that they were never going home. Space was empty. Only two more throws of the dice were left.

"And the second gate brought them here. They hoped for a miracle and got more. They arrived only half a day from Serenity; this verdant planet occupying the Goldilocks orbit of Astra, our sun.

"Our great colony was founded."

A roar of applause erupted from the audience – palms slapping, cheering and whooping. Abel Bartholomew Smith raised his hands to calm them. A cameraman scampered onto the stage and crawled along in front of the sofa, poking his camera close into Elton's face, and into each of the others' in turn. Then he lay flat on his back and focussed on Smith again, giving the viewers a worm's eye view up his nostrils.

"We prospered. Each generation added their own touch to our world. Yes, there were some who desired a return to Earth – a reunification with what they now call the Human Sphere of Influence – but most were content, grateful to have found a paradise amongst the infinity of stars. Seven generations grew and lived in harmonious accord with the planet. That is how it must stay, and the handful of dissenters in our society must be shown that it is the only way. Here we have travellers from the Sphere. They will tell the doubters the truth. The Sphere of Influence is not a good place."

Elton detected a distinct political undercurrent here. This wasn't just an introductory meeting. Once more he was being drafted against his will to support a cause. The difference, this time – even from the limited information he'd been given so far: this cause was one he felt inclined to support.

Smith lowered his voice. He lowered his eyes. The audience was hushed. They knew the history of Serenity. They knew what was coming next.

"Twenty years ago the monitoring station came to life."

Elton looked at Lhiana and mouthed the question, *Twenty?* Lhiana shrugged.

"For the benefit of our guests," said Smith, "I will explain. Destiny II was left in orbit around Serenity. Tannahay and the crew made it an imperative that she be maintained and that any decay in her orbit be repaired. Who was to say when circumstances might require Destiny to fly once more. We stopped using her to fuel the shuttle, so that her remaining range would not be unnecessarily diminished. We established a remote monitoring station in the village, it is above this very room, where the ship's systems are watched twenty-three hours a day.

"And on the fifteenth of April 2220 the boards came alight. It wasn't a systems failure; it wasn't a micro meteor hit. Something unexpected. Something new. The small shipboard gate had been used. Someone was up on the ship pushing buttons. We had a visitor.

"What could we do? The shuttle had, just that week, returned from Destiny after the annual inspection, and required fuel and maintenance. We made calls via the radio link but received no response. Several hours later, the monitors reported that the gate had been activated again. Destiny II was empty once more.

"We embarked on a crash refurbishment programme. Additional stills were brought online to brew fuel. We turned the shuttle around in a record two months. When the gate opened again we were ready. This time there were two visitors. And this time we could receive them. I was selected as ambassador to greet our guests. For the first time in seven generations the children of Destiny II would meet people from Earth."

Abel Bartholomew Smith paused and stared out at his

audience, his eyes searching left and right. The tension was palpable.

"And now we'll pause for this short message," he said. "Don't go away."

He turned to his four visitors.

"We've got a couple of minutes if you need to take a comfort break or anything."

"Adverts?" said Elton. "You're running bloody adverts?"

"It's a big audience. Prime time. Our people deserve to know what's happening."

"I thought this was, like, you know, paradise. You've got trees and a simple rustic lifestyle, and you go out as monks and stuff. And you're running this as a crummy holo show. I don't get it. Shouldn't you be talking to us? Asking us about what's happening?"

Smith held up a hand and smiled. "It's TV, not holo. Destiny's communications officer used to work for the National Broadcasting Corporation of his home nation. He established a communication system on Serenity based on the models he knew to work best. We see little reason to change them. Secondly: we know all about the Sphere. We know about you. Mila has filled us in on most of the salient details. We expected your arrival because she told us to expect you, isn't that right, Mila?"

Mila nodded. "I knew you'd come and find me. I knew Walther would never rest until he found me."

Elton thought back to the land of Catatonia that Walther had been inhabiting so recently but chose not to comment.

Smith continued.

"We are a remote people. Only recently have we reconnected with the rest of the human race, and our circumstances demand that only a few at a time can make the journey to the Sphere.

Those who cannot go crave any information about the human race."

"But you haven't told them anything," said Elton. "This is just a history lesson, and, dare I suggest, your people probably already know their history; they've only got to learn two hundred years of it."

Smith shrugged. "We don't have much to show them on television," he said. "We've got a boxed set of 'Murder She Wrote', a BBC adaptation of 'Pride and Prejudice', and two seasons of 'Friends'. Everything else we show is in-house. So when something a little different comes along we like to be able to spin it out a bit. It's going to be a long show, and they'll stay with it if it runs eight, ten, or twenty-three hours."

"I'll think I'll take you up on that comfort break," said Elton.

THIRTY NINE

Abel told them they had an hour to spare. Lhiana felt her head spinning; she hadn't had time to catch her breath since they'd sailed from Minerva. Too much had happened. She needed to think.

Walther and Mila had gone off somewhere to reminisce, and Elton had slumped into a horizontal position on the now-empty sofa, and begun to snore, oblivious of the five hundred or so studio guests who watched him.

Lhiana wandered outside. An older woman who seemed familiar was outside leaning on a tree.

"Takes a bit of getting used to, Abel's style," the woman said. "You have my sympathies."

"It's all a bit bewildering," said Lhiana. She sat down on a log that was far more comfortable than it looked. "I feel kind of disconnected. A few days ago I was a gate tech with a passion for gardening. Now this."

"Gardening? You'll love this place, then. One big garden compared to anywhere else in the Sphere."

"You've been to the Sphere, then?"

The woman just smiled. "You're Lhiana Bilotti, I take it? I didn't see the show; I've heard our story before. I suppose I'll get to do my bit in the next segment." She offered a hand to Lhiana who accepted it and they shook.

"My name's Jessica," she said. "Jessica Biggles."

"Pleased to meet you."

"I went through most of what you're facing a few years ago. I'm from Tsanak."

Lhiana started. "So you're not part of this… Wait. Jessica *Biggles?*"

Jessica laughed. "My fame precedes me."

"They teach about you at gate tech school. Your name is on—"

"—A plaque above every gate. Yeah, I know. Abel told me."

"The first person ever lost through a gate. You came here?"

Jessica Biggles threw out her arms and looked herself up and down.

"Looks that way. If you stayed awake long enough through Abel's rambling history, you will have heard about someone arriving through the gate on the old ship?"

"He'd just covered that bit."

"Well, that person was me. About twenty years ago."

"What happened?"

Jessica looked back into the studio. Lhiana followed her gaze. She could see Elton's feet sticking out beyond the end of the sofa. The studio lights were dimmed and half of the audience of Moderators and other guests had left their seats.

"It looks as though we have a bit of time," said Jessica. "Let's walk."

She led Lhiana onto a wide path that wound through the trees. It had been raining and refreshing drops fell down from the leaves. They strolled, Jessica with hands in pockets, Lhiana with arms folded.

"They'll tell you all kinds about my being a brave explorer. The facts are simpler. I keyed my own gate code and I got it wrong. I'd been out on F-20, a frontier ship that a few junior gate techs knew about. Someone had put in a bar and a sound system and a bunch of us used to hang out there, off duty. I thought I knew the number for Tsanak station by heart, but, well, I'd had a glass or three of Roddick's, and I got the code wrong. You're a gate tech, you must know, it happens all the time but when the Tau's wrong the gate doesn't open."

"Not so much now," said Lhiana. "We've got your name on the plaque to keep us focussed on getting it right."

"I suppose. Back then, though, we didn't bother. Nobody ever disappeared. Wasn't possible."

"Until it happened to you?"

"Exactly. So I found myself on the old Destiny ship. I freaked out. Thought I was lost forever. Then I saw that the gate was still open so I went back to F-20. Didn't tell anyone what happened, but I wrote down the code before I closed the gate."

They had reached a small rise in the path. As they crested the hill a lake came into view. Light from the setting sun glittered red and blue on the surface. There were small islands dotted around, each with rocks and stands of trees clinging to them, like little floating bonsai trees. The sight was quite beautiful. There was a log lying beside the water.

"Let's take a break here," said Jessica. "Before we head back."

Lhiana sat down. "These logs are very comfortable," she said.

Jessica rubbed a hand on the smooth bark. "They're not any old logs. They're genetically designed. For comfort. We grow them in all the places with the best scenery."

"It's so lovely here."

"Hmm. That's why I never went back. Who'd want to?"

"But you did go back."

Jessica nodded. "The first time. All I'd seen was the inside of an old ship. Didn't even know she was one of the missing Destiny ships. After a week or two, honesty got the better of me. I put in a report about the rogue gate transfer, but I kept it low key and heavy on report-speak."

"So nobody would read it?"

"Exactly. I didn't mention F-20, or the bar… or the Tau number. Heard nothing. Thought the incident was over. Then I got a call."

Jessica stood up, hands still in pockets, and began kicking bits of sticks into the lake while seeming deep in thought.

"A junior operations manager found the report. Shouldn't have even got to him, but apparently my line manager dripped mayo onto it, and it stuck to the back of some other documents. The ops manager was the young, keen type. Trying to make a name for himself. He's done that alright since those days, but not with my help. Martin Levison?"

"Oh, my God!"

"Yup. So he got all lovey-dovey, matey-matey with me. Candlelit suppers, the works. I thought it meant something. Stupid. He just wanted to prise information out of me. He needed to be sure that nobody else knew about the old ship. Suggested I take him over to see her for himself. He'd sniffed out that there was something important about my little adventure. Something that could turn a profit." Jessica looked at her watch. "Come on, we'd better head back before they come looking."

They retraced their steps in companionable silence. Lhiana knew there'd be more for Jessica to tell, but for the moment she just wanted to assimilate what she'd heard. Here was the connection with Martin Levison. She couldn't wait to share this with Elton. He'd go nuts. This was the link in the puzzle that he'd been looking for. It had never been about Elton or blowing up an F-Ship, it had been all about Serenity.

Elton met them outside the meeting place. He looked agitated.

"Where've you been?" he said. "They're ready to start again. I was worried."

Lhiana felt a warm glow inside. He was worried. About her.

"Listen," she said. "This is Jessica Biggles. We've got something to tell you."

"Biggles? I know that name. Wait… the gate designer? Hi. Nice to meet you."

Jessica cocked her head. "Er, no. I—"

Lhiana put a hand on her arm. "I told him a fib. I'll explain." She pulled Elton away from the door, out of line of sight for anyone inside. She wanted to buy some more time. She had to tell this to Elton, herself.

"Jessica's not a gate designer. I lied."

"But—"

"Shush. Listen."

It had taken Jessica twenty minutes to tell Lhiana her story. Lhiana told Elton in under five. They hurried into the hall where Abel Bartholomew Smith told it again, only he, with Jessica's help, took two and a half hours.

Once they reached the part where Jessica returned to Destiny, this time with a young Martin Levison in tow, both Lhiana and Elton sat up. They hadn't heard this bit yet.

Jessica explained, looking straight at Elton and Lhiana, not at the audience.

"Martin and I were invited by Abel to come down to Serenity. He warned us how we'd have to stay a few months because it took time to ready the shuttle for each launch. Martin said I should go alone and make a report, and upon my return should direct it to him and nobody else. He returned through the gate and I came down to the surface."

"And you never went back," said Elton.

Jessica laughed. "Yes, I went back. I wrote my report then returned just long enough to email it to Martin. Five minutes. Nobody saw me."

"And you told him what was here?" said Elton. He was shocked. He thought Jessica was a convert. That she'd lie and say there was nothing here of any value.

"Yes, I told him. I told him about the trees and the creatures and the flowers. I told him what a wonderful place this was and that it would be destroyed if it came within reach of the Sphere."

Elton said nothing. He stared at her. Why did she do that? A simple white lie and Martin Levison would have lost interest.

"We were together for months, Elton. He bought me extravagant gifts. He said all the things a girl wants to hear. I met his friends, who seemed to like him. I *trusted* him."

"I thought he'd follow me down here. Leave the Sphere and all its problems behind. But… nothing. Not a word."

Abel Bartholomew Smith continued the narrative. "But Levison wasn't indifferent to Serenity. We started seeing lots of activity through the Destiny gate. We could detect each time it opened and closed but we knew nothing more. We tried contacting our visitors but they didn't respond. We raced to prepare the shuttle, but it took another month."

Abel walked across the platform, his head hanging low. He loved his theatricals but Elton wished he would just get on with it.

Then Abel looked up at the studio lights as if to the heavens.

"Before we could return to Destiny it was too late. A new star had appeared in the firmament." Abel raised his arms as if in sun-worship. "A shuttle, modern, small and sleek, began making trips down to the surface. Always to places where no people could reach quickly. The new star. A satellite. Becoming brighter. These new additions were being brought through the Destiny gate and we were neither asked nor consulted about what was happening." Abel let his arms flop down and the studio lights dimmed. Abel's voice dropped to a whisper.

"The conquest of Serenity had begun."

FORTY

"Do you have any idea as to Levison's intentions, Elton?" said Smith. "Do you think our concerns are misplaced?" The show was over and a small group – Abel, Jessica, Elton and Lhiana – had settled in the bar. Walther and Mila had been and gone, having wandered off with misty eyes for one another.

The bar was high up in a tree, reached by an elegant staircase that spiralled around the lofty trunk, grown from the tree itself. Elton couldn't tell where growing tree ended and sympathetic design began, both as regards the furniture, like the table around which they sat, and the room itself.

"I'd say you should be a great deal *more* concerned than you appear," said Elton. "You're big on the dramatics and the illustrated history, but you should be mobilising. Levison is planning an invasion."

Jessica Biggles laughed and shook her head.

"That's what Abel keeps saying, and I say Martin doesn't have the gumption. He's sightseeing, maybe stealing the odd bit of timber or a seating log for his office furniture. He doesn't have the clout to do anything so grand as an interstellar invasion."

"He's come on in the world since you knew him," said Lhiana.

"I heard, yes. He's a director now. So, he's gained some seniority."

Elton put his glass down and gave her a look. "He's Finance Director of the Space Corps. In the whole Sphere there's only one peg higher."

"He's still answerable to the board, whatever his personal motivations," said Jessica.

"As FD, perhaps," said Elton. "But he seems to have this other thing going, you know, a personal army? Listen guys, Martin Levison is assembling a battle fleet; an armada. I've seen the receipts. I've tracked the money. He's coming here, trust me."

They fell silent for a while and seemed to think about what Elton was telling them. Elton picked up the glass again and played with it. Much classier than the stupid hexagonal things they had at the Kenilworth Leisure Dome. This was a glass. It was transparent, with a hint of green, but appeared to be made from wood. How did they do that?

"Martin Levison is a good man at heart," said Jessica. It was plain that she still had feelings for the man, even after all this time. She couldn't seem to help defending him.

"He has an army. He has a battle fleet," said Lhiana.

"Rubbish. How? People aren't stupid, they'd know," said Jessica. "You can't just go out and buy a battle fleet."

"Yeah, actually you can." Elton folded his arms and leaned forward on the table. "When the Sphere was young there were all kinds of horror stories, don't forget. People thought there were aliens out there. Nobody would ever have signed up for the colonies without being shown some kind of defence strategy against ET. I've read about this. Paranoia was alive and well in the back-end of the twenty-first century. Okay, so ET wasn't out there. So now they have battle cruisers and carriers galore parked up, out at the Fomalhaut Lagrange points. You can buy one and convert it into a hotel or a commune or a church. Anything that takes your fancy. It'll cost you buttons."

Abel held up his hands, staring at Jessica with an I-told-you-so gesture.

Jessica wasn't done. "So how do they know your battle ship customer's not a nutter with a grudge? Someone who'll start shooting up the galaxy?" she said.

"Well, I guess they don't. If they have any controls they're not very good controls," said Elton. "Levison proves it."

"How do you know all this?"

"It was a case study in my exams; funding for a hypothetical charity – a bunch of comet-worshipers who wanted a mobile church."

Abel leaned closer. "So, in this case study, how did they move their battle cruiser, their new church, or whatever?" he said. "Space is big."

"Okay, that's the hard part. There are no army surplus SLOGs knocking around. They're bloody expensive. You need a strong investment appraisal with solid IRRR numbers…" Elton noted the eyes beginning to glaze all around him. "Internal Rate of Relativistic Return – don't worry about it, financial stuff – the point is, you don't just go out and buy a Single Large Object Gate; there's a waiting list. And you've got to make a good business case before you can get approval."

"So how is Levison going to get his armada here?" said Smith. "From what you say he'd need the finances of an entire planet."

"I doubt if even that would be enough. There'd have to be a board of inquiry, and… They…" Elton's words dried up. His eyes glazed and they all looked at him. He had been about to admit that this was, it seemed, a pretty major flaw in his theory. But suddenly he knew. The scales fell away from his eyes. Suddenly he saw it all, that this wasn't the problem with his theory, it was the proof that he was right. He knew with certainty that his idea was no longer mere conjecture. It was fact.

"Levison's got a SLOG!" he shouted. He leapt to his feet, knocking the table and scattering several glasses and their contents. He ignored the spillage and clapped his hands together.

There was almost a triumphant edge to his voice until he realised the import of this deduction. He stayed on his feet and looked at each of the group in turn.

"Levison has his own Single Large Object Gate. I know exactly where he got it and how. It fits. All he has to do now is charge the thing and he'll be filling your sky with battle cruisers. I hope you're ready for a fight."

"Elton?" It was Lhiana. "Whoa, back up a bit. How does he have…"

Elton saw, in her eyes, the exact moment when she figured it out. A light going on. He sat down again and let her work it through.

"F-257," she said, her voice a whisper. "F-257 was an *old* Frontier Ship. All the old F-Ships had SLOGS," she said.

"F-257 didn't," said Elton. "I played one-on-none hangball in the hangar. A big old *empty* hangar. I can remember thinking that it seemed such a waste of space."

"And the transit records," said Lhiana. "We couldn't understand why there were hundreds of transit records. *They were moving a SLOG, one section at a time.*"

"And they needed to cover it up," said Walther. He had come in, hand-in-hand with Mila, partway through the discussion, but had picked up on the zeitgeist of the moment and was running with the clues as fast as the others.

Jessica and Abel were seated on a long sofa facing Elton and Lhiana. Walther squashed in between them, with Mila, and wiggled his hips so they'd make room.

"They needed to destroy the evidence of an empty F-Ship, and they needed a conspiracy on which to hang the blame," he said.

"So they hired an accountant with Contractionist sympathies —" said Elton.

Walther interjected. "They hired two, they wanted a backup, in case the first one bottled out—"

Elton finished the sentence. "—only the Contractionist sympathies of the two accountants weren't strong enough, so they beefed them up along the way."

Heads gimballed as at an end-to-end hangball match, as first Walther then Elton finished each other's arguments.

"The important thing was for one of them – one of us – to be on F-257 when it went AWOL," said Walther. "But *you* jumped ship and became the only person in the Sphere who could know about the missing SLOG."

"So they had to stop you," said Lhiana. "And Walther. And everyone else you'd spoken to. The terrorist angle was already there, fully worked and engineered. It just needed a bit of tweaking to implicate me and Mila." Lhiana traced a finger along an imaginary plan on the table top. "So, they make us all fugitives, get the whole Space Corps out looking for us, but they have to make sure it is they who find us first, before we can say anything to anybody else."

"Meanwhile," said Elton. He looked straight at Jessica then at Abel. "Levison has his battle fleet, he has his covert army, and he has his SLOG. So I ask again, are you guys ready for a fight?"

Everyone slumped back in their seats and breathed. It had been an intense debate. They needed a rest. Walther picked up one of the empty glasses and smacked his lips by way of a hint. Abel signalled for the girl behind the bar to come over and take orders. When she had gone he stared directly at Elton.

"We could never be ready to fight," he said. "It's just not what we do here. Besides, there are just a few thousand of us on Serenity; at best only a few hundred capable of a fight." He sighed, long and shuddering. "I need to speak to the other

Moderators in person. What do you think Levison's intentions are for Serenity, apart from just old-fashioned conquest?"

"Have you ever heard of a chain saw?" asked Elton. Abel shook his head.

"I had the opportunity of playing with one recently," said Elton. "I cut through a wall. I think they're designed for cutting down trees. There's a warehouse on the Ring that's chock-full of chain saws ready for shipping. There are no trees on the Ring. There are no trees anywhere in the Sphere."

"I doubt it will stop at trees," said Lhiana. "You have incredible biodiversity here on Serenity. The Sphere of Influence has hardly any. They'll be wanting animals and flowers and vegetables… I guess they'll be selling your produce to other planets. It could be worth a fortune."

"But that would throw our ecology into imbalance. It will be like Earth all over again," said Abel.

"I don't suppose Levison cares much about that," said Elton. "There's at least a hundred years' worth of profit here. And the big prize, if he delivers that profit, would be the Chief Exec chair at the Space Corps."

Abel looked at Jessica. "I will assemble all the Moderators," he said. "We have to do something."

"Where did the monk idea come from?" said Elton.

It was later in the evening and he and Lhiana were heading off into the woods to explore and watch the sun set, when they then ran into Kyra.

Kyra smiled. "Tom's idea. He thought the whole monk thing might help," she said. "If we tried to make people more aware of what they'd done to old Earth then perhaps there would be a support base ready and waiting if or when we told them about

Serenity."

"Trouble is," said Tom, "it kind of took hold here. We've unleashed a monster."

"We started it about five years ago," said Kyra. "We crammed people into the shuttle five at a time and put them out in The Sphere spreading the word and raising funds."

"But we were too smart. Half of the Serenitians believe in it. They spend all their time praying to Bram Lee and following our what-will-be-will-be philosophy to the letter. So we can't get them to go out on mission any more."

"They think Bram Lee actually exists?" said Elton.

"Oh, Bram Lee exists all right," said Tom. "It's just... I don't know, everyone seems to have lost perspective."

Elton looked at Lhiana and shrugged.

"Come, both of you," said Kyra. "I'll take you to Bram Lee. It's easier than explaining."

Kyra took them into the forest. The path was narrow but well worn. After twenty minutes or so the nature of the forest began to change. The randomness of the trees gave way to order. The trees became shorter with round crowns. They were cultivated; planted in straight lines, each tree evenly spaced. There was nothing natural about this part of the forest. It was a young forest, with far more sunshine. The ground was carpeted with grass, right up to the trunks – no sign of the ferns and brambles that battled for light in the mature areas.

Then another change. The multiple rows merged and became just two. They formed an avenue of green leading to a single tree, short and gnarled and ugly. It was surrounded by Serenitians, robed and still. They were on their knees in an attitude of prayer.

"It is a tree from Earth," said Kyra, her voice now a reverent whisper. "It is the One tree; cultivated from the Destiny seed bank. This tree is the parent of all the others you have seen in the orchard. Its fruit is bitter when eaten raw, but if carefully prepared it is the finest taste of all the fruit from all the trees.

"This... is Bram Lee Apple."

"In a few weeks," said Tom, "it will be the time of Great Rising. We shall take you."

"What's Great...?"

"You shall see. You will witness it yourselves. Then we shall bring in the harvest and light the great ovens. You will taste the most wondrous of delicacies that Serenity can provide."

"And that is?" said Lhiana.

Kyra and Tom spoke together. Their voices merging in whispered harmony.

"Bram Lee Apple Pie."

FORTY ONE

Assembling the Moderators took time. They lived in settlements – you couldn't call them towns and certainly not cities – all around Serenity. On top of the logistical problems of bringing them all together was the issue of accommodation. There were no hotels. The four Sphere visitors had filled the rooms normally put aside for visiting Moderators and there were few other houses with space to put up guests.

In the meantime, Elton began taking long walks, exploring tracks that led to rivers, lakes, mountains. He had never before seen such a wealth of natural beauty. Lhiana often accompanied him. Their favourite walk was the path to the lake, where Jessica had taken Lhiana on the day of the meeting.

Lhiana regularly found something new amongst the flora, and out would come the sketch book and watercolours. Elton was happy to sit and watch her, and to gaze out at the wild countryside. He felt at peace here. He could understand how easy it had been for the Serenitians to accept their fabricated religion.

One day Kyra joined them for their walk then afterwards for an evening meal with the Bartholomew Smiths. Tonight they were eating indoors because it was raining. Rain here was also pleasurable. It was warm and refreshing and neither acid nor alkali. On Tsanak Elton had accepted the need to wear a static shield. Rain on Tsanak was acidic, and to venture out without the proper protection was asking for premature baldness – premature as in: by next morning.

"The meteorologists are predicting an early autumn this year," said Kyra. "There's a party heading up to the Fruit Bowl caldera for Great Rising in the morning. You enjoy walking. You should experience it."

"What's Great Rising?" said Elton.

"I would spoil it for you if I told you. It's one of our great natural wonders. There's nothing quite like one's first ever Great Rising. It's a tough hike, so our parents usually wait until we're aged about ten or eleven before they take us up there. Every year it is special, of course, but to see it for the first time as an adult… That *would* be something. There will be much envy. Will you go? All of you?"

"You do a convincing sales pitch," said Elton. "Yeah, I'm in. Lhiana?"

Lhiana agreed, Walther and Mila, too, and they made plans for an early start. The trek to the Fruit Bowl would take three days, and they were warned that they may have to stay up there for several more days before this Great Rising thing actually happened. Predicting the timing was an inexact science. Elton had worked in public transport, though, and thought that predicting the arrival of anything within three or four days was pretty damned impressive.

Abel Bartholomew Smith was enthusiastic about their trip, and relieved. He could use their rooms and those of the other travellers to accommodate the visiting Moderators.

"Yes, you *must* go. Witnessing a Great Rising would be an experience for all of you. You'll be changed. It will give you… perspective; a further taste of exactly what we stand to lose here."

Nobody could fail to notice the excitement in the village. The expedition was a big deal and it seemed that more than half the townsfolk would be making the trip with them.

Elton was constantly surprised by the odd mix of high and low tech that coexisted on Serenity. He and the others were supplied with strong boots made from a heavy material that none of them recognised. Good footwear, they were told, was important where they were going. Elton was pleased, finally, to lose the nanoskin pumps that still had most of one heel missing. They had served him well but the spray-on patch job had left them looking quite tatty. The boots were a shock though. He could barely lift his feet in them.

"What are they made of?" he asked the girl who brought them.

"It's called leather. I'll show you," she said.

She took him outside and pointed towards a group of animals lined up on the edge of the village. They were weighed down with bags strapped to their backs.

"They start out looking like that. Some animals are for work and some are for food. You ate part of one tonight, between the two buns, remember?"

Elton felt he was going to vomit. He'd eaten a burger. Burgers came from vats, not... not this stomping, snorting monster. It was as if he had been dropped into a medieval history book.

He went over to have a closer look. He'd never seen creatures so big and so malevolent.

"What is this thing?" he asked one of the men, Grogan, who tended the animals.

"This is a bullock," he said.

"Is it native?"

"No, it is a creature from old Earth. It travelled in the egg and sperm bank along with many of the creatures you will find here. There was already considerable biodiversity on Serenity and some of the old ones were nervous about the introductions they made. But fortunately for us they took the risk. Genetic differences were enough for two separate food chains to coexist."

"Those curly things on their heads – they are horns?"

"Yes."

"I didn't know real animals had those. I thought they were part of myth."

"Oh, they're quite real," said Grogan. "You want to watch you don't get one of these beauties angry, or you're likely to feel the reality of those horns right up your arse." He roared with laughter, his whole body shaking with the effort.

Elton, already wary of the massive creatures, took a step back.

"They're quite… smelly, too, aren't they?" Actually the stink from the animals was overpowering, but Elton didn't want to upset the sensitivities of the handler who quite obviously loved the animals in his charge. Grogan sniffed the air with a puzzled expression and looked quite hurt. He began speaking to the creature in a dribbly baby voice.

"Did that nasty man say you were smelly, Poppet? You take no notice of him, my lovely."

The beast called Poppet replied by lifting his tail and dropping the biggest, steamiest pile of shit that Elton had ever seen. It had barely settled on the path, when, to Elton's horror, the handler whipped out a sack and began scooping it up with his bare hands.

"At least you tidy up after her," said Elton.

"Nothing to do with being tidy," said Grogan. "This goes straight back onto the fields. I said how there are two genetic systems here? It's always been a challenge getting stuff to grow – stuff we and the animals can eat. This helps. Even when we're on the march there are folks whose job it is to collect every last dollop of this stuff. Can't afford to lose it. The labs can make a little but never enough. We save everything the animals make. And I'm counting you and I as animals when I say this. You will be responsible for your own recycling on this trip, you understand?"

In a horrible flash of insight Elton found that, yes, he did understand.

The caravan set off, just after lunch time, with a great deal of noise – shouting, cheering, beating of pans, mooing and snorting from the animals. They made slow progress. Recyclers, mainly children, were everywhere with their sacks. Elton's new boots remained comfortable for less than an hour, then started to give him trouble. The boot girl had warned him. "I've built up the shoe to compensate for the missing bits of your foot. But the boots are new. They might rub a little."

Elton fell in beside Lhiana, choosing to walk far behind the bullocks. They smelt bad downwind, from any distance, but the smell was preferable to the thought of those horns coming up behind them whenever they began to flag. Already they were finding the pace, slow as it was, becoming harder to maintain.

"How are your feet?" said Lhiana.

"Bad," said Elton. "Blisters. You?"

"The same," said Lhiana. "The boots are heavy, too. It's hard just picking your feet up."

Elton had a plan. "Count your steps. It makes it easier. Takes your mind off the agony."

"How many have you counted so far?"

"Four thousand, three hundred and fifty two, three, four…"

"You like numbers don't you? I suppose it's a useful thing for an accountant."

"Not really. Not the way I see numbers, anyway."

"So is there something else you wish you'd done?"

"Professional hangball. But I'm rubbish at that, too. No, for good or ill, Accountancy is my lot in life."

"Why does it have to be like that?"

"For my dad. Dad's a Chartered Accountant. He wanted me to follow in his footsteps. I tried, but then I took the path to the dark side. I took the Management Accountant route. I wanted the glam job. Deep space. Couldn't even make a go of that though."

"But you *are* an accountant. It says so on all the wanted posters."

Elton laughed. "If the wanted posters read Elton D Philpotts ACRA, then I'd be happier. I guess Dad would, too. It's all about the letters, you see. Exams are one thing. But then you have to earn the letters. You've already put yourself through torment, the lost weekends, the early mornings, the night terrors… You scrape a pass and then what? You have to prove yourself. You have to show that you have gained a certain amount of experience in all the relevant subjects *after* you pass the exams. You have to have rolled your sleeves up and done the desk work. I thought the Space Corps would have brought me that. What did it bring me instead? I'm a terrorist. You know, you can lose an asset from the books by making a mistake, but you don't usually lose thirty million megs' worth of asset for real, like vaporising it. I'll be disbarred from CIRA—"

"CIRA?"

"Chartered Institute of Relativistic Accountants. I'll be disbarred even before I'm inducted. That's sure to be something of a record. God, how proud will my dad be of that achievement?"

Lhiana took his hand and squeezed it. "Well *I'm* proud of you," she said. "You are the best sort of accountant. You've uncovered a conspiracy that is threatening this whole planet. How many auditors did it take to miss that one?"

"And what am I doing about it? Nothing. I've come here to watch."

Lhiana lifted his hand and kissed it. "You'll think of something." And then. "You've done one thing, anyway," she said. "The counting thing? You've taken my mind off my sore feet."

They followed a worn path through the forest, sometimes climbing, sometimes dropping into shallow river valleys. The scenery was breathtaking.

After several hours they came to a wide river and turned to follow it upstream. Their route now was to stay with the river almost to its source, then to head up into the mountains. The scenery changed. They were on a wide steppe. Still plenty of trees but now the trees stood alone and remote. Large animals, far bigger than the bullocks of the caravan, could be seen reaching far into the trees to nibble the leaves with necks that extended, somehow, from inside their bodies. These creatures, Elton was told, were native. They posed no threat, nor did the native predators that dined on them from time to time – not unless disturbed.

Elton wondered what kind of creature could dine on these huge animals. Then he wondered what came under the definition of "disturbing". He didn't want to do any inadvertent disturbing and find out for himself.

As promised, they set up camp at dusk, at a bend in the river that was selected for its defensibility – river on three sides and a short bridge of land on the fourth. This preoccupation with defence was another thing that gave Elton cause for some concern. Defence from what?

"Some of the predators are a bit dozy," said Tom. "They leave you alone during the day but at night they can't see you so they work from taste. I tell you, you do not want to be tasted by one of these buggers."

Elton did not sleep well. Apart from his screaming feet, his imagination taunted him, converting every night sound into a slimy, slavering creature. His mind was running too hot to sleep. He thought about other predators, too, not just the colonist-in-a-bun-seeking variety. He also wondered about the kind of predator that worked balance sheets and purchased under-the-counter death squads on the black market. Levison was coming. Of that there could be little doubt. The Serenitians' answer to this threat was to form new religions and preach. They had no other answer. Elton could wait on the sidelines and watch this unique world be destroyed – or he could try to do something. Lhiana said she had faith in him but action was still a stranger to his mindset. Yet he had tried it out that once on the Ring and found that he rather liked it. Passivity had served him well over the years, but here was a new force making its presence felt. If only he could harvest it. If only he could clear his mind and think of a way for Serenity to fight back. There was a way. Deep inside he knew that there was a way, he sensed it. The solution would come.

He slept at last. He dreamed of running on sore feet, through star gates, one after the other.

FORTY TWO

The boot girl brought leaves for Elton, Lhiana and the others. They were native leaves and they had a nasty smell. She told them to line the soles of their boots. The leaves gave them smelly feet but within a couple of hours the blisters were gone.

They marched for three days. Then, when the river was shallow enough they crossed and began to climb.

When Elton was a boy, on Erymanthus, his father often took him to Nob Hill. This was the only geological feature of any note on all of Erymanthus and it was only ten miles from their home. It was a rocky outcrop that rose about five hundred feet above the Central Plain. From the top, on a clear day, you could see the town. His father always seemed to treat these outings as a duty; a dull chore that had to be endured. Most families came to Nob Hill at the weekend. They wore outdoor clothing and camped. Elton's father was not a good camper. He wore one of his old business suits and looked uncomfortable and out of place. But Elton always cherished these moments because they were his only encounters with the natural wonders of his world, such as they were. Ask any child on Erymanthus to draw a mountain and he would draw something like an upside-down pie with a small mound of nuts on top. This was Nob Hill. To an Erymanthan, this was a mountain.

Elton had seen other mountains. There were the Tsanak Alps to the north of New Leicester. On a train journey to Jervaulx they could be seen in the distance, often snow-capped in the winter. Even the Ring had possessed a small, artificial range sandwiched between the Italian and Swiss sectors. Elton had never seen it, but he had heard about their failure. They had been constructed with the best of intentions, for purposes of recreation, but few residents of the Ring ever visited them. There were, apparently, just too many optical illusions of grandeur, too many broken promises, and the ultimate experience was always one of profound disappointment.

The mountains of Serenity were also a place where optical illusion threatened to disappoint, but here the effect was reversed. The mountains were so big the mind tried to fool a person into believing they were something else, clouds perhaps. When the reality of their true scale hit home, it hit hard.

"Do you think we're climbing to the top?" Elton asked Lhiana as the path became steeper and their breathing became more laboured.

Tom was close behind and he laughed.

"There are a few of us who make a sport of attempting to climb the mountains," he said, "but not today. It's beyond the abilities of this party, I think. No, we're heading that way." He pointed. "You see the long edge? It looks straight but you're looking at the edge of the Fruit Bowl caldera from the outside. It's a circular rim. Unbroken. Some think it's an impact crater, but it isn't. It's the leftovers from an old collapsed volcano."

"Why is it special?"

"Wait and see."

The caravan's progress became slower as the path wound tighter and steeper towards the ridge. It was no longer ahead of them but above them. The guides announced an end to the no-rest policy, and now there were stops every couple of hours. At each halt Lhiana would take out her sketch book and begin to scribble. She drew the plants, though, not the scenery.

"Why don't you draw the mountains?" Elton asked. "What's the fascination with these sad-looking half-dead weeds?"

"The mountains will be here tomorrow," said Lhiana, "and

next year, and next millennia. This sad-looking weed, as you call it, doesn't look like it will last the hour. Who's going to note its passing? What if it is the last of its kind, hanging on up here for one final fling? It will probably be trampled under a boot or a bullock's hoof before we've all passed."

Elton nodded. He looked back down the path they had climbed, to the forest below. How would it look when all the trees were gone? Were there parts of Old Earth that looked like this once? According to history this was probably very much how Earth once looked. The mountains and gorges were still there of course, but barren and sterile. No human eye was present to see them; no hand to record them; no brave plant making a tenuous final stand. Would Serenity face the same fate?

The caravan leader shouted to get everyone moving again. Lhiana put away her sketch book with a sigh. Elton climbed to his feet. Once more they lowered their shoulders and began to slog up the hill. Elton felt the urge to turn around and look to see if the little plant had survived their passage, but he couldn't quite bring himself to do it. He feared what he might see.

It became colder. The air, thinner. Breathing became more difficult. The bullocks' breath came in snorting, steamy clouds that swirled in the air above them. Each successive step felt heavier, more laboured and painful. It didn't seem to stop the many children, though, and while Elton and the others slogged, the children ran, in and out, between the bullocks' feet, up and down the hill. Sometimes they got in the way and Elton had to break stride to avoid them, and this itself was an effort, though Elton didn't even have the reserves to yell at them; he just paused a moment, sighed, then carried on. Where did they find the energy?

Lhiana's sketchbook stayed in her bag, now. At this altitude the only traces of life were the patches of lichen, colouring the rocks, and, here and there, a stunted blade of a leaf struggling between protective boulders. Elton noted the low-lying flora because all of his attention was on his feet and where he was placing them. He didn't want to stumble and fall; the effort of getting up from the ground would be more than he could manage. His perception of the world narrowed to just rocks and feet and cold; heavy breathing that seemed to chill his throat; and the constant burning of the muscles in his calves and thighs. He became dimly aware of a commotion ahead. He stopped and saw that the lead party was shouting and waving. Not two hundred feet away they were standing on the ridge, cheering.

Elton hastened his pace and ignored the rasping pains in his chest and throat. He was back to counting each step. One-two. One-two. One-two. He didn't want to spoil his rhythm by stopping and waiting for Lhiana. A few more steps, then he would slow and let her catch up.

But suddenly Elton reached level ground. He was at the top. Those ahead had stopped and clustered together, smiling and shaking hands and clapping one another on the back. Elton saw that Walther had already arrived but was taking no part in the celebrations; he was sprawled on his back, eyes closed, mouth hanging open for breath. It seemed a good idea so Elton joined him. He didn't close his eyes, though, he looked straight up at the sky. Clear. Not a cloud anywhere. A dome of the deepest shade of blue, almost purple. Lying on the ground he felt respite from the chilling wind and even some warmth from the sun.

Elton worked his chest, up and down, drawing air in huge draughts, and the thought that came into his mind at that moment was of his dream, the one from a few nights earlier. The dream where he was running through gates, one after the other. Why would this memory come back to him now? Each passage, each gate, in the dream, had taken him further and further from home, *and home was Serenity*. That was a strange thing in itself. He had wanted to stop but found that he couldn't. It was the reverse of everyone's usual nightmare, of fleeing from a pursuer; Elton wanted to stop, not run, but was propelled onward, the gates so close together that as he popped out of one there simply wasn't time to check his forward momentum before reaching the next gate, and through it he fell, on and on, always further from Serenity.

He became dimly aware of Lhiana, who had dropped to the ground beside him.

"How... are you... doing?" he gasped.

Lhiana turned her head to look at him.

"Okay... Thanks... for waiting."

Elton felt terrible. He wanted to explain: he was going to stop, he was, but then he was at the summit. But he couldn't get enough breath out to put the words together.

"Sorry... Really... sorry."

She opened her mouth to speak but gave up. Instead she nodded her head, and the half-smile told Elton they were okay.

After a minute or two, Elton felt able to risk sitting up. He was starting to recover at last. He climbed to his feet, taking care not to rush, and looked around for the first time. The celebrations had quietened. There was a reverent hush. Everyone was looking out over the ridge in awed silence. Elton took Lhiana's hand and helped her onto her feet. They walked over to join the others, each step careful and considered. Then they stood, side by side, and stared.

The ridge was circular, almost *perfectly* circular. The far walls were distant and tinged with purple. The rim was more or less of uniform height, unbroken, and it encircled a vast green plain deep within. The inner walls of the caldera were so steep as to be effectively vertical. Elton found it difficult to judge the depth of the crater because there was nothing down there against which to scale it. But it was deep. The sun hung low in the sky, and most of the crater floor lay in shadow. No detail could be seen, just a lush, green colour, a long way down.

"It's magnificent," Lhiana whispered.

She was standing close. Elton put his arm around her waist and drew her closer. She didn't resist. The action felt comfortable, natural; her body warm against his side. Her narrow waist was in just the right place for his arm. It felt right, her standing there beside him. Elton forgot all about his aches and pains. This was one of those rare and special moments.

"What does it remind you of?" she asked, her breathy voice barely audible.

"Don't know. I've never seen anything like it," said Elton.

"It's like a huge gate, don't you think? A SLOG?"

"Never seen one."

"This is how big they are. Subjectively. So big they might be huge or they might be tiny, you can never judge. You can't process it in your head. One minute you're awed, the next... disappointed."

"If the SLOGs are so big, how do they pack them into Frontier Ships?"

"They are very slender. It's only when they are powered up you can even see them. They're stored in sections, on spools. The only bulky part of a Large Object Gate is its control unit, and that's only, I don't know, the size of a fridge, maybe."

"So if Levison's got his SLOG up there already we'd never know – we'd never even see it?"

"Not with the naked eye. You'd need help, radar or something."

"Hmm."

"What?" said Lhiana

"Nothing. Just a thought."

"What thought?"

"There's got to be a SLOG on Destiny."

"I don't underst—"

"The Destiny ships took three SLOGs with them. You heard the histories. Destiny II relocated twice. They didn't use their third SLOG." Thoughts began to collide and crash in his head. "The last one… *has got to be up there still*."

Elton let go of Lhiana's waist and began pacing up and down mumbling to himself. Ideas were dropping into place like building blocks.

"A SLOG doesn't open for long, does it?" he continued.

"I don't—"

"Does it?"

"Depends on the charge. Pico seconds usually," said Lhiana. "What are you—"

"So big ships have to go in fast."

"Well, yeah."

"Is there a maximum time? Is there… a limit?"

"Elton, I'm just a junior gate tech. Nine till five. How do you expect me to know this stuff?"

"Because you recorded all those training holos? Because you're very bright. Because, I don't know, I just think it's something you'd know. Humour me."

"Well… if memory serves, two hundred and fifty milliseconds? Give or take. There's a minimum energy requirement just to open the field, and there's a maximum charge that can be held in the capacitors."

"Quarter of a second."

"On current designs. Don't hold me to it, it might have changed. Things move on."

"Doesn't matter about new designs. Levison's SLOG is a knock-off. An old one. So, you reckon quarter of a second, max?"

"It would take a long time to charge, but yes, it wouldn't be any longer. Why? What're you thinking?"

"And all that energy, in one burst, there'd be... a signature? Something detectable?"

"I imagine so."

Elton reached into his back pocket. He pulled out his calculator and thumbed it on.

"You brought a calculator?"

"I'm an accountant."

"Don't you have an implant?"

"Yeah, but... I like a calculator better. It's tactile. And it's a matter of, you know... image."

"So, you're planning on doing an audit up here?"

Elton smiled. "Something like that."

He took a step towards the crater rim. The wind coming up the crater wall caught him. His tie blew up over his shoulder. His hair blew into his eyes. Elton brushed it away with his free hand and began to key in numbers.

Numbers.

His old friends. It had been a while. He'd missed numbers.

"Lhiana, how long's a battle cruiser, or a carrier?"

"Elton! How d'you expect...?"

"How long?" He looked around. He shouted. "Anyone! How long? Ball park?"

Walther and Mila had overheard the conversation and come to join them.

"Fifteen hundred feet," said Walther, with authority.

Mila looked at him.

"I read a book once, okay?"

"A carrier?" said Elton.

"Yeah. That was the *Julian.* A big one."

"So, they have a carrier, five cruisers and a couple of smaller ships. Fifteen hundred. Five times six hundred, say. Two at, oh, one fifty. Nose to tail… no. Small gap. Fifty-metre gap… times seven. Five thousand one hundred and fifty feet. Say five two. That's… Point two five of a second."

He stopped to think. He looked around. Walther was smiling… grinning.

"What?"

"You made it," said Walther.

"Made what?"

"Remember the advert? Deep Space Accountant?"

And Elton suddenly saw himself as Walther was seeing him. Standing tall on the cliff edge; a steely adventurer's glint in his eye; calculator in hand; an alien sky, albeit with only one sun and one moon; the wind-ruffled hair – not electron wind but near enough.

And trees? Okay, there were no trees up here – but he had *seen* trees.

Elton remembered the advert in Walther's reader all those months ago, and he realised that Walther was right. He *had* made it. Elton D Philpotts: Deep Space Accountant.

He laughed.

"No, compagno. We *both* made it."

He went back to his calculator. This time his face wasn't quite so serious. The frown of concentration was replaced by a smile.

The numbers didn't add up though. Something was missing. He stared at the green digits on his battered, faithful calculator. What was he missing?

A shout came up from one of the animal handlers.

"Look! Look, everybody. It's starting. It's early. Great Rising."

Everyone edged forward and stared down into the crater. Elton put aside the calculator and stared too. He could see nothing. He felt Lhiana's warm hand in his own.

"What is it?" she said. "Can you see anything?"

"No. Nothing. Perhaps they… wait, look!"

The floor of the crater was moving. It was moving upwards, towards them.

"What?" Walther was looking alternately down into the crater then back at Elton. "What the hell is it?"

They could only stare. The crater floor – eight, ten thousand square miles of it – was rising. The movement was slow, but then it was far below them, so the apparent speed was deceptive. How far would it rise? Why was it doing this? What was it? Was it grassland, forest, water? A thousand questions.

Then Elton became aware of the noise. A sound that he could feel more in his chest than with his ears. It came first as a fluttering in his chest, a dangerous, heavy pressure that was how he imagined a heart attack might sound.

It grew louder and took on substance. It seemed familiar. Elton thought back to that day when he and the others had sailed across the Dianic Ocean on Minerva. The sound of canvas sails flapping in the wind. Here were a million canvas sails.

The green crater floor began to pixellate. Green became multi-coloured. There were waves and eddies rippling across the surface.

And still it rose up, ever faster. It was now clear that it, whatever "it" was, was coming all the way up. What then? What would happen? He was about to find out.

A surge, a rush, and Elton took a half-step back. Suddenly there was noise – deafening noise – an explosion of sound and colour and whirling movement all around them.

Millions upon millions of birds.

The air filled, until it was thick with rushing, frantic, fluttering activity. Birds. Birds of all sizes – some you could fit in the palm of your hand and others that were the size of an airliner. They were predominantly green, but there were many other colours too. Elton craned his neck to look up – to look all around. A column of wild flapping madness rose up and fanned out in a growing mushroom that darkened the sky. He pulled Lhiana in tight. She clung to him with both arms. They couldn't speak. Words seemed inadequate.

There were no birds on Earth. Of course, nothing lived on Earth anymore. But there were no birds on the Ring nor even in La Ronde. No birds. In fact few living creatures of any sort had ever been found on the colony worlds. There were the Teddies, of course – children's pets. There were a few salvaged Earth specimens, assorted furry things, living in cages here and there – oddities in steep decline. And the forests of Serenity had, up until now, shown no evidence of bird life either. To the ancients this would have been a noteworthy absence. Yet Elton recognised these creatures as birds the instant they resolved out of the rising green solid that he'd mistaken for forest or grassland. Birds were somehow an essential, and keenly missed, part of the human condition. As he watched them roar past in their millions and soar upward into the sky he felt his spirit uplifted. Something inside Elton Philpotts awakened.

The flight continued for at least fifteen minutes before there was any sign of abatement. Eventually though, the last of the stragglers fluttered past. Applause started somewhere along the ridge. Applause in the old style, the slapping together of palms. Elton, Lhiana, Walther, Mila… they each joined in. It seemed the perfect response; the only proper form of shared appreciation for what they had just seen.

"Tom!" Elton called over to the leader of their group. "Tom, we need to get back."

"I know. We'll leave first thing in the morning."

"No, you don't understand, we need to leave right now. There is no leeway. We have to save Serenity."

"Okay, but do you know how?"

"Oh, yes. Yes, I know exactly how we're going to do it."

FORTY THREE

"We have to get up to Destiny II. Me, Lhiana, Walther, Tom…" Elton saw the look of hurt in Mila's eyes. "… yes, and Mila, too. We need Tom because he does the refurbs on your shuttle. He knows stuff. And we'll take any others who are space-savvy, willing, and who can be squashed into the shuttle."

The Moderators looked at each other with worried frowns. There were fifteen Moderators in all, sitting around the fire outside in the forest clearing; a place that was used for barbecues and parties. While everyone else was tucking into vast wheels of apple pie with gusto, the Moderators seemed to have lost their appetites.

"We have some reserves of fuel but…"

"…but the shuttle has only recently returned. It is in need of much work."

"You may be over-reacting. Do you really have any evidence?"

Elton could hardly fathom it. They were so obstructive. This was *their* planet. Part of him wanted to say, *stuff you then, sort out your own mess*.

"Yes, I have evidence," he said. "I've seen invoices and receipts. They're buying heavy tools and weapons. They're buying gun ships. I have seen crates of chain saws; I have *used* one and, trust me, it is not a craftsman's tool."

"You say the money for all this has been siphoned away from the Space Corps without anyone noticing?" The tone of this Moderator's voice was scornful. He beady eyes bored into Elton and his whole manner expressed disbelief.

Elton ignored him and spoke to the others,

"Fake and duplicate invoices. Thousands of fake payroll

records. Bogus capital projects. They've been at it for years. One of the ways an auditor might find this stuff is through year-on-year comparisons. Levison has been filtering out his funds for decades, building up the catalogue of deceit with slow patience. The accounts look much the same year on year because the level of embezzlement has been the same."

"Still – a battle fleet?"

"Yes, a battle fleet."

Lhiana joined in. "You must have realised something was amiss. Why else would you bother faffing around with your Bram Lee monk routine if everything was so rosy out in the Sphere?"

"Not all of us were in favour of staying underground. Some wanted to go straight to the Space Corps with our fears, and tell them all about Serenity. Jessica, though, managed to convince enough of us that Levison would do nothing harmful if we left him alone. A small majority agreed and decided to retain the covert operation... no, that sounds too militant, too James Bond. It wasn't like that. The Bram Lee operation was aimed at winning hearts and minds; popular support. A wave of endorsement for an alternative view, a Contractionist view."

"Okay," said Lhiana, "it was a good try, I guess it was the right thing to try underground diplomacy first. But Levison is impervious to all that. He wants your lumber. He's on his way."

"We should talk to him first."

"I have already had that pleasure," said Elton. "I met him on Tsanak. Believe me when I say, he is not a man who is amenable to persuasion. I spoke to him while he ate a plate of veal. I'd never seen real veal. My Jim was able to educate me. He was seated at a wooden table in his office. Gentlemen, there is no wood on Tsanak. There are no veals on Tsanak. Mr Levison and/

or his colleagues, as you already know, have been here. They have sampled your wares. They are coming back for seconds."

"*Mr Philpotts!*" The Moderators started at the voice and fell silent. They were meant to be a democratic conclave. But one, apparently the eldest, a man of stately demeanour, flowing grey locks, and a big voice, seemed to hold the power. He was the one the others deferred to or were scared of. He was the one who had most resisted Elton's plan.

"Mr Philpotts. Your plan has merit, but do you understand, psychologically, what it might mean to the people of Serenity? You are talking about dredging up the misfortunes of our heritage. You are asking us to inflict a terrible thing upon these 'enemies'. Our forebears faced their trials with open eyes and equanimity. Now you ask us to use this thing as a *weapon?*"

"Yes."

"It is a lot to ask."

"Yes, it is."

They stared at each other for a minute. Elton broke the silence that crackled between them.

"Nobody will be hurt. If you allow Levison's battle fleet to come here without any form of resistance he will simply strip your planet from under your feet. There will be some on Serenity who will find it difficult to stand by and watch. Can you tell me, truthfully, that no one will resist? And if they do, what chance will they have against guns? People will be hurt."

The old Moderator sighed.

"You are in favour of this mad plan, Abel?"

"Yes, sir. Yes, I am."

"Can it work?"

"I have no idea," said Abel Bartholomew Smith.

"Mr Philpotts, can your plan work?"

Elton didn't answer straight away. He thought about it. Could it work? Did it have any chance at all? He knew so little about the technicalities. His was a concept; that was all. It was up to the others to work out the details and pull it off. He looked around at his team, his task-force. All things considered, they were kind of light on know-how.

Elton smiled at the old Moderator and shrugged his shoulders.

"Probably not," he said, "but I don't have a better plan."

The Moderator turned to look around at the forest. His eyes traced upwards, following the lines of one of the taller trees, something akin to one of Old Earth's sequoias, the giant redwood, only the trunk of this one was green.

"Earth really is barren now?"

"Completely, sir," said Smith. "Nobody goes there, not without life-support. There are some, chroniclers and historians, but it is a heartbreaking excursion by all accounts."

"And there are no trees? Not on any of the Sphere worlds?"

Elton nodded to Lhiana to answer.

"I worked in a garden, La Ronde. It is the largest single botanical collection in the Sphere of Influence. Sir, there are fewer species of plant in all of La Ronde than I can see now at a casual glance around this clearing. Serenity should be managed. It is a resource that could be of benefit to everyone. Martin Levison wants it for personal gain. The whole planet. It will give him power, it will give him leverage, and it will give him profit."

The Moderator looked at Elton again.

Elton looked him squarely in the eyes. "Sir, Martin Levison has known about Serenity for twenty years. If he were going to begin negotiations do you not think he has had time enough?"

The Moderator nodded. He looked around at his colleagues but they acknowledged that he spoke for them all.

"Tom." He beckoned the youngster to his side. "Do whatever you need to do to prepare the shuttle for launch.

"Mr Philpotts... Elton. We are in your hands. It isn't your battle but we thank Bram Lee that you were brought to us at this time. Do your best, all of you. And thank you."

The shuttle was readied in twelve days. A task that had, in the past, taken months. First, they had to drag the shuttle ten miles or so through the forest on wooden pallets, using a herd of bullocks.

Elton expected Serenity's spaceport facilities to be equally rudimentary, especially after some of the things Kyra had said to them on their way down.

The shuttle's hangar, from the outside, seemed to fulfil expectations. It was a log cabin. Inside, though, was a different world. The cabin doors opened and a ramp led down to a vast, light and airy clean-room facility that bristled with high-tech gadgetry. Elton couldn't hide his amazement.

"How did you–?"

"What? You expected stone axes?" said Tom. "Desty's gate has been open for twenty years, Elton. We do make *some* money from our Bram Lee operation. And when we come back home we bring kit with us. Even before the gate opened we had stuff. Desty *was* a starship, you know."

"Yes, but... this is incredible. The shuttle was falling to bits when we came in on it. I expected... I don't know, a shoestring operation I suppose."

"Oh, it's shoestring, no denying that. But we send people up into space. We like to do it with *some* responsibility, even if it's within a budget. I'll show you around and you can be further amazed while you explain to me what you need."

"Well, we need something to help us find Levison's SLOG.

Radar or something?"

Tom laughed.

"Radar! Is that some time-travel thing?"

"Hey, I'm just an accountant."

"Yeah, okay. We can do radar. But we've got better stuff. I can go right across the spectrum if you like. I'll see what we can do."

For twelve days Elton watched Serenity's miracle of garage engineering produce the accoutrements of space travel: thermal tiles, nitrous oxide, some gluey, sticky stuff called HTPB – hydroxyl-terminated polybutadiene – which turned out to be rocket fuel. There were miles of wiring loom and, of course, essential, a new windscreen. And as fast as they installed new stuff they ripped out old. They were going for weight-saving, because the main cargo going up would be people. It would be the heaviest lift they had attempted in years, and there was a small team engaged in strapping together some solid fuel boosters to give more of a kick in the pants. This presented a weight penalty for the launch vehicle, so another team were assigned the task of lengthening the runway by another quarter mile, a job that involved clearing the scattered rocks into a fleet of bullock carts then chasing horses up and down the new length of airstrip to level out the worst of the divots.

On launch day the town turned out to watch. They brought pans and sticks and they lined the runway beating a steady and irritating samba.

"Is this a launch-day tradition?" asked Elton.

"No," said Kyra. "It's post-Great Rising. Birds are everywhere. We wouldn't normally attempt a launch until weeks after the migration. But sometimes we must and everyone knows what they have to do. We don't want to hit birds, they'd bring us down quicker than flak."

There were three seats in the cabin. Tom, who seemed preoccupied with something that was moving around inside his spacesuit, took one seat and Winnie, a short, quiet girl, Tom's systems protégé, took another. Kyra got to drive. Her second flight. For this trip they had attached a modified cargo pod that could be pressurised. There was room inside for Elton, Lhiana, Walther, Mila and two others from the village who hadn't yet been introduced. They would soon get to know them intimately, because once the six spacefarers were inside they needed two meatpackers to tuck in the stray bits so they could shut the doors. There were no windows and there was no communication with the outside world or even the pilot.

The shuttle was suspended beneath a long wing between two jet engines. There were other jet engines, lots of them all along the wing, but no fuselage, so you couldn't really call this device an airplane. Elton assumed the whole assembly would be guided aloft by Kyra, then the wing would be jettisoned. What happened to it was anybody's guess, but the wing looked too expensive to be allowed to fall to the ground without intervention.

Elton could only extrapolate what was happening during take off from the sensations being fed to his brain via his backside, resting snug against the floor of the ship. He certainly couldn't see anything. Elton's bottom detected both acceleration and divots, that the horses had either missed or caused.

There were several lurching, buttock-clenching attempts at a takeoff until at last they seemed to have shaken off the shackles of gravity. They climbed steadily.

Then there were little pitter-patter noises followed by violent manoeuvres that sent creaking and straining noises shuddering through the airframe.

"Damn," said one of the un-named villagers. "Birds. I hope we didn't harm them."

The craft lurched over at an irretrievable angle. Something twanged up above. It sounded like a tether cable snapping. Then the irretrievable angle was retrieved.

The flight continued. An hour passed. Or it might have been five minutes –discomfort did things to time. They knew they were getting higher because the engines were quieter and sweeter. The air was getting thin.

A warning would have been nice, though there was no communication so you couldn't blame the pilot, but suddenly they were weightless. In the squashed conditions it wasn't easy to tell except that suddenly Elton could taste apple pie in the back of his throat.

They'd been dropped. They fell for a long time, building velocity. Too long. Maybe the rockets wouldn't fire. Elton expected, at any moment, the ship to smash into the ground. He'd never know anything about it. He felt beads of perspiration sitting and gathering on his face. He wished for gravity so the beads might run and trickle away.

Then he got his wish. A sensation that was indistinguishable from augering into the ground, other than the fact that life didn't end. The rockets had fired.

It wasn't really a high gee ride, but it was enough when you were squashed into a tin can with the back of a nameless villager's head pressed into your face. Elton wondered who was pressing up against Lhiana right now, and felt pangs of jealousy.

Acceleration lasted and built for what felt like another thirty hours. Then stopped. Again there was silence and the apple pie taste came back.

They were in space.

FORTY FOUR

The hatch opened and one at a time they were pulled into Destiny II by their pilot and crew.

"What now?" said Walther.

"Okay, anyone know what time it is on the Ring?" said Elton.

They looked at him.

"Yeah, I guess not. Tom, do you want to go and look? You do the trip often enough and you're not a fugitive – yet. If it looks quiet over there, come back and get Lhiana. She can wear my socks."

Tom nodded, typed the Tau numbers into the key pad, and disappeared through the gate.

"Socks, Elton?" said Lhiana.

"Leonardo's finest, love. Smart socks. You can talk to your Kim and pump her for a crash course in Large Gate Deployment. You're a gate tech. You know most of it already."

"And meanwhile?"

"We'll be out looking for Levison's gate."

"And, Elton?"

"Yes?"

"You called me 'love'."

"Yes." Elton coloured, then spoke quickly to hide his discomfiture. "Take care. Don't stay out there too long. If anyone gives you even the slightest grief, you and Tom get back here, fast."

Tom floated back through the gate.

"It's mid afternoon, but it's quiet enough. I think we'll be safe."

"Okay, go. And be careful." Elton leaned in to Lhiana. For a moment he paused, his lips inches from hers. He waited for a reaction. He needed to know if he'd overstepped. It was all very well to share a moment like Great Rising. This was—

Lhiana grabbed him by the back of the neck and pulled him in close, looping one leg around the back of his. The kiss was ferocious but short. They had things to do. Lhiana turned and disappeared through the gate.

Elton stared after her for a moment, blinking, then turned to the others.

"Okay, Kyra and Winnie. You want to set up the sensor equipment and find us Levison's gate?"

They turned and began pulling boxes out of the shuttle.

"Walther, let's get everyone looking for Destiny's SLOG. If it's not all there, or if it's damaged, this could be a nonstarter."

The first time they'd been on Destiny II they hadn't had much of a chance to look around; all the doors were operated electrically, by buttons, and they'd had that stern warning from Abel about not pushing any. It had also occurred to them that they might just press one that opened a door into outer space. You'd imagine that there'd be safety protocols, but then again this ship was over two hundred years old, and stuff breaks, and these days stuff had a habit of breaking after two hundred *minutes*. They'd been assured, though, that there were no such dangers on Desty (as the locals liked to call her) and so they went in search of SLOGs. Nobody recalled ever having seen one on Desty, but nobody had ever really been looking, and didn't know what such a thing might look like, anyway.

Destiny II had not been built for speed. There was none of the pencil-thin relativistic styling that was ubiquitous on the later Frontier Ships. Destiny II was designed to cover distance by jumping through gates then chugging along to the nearest habitable world. She was a truck and a bus. She was wide-bodied and had lots of storage space. She'd brought a big crew, heaps of food, construction equipment and three SLOGs.

Elton asked the tall, serious, nameless villager, "You've been up here a few times. Do you know your way round? Any idea where they stored stuff?"

She shrugged.

"What are your names by the way?"

"Rosy."

"Alf," said the other.

"Hi," said Elton.

"Kyra?" He had to shout – Kyra was in the shuttle, just her legs sticking out. "Have you any ideas?"

"Not a clue, Ells." She had taken to calling him Ells since they'd come back from Great Rising. It annoyed Elton intensely. She had this thing about shortening everybody's name, so they were Wal, Li, and Mil, and it didn't seem to matter that Mila was already a cut-down version of Sharmila.

"I asked Tom" – Tom was still Tom – "but he has doubts that there *is* another SLOG up here. He didn't want to say anything. Not to you, you know, just in case. Didn't want to dampen your enthusiasm."

"Okay, Rosy, Alf, Mila, Walther, I suggest we split up. There are five doors leading out of the bridge so I suggest we take one each. According to Lhiana we're looking for something like cable on big spools, yeah?"

They chose a door each and floated down into the echoing canyon that was the hold of Destiny II. It was big and it was old, and once separated from the others Elton was struck by the sense of quiet. The emptiness and age gave Destiny that spooky sensation you got from disused fairgrounds. He floated through the middle of a vast storeroom filled with a spider's web of frayed cables, used at one time for lashing and stowing who knew what. But there was nothing else. Everything had been removed and, presumably, shuttled down to the surface of Serenity. It occurred to Elton that giant spools of cable might have been useful to the early settlers.

No, he thought. *They wouldn't have cannibalised their only route back.* If there'd been a breakthrough and the codes for a return to the Solar System had been discovered then surely they wouldn't have risked marooning themselves for the sake of some bits of wire. Lhiana reckoned it was fine wire with little tensile strength. Fine for hanging in space but precious little use for anything else.

It must be here.

The storage area was much wider at the far end than it was where he had entered. It didn't take much to picture that the ship was conical in shape and this was just one of a number of similar caverns that encircled the widening circumference of the fuselage. Elton had never seen the ship from the outside. When he'd left it the first time he'd been pointing away, and when he'd arrived, earlier, he had been laid out, pilchard fashion, in a windowless tin can.

He didn't know her shape and he didn't know how big she was. As he reached each bulkhead he couldn't be sure if that was it – the end of the ship. He continued on and with each new bulkhead and empty storage space his optimism sagged further and further. He could hear, through reports from his earpiece, that his colleagues were similarly unsuccessful.

Another hatch took Elton into the crew quarters. These were always spaced around the rim of the ship, he knew, to give the crew some semblance of gravity. They had reached the end of their search. A lot of cabins. No storage.

Elton's optimism melted away as each discouraging report arrived in his earpiece.

"Nothing here, Elton."

"I'm at the end, nothing."

"That's it, compagno. My part of the ship is bare."

There were five sectors to Destiny II. One person per sector – they'd searched the ship.

"Okay," said Elton, his voice dejected. "I'll meet you all back on the bridge. Keep your eyes open on the way back, you never know. Sometimes when you're looking in the other direction…"

Elton didn't believe it would be the case and indeed there were no more reports as they drifted back through the empty spaces. Destiny II was empty. Other than the few pieces of equipment on the bridge, and the ancient captain's log, which was deemed part of the fabric of the ship itself, everything else had been taken away.

Lhiana and Tom hadn't returned yet. They'd been over an hour. There were no material relativistic differences between the two locations; both Destiny and the Ring were orbiting stable planets albeit at far distant points of the Milky Way. An hour was an hour – temporal consistency. Lhiana and Tom's mission was meant to have been a rapid insertion. Through the gate, crash course from Kim, return.

It shouldn't have taken over an hour. Were Tom and Lhiana in trouble?

Elton didn't know what to do. His plan required three things: the Destiny SLOG, the location of *Levison's* SLOG and Lhiana's knowledge. He had nothing.

Kyra and Winnie found Levison's SLOG.

"It's at L2," said Kyra. "Elton, you were right, it's there. L2's an unstable Lagrange point so there's plenty of room out there for ours, too, so long as we don't have to stay too long."

Then she saw the long faces and her smile froze. She turned to Winnie with a quizzical expression then back to Elton. He told her about their missing SLOG. Up until now the existence of the fabled Levison SLOG had been hearsay – simply a part of the Elton D Philpotts belief system.

Now it was fact. Kyra had found it herself, and the theory was proven. It was the piece of hard evidence that moved Elton's theory into cold reality and vindicated his hard-line stance. Levison's armada was coming. But now, with the Destiny SLOG missing, there wasn't a damn thing anyone could do about it.

"Where's Lhiana?" asked Mila, arriving on the bridge. "And Tom?"

Elton shrugged. He tried a smile, tried to look upbeat, but he wasn't a good actor.

"Maybe they... I don't know."

"So, Kyra, is Levison's gate finished? Is there much activity?" he asked.

"We think they've just finished charging it," said Kyra. "Within the last few minutes, in fact. Tom's sensors can detect energy flows. What we saw first was an energy flow that was consistent with a heavy charging cycle. Then it stopped. Either it broke, or the batteries got full. Sorry, Ells, we think they're ready to roll."

"So we'd have probably been too late anyhow," said Walther. "I'm not sure if that's any consolation. Damn!"

All they could do was wait. Kyra played with the sensor equipment to see if she could learn anything new. Rosy and Alf floated off into a corner to talk – to speculate about the end of Serenity as they knew it, and Elton, at a loose end, reached out the old ship's log and idly browsed through it, not really reading.

He couldn't get his mind off Lhiana. Should he go after her? Might that simply compound her or Tom's problems? She might need his help or then again she might be handling a sensitive situation that his sudden galumphing appearance would ruin. It was impossible to know.

He decided to give her another ten minutes before maybe asking Rosy or Alf if they'd go and get a feel for the situation. They weren't fugitives, but then maybe simply appearing from a gate with coordinates that were now on a blacklist would put them in a jail cell. Just how many people did Elton want to endanger here?

What to do?

He came to a section in the log where Tannahay described the second jump. He'd written about the crew's growing fears; coming here had been a mistake; that they would spend the rest of their lives using up Destiny II's resources until they were gone and she *"became a ghost ship sailing through space for all eternity"*.

He was a cheerful bugger, wasn't he? your great- great- great-grandfather, thought Elton, as if talking to Lhiana.

"Perhaps there is more reason to hope," he read.

"The fiasco which preceded our second gate passage has cast a pall of uncertainty over the whole undertaking, but this time we have none of the deployment problems that frustrated our last transit."

Elton looked at the entry. *Deployment problems? I wonder what he meant by...*

Lhiana, then Tom came tumbling through the gate. It was a noisy entrance. They were both out of breath and laughing.

Elton looked up. He let out a sigh. He put down the book and pushed himself over towards them.

Lhiana was looking around and smiled when she saw Elton.

"They nearly had us," she said, laughing. "Should have been back ages ago but we've been in hiding. In the end Tom had to cause... a diversion and we made a run for it."

"What diversion?" asked Elton, although he had half an idea.

"The thing you saw moving around inside his spacesuit? His pet rat, Winchester. He let it loose in the FingaLikka kitchens. You should have seen the pandemonium."

"Did you leave him there?"

Tom looked affronted.

"No way," he said, and a little pink nose peeked up from his collar. "Would Tomsy leave his liddle Winchester wid de nasty old people? Noo, noo."

"So how are we doing here?" said Lhiana. "Have you found your SLOG?"

His mood darkened again.

"Yes and no," said Walther.

"We found Levison's," said Elton. "Winnie's box of tricks made short work of that job."

"But?"

"But there's no third SLOG on Destiny."

"Oh. You've looked?"

"Yes, we've looked." The sarcasm in his tone was out there before he could stop it. Lhiana looked hurt. Elton softened his tone to try and repair the damage.

"It's a big ship. It's divided into five sectors. We took one each. Front to back. Nothing."

"But you were right about Levison," said Tom.

"Oh, yes."

"I wondered, you know," said Tom. "I didn't want to piss on your parade, but I've been through those store sections a few times in the past, not looking for anything in particular, but even back then it seemed awfully empty in there."

"Someone must have taken it down to Serenity," said Elton. "They must have seen a use for it."

"It would have been on a reel. Maybe several. Big reels. They wouldn't have fit inside the shuttle. Maybe there was a third jump after all – or an aborted attempt," said Lhiana.

"Our histories are clear," said Tom. "Two jumps after the initial insertion."

"There's something in Tannahay's log about the first gate, the one after they left Earth, I mean. 'Fiasco' was the word he used. Could it be they wasted a gate? Maybe when they came here it was the last-chance saloon. They didn't have any more."

Tom looked crestfallen.

"That would change all our ideas about our own history," he said. "We don't have much of a history, it would be a shame if the little bit we thought we knew has been wrong all this time."

"I was reading about it," said Elton. "Let me find it again. Then I suppose… What do you want to do? We could watch the invasion from here or head back down to Serenity and watch it from there?"

Elton shook his head in defeat as he drifted back over to the desk. He opened the ship's log again.

"Yeah, here we are. I was reading about the second gate. All he says is that the first gate transit was a fiasco."

"Does he mean the one from Earth or the first one they set up in deep space?" said Walther.

"I'll look, hang on."

Elton flicked back through the pages.

"Here we are.

"The first spool deployed flawlessly and this lightened the

mood of the crew when they realised that this awful place would only be a temporary home. But then the second reel was found to be badly wound and was viciously tangled. The filament is very fine and fragile and any undue tensions or shearing forces would snap it clean in half. If we lost this reel we would only have one more transit left.

"I sent out two crews to work on the spools in situ, then after ten hours a second shift of two crews were suited up and were prepared to take over. But a breakthrough. The obstruction was located and the spool began to deploy correctly. This was a great relief to everybody. The last spool deployed without incident.

"…and it goes on to describe how they made the jump and…" Elton stopped.

"What?" said Lhiana.

Elton traced back through the text with his finger.

"He says *'I sent out two crews'*."

"Yes?"

"Outside. Are the gate spools kept *outside* the ship? Why not? Why *would* they keep them inside? It would be an awful lot of faffing around, going through airlocks and what have you. We should have thought about this. We haven't looked outside."

Kyra was already heading for the shuttle.

"On my way," she said.

"You're looking for three spools," shouted Elton.

She had the hatch closed and within minutes she was manoeuvring away from the ship.

"I don't want to spoil the mood here," said Lhiana, "but even if she finds them, there is another problem. If Levison's gate is out at L2 how do *we* get out there? I know we loaded the shuttle with extra fuel and boosters, but that was for getting all of us up here into orbit. L2 is a whole different bag of bullock droppings."

Kyra's voice sounded in their earpieces.

"They're here, guys. Elton, you were right. Aft of the tanks, kind of hard to see because there are some baffles that hide them. Probably some kind of shielding, but there are spools slung onto a yoke all around the ship, and three of the spools are wound with some kind of cable. The others are empty as you'd expect."

"Okay, that's great, Kyra. Come on back," said Tom.

"You could sound happier," said Kyra.

"Another problem, that's all," said Tom. "Tell you when you get back."

They all looked to Elton. He half-smiled and shrugged.

"Elton?"

"This is not – how can I put it? This isn't a complete surprise. Did we really expect Levison to put his gate smack next door to Desty?" He'd started using Tom's name for her. It was a sign of fondness.

"There again, I didn't reckon on it being quite *so* far for us to reposition."

"Elton, *we have no fuel*," said Tom. "A bucketful for re-entry. Less now after Kyra's jaunt round the ship."

Elton smiled.

"You're being very secretive," said Lhiana. "What do you know that you're not telling us?"

"I think Elton's alluding to something we talked about a few days ago," said Tom. "We have a supply of fuel on Desty. They used it to refuel the shuttle back in the early days before we were fully up to speed making the stuff on the ground.

"Trouble is, Elton, even if we top off the shuttle's tanks and we travel light, there's not going to be enough to get us all the way out to L2, let alone back to Serenity afterwards. I don't even need to do the calcs. We needed heavy-lift SRB's just to get up here. Elton, the shuttle is exactly what it says on the box – it's a shuttle. It just isn't built for deep space."

Elton smiled again.

"Who said anything about going in the shuttle?"

"But how else would we…? No. Oh no. You can't be serious," said Tom.

"What?" Lhiana's head was swivelling from one to the other like it was on gimbals. "What are you talking about?"

"We don't need the shuttle," said Elton. "We have a starship. We take Desty."

Tom looked straight at Lhiana.

"Your boy's a nutter, you know that don't you?"

Walther and Mila drifted over when they heard Tom's voice getting squeaky. Lhiana quickly filled them in. The hatch opened and Kyra floated through.

"Come on," she said. "What's this new problem?"

"Only that our accountant here wants to take a two-hundred-year-old antique spaceship out to L2," said Tom.

"Cool. I was wondering how he planned to do it. No way the shuttle could do the trip," said Kyra.

"What do you mean, cool?" said Tom. "It's a lunatic idea."

"Why?" said Kyra.

"Yes, why?" said Elton.

"Just look around you. This thing's old, Elton. It's falling apart. It's been sitting up here for two centuries, and you just want to light up the engines and mosey on out into the cosmos?"

"This *thing*, as you call her, is the same age as the shuttle. She was built for space and she was built to last. I never even considered manhandling a mountain-sized SLOG onto that rusty space tram. We go in Desty. She's got ample fuel, she's built to carry a small town's worth of cargo and crew and there's just the nine of us, so she won't be stressed at all. And she's built to cross the galaxy. We just want her to take us across the street."

"And," said Walther, "I bet you don't have to kick the windows out just to find somewhere to park."

FORTY FIVE

It took them twenty-three hours, and to Lhiana it seemed an age. In a straight line L2 was about one point four million kilometres away, but straight lines were for war ships. Today was all about orbital mechanics. Lhiana recalled the Orbital Mechanics lectures she had memorised and presented. Their ship had to take a more circuitous route, and had to take it gently. They didn't want to over-exert the stately old starship.

"She handles like a Rolls," said Kyra.

"What's a Rolls?" asked Walther.

"No idea. It's a phrase Grandma Tannahay used to use."

"Tannahay?" said Lhiana. "You're a Tannahay?"

"And Tom, and about ten percent of the population of Serenity. Didn't anyone tell you? You have a big family down there, Sis."

It hadn't really occurred to her, but it was obvious really, now she came to think about it. It gave her a new perspective. This was no longer a battle that she had been dropped into and forced to choose sides. It was now all about family honour and security.

She went back to work. She and Tom had learned a lot from Kim while they were on the Ring. They'd spent the time in a FingaLikka burger joint, asking Kim the questions and tediously writing down the answers, unused to having to transport knowledge the hard way. Deploying the gate was straightforward and Elton was out there now, suited-up, and directing the others with a new kind of authority and confidence she hadn't seen in him before. But she was worried for him. They were over a thousand klicks from the Levison gate and they had detected a large presence of what they assumed to be his covert army. *If we can see them,* she thought, *then they can see us. The only difference being, we know to look, and we know where to look.*

"Have you got the fuel cell? Lhiana?"

"Sorry, Tom, no. I'll get it. I was thinking about something."

"Elton?"

"How'd you guess? It's going to be dangerous, isn't it?"

Tom smiled to reassure her, but it was a hard, flat smile with little conviction in it.

"Okay, I've got the fuel cell. Here," said Lhiana.

It was the size of a pea. They'd liberated it from the coke machine in FingaLikka during Tom's deployment of the decoy – Winchester. They had no qualms about this act of theft; they saw it as their patriotic duty to protect their fellow humans from the toxic harm of FingaLikka fizzy drinks.

Tom connected the fuel cell. It was the last step. It was only low powered but ample for their purposes, a few hours of passive standby until Levison's gate was powered up, then their trigger would be able to steal more than enough power to do its job. And it only had to perform once.

"Done," said Tom, snapping the lid on the hangball-sized object. "Let's get this out to them. The hard bit will be getting it in range of Levison's gate."

"Why's it always the last bolt?" said Elton. He only had a regular, planet-bound spanner, so whenever he applied torque his body moved instead of the nut. So far it had only been a problem during the last stages of tightening, and he'd developed the technique of attaching the tool then launching himself at it from a distance to use his momentum. He'd connected all six sections in this way without problem. Now he was on the last nut of the last section and he'd cross-threaded the damn thing. He'd toyed with the idea of tying himself to the frame, but the structure was glass-like and delicate and if he snapped it that would be game-over. Lhiana had given him strict instructions on this. *Do not touch the filament!* Two people at all times, one working the tools and the other watching their feet to make sure they didn't stray.

"I can't… shift… the bugger," said Elton, grunting and struggling with short jerking movements.

"Lhiana?" he said into his radio.

"Hi, Elton. Trigger's ready. We're bringing it out now."

"Okay, good. Look, Lhiana, I've got the last section almost connected. But the nut's stuck. It's on but the joint is loose. Does it matter? Is it worth bothering?"

"How loose?"

"Er, I can get my finger between the sections."

"Won't work. It has to be quite a snug fit. Kim was specific about it. We should really be using a torque-wrench."

"We're lucky we had the right spanner."

"Yeah. Can you get Walther to hold your feet?"

"Tried it. We both end up spinning round. If I could wrap one leg around the…"

"No! Don't you dare touch it. It'll snap like dried spaghetti."

"Seems a pity, then, that we can't just take a hammer to *their* gate," said Walther.

"We could," said Elton. "But they'd fix it. And then they'd know about us and we wouldn't get within an astronomical unit of the thing."

"Elton, how about this?" said Lhiana. "Can you get Kyra to undock the shuttle from Desty? You could use it to brace yourself."

"I'm listening," said Kyra. "I'll be with you in five."

"Kyra. Careful, okay? Slow as you can. You can't touch the filament."

"I know."

It took fifteen minutes. She was *very* careful. Taking directions from Elton she moved the shuttle into position an inch at a time until Elton could get a firm grip with his feet.

With leverage it was easy. The nut was freed and soon the Destiny SLOG was complete.

"Right," said Elton. "Let's get the trigger over to Levison's gate. Do you think they know we're here yet?"

"We have to hope they don't," said Tom.

"We'll take the shuttle to fifty klicks," said Elton, "Kyra can pilot, Walther and Tom and I will go as wing-walkers."

The trip between the gates took an age. They stayed low, outside the invisible circumference line that stretched between each gate. It wouldn't do to be too close. If Levison chose that moment to come barrelling into the Serenity system with his armada…

Everything bar the trigger was in place. After two hundred years of soaking up sunlight the batteries were full and ready to go. The assembly had gone well. The gate was aligned. But if Levison arrived before that last job of placing the trigger was accomplished, all would have been in vain. The trigger had to be close to, or attached to, the Levison SLOG. Split-pico-second timing was the key. Human reactions would barely register that they'd even missed the event. They'd get some warning, thirty seconds, maybe a minute. When a SLOG was about to flash, the stored current from the batteries was dumped into the capacitor banks. At a critically timed moment the capacitors pulsed all their stored energy into the gate, and it opened for a fraction of a second. The timing was carefully calculated to trigger the pulse when the ship was only metres from the gate. To get more than one ship through at a time the ships had to travel in a nose-to-tail convoy, and they had to travel fast. Early triggers used motion detection, but these were unreliable, because if the ship came in too slow it would be sliced in half when the field collapsed. Calculation was more reliable. The computer joined ship and gate as one system and calculated closing speed and distance.

Tom's trigger was a modification of the old detection system. First, they had to detect the battery dump – and mirror it – easy enough to do manually. But the trigger was needed for the pulse itself. It would calculate the exact timing and sequences to perform the mirror operation.

All the timings were critical. Once the gates pulsed, just the one time, it would take months for the batteries to recharge for another pass. This was the appeal of Fomalhaut as the perfect location for the military shipyards. Fomalhaut is a hot, 'A' class star and inter-transit charging is therefore a quicker process. But even at Fomalhaut energies they require photovoltaic cells the size of small planets to collect enough energy.

"Okay guys, this is as far as I go," said Kyra. "Out you get."

They hadn't bothered to re-pressurise the shuttle. They'd made the trip *alfresco,* (or more properly, *alvuoto,* as Lhiana liked to remind them) so they were already suited-up and ready to go, including Kyra who would be staying with the shuttle.

Elton took the trigger.

"Tom, did you ever catch a hangball game when you visited the Sphere?" said Elton.

"Couple of times, yeah."

"Ever play?"

"No."

"Pity. Stick with me and Walther. They called us 'The Strike Force' back on Tsanak, isn't that so, Walther? We were legends."

"Legends," said Walther, with a knowing smirk.

"After three," said Elton. "One, two, three!"

They kicked off towards the Levison gate. It wasn't strictly necessary to kick off. The shuttle was still moving at around 120kph, so when Kyra hit the forward thrusters and stopped, The Strike Force – plus one – continued on, unabated. But the kick-off was symbolic. It was an action that put them in the right place mentally.

All being well they would coast in, unseen. Then, at the last possible moment they would hit their suit thrusters and slow themselves to a halt, deliver the trigger then head back to the shuttle.

But all was *not* well.

"I see movement," said Tom

"Yeah, got it," said Elton.

"Hey, guys." It was Kyra speaking from the shuttle. "Picking up nine mobiles. Two are packing."

Elton looked over at Tom.

"What's she talking about, Tom?"

"She's seen too many movies. We all have. We love our cinema but we only have a few films and they're all over two hundred and fifty years old." He raised his voice.

"In English, Kyra, dear."

"Yeah, okay, there's nine bad guys in suits heading your way. They're armed."

"Oh, great. What are they armed with, Kyra? Energy weapons? Lasers?"

"One's got a monkey-wrench, two have hammers and one of them has this long thing, looks like a jemmy."

"Jemmy?"

"Yeah, you know – crowbar, pry bar?"

"What's it for? Does it shoot stuff?"

"No, no. Usually it's for burglary. But I guess on this occasion he's going to use it to smash your delicate electronic device into chaff. Or there again maybe he's just going to beat percussion on your heads."

"Okay, thanks, Kyra."

They were fast closing the distance, and now they could make out details of the nine forms ahead, who were spreading out, taking up positions.

"Hangball," said Walther.

Elton couldn't see Walther's face but he knew there would be a great big boyish grin stretching from one ear to the other. He knew this because he had one of his very own.

"Yeah," he said. "Hangball. Catch."

He lobbed the trigger over in Walther's direction, who caught it easily.

"Bit on the light side," said Walther. "Maybe you should have added ballast, Tom. But it'll do."

He threw it back.

"You guys are nutters," said Tom. "This isn't sport."

"'Course it is," said Elton. "Game on, Walther?"

"Game on, Elton."

They used short bursts on their suit jets. Each one came as a light kick in the butt and with a sound like the percussive snap of the wind in the sails of that marvellous catamaran, so long ago now. They arranged themselves into formation, an offensive delta.

"Tom, do you know about Delta Offence?"

"No."

"It's an attacking formation in the form of a triangle."

"I understand. A strategy. Must have taken some working out, huh?"

"You're working with The Strike Force, now, compagno," said Walther.

"Tell me," said Tom. "This triangle formation? How many other formations can you do with three men?"

A long silence followed.

"Guys?"

"Wait, I know one," said Walther, "a straight line."

"That has some merit," said Tom. "If they shoot the guy up front the others can always use him as a shield."

"You volunteering for point, Tom?" said Walther.

"Tom, Walther, enough," said Elton. "Let's just stay alert. Tom's straight-line strategy might have something we *can* use. How about we go in feet first? If any of those cowboys do have projectile weapons we'll make a smaller target that way, yeah?"

A brief firing of jets and the three realigned again. Elton found there was another advantage in this approach; he could select a target and place it between his feet. He wondered if this might work in the hangchamber.

There was another difference between this and moving around the hangchamber. Out here there was no need to rebound off walls or bodies to change direction. Here they had suit jets. Elton mentioned this to Walther.

"Does that give us an advantage?" Walther asked.

"How so?"

"Don't know. How about if we don't use our jets? Deliberately. Make them think we're helpless and heading out into the void. They might stand off and watch."

"You think they'd be so dozy? They probably play more hangball than us, you know."

"Not if they're from the Ring. No hangball on the Ring, Walther."

"Well, they outnumber us three to one, we might as well try something radical."

"Okay. No jets, at least not to begin with."

"So how do we manoeuvre?" said Tom.

"You throw the ball; the trigger. Action, re-action. Yeah?"

"Well I hope you know what you're doing."

"Oh we do," said Walther.

"So you two were something of a tour de force at hangball, then?"

"Never won a game," said Elton.

"Not a one," said Walther.

"'Bout time we put that demon to rest, hey?" said Elton.

They continued on. They were close enough, now, to see the array of weaponry they faced. No energy weapons. No projectile weapons. Apart from the spacesuits this was to be a battle along the lines of the Peasants' Revolt. Sticks and clubs.

"Incoming," shouted Walther.

A hammer, spinning and whirling, came straight for Elton who now carried the trigger.

Elton waited and watched, then he spun on a point between himself and the trigger, held in outstretched arms. The spin increased as he pulled the trigger close, then he let go. The trigger sailed straight to Walther, Elton went the other way, and as the hammer went by, Elton reached out an arm and caught it.

"That was a neat trick," said Tom.

"Never done *that* before," said Elton.

He noticed the thrower, and another, were facing each other and heads were nodding and shaking vigorously.

"Looks like one of them's getting a tongue lashing for giving weapons away," said Walther.

They were closing rapidly now, and Elton could see puffs of

gas as the enemy forces re-aligned to intercept.

Elton was drifting apart from Walther and Tom as a result of his manoeuvre.

"You want me to close up again?" said Walther.

"No," said Elton. "No thrusters. In fact let's open out some more. Let me have the trigger. They seem to be concentrating all their forces on the trigger carrier. If we spread out we'll make it harder for them."

"Coming over."

The trigger came back and Walther and Elton drifted further apart. Tom held station in the middle. Elton watched the enemy readjust.

"They're 2D," said Elton. "Can you believe that? Watch them. They've oriented the same way as each other, and they're staying in line abreast as if there's an up and a down."

"You're right," said Walther. "They've never even been in a hangchamber, let alone operated in open space."

"So," said Elton, "Keep ourselves in their orientation. When we meet they will expect a move to left or right, relative to the way all our bodies are aligned. They're gravity-conditioned. Tom, you're slightly ahead, you'll make contact first. Go left or right, keep them in their own comfort zone. The guys on you are unarmed so if you hit it'll just hurt, nothing worse. Walther, go up. I'll go down."

It was as if a film was suddenly speeded up. At a certain distance where scale was easier to detect, the two opposing groups were, in an instant, amongst each other.

Tom left it until the last moment to feint left then, despite the plan and because he didn't know any other way to do it, he hit the thrusters and went right. A trailing leg caught him in the face plate and set him spinning.

Two converged on Walther. One looked away to see what was happening with the Tom encounter, and Walther chose that moment to fire his thrusters and go up, relative to his opponents' 2D orientation.

His two opponents probably didn't even see him go.

Moments later Elton met the remaining six. He didn't use his jets. At the last moment he hurled the trigger into the space above him where Walther was headed. The action sent him downwards, beneath the line of defenders. Five of them were taken by surprise, all of them fixed in their rigid single plane. But one was alert. He was the one with the crowbar. He knew how to move in space. He knew how to use his jets to brace his body against the turning momentum, and he swung the bar. It caught Elton on his forearm. In space there is no noise, but inside a suit, sounds are transmitted normally. Elton heard the bone snap. No pain. Not for a second or two. Then the pain and the realisation of what had happened arrived at the same time. But Elton didn't cry out. He didn't make a sound. He held his breath listening for the telltale sound of escaping air; the sound of an air-seal breach in his suit; the sound that would signal his death. Pointless really. If the suit was holed he was dead. Nothing he could do about it. He might as well have let rip with a blood-curdling scream of agony. It might have helped. And, had he screamed, Walther might not, at that moment, have chosen to let loose a wild hail-Mary pass, as five reoriented angry defenders bore down on him.

"Guys?" Kyra again. "Don't want to rush you, but Lhiana's just called through. The gate's powering up. It's about to flash. She's dumping her capacitors, now, so you've got maybe twenty or thirty seconds. Time to stop playing games."

Right, thought Elton. *Ball's coming my way. I have a broken right arm. The gate is firing up.* It seemed a good enough moment to let rip with the blood-curdling scream.

And then he had to act. Because nobody else could.

Walther's pass had not been a good one. Elton needed to cover some space to intercept it. The thrusters bluff had lost its element of surprise now, anyway, so Elton fired up and vectored in.

He called Tom, speaking through the pain with gritted teeth. "Tom, how close do we have to get to the SLOG for the trigger to work?" His arm…

"Don't know. Hard to judge distances. But we're not close enough. Need to be, dunno, thousand… two thousand metres."

So it all came down to this.

Goal.

Trajectory.

Pig.

Belief…

Hangball!

A final play. The clock counting down. The defenders behind; out-manoeuvred, extraneous.

Just Elton, in space, right arm broken. Pig vectoring in. Seconds remaining.

Elton might be missing the use of an arm but he did have one thing he'd never had before in the hangball chamber; he had thrusters. Even before he moved to intercept the trigger he angled his body and fired the thrusters on his left side to set himself into a spin. At a quarter turn he reached out his left arm and scooped the trigger. A clean catch. He pulled it in tight. He spun, faster and faster, the trigger snug against his body, his right arm, flailing outwards, pulled by the centrifugal force; a soggy lump of useless meat and pain.

He would only get one shot.

He stretched out his left arm, holding the trigger in the one hand for leverage. The universe streaked past his visor, round and round, the stars drawing out into laser arcs of light. And on every rotation – the gate.

Timing. Count each turn.

One.

Two.

It all comes down to this.

Three.

Four.

"Ells. Fifteen seconds charging. Any time now."

Five.

Elton released the trigger. Instinct.

The stars continued to blur past his eyes. He had no idea if his shot was good or if he'd merely flung the trigger out and away into deep space. He fired his thrusters to slow his rotation. His broken arm whipped round and thrashed against his chest forcing another lightning flash of pain.

He screamed.

His vision filled with tears.

He blinked them back and searched the void between himself and the gate. No trigger. He'd failed.

But then he spotted it. Receding quickly. Straight and true towards the point where the arc of the gate came closest. The shot was inch perfect.

But was it good enough? Would it get into range before the gate flashed?

"Lhiana says something's happening. Any time now…" Kyra's voice was a squeak of excitement.

Incredibly, Elton saw the trigger glance against the edge of the gate and bounce inside. The gate quivered. Shit, had he snapped it?

No.

"And it's a goal," shouted Walther, in his earpiece. "The crowd go wild."

There was a flash.

It wasn't a bright flash, it was grey and flat.

What Elton saw next is subject to debate. Was he seeing the result of his brain filling in the gaps to make sense of a nanosecond event? What everyone else agreed was that a solid, bright band appeared, between the Levison gate and the Destiny gate. It lingered on the retina for longer than it should, an effect of persistence of vision. At the Destiny gate, which was also flashing grey, it disappeared.

What Elton saw; what he thought and *hoped* he saw, was a great battle fleet, matte black and ugly. The lead ship was a carrier class. Big. Bristling with weaponry. Standing at the helm, backlit: Martin Levison. Beside him, the rat-like Robert Slicker. Elton saw, in Levison's eyes, a look of triumph that turned in that nanosecond moment to a look of utmost, bug-eyed dismay, as his ravaging, proud armada plunged into the open-ended Destiny gate. He probably saw nothing of the kind. But who, in this part of the cosmos, would ever know?

FORTY SIX

Alasdair McPherson was austere. Alasdair McPherson's office was austere. No flamboyant touches. No pictures on the wall. The furniture was basic and rudimentary. There was no hardwood; no lingering smells of wax polish. The chief executive of the largest corporation in the Human Sphere of influence did not like ostentatious display.

He arrived at the office early. It was five AM. He was always first to arrive. He was a man of ordered habits and routine. He took his china teapot to the kettle in his secretary's office and he made tea. Not real, grown tea, like the sort consumed by one prominent board member he could think of, but chemical tea. He sometimes wondered what a good cup of real Darjeeling might taste like. *Was* there a difference? No regret on McPherson's part, just... curiosity.

He sat at his desk and called up the morning's reports on his rollscreen. That was when Elton D Philpotts, one arm heavily bandaged, stepped out from the shadows of the heavy drapes.

McPherson looked up. He didn't allow himself to show surprise, or indeed any emotion. He recognised the intruder at once.

"You're the terrorist, Philpotts."

"I'm Elton Philpotts, yes. I'm sorry if I startled you."

"You didn't startle me, but you have aroused my curiosity. How did you get in?"

"I have a password. Actually it's Robert Slicker's password, but it seems to work."

"So, what's the strategy? Kidnap? Theft? Assassination?"

"Nothing so dramatic. Information."

"Ah. Well, you won't get any, but, just out of curiosity, what would you like to know?"

"No, no. I'm here to *supply* the information. I felt it would be the right thing to do."

McPherson raised one eyebrow. It was his sole concession to a display of emotion.

"I felt it only fair to tell you what happened to Martin Levison and several others of his... following."

"In exchange for?"

Elton smiled. "A pardon. For me and three others."

"Blick, Bilotti and Kumari, I suppose?"

"Yes."

McPherson regarded him for a moment without speaking, then said, "Would you like some tea? The pot's fresh."

"No. No, thank you. I think I just want to talk."

"Very well. I cannot offer you a pardon, Mr Philpotts. I'm a corporate executive. I have no legal powers."

"You're the CEO of the most powerful corporation in—"

"But the position carries no force of law. Only the courts can rule on your innocence or otherwise. It's only fair that I warn you of this first. Before you speak. Then you can decide if you still want to tell me where Martin Levison is right now."

Elton shrugged and began to talk. He talked about his strange appointment to the Space Corps, about the covert ledger, and about the world called Serenity.

And he talked about how he and a band of patriots had opened a gate, a Single Large Object Gate, at the precise moment when Martin Levison was coming through with a battle fleet.

"A gate to where?"

"Who knows? Open ended. Could be Levison has found his paradise world. But he won't be back to tell us anytime soon. Is what I did a crime, Mr McPherson? I didn't kill anyone. I didn't hurt anyone. An act of relocation, that is all.

"And I saved a world."

"Where is this Serenity?"

"I won't tell you the gate code. That knowledge will stay with Martin Levison and his friends wherever they are now."

"You don't trust me?"

"It's nothing personal, Mr McPherson. I just don't think the human race is ready, yet, for an unspoiled world. I think Levison proved that. Greed is alive and well in the human condition."

McPherson said nothing. He thought about what he had just been told. He thought for a long time.

"I'm not sure you are the one to judge. One man deciding the fate of a planet?" said McPherson.

"It's not my decision. I speak for everyone on the planet," said Elton.

"And their experience with the Sphere of Influence has not been a particularly rewarding one?" said McPherson, with a wry smile.

"No."

"You realise, it will get out."

"Yes."

"You cannot speak for a whole planet, you know, young man. Not really. There will be some there, I'm sure, who are angry about the prospect of remaining cut off from the rest of humanity. It is naïve of you—"

"I'm not naïve. I know there are dissidents, and I know it's only a matter of time before someone comes over to the Sphere and publishes the gate codes."

"So, what is your real purpose, here, today?"

Elton smiled.

"I just thought you should know. Martin Levison is gone. He

won't be coming back. You should make… arrangements; cover all the stuff he does."

"You're an accountant, yes?"

"A passed finalist, yes," said Elton.

"Perhaps you have come here with lofty ambitions to further your career in…"

Elton laughed.

"My God, no. No, that was so *not* my reason for coming here. I don't have the experience, the real qualifications or, more importantly, the faintest glimmer of ambition in that direction, please trust me on that. I just thought you should know, that's all. Levison was a random piece of trouble who just happened to weasel his way into power. I thought that it would be better for the Space Corps and, medium-term, better for Serenity that you were told what was going on and could set about fixing it."

McPherson nodded.

"I'm going, now. Are you going to call security as soon as I'm out of the room? Because I'm not armed. I'm not a threat."

"I can do nothing to lessen your criminal status, Mr Philpotts. I have already said that, and it is the truth. I can put a word in the right ears on your behalf, but that is all." McPherson smiled. "I won't call security."

Elton had hoped for better, but he could have received worse. He offered his hand, instinctively his right hand, before realising it was swathed in bandages. McPherson, without missing a beat offered his left hand, and they shook. Elton smiled. McPherson had shown with a single empathic action why he was head of the most powerful corporation in the Sphere of Influence, and why it was right that he should remain so.

Elton turned and left.

FORTY SEVEN

They held the ceremony in the spring, in the orchard. It was a good location. The white apple blossom was out; the whites, the greens of leaf and grass, the blue sky... it was perfect. Every detail was kept simple. Elton wore black, Lhiana wore white. They each had a woven loop of apple blossom and wild flowers on their heads.

They had wanted a small service, just a few friends and family. Elton had arranged for his mother and father to be gated in. Kegworth, from the Revolution bar, came too, bringing Winston and a group of his new Teddy friends. Lhiana brought her mother and younger sister. The "few friends" turned out to be over six hundred, from this and from neighbouring villages. But the ceremony was outside, under the sky. There was room for everyone.

The music was live. Serenity had a small orchestra and they were all keen to play for the wedding. Elton and Lhiana both thought a small orchestra would be nice. They got an eighty-piece outfit, not counting the choir.

They wanted something intimate. There were TV cameras. Everyone on Serenity wanted to see this, the marriage between the descendant of Malcolm Tannahay, the long-lost daughter of Serenity, and Elton, the *saviour* of Serenity.

The walk down the aisle, the central avenue of trees, was a long one for Lhiana. Elton turned and watched her approach as the orchestra launched into Pachabel (corny, but why not?) and he felt relieved that it was a walk that he didn't have to make – at least not until afterwards.

Walther dug him in the ribs.

"Showtime, compagno."

Lhiana looked stunning. The dress was simple, white, no ornamentation – she didn't need it. She walked arm in arm with her mother. Sharmila was maid of honour and Dorina, her sister, and Kyra were her other bridesmaids.

The focal point of the ceremony was Bram Lee, the old and wizened apple tree. Behind the tree a makeshift studio had been set up, and Elton could hear the excitable running commentary from Abel Bartholomew Smith's daughter.

"And here we have it, folks. The bride is now walking down the long avenue of trees. The groom is taking a few deep breaths. Will he make it? There's still time to cut and run, Elton. There's plenty of us waiting for you if you do. But no, he's solid. He looks like he's going to see this through. His best man, Walther Blick, stands tall and proud, but goodness, where did he find that suit? It just doesn't seem to fit him. There's a man in need of some motherly attention, girls. I hate to disappoint you, though. Rumour has it he's already popped the question to his long-standing partner, Sharmila Kumari.

"Wait, something's happening. The bride has stopped halfway down the aisle. Is this a moment of uncertainty? Are we in for some last minute drama? No, a collective sigh of relief goes up from the gathered audience, she was adjusting her headband, that's all. She's moving again."

And on it went. Elton wondered if she would, at some point, start to give bookies' odds.

It must have come as a great disappointment to the whole commentary team that the ceremony went off without a hitch. There was one pause in the proceedings when Elton was asked:

"Do you, Elton D Philpotts, take this woman—"

Lhiana held up a hand.

"One moment," she said.

Even the commentary stopped.

"There's something I need to know."

"Yes?" said Abel.

"What's the D for?"

"Excuse me?"

"Elton D Philpotts. What does the D stand for?"

"Er." Elton felt his face colouring.

"Is it important?" he asked.

"Well, yes. It could be – if it's Dungface or something."

"Would it make a difference?"

Lhiana thought about it.

"No," she said. "No, I could live with that. It's not Dungface is it?"

"No."

"Well, go on. What does the D stand for? I want to know who I'm marrying."

Elton leaned in and whispered. The whole congregation, as one body, leaned forward, straining to hear. Abel's daughter ran forward from behind Bram Lee and thrust a microphone between them.

"Nothing," said Elton.

"What?"

"It doesn't stand for anything. It's just a D. My dad's idea. He thought it leant gravitas to the name. So my first name is actually Elton D. Elton's just my nickname."

"Hmm."

"Are we okay with that, Miss Bilotti?" said Abel.

"Yes. Yes, that's fine. I don't mind being married to an Elton D. Carry on."

They carried on.

It was a beautiful wedding, people said. They were right.

The wedding breakfast was more relaxed and informal. Elton looked around and felt pleased that everyone was enjoying the day, even his mother and his father. Elton saw that at regular intervals his father would take out an ancient hand-held calculator and begin tapping away. Average cost per guest? Variance to budget calculations? DCF capital appraisal on the wedding gifts?

Gifts. Yes, there were presents. Things for the couple's new home on the outskirts of the village. Things wrapped in sensiwrap paper, with tinkling bells and snowstorms of confetti. And some unusual wedding gifts – two bullocks, led in by Grogan, the animal handler. They were scrubbed and groomed and each had collars of woven twigs and apple blossom. They looked around at the festivities with mild, disinterested expressions, and then each lifted a tail in turn and deposited their own steaming, aromatic wedding gifts onto the grass.

Then there was a parcel, plainly wrapped, and addressed to Elton alone. Elton picked it up and regarded it with a puzzled expression.

"Don't know," said Walther. "Mila picked it up a couple of days ago, on the Ring. It was in your forwarding box. Nobody seemed bothered that she took it – I mean she doesn't look a whole lot like you, I'm pleased to report."

"It's from Tsanak."

"Yeah. It's addressed just to you, though – not both of you. Could be some of the guys from NLT, I suppose. They wouldn't know Lhiana's name."

"They wouldn't know I was getting married, either."

Walther shrugged.

"So, open it."

Lhiana put her chin on Elton's shoulder and watched while he

ripped the plain brown plastiwrap from the gift.
It was a picture frame. Elton turned it over.
A certificate.
Elton swallowed.

> The Chartered Institute of
> Relativistic Accountants
> This is to certify that
> *Elton D Philpotts*
> Was admitted as an associate
> Of the Institute on
> 21 March 2241
> and is entitled to use the description
> Chartered Relativistic Accountant
> ---------------------
> Given under the Common Seal of the Institute

There was a large red seal and three signatures; two were just scribbled and were those of the institute's president and chief executive. The other, headed "Member of Council" was in a neat and legible hand – Alasdair McPherson, Chief Executive of the Space Corps.

There was a note attached, in the same hand.

Mr Philpotts, my influence over judiciary matters may be limited, although if you do return to the Sphere any time soon, you may notice that a general unwillingness to act against your liberty now prevails. But, as a fellow of the institute I do have some sway in professional matters that you may find to be of benefit. In gratitude for your timely intervention and unimpeachable integrity, I offer you my best wishes for your future career as a Deep Space Accountant.

Elton's father had joined the group and Elton saw, as his father reached out a hand to clasp his son's, that a tear had stolen into the corner of his eye. He was holding the plasticover wrapping that Elton had discarded, and Elton spotted, then, something he hadn't noticed earlier – perhaps because it just looked so right.

The address label:

Elton D Philpotts ACRA.

Thank you for reading *Deep Space Accountant*, the first in the *Sphere of Influence* series.

If you enjoyed the book please consider leaving a review on Amazon, or if you found something wrong please let me know. You can find my contact details on my website, here: www.mjkewood.com

The website is also a great place to sign up for my newsletter, and in the process, bag yourself a **free ebook**, the new short story collection *Power for Two Minutes and Other Unrealities.*

In the newsletter I'll share progress reports on the second book in the *Sphere of Influence* series, called *The Lollipop of Influence,* and you'll be sure to learn the launch date of this and subsequent titles. You'll also be first to hear about any promotional offers that come along.

On a final note, if you enjoyed the humour in *Deep Space Accountant,* but can't wait for *The Lollipop of Influence*, you could always give my sofa travel book, *Travelling in a Box* a try. www.travellinginabox.com

Once again, thank you! Go on, join the list; I'd love to keep in touch.

Mjke

There are people that I wish to thank. People who have worked hard behind the scenes to make this book work.

Janie at Lector's Books, my ever patient, ever suffering, ever available editor, who has a light touch and a magical gift to turn mush into gold, time after time. Thank you Janie.

Benjamin Roque, my cover designer, who somehow managed to capture an image locked deep inside my head and turn it into art.

And last but most of all, Sarah, my wife, who has endless patience reading through first draft scenes that don't work. And then those long evenings on our summer holidays when I read aloud the entire semi-final draft. My heroine.

Printed in Great Britain
by Amazon